The Most Wanted

Also by Jacquelyn Mitchard

The Deep End of the Ocean
The Rest of Us

JACQUELYN MITCHARD

The Most Wanted

VIKING

VIKING
Published by the Penguin Group
Penguin Putnam Inc., 375 Hudson Street,
New York, New York 10014, U.S.A.
Penguin Books Ltd, 27 Wrights Lane, London W8 5TZ, England
Penguin Books Australia Ltd, Ringwood, Victoria, Australia
Penguin Books Canada Ltd, 10 Alcorn Avenue,
Toronto, Ontario, Canada M4V 3B2
Penguin Books (N.Z.) Ltd, 182–190 Wairau Road,
Auckland 10, New Zealand

Penguin Books Ltd, Registered Offices:
Harmondsworth, Middlesex, England

First published in 1998 by Viking Penguin,
a member of Penguin Putnam Inc.

1   3   5   7   9   10   8   6   4   2

Poems by Sharron Singleton. Copyright © Sharron Singleton, 1998.
Illustrations by Joanna Roy. Copyright © Joanna Roy, 1998.

ISBN 0–670–87884–7
CIP data available

This book is printed on acid-free paper.

∞

Printed in the United States of America
Set in Adobe Garamond
Composition by Creative Graphics, Inc.
Designed by Francesca Belanger

For my daughters, Jocelyn Marie and Francie Nolan

Mi más queridas

And for Luz

ಆಶ್ ಲ್ಶೂ

Acknowledgments

Like a pole barge going slowly up a river, this book got finished only because of all the toting and cheering from the shore.

I first need to thank Michelle LaVigne, a true friend and a good writer, who allowed me to model the character of Annie Singer on her slender and lawyerly bones. To the many people who helped me have at least some sense of Texas and its culture, including Maria, Joe, and my beloved Elizabeth, whose heart is bigger than the big Republic; to Ken and Gloria for help understanding why some of us cross the line of the law; to Linda Bubon, classmate and friend, owner of a unique Chicago bookstore, who, in the spirit of fun, let me borrow its wonderful name for Anne Singer's law firm: thank you all.

A cherished network of family, co-workers, and friends again surprised me with loyalty and sheer intelligence. For heroic forbearance, I thank my cadre—Susan, Michelle, Pamela, and Patty. For simply showing up at the site of the cyclone, Sandy, Karen, Lilia, Amy, Kevin, and Pam. For provocation and uncommon gentleness, my sons, Robert, Daniel, and Martin, I love you best. Ann K.,

Anne D., Jane H., Laurie, Franny, Brian, Jean Marie, Tory and Steve, Stacey, Hannah, John and Georgia, Rick, Sylvia, and all the "we of me," you know where I'd be without you.

To the strong and good women who publish my work, Barbara Grossman, Susan Petersen, and Phyllis Grann, thank you. I wish also to thank Penguin Putnam artists Gail Belenson and Francesca Belanger for their superlative grace notes, and Beena Kamlani for once again making me look smart.

To my agent and once-and-future-best-pal, Jane Gelfman, all my gratitude; and to the staff and supporters of The Ragdale Foundation, a writers' residence in Lake Forest, Illinois, who helped me through substantial portions of this book in 1997.

Finally, though several beautiful original poems appear in this book, they did not come from my mind or pen.

The love poems of Arley and Dillon are the work of Sharron Singleton, a luminous writer and a tender friend, who found her way into the souls of characters she didn't know and made them speak, almost before the person who created them was able to do that.

So far as Sharron and I know, this kind of collaboration between two writers of different genres, in a single work of fiction, hasn't been tried in quite this way.

It was a startling adventure, as all of this has been.

January 8, 1998
Madison, Wisconsin

Dreams
by Sara Teasdale

I gave my life to another lover,
　I gave my love, and all, and all—
But over a dream the past will hover,
　Out of a dream the past will call.

I tear myself from sleep with a shiver
　But on my breast a kiss is hot,
And by my bed the ghostly giver
　Is waiting tho' I see him not.

The Highwayman
by Alfred Noyes

I

The wind was a torrent of darkness
  among the gusty trees,
The moon was a ghostly galleon
  tossed upon cloudy seas.
The road was a ribbon of moonlight
  over the purple moor,
And the highwayman came riding—
    Riding—riding—
The highwayman came riding,
  up to the old inn-door.

He'd a French cocked-hat on his forehead,
  a bunch of lace at his chin,
A coat of claret velvet,
  and breeches of brown doe-skin;
They fitted with never a wrinkle:
  his boots were up to the thigh!
And he rode with a jewelled twinkle,
    His pistol butts a-twinkle,
His rapier hilt a-twinkle,
  under the jewelled sky.

Over the cobbles he clattered
  and clashed in the dark inn-yard.
And he tapped with his whip on the shutters,
  but all was locked and barred;
He whistled a tune to the window,
  and who should be waiting there
But the landlord's black-eyed daughter,
    Bess, the landlord's daughter,
Plaiting a dark red love-knot
  into her long black hair.

And dark in the old inn-yard
   a stable-wicket creaked
Where Tim the ostler listened;
   his face was white and peaked;
His eyes were hollows of madness,
   his hair like mouldy hay,
But he loved the landlord's daughter,
    The landlord's red-lipped daughter;
Dumb as a dog he listened,
   and he heard the robber say—

"One kiss, my bonny sweetheart,
   I'm after a prize to-night,
But I shall be back with the yellow gold
   before the morning light;
Yet, if they press me sharply,
   and harry me through the day,
Then look for me by moonlight,
    Watch for me by moonlight,
I'll come to thee by moonlight,
   though hell should bar the way."

He rose upright in the stirrups;
   He scarce could reach her hand,
But she loosened her hair i' the casement!
   His face burnt like a brand
As the black cascade of perfume
   came tumbling over his breast;
And he kissed its waves in the moonlight,
    (Oh, sweet black waves in the moonlight!)
Then he tugged at his rein in the moonlight,
   and galloped away to the west.

II

He did not come in the dawning;
   he did not come at noon;
And out o' the tawny sunset,
   before the rise o' the moon,

When the road was a gipsy's ribbon,
  looping the purple moor,
A red-coat troop came marching—
    Marching—marching—
King George's men came marching
  up to the old inn-door.

They said no word to the landlord,
  they drank his ale instead,
But they gagged his daughter and bound her
  to the foot of her narrow bed;
Two of them knelt at her casement,
  with muskets at their side!
There was death at every window;
    And hell at one dark window;
For Bess could see, through her casement,
  the road that *he* would ride.

They had tied her up to attention,
  with many a sniggering jest;
They had bound a musket beside her,
  with the barrel beneath her breast!
"Now keep good watch!" and they kissed her.
  She heard the dead man say—
Look for me by moonlight;
    Watch for me by moonlight;
I'll come to thee by moonlight,
  though hell should bar the way!

She twisted her hands behind her;
  but all the knots held good!
She writhed her hands till her fingers
  were wet with sweat or blood!
They stretched and strained in the darkness,
  and the hours crawled by like years,
Till, now, on the stroke of midnight,
    Cold, on the stroke of midnight,
The tip of one finger touched it!
  The trigger at least was hers!

The tip of one finger touched it;
   she strove no more for the rest!
Up, she stood to attention,
   with the barrel beneath her breast,
She would not risk their hearing;
   she would not strive again;
For the road lay bare in the moonlight;
    Blank and bare in the moonlight;
And the blood of her veins in the moonlight
   throbbed to her love's refrain.

Tlot-tlot; tlot-tlot! Had they heard it?
   The horse-hoofs ringing clear;
Tlot-tlot; tlot-tlot, in the distance?
   Were they deaf that they did not hear?
Down the ribbon of moonlight,
   over the brow of the hill,
The highwayman came riding,
    Riding, riding!
The red-coats looked to their priming!
   She stood up, straight and still!

Tlot-tlot, in the frosty silence!
   Tlot-tlot, in the echoing night!
Nearer he came and nearer!
   Her face was like a light!
Her eyes grew wide for a moment;
   she drew one last deep breath,
Then her finger moved in the moonlight,
    Her musket shattered the moonlight,
Shattered her breast in the moonlight
   and warned him—with her death.

He turned; he spurred to the West;
   he did not know who stood
Bowed, with her head o'er the musket,
   drenched with her own red blood!
Not till the dawn he heard it,
   his face grew gray to hear

How Bess, the landlord's daughter,
   The landlord's black-eyed daughter,
Had watched for her love in the moonlight,
   and died in the darkness there.

Back, he spurred like a madman,
   shrieking a curse to the sky,
With the white road smoking behind him,
   and his rapier brandished high!
Blood-red were his spurs i' the golden noon;
   wine-red was his velvet coat,
When they shot him down on the highway,
   Down like a dog on the highway,
And he lay in his blood on the highway,
   with the bunch of lace at his throat!

And still of a winter's night, they say,
   when the wind is in the trees,
When the moon is a ghostly galleon
   tossed upon cloudy seas,
When the road is a ribbon of moonlight
   over the purple moor,
A highwayman comes riding—
   Riding—riding—
A highwayman comes riding,
   up to the old inn-door.

Over the cobbles he clatters
   and clangs in the dark inn-yard;
And he taps with his whip on the shutters,
   but all is locked and barred;
He whistles a tune to the window,
   and who should be waiting there
But the landlord's black-eyed daughter,
   Bess, the landlord's daughter,
Plaiting a dark red love-knot
   into her long black hair.

The Most Wanted

Arley

Even now, years later, I know there are going to be those nights. Nights when I will wake up with my nightgown soaked to my ribs. When I will be taking breath from deep in my stomach, not my chest. When I will be sure that it's really not a dream.

Instead, it will be as though my very own safe room on Azalea Road is really the dream. As if my Desi, right on the other side of the wall, sleeping in her white bed under that wagon train mural we painted for her, all in the palest of pinks and yellows and greens, is just a wish that found its way into my sleep, when my mind was off its guard. As if I didn't get away; I didn't live to tell.

The fire dream, and the other one, the kiss, come back so round and full of sound that I could swear I'm back there again in that black little square of cabin on the night of the fire, watching Desi go out the door in that flickery red wash of light, afraid I will never feel her little stickpin fingers close tight around mine again, afraid I will never again smell her hair.

Once or twice, I've had both those dreams on the same night, and then I'm sick with the shivers and done with sleep until morning.

1

When I dream of the kiss, I don't hear the fire. I can feel my mouth open up under his as if that mouth had never done a single thing—not eat or breathe or pray—anything but wait for what it was made by nature to do, the only thing that made it feel satisfied, or useful, as if it had been not two years but instead two minutes. That scares me just as much as the other dream does. It makes me know that I am, at the core, as bad as he was.

I don't tell Annie. I guess I'm still immature enough, or prideful enough, that I don't want Annie to think she was right about Dillon all along. And we'll never know, not really, if she was totally right, because what he did on the porch that night . . . well, only he would know, and he's gone so long, there's no asking. Annie comes if she hears me crying, she comes as if I'm a baby that woke with a fever, and she just sits there, she doesn't try to hug me or anything. She's good that way. Actually, she's probably good in all ways. Still, I don't want to admit to Annie that I know I was a fool. I used to tell her, "Annie, I made this here bed, and now I'm going to have to lie in it." I guess I wanted that to sound like bold talk. But there was no other choice. I did wrong, and then I did more wrong, and I did it because I knew that what Dillon did was part my fault. That he did it in some sense for me, or maybe all for me, and one piece of me had to stick with him on account of that.

I guess, by that night, along with the police and everybody else, I had started to think of Dillon as almost a supernatural creature, who could do anything he desired and not be stopped. On TV, they called him "The Highwayman," just like he wanted. It was as if he'd made himself up a new self, a self I didn't know. I couldn't feel him moving in my chest or trace his jaw with my forefinger in my mind. And if I tried to make him come back to me and fit inside my heart the way he used to, he just wouldn't.

We weren't one anymore. All I would be able to think of was Desi. Of course, it was a mercy that I could let him loose that way, I know that now. But it felt then like being in hell. It was like I walked right down Kings Highway with my shirt bare off for everyone to see, did it on purpose, not having any clue why, not even seeing my shame until somebody showed me pictures of what I'd done. There are times when I think that none of it could ever have happened at all. And yet I know.

I have certainly got the proof.

When Dillon came along, he just filled up the sky over me, and I couldn't see around him to good or bad or wise or stupid or anything. I know how that sounds. But if you feel like that, it's more than love, it's like your mind getting turned over and emptied out like a drawer; you're so cleanly dedicated to that one person, it's as if all the rest of you was scrubbed off. It's like waking up from a dream into a dream and not knowing where one left off and the other began.

When I think back on the house in Avalon and Taco Haven in San Antonio, Mrs. Murray's class and the Bexar County library, Coach Diaz and the track team, it's all like an old film in black and white. And for a while, the future looked that way too, but not now. Now the future shows up in my sleep in all those pastel pretties Desi likes. So I'm not afraid to sleep most nights. It's not like I'm depressed. You don't have to be depressed to regret what deserves regret.

Did anyone else ever feel about anyone the way I felt about Dillon? Like he was a strongbox that would look gray and ordinary to anyone else but show its jewelly treasures inside only to the one person who had the key? If someone else ever did feel that way, how long did it last? I know one thing: nothing on earth can explain how I could know every breath and hand line of the boy

3

who wrote those poems for me, and have the very same boy be a stranger who did all those terrible things. If you ever felt love that crazy for somebody, you can't imagine that you would ever feel the other, a growing so far and wide apart you might see him on the street and not even have to swallow hard. That you might even think, Oh boy, there's trouble.

Of course, I can't ever know whether that would have happened to Dillon and me. Whether we'd ever have had fights or got divorced or started to hang around with different crowds. We never passed each other on a street or even held hands. We never got anywhere close to getting ordinary. It wasn't ordinary how quickly he became everything to me. It wasn't ordinary how quickly he had to become nothing. It wasn't natural: I only knew Dillon a handful of days. Most of the time Dillon was growing up and going to school and even making love, I never knew him. Maybe that was the real Dillon, and the Dillon I knew hardly real at all.

When I was a kid, the one time I ever got farther away from Avalon than the half-hour bus ride to San Antonio was when Mama and Grandma and my brother and sister and me went to visit my aunt Debbie Lynn in Galveston. I was almost six, and I didn't even know there was an ocean alongside Texas. No one ever told me.

Debbie Lynn took us to the beach in her car. The end of it was invisible, it was so long. And the white strip was so much a contrast with the green Gulf, water that seemed like a huge soft mattress, that I couldn't take it in all at once. I had to look down at my feet. Down there was this whole carpet of tiny shells, no bigger than my thumbnail, with colors I'd never seen before except in a church window—rose pink and gray and shiny black. I started to scoop them up and stuff them in my pockets and even my undershirt, peeking around at everyone else on the beach and wondering why they weren't doing the same thing. How could anybody keep from wanting them, these beautiful things just sitting there, free for the taking?

But later on that night, when those shells dried off, I almost cried. They still had their tiny fan shape. But they didn't have their colors anymore. They were dull. You could barely believe they could be those same ones that lay gleaming, washed in the sand.

I remember asking my aunt, Which are the real colors?

But she was like my mama: nothing drove her more nuts than a child asking questions. So I decided myself about those shells, the way I had to decide most things when I was little. I studied it without the information a grownup could give you.

And I decided that both colors of the shells were real.

It just depended on where you were.

CHAPTER ONE

Annie

That morning, I had crawled in to work, my pressed white cotton blouse already damp and crumpled at the waist just from the ten-minute drive to the office. I was beat from the heat and sapped from a major wee-hours bicker with Stuart. We didn't fight, Stuart and I. I don't think we ever really had a fight—not a blowout of the kind my sister and her husband have twice a month and laugh about later. Don had such a habit of hurling the contents of a cup or a bowl at the ceiling during his rants that one year, for their anniversary, Rachie hired an artist to paint a mural of stains—from coffee to ketchup—on the kitchen ceiling, so Don's outbursts wouldn't show. "He's just loud," Rachael said, "not dangerous."

Don loved the mural. He beamed at Rachael and said, "That's why you're my best girl."

"Enshrining their dysfunction," Stuart commented when I told him about it. "Well, to each his own."

What Stuart and I had instead of fights were long, tortured, semantically dissective chats, in which each of us would try to out-lawyer the other—as if anybody ever prevailed in a personal disagreement through the use of logic. The night before Arley

Mowbray turned up in my office and overturned my life, the chat had been about our marriage, which either was or was not imminent, depending on which of us you talked to. Stuart had been pulling cruise folders out of the Sunday paper and leaving them on my nightstand for months, as well as speculating aloud about getting La Casita to cater its famous ranch eggs for a brunch. But I, for my part, was not picturing a beige linen frock and a straw hat in my near future—though that was actually the only sort of wedding outfit I thought I could endure.

Stuart especially thought it would be fun to fly to Las Vegas and get married early in the day so we could spend the night at the blackjack tables.

"Don't you think that would be cool?" he'd razzed me that night, as I rinsed the leftovers of Greek salad from the Fiesta ware we'd just bought. "We could get one of those heart-shaped tubs. Like those old ads for the Poconos." I had to laugh, picturing Stuart and me in a red enamel tub, disporting ourselves among the suds. I wonder now whether Stuart felt the boat rocking for us, that fall, long before I did. He had ratcheted up his suitor act a couple of notches, though at the time I couldn't imagine why.

People always say they know their lovers better than they know themselves, but when Stuart said that, it was literally true. Three days before I'd get a cold, he'd predict it by noticing a change in my eyes—and he was never wrong. He could gauge how bad my day had been by how long it took me to turn the key in the front door, and he'd be ready to offer a back rub (which, unlike another man's, would not turn into a front rub within the first three minutes). My parents loved Stuart from the moment they met him, but I forgave him that, even though he sometimes teased me by urging my mother on the phone to exercise her parental rights: "Miriam, she won't set the date. Why can't you just give me her hand? I thought that was how this worked." Long silences afterward, during which Stuart would simply smile and nod, made me assume my mother had launched into her own visions for my wedding. Marrying off the plain older sister would, for her, represent a major victory. Given her way, Mom would have the lamps on the dinner tables encrusted with pale-pink furled rosebuds and would fly little second cousins in from Chicago and Flagstaff to strew petals. I would hate this, but Stuart wouldn't have minded. He was a real person in that respect, adaptable and forgiving, and he proclaimed himself up for any kind of ceremony, large or small, that would end with my being his one and only. As for me, I'd never thought seriously about Stuart and me being married. Or about our being apart. Both things had always seemed excessive.

Since we'd met in Chicago, where we were both public defenders and Stuart was just beginning his novitiate as a capital punishment abolitionist, we'd marveled at our easy, undemanding fit. Displaced New Yorkers greet each other with pathetic relief no matter where they wash up, but almost instantly, it was clear that Stuart and I had a shared sense of things that went way beyond a common city of origin. We agreed on things no one else even considered. We both thought Dionne Warwick could sing rings around Whitney Houston. Locked in separate rooms and allowed to make only one phone call, we would each order pizza with green peppers and pineapple, easy on the cheese. We both thought Jack Nicholson was the world's most overrated actor and Jackie Gleason the most underrated.

"You can have all of them," Stuart said the night we met. "You can have *Chinatown*. You can even have *The Godfather, Part Two*. There is only one real movie. *The Hustler*. *The Hustler* is my life."

I could count on him never to say "presently" when he meant "currently." He could count on me to be able to sing all the Belmonts' parts if he sang the Dion parts on "Runaround Sue."

Ten years later, our routine was still just as predictable and satisfying. We worked all week like dogs and then gave ourselves over utterly to our daylong Sunday date, which only an execution, or the threat of one, could derail. A long, late breakfast and then a drive to one of the hamlets sprinkled around San Antonio. Thirty minutes by car, and you'd feel time had dialed back thirty years—that's how small those towns, like the towns Arley and Dillon grew up in, really were. People sold Miz Stern's settee or Miz Brainard's quilts for the equivalent of East Coast pocket change. Not that Stuart and I bought anything much. The rare tchotchke aside, our antiquing journeys mainly amounted to wishful foraging, in the spirit of a more roomy and prosperous someday we somehow never really articulated. "We should just keep the furniture we have, Anne," Stuart told me once. "By the time we get around to a house, this stuff will *be* antiques."

Do I remember the words and thoughts I had the night before I met Arley so clearly only because it *was* the night before? Do things seem more meaningful because subsequent events etch certain cues into a framework that has more weight? I remember rinsing the plates and listening to Stuart sketch increasingly weird motifs for our wedding, and I remember that I suddenly thought, Who will get the Fiesta ware? Why did I think such a thing?

It scared me. "Well, Stuart," I'd said finally, "at least it'd be a story to tell the grandchildren. Except there wouldn't be any grandchildren."

And that started it, not a new discussion but a thinly disguised variation of a debate we'd had six times, this one distinguished only by its more urgent tenor. I could make Stuart see all the reasons why I didn't want to get married unless we were going to have a child, and I could even get him to understand them. But I couldn't get him to feel the same way. A child was beside the point, he would insist. The point was that "living together" at our age was just laziness or perversity—trying to prove something to an audience of people who were either dead or no longer gave a damn.

I, personally, thought that it was Stuart who was trying to prove something. Despite all his stalwart cheer, what I really sensed in Stuart about getting married was a great giving up, like the big get-it-over-with sigh he gave every morning as he got up off the couch to run, after lying coiled in the fetal position, his shoes unlaced, for fully ten minutes. He seemed to believe that marriage, like running, would be healthy for a person, even if initially strenuous and cumbersome.

"Stuart, you don't regard getting married as an adventure," I told him that night.

"You don't regard it as an adventure, either," he replied.

"But you shouldn't get married after ten years just because you've run out of other things to do."

"I haven't run out of other things to do. I assumed that we'd get married one of these decades, Anne. We're the oldest living cohabitators in America."

"Not so," I told him, picking up a bolster to throw at him. (I hate this trait in myself, this willingness to cut the tension in a debate with jabber and slapstick when I should say nothing and let the frosty silence work my will, the way other women do.) "Your uncle Stan and Missus LePollo are."

"They're trying to avoid losing their Social Security. Pretty soon we'll be doing the same thing. So how about it, schweetie? What've you got lined up for a week from Saturday? Or Sunday, if you're busy? Let me make an honest woman of you, even if you are a lawyer."

"You mean that's what you want to do? Just mosey on over to the Bexar County Courthouse and lasso up a judge?"

"I already said it would be romantic to just elope."

"To downtown?"

"Well, you didn't seem to like the Elvis Chapel idea. So what do you want to do? Rent the back room of Mister Allegretti's in Hoboken? Or did you want a chuppah, and a lightbulb to step on?"

It was kind of entertaining. And because of that as much as anything else, I didn't want to rev up the child thing. It wasn't that I craved reproduction with every waking breath. But I was thirty-nine that winter night, and I figured that if I was going to give the matter an honest chance, it would have to be soon. In fact, I'd been sort of madly dicing around with our birth control in recent months, not really taking any reckless chances, but not covering every base, either, just to see if anything happened. Nothing had.

Unlike virtually every one of my single friends, I'd never had an abortion or even a serious pregnancy scare. My period marched in unremarkably every month, took off its cardigan, and stayed for the exact same four days it had since I was thirteen. Was I that careful? Or that sterile? In the past few years, the distinction had begun to matter. And so I dithered around that night: I wasn't ready to have a child right now. I wasn't ready to say I never wanted one. I didn't spend my days at Women and Children First spinning fantasies about my own nestlings, but it was becoming increasingly difficult for me to see what reasons I had for choosing not to be a mother.

"Stuart, I think the way it goes for most people who stay

childless is that they're tempted to have children but they know they have good reasons not to. I just don't have those good reasons."

Didn't that sound sensible?

"A person doesn't have a child because she can't think of a reason not to, Anne. And you do have reasons not to. You have a demanding, draining job—"

"Which I don't even want half the time," I interrupted. "I could do fifty other things. Part time, even."

This was the major difference between us: I found my work interesting and even compelling, but it was not a calling, as Stuart's was for him. This often made things easier: when Stuart got the chance to work in Texas (the equivalent of Jerusalem for a death row lawyer), I could tag along, certain I'd find a job. And I did. I could even see myself working in private practice one day. It would not put my soul in jeopardy to make more than thirty thousand dollars a year, and I was still a doctor's daughter: I liked my sheets to have the two hundred thread count, and I bought new running shoes twice a year, while Stuart wore his until they were as thin as ballet slippers. Capital punishment, the Knicks, and I—in that order, I sometimes felt—were the reasons Stuart got out of bed in the morning.

"You're getting to a dangerous age," he'd told me that night, making his opening argument for the prosecution.

The defense objected: "People have kids much later now, Stuart. You know that."

"And there are already too many children in the world. . . ."

"There are too many lawyers in the world too."

"Anne," he pleaded, "you know what I am. You know what I do. When I think of that mix with a child in it . . ." It wasn't just the hours, the strain, the pitiless economic pasting they took (Stuart and his colleagues at the Texas Defense Center made salaries that didn't seem horrible on paper, until you factored in days that lasted seventy-two hours, none of them billable). All that did make for a fragile personal life, true enough. But the real reason death row lawyers didn't have children was that life was incompatible with death.

For Stuart's clients, everything that could go wrong with life had. "The mental slowness we pleaded was no stretch. The guy was a rock—he was plant life with a tongue." So Stuart's best Texas friend, Tarik, once said of Willert Styles, a spree killer Tarik had battled three years to save, whose date with fate (Stuart and his friends called an execution "dinner and a movie") took place just a couple of months before. "He was a bag of lawn clippings with legs, and his parents would have treated lawn clippings better."

"If they're so worthless," my girlfriend Jeanine used to ask Tarik, "then why is it so important for them to live?"

"It's only important for them not to die," Tarik would tell her.

I'd heard it all so many times. I even believed in it. I was proud of Stuart's convictions. Still, an overwhelming lassitude seized me whenever Stuart pulled the "what I am" card in one of our discussions. From that moment on, it would be like running in cold syrup. We'd pirouette around the impasse like smart people: Stuart would say his work was just like having a baby; it ruined his sleep and trashed his social life. But it never grew up, I'd respond, it never got smarter and made you a valentine.

Back and forth. Back and forth.

Point, Stuart. Advantage, Annie.

The unspoken fact was that there was no way to compromise: one of us would have to blink. It was inevitable that we'd eventually wash up on the place where there was nothing left but to consider what would happen if we couldn't get married. Would we go on as we were? Break up?

I knew that for Stuart, remaining the kind of loverly pals we'd always been, in bed and out, was a life goal. But I didn't know if it still was for *me*.

So that night I started to feel really sorry for both of us. How poignant it was that, despite neither of us really being wrong, nothing could really be all right. Sad, even contrite, Stuart began nuzzling my shoulders: another of his life tenets was that a nice sexy interlude could bridge all human spans. I didn't exactly disagree with this prescription, usually. But this time, unlike other times, neither of us could even summon the will for sex. Looking back, I see that sense of something beginning to end must have prepared the ground for what took root between Arley and me. Of course, if you had asked me then, I would have told you that Arley's kind of trouble was the distilled essence of everything about Women and Children First that could grind a lawyer to a stump. Some nights, my junior colleague, Patty Flanagan, and my friend Jeanine—an adoption social worker—would end a just-girls night at our favorite haunt with a toast to Louise Marker Drew. Mrs. Drew was the Texas whiskey heiress who stunned her kin twenty years earlier by bequeathing her entire estate to found a legal support center for women in trouble. "To Missus Drew," Jeanine would say, "defending the sacred right of women to make piss-poor life choices!"

Patty and I didn't really feel that way about our clients, not usually, not any more than Jeanine believed in chastity belts for her serial-birth mothers. Some of my clients squeezed my heart with their courage and gallantry. But others . . . you did get weary. A young woman would show up with a fat lip and a big belly, and you'd get her sorted out—a training job, a place to live—and eighteen months later she'd be back, with the same fat lip and big belly. After seven years, burnout was not just a concept. At first—in fact, for a long time—I fooled myself into believing that my involvement with Arley was so intense because it constituted a career crossroads, either a new beginning or a last hurrah. It was never that. It was, from the beginning, a person-to-person call, a near-biological obligation. I hadn't had such an experience before—how could I have recognized it?

That morning in December, all I wanted was for the poor and downtrodden to get their asses in gear and quit flopping over like carp for anything with hairy legs stuck in a pair of snakeskin cowboy boots with lifts. I was sick of hearing about how much some crankhead fruitcake looked like Michael Bolton and how, no matter how bad he was, no one else really understood how good he was inside.

The name "Arlington Mowbray" was taped across the top of the first intake file in my In box. It was real Texas. Everybody seemed to have been named after a character in *General Hospital*. I took one look at the top line: "Female, aged 14, married, wishes to obtain . . . ," picked up the file, and went out into the hall, ready to pass it off to the first sap I ran into, Matt or Raul or Patty. After all, I was the boss. Why did *I* have to lead the charge into the valley of the doomed every damn day?

But as I was searching for my intended victim, I saw her. She was sitting in the lobby, just under the big plant shelf. Lilia, our secretary, was obsessively sponging off the philodendron, and the tall, dark-haired teenager didn't even seem to notice the drops of water that spattered her purse, her arms, and the folder on the chair beside her. It wasn't just that she was beautiful, though she was. What was remarkable was that she seemed not to have been

touched by teenhood to the slightest degree. Her rope of shiny
dark-brown hair hung over one shoulder in an ordinary braid.
She wore no jewelry; her ears weren't pierced with even a single
punch—a fashion statement most girls would have considered
wildly conservative if not worse. Strangest of all, she had no
blemishes. Except for the thick wings of her brows, her skin was
as pure as an eight-year-old's.

As I watched her that first day, I saw her reach around reflec-
tively to grab hold of the thick brush formed by the end of her
braid and sweep it across her lips, a gesture I would come to
know as intimately as the smell of my own pillow. Arley was reading *Seventeen*, and she was reading it the way *I* used to read
Seventeen, as if she were studying for SATs. I saw her run her
thumbnail furtively down the inside gutter to slice out a page,
then fold it with the speed of a magician into the front pocket of
her jeans, which, I noticed, were ironed. I knew what she'd do
later on: she'd try to duplicate that stunningly coordinated
ninety-dollar outfit with something in the same colors at Kmart
for $15.99, which she would wear with self-conscious delight for
three weeks, until it opened at the seams and unraveled.

I can think of half a dozen possible triggers—my biological
clock, Arley's touching intelligence—but none of them would
fully explain the immediate fusion. I'd seen a great many young
women in trouble, all needing my help or my protection, needing
the things my credentials could provide. And a few had extraordi-
nary potential.

But of all of them, only Arley—without the worldly wisdom
to understand her presumption—tried to offer me something in
return. Propelled, and later terrified, by her own need, she recognized mine. I don't know why.

I don't know how long I watched her; knew only that after a time, I realized I felt like a peeper and should say something. But I couldn't. I couldn't summon the words. I saw her look at her hair in the mirror, lift it up on the back of her neck and turn, gazing at her reflection in the fish tank across the room as if she were peering into a pond. She tried a haughty look. She tried next to look deliriously joyful, putting on one of those open-mouthed smiles that seem to have caught someone in the midst of saying, "I'm having the time of my life!"

And when I saw her do that, I was lost; I know that now, and she knows it too. Those first moments, I was swamped by a tidal current of memory for my sophomore self, when I was so desperately unhappy that I kept threatening suicide, until my mother finally said, "So kill yourself already. Just shut up about it."

"Don't ever cut it," I finally said to Arley that day, forcing myself to stride into the room, holding out my hand to shake.

She grinned. "I'm not going to cut it. I'm just going to hate it, every day from now until January, when the weather cools off."

"And when it's cooler?"

"Then I'll feel like a princess."

"So it's worth it? Or is it only half worth it?"

That stopped her. She seemed to think I was scraping deeper than the topic of hairstyles, and maybe I was. "I need to see the lawyer," she said then, a splash of color lighting her dark skin. "I have to do this"—she pointed to her file—"because I have to go back to school."

"Are you in college?" I asked, just to see what she'd say.

"I was going to say I am," she told me, with a level look. "But you all got the facts of me right in front of you. I'm only in high school, ma'am. Freshman year."

"So what brings you here?"

She brushed her lips with her braid, thoughtfully. "I guess because I think they should respect a person's civil rights."

"This person is you?"

"Yes. Me and my husband. My husband Dillon."

"You really are married, then?"

She stared hard at me. "Are you the lawyer?"

"I'm one of them, yes."

"Are you *my* lawyer?"

"I might be, if it turns out that you need a lawyer."

"Then you already know about what I'm here for. I told the lady."

"Why don't you tell *me*?"

"I am legally married. Even though I'm . . . well, I'll be fifteen."

"When?"

"In April."

"And, Arlington, just how—"

"It's Arley. Arley Mowbray. Well, now it's really Arley Mowbray LeGrande. I'm sorry to interrupt, ma'am."

"Pretty name."

"Arlington is the name of a town. Between Dallas and Fort Worth."

"Is that where your family is from?"

"No, I . . . we're all named after towns in Texas, my sister and my brother and me."

"Why?"

"Well, my mama—" she began, and then said, "Does that matter?"

"No, of course not. Just making conversation."

"Yeah."

"So how did you come to marry so young?"

"It's not *so* young. We just read *Romeo and Juliet*, and she was exactly my age." I couldn't help but smile. She saw it.

I said, "Yes, but that didn't work out so well."

"This will."

"I hope so."

I took her into my office, and she immediately began playing with the perpetual motion gadget on the desk, just the way every child who came into that space did, instantly and with utter concentration, experimentally plomping the steel balls on strings one against the other. I paged through the intake forms again, thinking almost exactly what Stuart would say later, that Arley's story was fit for the Hallmark Hall of Fame of bad ideas. Not everyone goes to prison for just cause, particularly in the republic of Texas, but from the facts, Dillon LeGrande came from the kind of people who could have found trouble in any quarter of the lower forty-eight.

The eldest of four sons of a mother widowed once by a refinery explosion and once by a knife fight, Dillon seemed to have more or less raised himself in the little town of Welfare, one of those single-tavern burgs on the ragged hem of San Antonio's outskirts. Arley's family lived only a few miles west, but their orbits didn't seem to have overlapped, despite their having attended the same magnet school in Alamo Heights. Dillon's brothers were roughneck punks, in and out of foster care and baby jail for the usual drinking-fighting-truancy stuff, but Dillon seemed to have stayed out of trouble—officially, anyway—until the night he and his brother Kevin decided to take a friend and his handgun and hold up a gas station in Comfort, a few miles north of their home. The hapless kid working the cash register ended up with his left arm shattered by a gunshot wound, and Dillon and Kevin

wound up in Solamente River Prison. As the elder and, supposedly, the shooter, Dillon had been given eight years.

Arley and Dillon had begun corresponding in September.
She'd visited him once. He'd pledged his troth. For two full
weeks, they'd been husband and wife.

I sighed. Ordinarily, I started interviews with a stab at outlin-
ing goals: Why were we here together? What had happened and
what was needed? But for some reason I found myself eager that
day to influence a situation I knew very well was none of my
business.

And so I asked Arley, "What possessed you to do this thing?
What possessed your mom to sign for it? Was he your boyfriend
before he went in?"

Arley shook her head. "I didn't have a boyfriend before him. I
just got to know him through the letters."

"Three months ago."

"Three months." She squared her shoulders then and said,
"He's really good." And I knew what she meant—good in the
sense that applies to a child, or to a nun. "I know what I'm doing.
I might only be fifteen—"

"You're fourteen."

"Okay, but I know what I'm doing. I know what I'm doing
when it comes to this. My husband—Dillon—has a clean record
for his . . . incarceration, and he really should be out in less than
two years. It's all right there."

"So what's the problem?"

"Ma'am," said Arley, coloring deeply, "he needs me to be with
him before that." I could tell it was killing her to do this, and I
felt like a shit. She would not have said any of this for worlds, except that Dillon mattered more to her than her sense of decency. I
didn't realize then what an exaggerated sense that was, or why,

though I would come to see that Arley's decency was exactly like her skein of heavy hair—equal parts discomfort and joy.

"He wants a conjugal visit," I suggested.

"And I do too."

"It's been denied."

"Yep."

"You want to have sex with him."

"I want to . . . be close to him."

I put my face in my hands. "Well, Missus LeGrande, unless there is something that you are not telling me, unless there is something I learn about your husband that you have not told me: for example, that his record suggests that he constitutes a risk to your health or well-being"—beyond the obvious, I thought—"or a risk to the security of Solamente River Prison, your request and his petition together should work. Now, your responsibility—"

"I can pay. . . ."

I sighed. "Well, you pay what you can pay. We generally work those things out fairly well. But what I was going to say was, your responsibility is to tell me the truth and give me some patience while I try to work this out without litigation—that is, without having to—"

"Without going to court."

"Exactly. Because I think that would be best for everyone involved, including you and your husband and the state of Texas and, God knows, me."

"Well, I can be patient."

I hope so, I nearly said, looking at her and thinking, You haven't been a bit patient so far; why can't you be patient enough to grow your last inch or two before you load all this on? I wanted to say, Kid, this barge is never going to get any lighter, and it will only sink lower in the water, no matter how fast you pole or bail.

But there was something in her gaze, a kind of pleading, that suggested she already understood everything—the sorry way this looked, the inappropriateness of her claim, the risk of shame—about this thing she'd launched, and that it was beyond her, entirely beyond her, to correct the path of flight.

And I sensed what I would later know: that Arley needed no help from me at experiencing guilt or regret. That she'd seen the world as mostly a place of recklessness all her young life. I'd learn that she had created a plan on paper, her Book of Life Goals, out of fear of growing up the way she'd been raised—that is, recklessly—and that, much as she loved Dillon, it hurt to see her carefully written entries on sports and clothes and manners become so many sticks and ladders, marks in rainbow ink, meaningless as bird tracks.

As we stood up, I managed to avoid the impulse to pat her shoulder. Suddenly she pointed to the purple folder she carried and said, "I'm going to leave this with you all now. But there's just one thing."

I sighed. "What?"

"In our letters. In here. You'll see that I lied at first. I said I was older."

"I see. But he knows now? Everything?"

"Yes, ma'am. Everything. And he doesn't mind." I looked at the lean curve of Arley's waist and thought, I'll bet he doesn't, I'll just bet he doesn't one bit, but all I said was, "Well. Then it's no problem for me, I suppose."

I watched her close the door behind her, and said to myself, Well, we will just have to find a way for this girl to land as softly as possible. Then I sat down with my cold coffee, to read the "evidence" in her purple folder, which she'd labeled in filigreed sticker letters, "Dillon and Arlington LeGrande."

CHAPTER TWO

Arley

I used to think none of this would have happened if I'd been raised normal. But maybe it doesn't change everything. Once I met a girl who grew up in a rich family in Dallas—her father was even a doctor—and she told me that in high school she was drunk every day; she drank milk and Scotch out of a thermos every morning. It had to be her parents' fault, but I couldn't see how. She told me they did everything for her.

The way I see it, everything came out of me getting the job at Taco Haven. It was my first step. The way it worked was, Elena talked her mom into letting her get a part-time job. She told her mother it would make her "more responsible," even though she didn't even know whether she could find a job at that point! Then Elena went over to see Ginny Jack, the owner of Taco Haven (which was just across the street from our school, where Alamo Heights merges into San Antonio). She convinced Ginny that the two of us should work there, and that we should work the same hours—which she told Ginny was for safety but was really just so that we could goof around and be together. Then I had to talk my mama into letting me take the job. Which was not easy, but I was pretty set on it.

It was going to be part of my master plan, anyhow, a way to save money for college or for moving out on my own. Some teachers were starting to say I could get a scholarship.

Mama just said forget it. No way was I working Saturdays. She told me it was because she didn't like me hanging around with Elena, not because of why you would think—that Elena was a little wild—but because Mr. G. had his own construction business and all. She didn't want me getting ideas about what I should have or not have, I guess, but she acted like it was because the Gutierrezes were Hispanic and we were somehow better than them, which is a big laugh. We didn't have much room to talk about social class. City people would have called us hillbillies or worse, though there are no hills right around where I lived.

Well, I said I still wanted a job, because then I could pay for my own clothes. Mama said she'd think about it. Of course, she came right up with another objection. One night, she waited up to see me, even though it was a lot of trouble for her, being as how her shift started at six and she usually worked until five the next day and didn't get home until seven. "No way are you leaving this house on Saturday," she said. "Any Saturday. That's your day to get your work done here. I can't work these kinds of hours without you take care of this house, see? *That's* your job. That's your keep." I wanted to defy her. But I knew she would give me up as incorrigible. Lots of mothers said to girls they'd give them up to the state if they didn't behave, but they didn't mean it. Mama truly did.

I did sass her, sort of, one of the only times in my life I ever said anything back to her. I said, "So it isn't really about Elena's family."

"Well, I don't really care if they adopt you," she told me. "If they're so successful, they could use another kid."

Elena's mother actually did treat me like another kid in the family. And she was happy when Elena and me started being best friends. We'd always kind of known each other. But then, in eighth grade, Elena cheated off me in a math test, and when I caught her, she started to cry. That surprised me, because I always thought of her as so tough. So when the teacher noticed how good her grade was, I lied and said she didn't look. Elena said that was the most loyal thing she ever saw anybody do.

When we got the job, Mrs. Gutierrez said, "Well, at least Arley can be a good influence on you, Elena, and you can do like she does. She doesn't have half of what you have, and you look how hard she works." That embarrassed me, but you know, I was secretly kind of proud of it, and when I started hanging out at their house more, I would sort of leave my book reports around, so Mrs. G. would see how neat they were labeled and typed and decorated. I even kind of liked it when she said that I would end up a doctor or a lawyer and Elena would be, like, selling earrings at the mall.

"No way, Ma," Elena would pipe up. "I want to be a nude dancer. You know that."

Mrs. G. would mutter swear words or prayers in Spanish and go in the kitchen to get chips for us. The best thing about working, for Elena, was getting her mom off her case.

"She's such a royal bitch," Elena would say. But Mrs. Gutierrez wasn't a bitch at all. Elena just didn't know there were mothers who wouldn't even know what year of school you were in. When Mrs. G. would go, "Did you study for your English test, Elena Louise?" she thought it was a way of controlling her. To me, it was like tucking her in at night, or something, and when I would stay over on Saturday nights after Elena and me went to the movies at the mall, and her mom started nagging me, too, about how I would wreck my complexion eating so much grease or whatever, I totally loved it. I would even show her my report card, and she would make me promise I would never waste that good mind on just being a housewife, like her. "Go on," she would tell me. "Say, 'I promise, Luisa.' " I couldn't really call her Luisa, though, but I did, sometimes, quietly call her "Ma." The way Mrs. G. must have felt about me at first, about what I did, was one of the things that hurt the most. They had one of those big, close Hispanic families, where they watch out for the girls like they were made of cake sugar that would melt in the rain. Not that this had much effect on Elena's oldest sister, Gracie. Connie was the nice sister, but Grace was a desperado, who'd once even spent a few months at the Evins Center in Edinburg after she refused to go to school so many times Mr. and Mrs. G. had to call the authorities. Connie, on the other hand, was in college now, at Midtown Tech. I never even thought too much about college before Elena's mom started saying how different I was from other girls my age. How serious. It made me think maybe my life was more than just a thing Mama could do with whatever she wanted.

The way it turned out, though, Mrs. Gutierrez wouldn't let Elena work Saturdays, either. She thought Elena needed at least one whole day for rest and homework. So we agreed with Ginny that we'd just work Tuesdays and Thursdays after school and afternoons on Sunday. Mama was just about to say no to that, too, but then Elena had this great idea: She said, why didn't I offer Mama some money every week? So I did. And Mama said okay, twenty bucks. I said no, ten. She said at least that was enough for smokes, so fine.

That's what finally did it. And it's a good example of what's so good about Elena. I can look at a chemistry problem and "see" it right away; but I can't see through people the way Elena can.

Taco Haven was no great shakes. Elena's sister Grace called it "Restaurante Cucaracha," but it wasn't all that dirty. We had fun there, and we felt grown up, getting a check every week with our names printed on it, even if the check was only for sixty dollars.

What if Mama had really put her foot down? Or what if we'd applied to be baggers at Oberly's or The Supershop? There must have been a master plan even bigger than mine. Annie says, "Everything is chance. People just believe in fate so they can think they're not to blame."

But even Annie goes out the door backward if she forgets her list or her keys and has to go back in. She tosses salt and makes *puffi-puffi* noises with her lips when someone talks about a tragedy. She insists that's not superstition, that it's Jewish voodoo. "Inherited insanity," she calls it. She never used to know how ideas like those would seize hold of me, such as that a child could be born looking perfect, with bad genes wriggling inside.

Early that Sunday at Taco Haven, I was thinking about boys, but not about having babies with one. I was thinking how weird I was, compared with other girls, for not having a boy in my Book of Life Goals. But the way Mama was about men—the way she went all dreamy over the doctors' hands at the hospital where she worked, and the way she used to bring home salesmen and cowboys about once a month, who drank all our orange juice from the carton—that and the big-haired girls my brother Cam had in his room all night, who came out smeary and smelling . . . none of these things exactly made me feel like having a crush. Back in seventh grade, every girl was wearing one of those red stickpins you got at Rangers games to show she had a boy. But I didn't even want one. Even as a high-school freshman, when everybody would ask who I was going out with, I would just smile. Elena said I had a mysterious smile and that I would make them all think I was going out with a college boy. But it was scary to me, scary like the time back in kindergarten when the kids locked the teacher out of the room and everybody laughed but me, and I got scared and took so many deep breaths I passed out.

At sleepovers, Elena and this other girl she was friends with for a while, Chita, would tell me all about how it felt to have a boy's tongue in your mouth. It felt like a live animal, they said, separated from the person, and at first it was sickening, but then it got to feel weird if you kissed and you didn't do it. And the way they would try to touch your top with their wrists instead of their hands so that they could act like it was an accident. Elena had made out from the waist up with three or four boys. And one touched her between her legs outside her pants. She said she liked it. The feelings made her wiggle. I'd say, "It sounds amazing." But I thought, what if he had mustard just before? What if I gagged? But I didn't say anything. I couldn't even see why a hot girl like Elena would want anything to do with a string bean like me, her with her little gymnast's body, calves that looked like she was always wearing heels, and her big red smile like Halloween wax lips. When we went out, boys would howl at her like coyotes in the hills; I was Elena's shadow.

That was before Dillon, of course. After that, being a real woman, in a physical way, seemed so easy. I was as good at it as I was at hurdles—a natural. I was beautiful from his first word to me, long before he ever touched me. I know that sounds silly.

That day in September, it was so hot outside that every time someone opened the door, the air would lick into Taco Haven like gas off a charcoal grill, and you'd start to sweat instantly. They lie about Texas heat when they say it's dry and you don't feel so bad. What it's really like is so humid sometimes and so dry others that you feel like you got up in the morning and, first thing you went out, you were wetted down and rolled in flour like a tortilla. That day, whenever I wasn't waiting on somebody, I stayed in the back, next to the freezer. I could count on my hands the times I'd ever been cold in my life. In fact, I never had but one blue-jean jacket until Annie bought me that green trench coat to wear to court.

I was waiting on a table of college kids, two girls and two boys, when Elena's big sister Connie came in. I tell you I almost dropped my pencil, she looked so unusual. The girls and the boys shut up too, and for a minute, the only sound in the whole place came from the old skinny man, Mr. Justice, who was always hanging around by school. He was singing along to Patsy Cline on the jukebox and fiddling on the fiddle no one could see but him. I'd been worried about Mr. Justice, because Ginny Jack said I had to throw him out after a third cup of coffee or he'd sit there all day, so half my mind was on that problem and half on trying to memorize the way the college girls had braided up their hair in back with ribbons.

But Connie made me forget everything.

"Jesus Christ," Elena said to her sister. "You look like you been embalmed." Elena is so smart sometimes. That was just how Connie did look: she was pale and smooth as a mannequin in Dalton's window, and she looked somehow assembled, like from separate parts—a cheek, an eyebrow, a lip.

"Shut up," said Connie, but nice and smiley. "It's the corrective makeup," she told Elena. "We worked on each other today. Can I get a Coke?"

The college girls must have been from four-year schools like A&M, because they looked at Connie like they expected her to be beamed up to the mother ship. I took their order right quick, so I didn't have to listen to them sniffing and saying stuff like, "Wow, I wish I could get my foundation to go on like that." I pinned their order up on the spinning rack outside the kitchen for Cully, the cook, and then I got Connie her Coke. Just so she'd know I'd noticed, I pointed my head over at those girls and said, "They're, you know, so full of it."

"I don't even notice, *querida*. Don't you worry," said Connie in that Tejana-girl voice she used to goof around, where she said "choo" for "you" so she'd sound like her grandma. All the sisters liked to pretend to be Grandma Gutierrez having one of her temper fits, flapping her shawl at you like a bullfighter. "I don't pay them no mind."

"All the same," I said, "what *is* different about your face?"

"Like I said, I'm studying corrective cosmetics." She took a sheaf of papers out of her big black bag then and spread them over the counter. I had to sit down when I saw.

There were pictures of a dark Hispanic woman with pouchy red scars all over one side of her face and of a baby girl that was the cutest thing except for this big ugly stain that started up under her baby hairline and spread all over one of her little cheeks.

"What happened to the baby?"

"She was born that way."

"It's not a burn?"

Connie pointed to the other picture, the one with the red, shiny scars. "That there lady was burned. Somebody threw scalding water," Connie said in a low, ominous voice. "She went around like that for six years. Little kids screamed when they saw her on the bus. She didn't have no self-esteem." Then Connie flipped the sheet over. It was the same lady, only the burns were *gone.*

"That's after she had surgery," I said.

"No, ma'am," said Connie. "That first shot was after she had surgery. The burns went so deep they couldn't hardly get grafts on at all. Either that or the doctor was an idiot, I don't know. Anyway, they used special makeup, which is nongreasy and waterproof."

"That is amazing," Elena said over my shoulder, passing behind me to give Mr. Justice his last cup of coffee. "So if it's such a miracle, how come you look like you dressed up for Halloween a month early?"

Connie ignored her. "Now, this baby girl here," she said, "she was born with what you call a port wine birthmark. That's 'cause it looks like somebody poured a glass of red wine on her. And her mama learned how to put Cover Creme on her so people wouldn't think that little baby was horrible-looking, because she can't have cosmetic surgery till her skin gets all grown, or whatever."

"What are you studying it for?" I asked her.

"Well," said Connie, "it's partly personal. I have what's called a nevus mark. See?" She lowered the neck of her blouse a little, and I could see this big blue bruise. "It won't never go away, and I got a big one on my butt and two big ones on my thighs too, which is why I never was one to go to the beach with boys, like Gracie."

I thought to myself that if those marks were the reason Connie didn't go like Gracie, they were probably a blessing, kind of like a protective shield. Then I thought about how happy it must have made that baby's mama and daddy to see her look so pretty, like she was meant to look, and how it would feel to be the person who gave them that gift. But all I said was, "That's way cool. Do you, like, teach people to do it on themselves? Can anyone learn it?"

"Maybe not everyone," Connie said lightly, gazing at Elena.

Elena caught the look. "It was me," she said, "I'd be studying doing that makeup thing on corpses, 'cause they stay still, and that's what *you* look like, anyhow."

"Elena La Braina, you ain't never going to no college, because you can't even find Texas on a map of Texas, girl," said her sister.

"Least I ain't got no convict boyfriend," Elena replied sweetly.

"Who? What?" I said. Then Cully rang the bell, and I had to go get the college kids' chicken-fried steaks, but I told Connie not to say one word, not a single word, until I came back. Mr. Justice got up to leave just as I was setting down the plates.

"You'd look better than them with scarlet ribbons," he told me softly, as he passed me. I guess he'd noticed, too, how rude those college girls were; still, it was so weird, an old man saying something like that. It was clearly the kind of comment you have to watch out for a man making to a young girl. But it didn't feel that way. It was more grandfatherly like. I just smiled; I was rushing back to hear Connie tell.

"Who's in prison, Connie? What do you mean?"

Connie smiled, secretly. "That's for me to know, Miss Arley."

"Come on! You know you can't *half* tell a thing! It's illegal!"

"I wasn't telling nothing at all," Connie said, drawing herself another Coke from the fountain (Ginny Jack didn't care about that stuff). "It's my little sister who's so little except for her mouth."

"Connie!"

"Okay, okay," she said then. "Don't wake the dead!"

"You got a boyfriend in jail?" This was so scary and so romantic at the same time, it sounded like something on *Melrose Place.*

"I've been seeing a man and writing to a man who is presently incarcerated," Connie said.

"Who?"

"His name is Kevin LeGrande."

I guess I was purely the last person in Texas who hadn't ever heard of the LeGrande boys. (Later on, they were known not just in Texas but in California, Oklahoma, and points east.)

Elena said, "You *some* college girl, Connie. You sure can pick 'em. Right, Arley?"

But I just asked, "How'd you meet a boy like that, Connie?"

"My auntie Grace goes to Kevin's mama's church. Actually, his church too. That English church—what does she call it? White Catholic? The mama is only a little thing herself, and she was telling my auntie her two boys were in Solamente River. Them in trouble only because this Indian kid from Austin got them to knock over a gas station, and he had a gun—"

"Did they kill somebody?"

"No, they never did. They didn't even but crease that boy's arm that was working there. And only that because he was hiding and he jumped out and scared them. And Spirito, the Indian kid, he's only sixteen. He went to the boys' farm, but Kevin got three years and his big brother, Dillon, got eight or nine 'cause he's, like, twenty-five or something, and he should have known better."

"How old is Kevin?"

"He's nineteen."

"You're twenty!"

"He's almost twenty. And anyhow, I've only been over to see him one time, and we just talked through some glass."

"Was it scary and awful in there?"

Connie looked far out the front window, to where the sun was lowering down on Alameda Street. "When they shut those big green steel doors behind you—"

"God, Connie!"

"But he is one fine boy."

"Why'd you go see him?"

"We've been writing for five months—this thing all happened way last summer. And finally he asked me if I wanted to go out—"

"Go out," Elena snorted. "That's a good one."

"Well, he asked me to be more than just a friend, is what. And pretty soon he starts getting contact visits, so you can sit next to each other and talk and all—"

"Watch he don't rub off your corrective cream, *querida!*" Elena hollered. I was glad there wasn't anybody in there except the old Mexican woman who kept house for the priest at Mater Christi, and she didn't look up once, just kept eating her chicken strips with *pico de gallo,* cutting them up in little tiny bites.

"Shut up, Elena. In fact, *stupida,* it doesn't rub off unless you use special cleanser and a towel, so there!"

"But why did you write to him?" I persisted.

"Oh, right. Well, his mama asked my auntie if she knew any nice Christian girls or boys, didn't have to be Catholic, if they would write to Kevin or Dillon because it would be good for them, they were so lonesome."

"Why'd you pick Kevin?"

"I wrote to them both, really, and Kevin wrote back, and he loves to dance. . . ." Connie got up from the round leatherette stool at the counter and did a few slow, snaky steps of the Catalina. "And I figured I was even better than whatever they are,

because I'm a real Catholic, not—um—Espiscopaliana or whatever . . . and he's real cute!"

"Aren't you afraid of when he gets out?"

"Why should I be?"

"Connie, jeez, he already went after a boy with a gun. . . ."

"It wasn't him did that."

"Not *that*," said Elena. Connie jumped like her little sister was
going under the cuticle of her nail with a needle file. I knew she
wanted to shut Elena's mouth for her.

"What *did* he do?" I asked her.

"He did some stuff. He's got no father. His daddy was killed
in this gross accident," Connie said.

"*What* stuff did he do?" I kept after her.

"Him and a bunch of boys ran some cows down with a
pickup—"

"Ran them over?"

"No, but they . . . ran them till they died, I guess."

"That's horrible. The poor things!"

"Arley, for God's sake. It's not like they were puppies or
something."

"It is to cows!"

"And that was all, except some little stuff—"

"Like?"

"Like drinking with the cowboys in the spring tent at the
rodeo. Like there's one whole boy from here to the coast who
hasn't got drunk by the time he's twelve! And school stuff, stealing
some stuff—"

"What?"

"Arley, I don't know! Like CDs or clothes or junk. He went to
the boys' school—"

35

"So he was in before."

"That's not jail!"

"Does your mama know?" I asked Connie.

"She knows I write him. She don't know I've been to see him." She aimed a blunt look at Elena. "Anyhow, Mama don't think there's a single person don't deserve another chance."

"Look at Gracie, for example," Elena put in. "She's had more chances than the state lottery."

"Why don't you write to that other boy?" I asked Elena. "Or maybe Gracie . . ."

"They'd have a lot in common," Elena said. She started wiping up the tops of the squirt bottles, which would get little hard collars of taco sauce around them in the course of a day, and I noticed we were all but ready to change over shift. "Me, I don't think no boy behind bars is going to be much fun."

She meant sex. When Elena said "fun" in her purry voice, that was what she meant. I didn't know then if she meant actual sex or fooling around. It turned out she only meant fooling around, because she wanted to know every move I made when I actually *did* it. Still, I hated when she tried to talk so big and tough, like she was Gracie and not her own sweet self under all that tangly pinned-up hair and black kohl shadow. She said, then, kind of nasty, "Why don't you write to him, Arley? You are so pure and all. You can make him see the sin in him."

Why ever do we do things? Half the time, because we're mad, angry mad, like I was then. All I remember was feeling the flush spread up from my neck and being glad I'm so dark—darker-skinned than Elena, though she's the one who's Mexican—that nobody could tell for sure I was blushing, though I tend to blush all the time. Elena thought she was so goddamned grown up compared to me. I was hot and a little nauseated that day, the way you are when you drink cold coffee and then belch, and I was tired to think I still had so much French to do, and tired of my mama treating me like a ghost if I didn't get her underwear folded colors separate from whites the way she wanted. I was sick of the stink of garlic and chilies on my hands, which would take two days to come out, and of the things wrong with me that ruined how pretty my hair was and how clear my skin was, and of my chest like a closet door with two buttons on it and of my nose, which was so flat and broad across you could balance a pencil on it. I was sick of feeling like a dumb little kid.

I thought, Elena, I'll show you.

"You give me his address," I told Connie. Elena just stared at me as if she could see my bones. "Come on. I mean it."

And I was stuck surer than a twice-doubled dare.

I went to Oberly's and spent half an hour looking at the stationery. Most of it was reeky. Puppies and flowers and rainbows and stars. Real juvenile. It looked like what a third grader would use to write to her grandma. Then, in the natural foods section, I found some stationery made of paper recycled from cut-up old cotton clothes. I knew right then it was the perfect thing; it looked just like the colors of sunset and cost six dollars. But I bought two boxes, and I never wrote one single letter to Dillon except on that paper. It was one of the things that became a tradition with us.

But I didn't know it would happen that way then. I just thought the store might run out, so I should stock up. It's funny how you find yourself preparing for things you don't even know will come.

To tell you the truth, I wasn't sure I'd write a letter at all. If I hadn't known Elena would mock me forever about it, I'd just have given up the whole thing right there.

Still, I put it off and put it off for days. It wasn't just that I was busy. I was always busy, but you're never too busy to do something unless you don't really want to. Until Elena asked me twice if I'd done it, I pretended it had just slipped my mind. In fact, I was sort of scared. What was I supposed to say, anyway, to a person like that? Was he violent? Was he pitiful? He couldn't be too smart. I knew I should feel sorry for him. But it gave me the creeps even to think of hands that pulled a trigger on a gun holding paper I'd held in my hands. Still, he was sealed up in Solamente, sealed up tighter than a coin roll. So what I really felt was the kind of fear you have waiting for the roller coaster at the Cinco de Mayo fair and already holding your ticket; you want to turn back, but you know nothing bad can actually touch you.

Even once I was going to do it, I had to plan it out. I couldn't go writing a letter at work. And I could just see my math teacher, Mr. Hogan, or Mrs. Murray or somebody else grabbing hold of it if I tried to write it in school, or Elena waving it around at the lunch table. I didn't want my stupid brother Cam seeing me, not that he'd notice anything in front of his face that wasn't edible or sung by LeAnn Rimes. The first time I decided to actually write Dillon, Mama was at work and I had chores. So I talked Elena into coming over and doing my midweek laundry. In exchange, I would coach her to an easy A on the history take-home test.

It didn't require much talking into, to tell you the truth. I couldn't ever understand it, but Elena always wanted a chance to come to my house. It must have been like a field trip for her. She thought everything there was interesting. It sure wasn't like her house, and not only because it was grungy and small. What was really different was that Cam and me pretty much lived alone; and since living with him was like living with a stuffed dummy, I basically lived alone. Mrs. G. was always running around, picking up things for Elena and reminding her of stuff. Elena couldn't believe that my mama never had to remind me of anything. She couldn't believe I didn't throw a big party every weekend, when my mother worked double shift. As far as Elena was concerned, I was setting a bad example for all the teenage kids of the world. "You're too good, girlie-girl," she would tell me when I couldn't go shopping or get fake nails or whatever because I had stuff to do. "You're just too obedient. You got to scare your parents once in a while. You should run away. I did that one time, because they wouldn't let me have a TV in my room. I stayed at my cousin's eight hours. My mom was crying and making a novena when I came home."

"Did you get the TV?"

"No. But it was fun. It taught her a lesson."

That night, Elena was putting the whites in the washer, and I was set up with my new stationery at the kitchen table, when Cam came slumping through the door. He had his blue jeans down around his bottom, and his shirt was longer than my whole body, and his hair, still so blond from summer it looked almost silver, was laced with leather in an Indian braid. He barely looked at me. But then Elena came banging back into the kitchen from the dusty shed where we kept the washer and dryer, yelling she was dying of thirst. She was flushed and sweating, all those wispy black curls clinging loose around her face and forehead. So far as I knew, Cam had only spoken to Elena once in all the times she ever came to our house—and that time, he just asked if Grace was her sister. But this time, he stopped on a dime and put down the orange juice container he was drinking from when she came in; and he looked at her and she looked back, and I saw that she was going to stare him down. She reached up and made her fingers into combs and drew both her hands through all that tangled wet hair and shook it up and back, all without taking her eyes off his. Old Cam finally sort of fell across the room and opened the refrigerator door and started looking inside as if a movie was on in there. Then he slammed the door and took these two giant steps to get into his room as fast as he could. The whole time, there was a coiled-up watching in Elena, like she was the one in charge, as if Cam was trying out for a team or something and she was the coach. She never got nervous, that girl. She still never does.

"What happened to him? He's a pretty boy now," Elena whispered when Cam was finally out of earshot.

"Pretty worthless," I answered. "The way he looks is the best thing about him. I think he's got him some kind of a genetic defect that he can't pick up his own underwear off the floor and even put it out there so I can wash it. Which I don't even know why I've got to wash it."

"You the girl," Elena said, grinning, carefully extending her shiny legs and laying one on top of the other and then admiring them like they were sculptures. She knew that she could usually get me going by saying something like that—that it drove me nuts how even in school the boys had it so much easier, how teachers would be giving them little hints all the time and looking at the girls like, What did you want, anyhow? But this time I didn't want to get into it with her. Why were we talking about Cam? What was I going to say when I wrote to Dillon LeGrande, 8477298372, Texas State Department of Corrections, Solamente River, Texas? Did I just talk to him the same as other people and ignore what he was really doing? Pretend he was away at school or something?

When she finally gave up on getting me talking, Elena pulled out her books, bitching about European history. "And I thought all this time they were saying, 'Hi, Hitler.' At least that makes sense."

"What *Heil* really means is 'hail.' Like, 'You're great.' "

"You mean like, 'Go, Hitler'?"

I sighed and just stared past her. My hair smelled like the laundry soap on my hands. I asked her then, "Did you know that the prisoners in concentration camps had numbers tattooed on their arms, and prisoners in our own country have numbers, too, that are used the same as their names?"

"Tattooed?"

"God, I don't think so. When I got this here"—I pushed over the scrap on which Connie had written Dillon's address— "I thought it was his phone number. But it's his, like, serial number."

"You mean that boy in jail? That LeGrande? You're not really going to write to him, Arley. I was just fooling. You don't want to get involved with no boy like that. All those LeGrande boys are bad to the bone, except the little one, Philippe, and that's only because he's too little to be bad."

"I'm writing a letter is all, and you were the one dared me." What did she think? That next thing I was going to start riding the bus two hours to bring him chocolate-chip cookies? In between doing this house and my job and my homework?

"I don't even see why Connie wants that Kevin, you know? Connie might have a big butt, but she ain't so bad she has to go to prison to find a boy."

"I think Connie's beautiful."

"Her butt looks like two pigs fighting in a bag. I say, 'Constanza, you can see every spoon of Choco-Mocho you ever ate.' She ought to learn liposuction along with the corrective makeup. Get herself a home unit she can plug in the wall."

It was Elena reminding me of Connie, and her cosmetics course at the technical college, that made me decide that I was going to lie to Dillon. I realized right then that one big thing I'd been worrying about all along was that no man of twenty-five, or whatever, was going to want to write to a little kid in ninth grade. So I would tell him I was in college. It would give me something to write about. And since I was never going to see him, anyhow, it didn't matter at all. Elena kept whining, "Come on, Arley, honey-girl. Tell me all about the Beer Hall Putsch. Like I have to know stuff like this in my life. I swear to God if Miz Hunter says one more time, 'You got to be fluent in your culture . . .' What culture? I live in Texas! Did you see she's sticking her keys in the bun on her head now, along with all those pens? Next it'll be Tampax. . . ."

I wanted to slap her one. All of a sudden, I was feeling as restless and full as I did on Saturday nights in summer when the Nevadas brothers drove their big metallic-red hogs past the house and the music from their stupid big boom boxes, lashed onto the backseats, came up at me in my attic room, broken in pieces by the wind, and though I felt nothing at all for Ricky Nevadas, I would be like in "The Raven"—"back into my chamber turning, all my soul within me burning . . ." Why not have a guy you write to a zillion miles away? It would give you something to show off to people in the hall before school. People who thought you were just dumb or naive because you didn't come from the big-house suburbs like Alamo Heights or Regents Landing.

"What do you think is the most interesting thing about me, Elena?"

"Your mother. Definitely."

"I'm serious."

"Well." She curled up on the bench, opposite me, and stuck her finger in her history book to mark World War II. "I guess it's that you are beautiful."

"Shoot, I'm not. *You're* beautiful."

"No. I'm hot." Elena's laughter rumbled up her throat like water bursts out of a faucet left off too long. "You *are* beautiful. Like, your hair. You could tell him about how you wash your face with table salt to keep from getting zits or that you never cut your hair in your life."

That was true. I only trimmed the ends and burned them with a match to stop the split ends. And I'd just learned to make my own shampoo from dishwashing liquid and honey and lemon. But so what? Guys don't care about your hair. I told Elena so.

"I didn't think you was thinking of him as a guy, Arley. Like a boyfriend. I just think it's interesting. You look like Pocahontas in the movie. Tell him that."

"I'm not thinking about him as a boyfriend. I just don't want to sound like a stupid little girl. And, like, how do you begin this? Do I say 'Mister LeGrande'? Or 'Dear Friend'?"

"How about 'Hi, Hitler'?" Elena suggested. And then we cracked up laughing.

It wasn't until eleven o'clock when I really sat down to write the letter. The wind was blowing in the window, and it kept floating the curtain against my face like a spiderweb. I looked down, and there was Ricky Nevadas out in his backyard, in nothing but his jeans, washing his bike in the light from the streetlamp and singing the same song he always sang, "Bye Bye, Love." He saw me in the window and whipped the towel around his head a couple of times. You could see the light shine off the drops of water or sweat on the hair under his arms. I pulled the curtain and sat on my bed.

And I wrote Dillon about my hair that hadn't been cut in twelve years, about how Cully, the cook at Taco Haven, had to get the big-size hair net—the kind he used for his dreadlocks—for me to wear in the kitchen.

I wrote about the music I like, zydeco and the Indigo Girls, about Cam, and how he thinks he's Kenny Wayne Shepherd or better, and I even told him that my mama had never been married—because you might as well be honest.

Except, then I wasn't. Because I wrote about the paramedical cosmetics, too, and being in college with Connie. It got kind of fun. I was philosophizing: "Anything that makes you different can be a cause of rejection, don't you think?" That got boring, so then I told him I ran track, because I knew it would make him think I had a good body. And then I didn't have anything else to say. That was plenty for a first letter, especially to someone you didn't even care whether they wrote back.

But it just didn't feel like enough.

So I told him about my dream.

What would have happened if I hadn't? If I'd just stopped there and left it with the problems I had with my hamstring stretches, what would have happened? Would it have been better, all the way around, if it had all stopped right there, without my ever knowing a thing about him, all that happened between us sucked right back into time like water into dry ground? Could I say that and still be true to Desi? To myself?

It doesn't matter now. I told him about the wagon dream, which I had pretty often, starting years and years ago, from when I was little. I kept having it too, until after Desi was born. The first time, I was in second grade and the teacher was telling us about the westward expansion, about how Texas had become an independent republic and a state. I wrote to Dillon: "She told us how deprived these families were, coming out across all those miles of prairie in covered wagons, how some of the babies starved to death because their mothers didn't have enough food to make their milk." The funny thing about the way I heard those stories, I thought it was "colored wagons." I could just picture them, all these bright colors, like sidewalk chalk—lime and pink and watery blue. I pictured them in my head, and I drew them for school, just strung out across fields of grass like soap beads. And when I dreamed about it, they would go up at the end, right up into the sky. "Sometimes," I wrote in that first letter to Dillon, "I think that dream was kind of a message, that I'm waiting for a train of colored wagons, waiting so I can get on and get on out of here." Then I was done. There just wasn't anything at all left of my life to tell. Anyhow, it was already three pages, both sides.

Three days later, I got a letter back. It was only a page, but it came express. The postman brought it right up to the door; thank God Mama wasn't home.

It said that my name was filled with "music" and my dream with "prophecy." And it finished up with these lines: "I can't abide cheap trading on real feelings. So if you think it would be a big laugh to tell your girlfriends you're writing to a man behind bars, find a different man. I'm sure there's plenty wouldn't mind. Now, myself, I'm hungrier than I can rightly explain for the pleasures of real life, and they've been denied me for two more long years. So if you want to write, I will answer you. If you honestly want to share thoughts with me, I will respond truthfully. It was that dream about rising up and out, out of this dusty redneck hell, that made me have enough trust to do it this first time. But if you're not that woman of energy and heart, don't write me back. I won't bear you ill will."

It was signed: "Yr. obedient servant, Dillon Thomas LeGrande."

I couldn't believe it. I wanted to cry, I felt so ashamed.

It was like he saw right through me. Saw me sitting there thinking maybe I could use him for some kind of status symbol at school, for proof that I wasn't little Goody Two-shoes. It was just what he feared.

The saddest thing, though, what really grabbed my heart, was that in spite of what he suspected, he still turned to me. He was so lonely, he had to take the risk of getting betrayed. And I was the one he turned to.

I couldn't foresee, from that first letter, what would happen with us. But I knew how it felt to be that lonely, to feel as though there wasn't one other person in the whole world who truly cared about your feelings or your thoughts. To feel you would never be free of everything that tied your hands. And so the pull from him to me was like the pull of the earth, all that loneliness a void to be filled.

Of course it's easy for me to say now, because I know what came afterward. But somehow I felt bound to Dillon from that first moment, simply by how much he needed me. No matter what else, I've never seen anything to convince me that being wanted isn't more powerful than wanting, that it's the most powerful thing of all.

Annie once got so mad at me when I was explaining this to her that she about went savage. She said Dillon probably tried that line about his loneliness on a dozen girls, that he was a professional manipulator, using self-pity to set the hook, and that he finally snagged someone. And maybe she's right. But I also think that from the very beginning, Annie was jealous of the power Dillon had over me, and jealous, too, of the way we felt. After all, she knew how you could fall in love—the kind of love anyone would recognize as love, the kind that's enough to have a life together, even—and still not feel how we did.

46

Or maybe it's just different for people like Dillon and me. Annie's not from here. She used to say she'd seen it all at her legal aid
agency, but seeing it's not the same thing. You're still a step outside the rim. Annie's mama would leave messages if Annie didn't
call her every single Sunday. But a phone call at the house where I
lived with Mama and Cam could be to tell you someone was in
jail up North or dead. You asked somebody, they'd always say kin
is kin. But that doesn't mean the same thing to people everyplace.
When you grow up with all kinds of love from your blood kin,
maybe you don't have that desperate hope for someone out there
waiting who can make up for all the things blood never brought
you. Someone who can look deep inside you and see things no
one ever bothered to tell you were there.

We both knew. Not right away, but early on. It was like you
had been waiting all your life, hungry for one sweet food; and finally you got it in your mouth, and you knew you would never
need anything else to fill you again. Like God didn't make one,
but two, and you were born knowing everything in each other
before you ever laid eyes on each other or said one word.

Dillon later said that what convinced him I was his special
waiting someone was the way I described my dream, the very last
thing I wrote, the thing I almost left out of my letter.

Dillon thought that numbers were significant, and he thought
that since the first letter I wrote him was about the first dream I
remembered, and because he was my first love, we were meant to
share that dream. I reckon that's at least one thing he never had to
lose.

CHAPTER THREE

Annie

There was no good reason to drive over to Avalon to see Arley that Wednesday. There was no good reason to see Arley at all, in fact, for the time being.

I had a dozen cases in which time pressed more urgently. But there were plenty of things to do for Arley's sake. One thing was to phone Ray Henry Southwynn, the warden at Solamente River, to see whether a few minutes of plain talk could derail the potentially expensive path of this petition somewhere short of court. But first, I needed to be more of an authority on the matter. For me, hell is being embarrassed. And there's nothing that can short-sheet you faster than a lack of information.

I flipped through Arley's file. I could call a few of her teachers. I could call her mother. I could do all those things if I could sit still, which I couldn't. A dangerous bout of buying anything I could find in the office vending machine and slathering it with frijole dip threatened, so I took a walk down the hall, looked in to see if Patty could be distracted into wasting some time with me, ended up settling for a bag of pretzels and the tepid coffee that was Lilia's specialty—today, everything in Texas would be boiling except the coffee in our office.

Back at my desk, I decided to call my sister. We hadn't spoken in weeks. I looked at my watch. She'd still be home, flying around the kitchen, stuffing clients' business plans and her sons' forgotten homework papers into the same huge, worn doctor's black bag (formerly my father's) that Rachael had used as a briefcase since graduation. I lifted the receiver and listened to the harsh buzz, but I didn't dial her number. There was something I wanted to ask Rachael. Something that pertained to my business with Arley. I just wasn't sure what.

Still restless, I sat on the windowsill and flipped open Arley's purple folder. Here was Dillon, in one early letter, on the night of the crime: "I should never have been used the way I was at the Humble station with Kevin and his buddy. I let myself get victimized by greed. The only thing that hurts is that I ended up taking the fall for everyone else. But there's no point complaining about it. I could tell you a great deal about that night that would put it in perspective, but it would only be scratched out by the censors (hello, gentlemen!), and it will suffice to say that I had never had a gun in my hand outside of the pasture back home until that very night—though I must admit, I am a dead shot. . . ." Nothing special here, or at least, not really. Lots of tough-guy talk and that ever-present savor of conspiracy. In Stuart's experience, he always says, plenty of bad eggs are eager to admit what they've done and treat you to the Technicolor version. But in my job I seem to encounter the kind of mopes who were always on their way to either choir practice or a tryout with the Mets when nasty fate intervened. I couldn't get what little I'd seen of Arley to stick comfortably to the flypaper of Dillon's quite ordinary self-pity—she seemed to have such preternatural grace and sanity for a girl her age. How had things escalated, in mere weeks, from ordinary lonely-pen-pal-in-the-pen chatter—"Gee, there's nobody like you"—to "Instead of going out on your first date, how about marrying an armed robber?"

I read on. It was all the fault of younger brother Kevin, who had been "wild as a hard rain since the day he was born and given our mom no end of suffering." But enough about good old Mom: Dillon quickly got back to number one. "If only that kid at the Humble had not jumped down on me like the damned Sundance Kid—I'm surprised he didn't kill us both—nobody would've been hurt. He didn't have to do that. He didn't have to be no hero. All Kevin wanted was beer money, anyhow. And now here I sit. I can see about four inches of sky through the window just across of my cell and down the hall. My big excitement for the week is when I see a storm cloud. The whole place gets jumpy when there's going to be a storm. We're like cattle in a barn, trying to feel changes in the air."

Well, there *was* that: he was smarter than most.

But guys in prison have nothing if not time, and those who can read do. They borrow from what they read; there isn't a con without a whole storybook full of naive, romantic, grandiose, unfocused plans. Dillon certainly had his down pat: He was going to trace his roots back to County Galway, Ireland, where his mother's people, the Dillons, were from. He was going to write poetry—after all, wasn't there some kind of kismet in the fact that he was named Dillon Thomas (never mind the spelling). And he was going to collect antiques, and get a big cattle spread like his grandpa used to have, before the old man was forced to sell off. "And a week later," Dillon wrote, "the land was punched for oil leases and ended up making every non-Dillon in sight richer than God." Sheesh. The dog probably died too, run over by the pickup truck. If Dillon LeGrande's family didn't have bad luck, evidently, they'd have had no luck at all.

My head began to hurt at the back, the place where I believe conundrums are stored like tightly capped jars of pickles and relish. Hadn't there been a single person in Arley Mowbray's life with enough brains to point out that this particular ladder of love was one any fool could see didn't have a safe rung to stand on? And even if every single person she knew had warned her, would it have mattered?

Any fool, I thought. My job had not done much to strengthen my belief in the common sense of women. From what I'd seen, for the love of a man, plenty of women would cut up their best friends and sell them for body parts. Good relationship? Lousy relationship? Didn't seem to matter much. Experience with that kind of psychology had made me sort of a handicapper for certain varieties of attraction—I could pick the couples who would wind up at our office in pieces just by looking at what special sorts of trouble they'd been raised on and were predestined to seek out for themselves when they grew up. It didn't explain, though, how a normal woman, with normal cells and an ordinary background, could pass Go at warp speed without a backward glance, headed straight for the worst man in the room. I myself had never had the kind of love that didn't sprout from friendship. In Stuart, especially, there was the essential buddiness that outlasted simple heat. And so it had been with the ones before him—only two major candidates, really—both candid, indoorsy English majors, versions of me who buttoned on the right.

It wasn't that I didn't believe in the charms of animal attraction. Attraction was a good thing. The involuntary tightening of tissues, the flutter, the sinking, the sense of wanting to steep yourself in another person's smell. Great sex was like a good massage—a gift of being alive you could not imagine doing without. But I would never have willingly danced in traffic for its sake, or any other sake. I'd learned from meeting scores of sad-eyed old ladies who'd had only thirty birthdays that life was too short for certain risks. You definitely didn't want it to get shorter.

I began chewing through a pen casing, a little stress habit I'd always had and never noticed until the bitter-grass taste of the ink broke through. We were talking about a fourteen-year-old here, a girl who still considered songs on the radio renditions of her real feelings.

But was that fair?

Didn't the radio sing to all fools?

How many times had I tried to suppress giggles when Stuart got choked up trying to sing along with "Up On the Roof," which reminded him fatally of Mary Sullivan, the goddess of his apartment-house terrace, who loved him with a ferocity that curled his toes, then left him for a seminarian. Twenty-five years later, he said he could still smell the vanilla of her red hair. And Jeanine. Jeanine was my best friend in Texas, sane as salt, the director of an adoption agency, who swore that, in her job, she'd seen every permutation on a loser that the Y chromosome had to offer. But she'd met Bruce at the airport and taken off with him to Key West, only to end up in an enlightening phone call with his (second) wife a week later.

And look at Rachael. I knew now why she was on my mind so much. Carlos. I found a fresh pen and settled down for another chew. My own saintly sister, the princess of prudence, a woman who actually planned, in high school, to become an accountant. Rachael and Carlos. How many years had it been since I'd thought about that? About the year my sister had spent cutting classes and running up my parents' gas cards to visit her bad-boy beau at the flat where he lived with several hundred aunts, cousins, and siblings?

My kid sister was no turnip. Rachael had a quick brain and a hot temper, but the temper emerged only when someone tried to interfere with the excruciating slowness that her every decision required, be it buying a bra or choosing a college. Except when it came to Carlos—that once. There had been no talking to Rachael, not that I'd tried. And why hadn't I tried? Well, Carlos had come along at an awkward time in our sisterhood—my first year of law school, which had consumed all I was and all I had. Still, Rachael was my only and beloved sibling. There had to have been more to it than that.

There *was* more to it than that. I gnawed my pen. I'd given up too easily, possibly because, like every sister at some point, I *wanted* Rachie to stumble, trip herself up.

And she did. Almost. For the first time, she'd gone to war with our parents. The slightest criticism about the merits of a long-term relationship between a Jewish doctor's daughter from the Upper West Side and a dropout Puerto Rican kid from the Bronx with a thing for lighters and litter bins simply rendered Rachael as impermeable as an oyster shell. Long-distance, from law school in Wisconsin, I marveled at my parents' restraint, as distinct from their ordinary behavior as Rachie's obsession was from hers. I remember now how jealous I'd been of their gentle patience with the spoiled brat, always their fair one. Now, of course, I see that it was their very self-restraint that finally allowed Rachael the room she needed to turn around. Had my parents not let her alone, Rachael could easily be right now sitting vigil on Saturday nights in some parish church in Jersey.

Once she was in college and dating solid citizens like herself, we both sort of behaved as if that time had never happened. I figured Rachael felt that she'd let everyone down. I guess I felt that I'd let *her* down. And I'd taken my cue from my parents: around me, at least, they'd never spoken Carlos's name again.

What the gap meant, though, was that there was a universe of things I didn't know about Rachael and Carlos. All the things I'd wanted to know but never asked—or never wanted to know? My sister and Carlos met one summer when her temple youth group tutored a select group of bright JDs. He was two years younger, sixteen, and their relationship had lasted a full twelve hours before they made love, Rachael's first time, standing up in the book-storage room of a public library—something my sister probably had imagined as likely to happen to her as running away with the Ice Capades. She'd confided as much to me, late one night over margaritas at our aunt's place in Florida, when we were having one of those "first time vs. best time" sister talks. Those kinds of revelations weren't ever off-limits between us. I've always thought Rachie's secrets and motivations were mine by birthright. But I hadn't taken the subject of Carlos further that time, nor had I since.

Okay, there was the fact that the whole thing was creepy. I did know that Rachael's adventure ended when Carlos finally had to choose between prison and the army. I imagined that I felt about the relationship the same way I'd have felt learning Rachael was bulimic but cured. Glad I knew. Glad I didn't know too much. Glad it had all worked out for the best without me.

Funny, at work I wasn't squeamish in the slightest. Nothing stopped me from wanting to know about the depths of other people's sordid experiences, down to the molecule. In lawyer life, knowing why people do things is my intoxicant, my power cell.

It's different, though, when it's close. Some things you just don't want to look at.

The reason I couldn't call Rachie right up, right now, and ask

her about Carlos was that it would seem too little too late, to
both of us. A dozen years and more had passed. How did she feel
today about her passion for her free-fisted black-eyed pyro sweetheart, the boy she once swore to love forever? Did the self who
loved Carlos seem, now, to have vanished in a puff of smoke,
even the smell of sulfur little more than a memory? There were
good and obvious reasons to talk about it today, a sort of need-to-
know situation. But even a parallel with a professional incident
didn't seem like a good enough excuse to explore what was probably the major blank spot in my relationship with my sister.

A trio of chewed-up Bics lay on the blotter before me. I was
worn out: all that introspection isn't easy for a lawyer. Weird how
a minor avenue of thought had become a huge time sink, sucking
up most of a crowded Wednesday. It was nearly three. By the time
I could get to Avalon, it would be close to four. Arley would have
to be home from school. Unless she was working.

I gathered my things and went out to the car. On the cell
phone, I called information and asked for Taco Haven.

The answering voice there said only "Jack."

"I'm trying to find Arlington LeGrande."

"This is Ginny Jack."

"Yes. I'm trying to find an employee, Arlington LeGrande."

"No one works here by that name."

"No Arley? A waitress?"

"Arley Mowbray, you mean. She don't work tonight. Can I
please ask who's caring about that?"

"This is Anne Singer. I'm, well, I'm Missus LeGrande's attorney, Arley's attorney."

"She in trouble?"

"No.

"Beyond the obvious, I mean."

"Ah, excuse me?"

"Missus LeGrande, indeed."

"Oh. Well. No, she's not in any trouble."

"She's a sweetie pie, you know that?"

"She seems to be."

"Got the wrong heritage, though."

"I don't know what you mean."

"Well, you meet little Rita, her mama, and you see why that girl's about half better than she should be, which ain't saying much."

"Excuse me?"

"No, excuse *me*. I shouldn't be saying this stuff."

"I appreciate it. Really. I don't know much of what has gone on with Arley. . . ."

"She's just such a nice, sweet kid."

"I know."

"She's too nice and too sweet to be involved in all this junk. I just ain't been able to think it all through straight. It happened so sudden."

"It sure seems that way."

"I knew Rita in high school. She was two years younger, but she was going like sixty before I knew what twenty was, if you know what I mean."

"Can I come by and see you, Missus. . . . Jack? I'm actually going to pass by the restaurant on my way out to Avalon today. . . ."

"Well. Maybe. Well, no. I need to stick my nose back where it belongs. I'm sorry. I got a late lunch rush here, ma'am, so you'll have to pardon me. I'll tell Arley you called."

I wanted to know more. Despite her critical error in getting herself married to a convict, Arley had made far fewer revolutions around the block than most of my clients, and their children, not to mention *their* children. I'd once hosted three generations of women from the same family, all pregnant by the same man. Just sorting out the genetics was enough to make you rip out fistfuls of hair, never mind the psychodynamics. I had only Arley's manner and appearance to work from, but she seemed pretty unaffected by her upbringing. So whatever else her former schoolmates thought about her, Rita Mowbray had to be a fairly protective, consistent parent, if not a plaster saint. I knew plenty of very good mothers who somehow never managed to buy skirts long enough to allow them to sit with their legs crossed. A taste for the fiesta didn't mark a woman as a poor parent, especially in Texas. And Rita Mowbray, as her daughter had told me, was a fully educated registered nurse. That alone took smarts and guts, particularly for a woman on her own. I was looking forward to meeting her, little Rita who went like sixty.

And then I did.

When I finally found the little white house, set back on a corner lot from the dusty, pitted surface of Jean-Marie Street, it was Arley who opened the door. Even through the screen, I could see her brown eyes widen and grow darker. They looked like horse's eyes, with that tightly strung combination of challenge and fear. "Hello," she said, but it was a whisper. It was the whisper that made me realize why I'd come at all—a sixth sense that Arley was in more trouble than even her bizarre romantic life indicated. That there was something she needed protecting from, and she was afraid to tell about it.

"Arley, hi," I told her. "I know I didn't call ahead, but I told you I'd be in touch."

"My mama's here," she said. "My mama is here, though."

"Well, that's okay. I probably should meet her."

"Who is it?" called a voice from inside, a voice that sounded like the inside of a hundred bars at three A.M., with the lights just blinked on, revealing all the straw papers and beer spills on the dance floor. "Who's there, girl?"

I gently shouldered Arley aside and walked in. I still don't know where I got the chutzpah—you have to understand people's boundaries in my work, and respect is the thing you most need to keep in mind. But I did what I did.

Rita was standing there, tapping her foot, watching a saucepan of water on the stove. When I saw her from the back, I thought right away she looked just like Cherry Ames, student nurse, in those books I used to read when I was ten. She had on the kind of starched and bleached uniform that seems so dated on a nurse today, it's almost like a costume. And yet it's somehow . . . what? Sexy? Baroque? Like seeing a nun under the age of sixty in full habit. When she turned around, though, I could see that Rita Mowbray's cherry days were far behind her. She had a face like a good boot, seamed and browned and yet handsome in its way. Like the central casting version of the dance hall girl with a heart of gold, rubbed to a faint sheen between the stones of experience, she looked like a woman with a good memory for the way nature had made her. Shiny, long, thick hair in a heavy blunt cut swept her shoulders, but it was a parody color, yolk orange, like a farm-fresh egg. One of her index fingernails was varnished blue and spangled with stars. She said, "Can I help you?" Her accent was thick South Texas, the "yew" a couple of syllables long.

"I'm Arley's lawyer. I'm Anne Singer," I replied, awkwardly covering the distance between us and holding out my hand, which she grasped delicately with three fingers—a thing that makes me want to slap women my age who do it. I couldn't help but notice that under her cap sleeves, Rita Mowbray's small arms were as incised with good muscle as Stuart's were; she could probably have whipped me over one shoulder had she cared to. She was, if anything, shorter than I am, and slender, and she had the strangest way of looking, as if she were listening to a great dirty joke on a hidden earpiece. Her white smile was as cold and eager as a dog's grin. It scared me. She scared me.

"I didn't know my daughter had a lawyer."

Arley cringed, seeming to shrink from her blossom-stalk carriage into a kind of crouch; even her hands crept up near her chest. I thought I'd got it then. She beat her. She'd let a succession of hang-arounds use the child sexually, perhaps so long ago Arley didn't even remember. There was nothing in this room but fear, fear so dull and accustomed no one even seemed to recognize it as such anymore. No wonder the kid had turned to the first kind of shelter she'd ever encountered: she was a hungry heart on the half shell for the likes of Dillon LeGrande. As it turned out, I was right, and I was wrong. Rita Mowbray never laid a hand on her daughters or her son. She had never needed to.

"I'm having me a hard-boiled egg," she said pleasantly. "It's my egg-fast day. I've had an egg-fast day once a week every week for fifteen years, and I never gained a single pound in my life."

"That's remarkable," I said, looking at the one egg in the pan. "I . . . ah, I'm sorry if I intruded on you."

"Shoot, no, that's just fine," said Rita. "I'm interested. I'm truly interested. Would you like to sit?"

It was basically a picnic table. Without my having asked, Arley brought me a glass of water with ice and then sat down beside her mother.

"My shift starts in half an hour," said Rita.

"Do you work at a doctor's office?"

"I'm a registered nurse, at Texas Christian. Surgical floor."

"You work nights?"

59

"I don't mind. You get more."

"Missus Mowbray . . ."

"Actually, it's Miss Mowbray. I've never been married."

"Okay. I . . . ah, my business is really with your daughter. It's about the suit she wants to help her . . . husband bring against the warden of the state penitentiary at Solamente River. . . ."

"Oh. That stuff. Then I guess it don't matter any to me."

"You mean it's okay with you?"

Rita Mowbray half turned on the bench. "Wake your brother up," she said to Arley. "He's about going to be late for work." Arley departed swiftly into a room just off the kitchen. I heard a loud *plong* from inside, as if someone had dropped a guitar (I would later learn that Cam often slept in a hammock with his guitar and tended to roll over on it). "Miz Singer, I was surprised to hear Arley wanted to get married. Not that they don't start earlier now. My daughter Lang had a boyfriend since she was eleven."

"You *did* give your formal permission for the . . ."

"Not because I was in favor of it. People will do what they want, anyhow. Teachers are always calling up telling me she's smart enough to be in college. I'm not her conscience."

"You're her mother."

"That's true enough. Good brains run in the family." She smiled, and again I found myself fascinated by those sharp teeth. I turned to Arley, in the doorway now.

"Want to go out for some coffee?"

Rita said sharply, "She needs to make dinner for her brother."

"You have a younger child, then, too? A little boy?" I asked.

"Hardly. He's six two," Rita said proudly, "and only sixteen. Hasn't got his growth yet."

"Is he disabled?" I asked, and Arley made a coughing sound,

which I realized a second later was laughter she was trying to hold back. When Rita turned, ever so slowly, and fastened that merry, malicious gaze on her daughter, and Arley went still and examined her sandals, my heart started to knock. I began wondering why everything about Rita had raised my hackles from the first instant, which I wouldn't really understand until that night at Texas Christian with Arley, many months later. This was our first meeting; I was being unjust. "No offense meant," I said quickly.

"He's not disabled more'n any male," she said. "Look, Miz Singer. If she didn't give him food, he'd just eat banana peppers and hot sauce out of the jar with a spoon, and after a while of that he'd get sick, and I'd have to pay for it. Arley's been cookin' since she was a child, and unless you all are going to find a way for her to move in over there at Solamente River and keep house for her man, she's going to go right on doing it here, or she can do it somewhere else I don't have to support her." She looked up at Arley, then down at me. "You really a lawyer? Or an assistant?"

"I'm a lawyer."

"How old are you?"

"Forty in January."

"You got any kids?"

"No. I don't."

"Well, I am thirty-eight years old, and by the time I was the age of my older girl, I already had me two." Rita was younger than I was. I felt like lying down. How did we look side by side? "My mama had me when she was sixteen. Her mama had her when she was sixteen. I waited. I was seventeen."

"I know children are a tremendous responsibility."

"Well, it's like we learned in biology. They'll survive. They're meant to survive you. All the while I was in school, day and night and day, I had to pay for those kids to sit in the day care at the hospital and draw with markers I couldn't never scrub off their clothes, and play with pretty blocks while I shoveled caked shit out of comatose patients' butts."

"You did it, though. You got your education."

"Well, what was I going to do? Cut hair? Tend bar? I could have took care of myself. Maybe found somebody who'd do it for me, too, at least when I was younger. But I had them all"—she pointed her chin at Arley—"and I wasn't going to go down begging for welfare on account of them. You can't live right off that, anyhow."

"But you wanted a family—"

"You don't have to want one to get one."

A door banged open, and a barefoot blond boy in surgical scrub pants and a T-shirt that read "Hell Freezes Over" stumbled into the kitchen. His was the strawberry-blond hair color his mother's must have remembered, and the topography of his smooth face gave him the beautiful, vacant look of a B-movie star. He nodded at us without expression. "Ma," he said. "Ma'am." A Texas kid will always say this when you meet him, and a Texas kid can make "Ma'am" sound like a four-letter word. But this boy didn't. He didn't have that much energy.

"I got to go if we are going to go," Arley put in, softly. Dazedly, I waved to Rita and Cam and sort of crab-walked out of the house. They stared at us as we got into my car.

Arley strapped herself in, smoothing her jeans, plucking at her rayon shirt. Her breath was coming in little chuffs, and she let her impossibly long hair fall over the side of her face like a tent flap.

"Arley?" I said, backing out around the motorbike I assumed was her brother's, which seemed constructed mostly of duct tape. She didn't answer. "Arley, your mother's one tough cookie, isn't she?"

She looked up at me then and blinked her eyes once. "Yes," she said. "She does what she wants."

"That must not be easy to live with all the time."

"She ain't hardly . . . well, she's hardly ever home all the time. So it doesn't matter so much."

She probably didn't need the advice. But I felt compelled to give it.

"Arley," I began, "you know from school that there are people who help kids out if they have trouble with their parents. No matter what kind of thing happens, it's already happened to some other girl before, and nobody has to put up with it. . . ."

"What do you mean?"

"Abuse, Arley. Hitting. Or neglecting you."

She smiled, and she looked patient and old, like one of the veiled and straight-backed señoras, of incalculable age, who prayed on the steps of the cathedral on the Feast of the Immaculate Conception. "Mama wouldn't never hit us."

"Do you feel . . . close to your mother? Even if she acts kind of distant?"

"No."

"Do you like her?"

"Well, this is going to sound awful, but I used to like her more when I was a kid."

"What changed?"

"The big thing was, when I got in school I started to see that things at our house weren't . . . normal."

Here it came, I thought. The cigarette burns. The "uncle" with the curious hands. The skin on my forearms prickled. "What do you mean?" I asked carefully.

"Well, it's hard to explain. Like, okay, I know that some people don't like to cook. Elena's mom, she cooks all the time, and it's like this big thing with her. She's always telling me how you have to make the food nutritious, but you also have to make it look good, or nobody will eat it." She drew a big breath, and I fidgeted, impatient with the teenage digression. "And Ginny, my boss," Arley went on, "she totally hates to cook. And she owns a restaurant! But my mama, see, I can't never remember her cooking, not once. I know she must have done it before I was big enough to do it. We'd have starved otherwise, you know? But I don't remember. Even on Thanksgiving."

She went on, describing a life so devoid of joy or recreation, it could have been lived inside a grim monastic order. Arley's mother barely spoke, and then only to give commands. When she was not at work, she was out dancing. She did not neglect her children; neglect might have required more concentration than Rita was able to muster up. For Arley, school was a respite, not another chore. Arley's mother simply did not love her, and not only did she not love her but she regarded Arley's school successes, as well as her timid attempts to involve herself in extracurricular activities, as a source of irritation, an obstacle that got between her and her right to cheap labor.

Arley's breaking away, to claim time for herself with Elena's family, to take her job, was not a minor teenage rebellion; it was an all-out revolution. No wonder Arley was tense, wondering what her mother would "do" to her about Dillon.

Dillon . . . With Dillon, Arley had probably traded more words and feelings than she'd ever expressed in the previous fourteen years of her life. No wonder she'd been knocked off balance by the force of his attention.

"Did you ever have people over? Family? At Christmas?"

"No. We once went to her sister Debbie Lynn's house in Galveston."

"So what do you do on holidays?

"Mama usually works. You get more if you work a holiday. Cam and me usually have a sixteen-piece bucket. You know, they're open on Christmas, too."

"What does your mother do at home?"

"Well, nothing. She just talks on the phone. Or she sits at the table and smokes. She never eats nothing; just sits there tapping with her boot and looking out the window and waiting for us to eat and get the dishes done. Or whatever. Then she goes to work. When I was little, I would talk to her sometimes. I remember once I told her about the tarantula in the glass case at school. She didn't really get mad at me; it was more like she could see right through you, like you were glass . . . no, like you were water." She smiled. "I sound like a real case, huh? It's not, like, at all as bad as it sounds."

I might have felt relieved. No lech uncle. No hidden bruises. But as we drove through Avalon to the drive-in restaurant, Arley's account of her life, though told without a trace of self-pity, left me feeling more bowed, more helpless, than I could recall feeling when faced with the most miserable case of spousal battery. You could name that. You could find that. If you could find that, you could fix it. Not easily. It would always be like drawing out cactus tines with a tweezers—every time you got one, you'd spot three more. But what Rita did to her children had no name, because it was nothing. Nothing that could be legally called abandonment. She walked the line. She was careful and correct. She did nothing more than let her children pass through.

We sat in the lime glow of the Dairy-Brite and sipped our cherry colas, and Arley told me that things actually got better, for her and her brother, when they got tall enough to use appliances and smart enough to remember the number of the Bexar County police and Rita's nursing station at the hospital. Rita switched to nights—more money—"because we didn't need anybody to take care of us when we were asleep. There were whole weeks when I never saw Mama, Miz Singer—"

"You can call me Annie," I said. "Your big sister, where was she?"

"Oh, she had to live at Grandma's."

"Your grandma took care of her?"

"No." Arley dropped her eyes shyly. "It wasn't like that." She swiped at her mouth with a tassel of her hair. "You know, Cam used to mind me. But now he can't do one thing. He's like dead from the neck down. He works at Electric Mirage three nights a week, but the rest of the time he just sits in his room with his guitar and his fiddle and smokes. Or he rides around with his friends. This is about a year it's been like this. I was really mad, at first. I, like, want to ask him if he has a genetic defect that makes him so he couldn't push a button on the washing machine." She smiled at me. "That's why I started laughing today. Mama lets him get away with it 'cause he's a boy. She just—she really likes men." A prostitute, I thought. That was the shoe that hadn't dropped. But then Arley added, "Not that she ever gets any of them. She hasn't had a date with a guy in, like, a year."

She was quiet a minute, then she piped up again. "Plus Cam can sing."

"Sing?"

"He has a really good voice. One night, he was at this tavern where Mama goes with my sister, whenever Langtry comes around, and Cam was there moving some boxes for the owner, and he just got up there and sang some Willie Nelson song, and Mama and Lang was knocked right on their ass. I mean . . . I'm sorry I swore."

"It's okay."

"So now, you know, Cam is a genius." Arley had even over-heard her mother, on the phone, telling a girlfriend that with his voice and that big cleft in his chin, he could be as big as Clint Black. "She told my sister a cleft looks bad on a woman, but it's sexy on a man. And you know, my sister does have a cleft in her chin. A little one."

"Her name's Langley?"

"Langtry. That's a town name, like all of us. Mama says people say you look at them from behind, you can't tell who's the mother and who's the daughter. At the bars, they get taken for sisters."

"What does Langtry do?"

"I don't know. I don't even know where she lives. She just comes and goes. She got her own place when she was sixteen. I didn't even know she moved away till Cameron—that's *his* real name—found all her stuff was gone out of that room up in the attic. I took that for my room then."

I asked Arley, "Didn't your mom ever want to marry?"

"She wanted to marry a doctor."

"And does she go out with doctors from the hospital?"

"Not really. I mean, once in a while she has. She worships the doctors. The doctor who fixed my leg when I broke it on the side horse in gym came over here once and picked her up. But he didn't come in. Mostly, she's dated guys that are kind of losers. They come around here, and they stay for a while. But then they leave."

"Is she really sad then?"

"She doesn't cry. She just rips all the pillowcases off to wash and tells me to throw out whatever they left. A razor or whatever."

"How did they treat you?"

"They never treated me any way at all, except one guy once

bought me some barrettes, but Mama had a hissy fit and stomped on them. They were mostly asleep in the day and gone at night. They'd get really thirsty, though. They'd drink all the juice."

"Speaking of thirsty, I could use another Coke. You too?" I asked her.

"I would," she said. "But I can pay."

"It's okay. Do you want anything to eat?"

"I really want onion rings. They have the best ones here. But I shouldn't. Do you know that if you eat that greasy stuff, it makes little grease bubbles in your blood? I mean, that's what they mean about clogging your arteries. Can you imagine having greasy blood?"

"I think you'd have to eat a lot of onion rings, over a long period, to get greasy blood."

"Well . . ."

"I love onion rings. When I was a kid in New York, we used to go to this one place where they would just give you a paper bag full of them, and the whole bottom would be soaked through in minutes—"

"That's just like here!" She smiled.

We got two orders, and Arley asked me suddenly, "You want to see where my grandma is?"

"Okay," I said, glancing involuntarily at my watch. She saw it. "It won't take long," she said, with a burble of laughter in her voice. "It's not like what you think."

She directed me a half block down the road to a little cemetery, almost invisible from the car. I followed Arley up onto a small ridge, through a choke of weeds and wildflowers. We came to a black marble stone, shaped like a square footlocker. "This is my grandma," Arley said softly. "Amelia Mowbray. My grandfather, I never knew him. He's buried somewhere else, I guess.

But Grandma I remember. I was about nine when she passed. She used to live right here, down on Miranda Street, with my mother's brother Randall, who has schizophrenia. He lives in a state home now. I always thought he was kind of nice. Grandma was nice too. She worried about Randall all the time, but sometimes she would come over and play checkers with me, and sometimes took me to bingo. Langtry, she stayed home with Randall, and they had a teacher come in once in a while because of a hardship situation. So Lang never had to go to school. She did the cooking and cleaning for Grandma, because Grandma had an ulcer. I wish Mama would have named me for her, instead of how she did."

"I think you have a beautiful name."

"It's humiliating, though, when you know how I got it. See, she named us after the towns where she was when they . . . when she . . ."

"What?"

"When she got pregnant. That's what she said. When I wanted to change my name to Amelia when I was about ten or eleven, she said, 'I named you what I named you for a reason. Just count yourself lucky you're not called Brownsville or Matagorda.' I told Dillon that right off. You can't imagine telling something like that to a stranger. That was how I knew there was something special between us."

Arley settled down on the tombstone like an old lady snuggling into her favorite settee. "Well," she said, clearly enjoying the chance to recite her life, "about a year ago was when I started my program."

"Your program?"

"I took stock. It was when Ricky Nevadas told me he saw Lang in San Antonio at the Alamo Plaza with his uncle Frank. It wasn't like some big surprise. She used to go out with older guys all the time. One of the gym teachers from the middle school went out with her. I heard that. And he got in trouble, because she was only fifteen or so. Not that I have any room to talk. But it's different for Dillon and me. I mean, it's like we are the same age. It's like I'm even teaching him some things, in a way. It's not just guys being older. It's what they are. See, everybody knows about Ricky's uncle."

"Knows what?"

"Well, he's . . . he's like fifty years old," Arley admitted, now brushing her lips furiously with her hair, as if trying to paint away her words. "But that wasn't it. He's . . . he's like in the Mafia. Or something. He's been on the news."

"Did you tell your mother?"

She laughed, a deep-throated little-girl hoot that made me want to cradle the back of her head in my hand. "Uh, no! I surely didn't tell her!" Arley's face clouded over again. "I just figured then I had to decide what I was going to do with my life. 'Cause I wasn't going to end up like Lang! So I took stock. I did it like . . . See, when Elena's father travels for business? He gets these maps from Triple A, with a big fat red line on a map and stars for all the places to change highways or stop overnight?"

That's how she'd laid out her teenage years. A map. There were choices to make. The girls she read about in *Seventeen* were all popular. Elena was popular, "though she's a little wild. But not really. It's all like a big act." Elena's big sister Connie was a nice girl, and really pretty, and played girls' softball all the way to state and was the first person in the whole Gutierrez family to go to college.

"I got out books on dating dos and don'ts and Christianity and low-fat cooking and color matching. I started making little charts about what I ate, and I decided to do one thing every day to improve myself, even if it was just flossing. I lined my poetry books up in alphabetical order by author, and I painted my room up there and made curtains, and I got on the track team." She looked at me shyly. "I could make All-State in the hurdles. You don't hardly ever get to do that in just ninth grade."

"And then?"

"And then I started learning about poetry."

"Do you like to write?"

"Well, sure, I mean—" She cast her eyes down at her broom of hair. "All girls like to write, I think. It's like you can't help it. You feel so much, it just comes out."

"But you're good at it."

"I'm not very good at it. Missus Murray says . . . well . . ."

"What?"

"That I have the eye. Just because I was writing about how the surface of leaves were like skin . . ."

"That's pretty creative."

"Not really. It's obvious. But that wasn't the only reason I got into it. . . ."

"Why else?"

"Because Missus Murray told me once that no matter what else you know or you don't know, if you can quote from poems, people will always think you're smart."

"Makes sense."

"But she said not just from one poem. Like, anybody can say, 'And miles to go before I sleep . . .' You have to know lines from a lot of poems. Like . . . Yeats."

"Yeats?"

"That's Missus Murray's favorite. The words are so beautiful, but they're hard to understand. You have to really concentrate, like being an athlete. When you're reading a poem, you can't think about anything else. It clears you out."

"I can see what you . . ."

"And, of course, that turned out to be a good thing because Dillon's really into poetry too, though not very many poems. . . ."

"What do you mean?"

"He . . . says there's no reason to study other poets once you know Dylan Thomas, because he's the best."

Right, I thought.

"I think it's because of his name, though, really."

"Sounds kind of juvenile."

She looked up sharply. "Not really. Lots of people could be really smart if they got the chance. He just didn't get the chance—"

"Well, he got as much chance as you. . . ."

"Not exactly." She started gazing around the cemetery, losing interest in her line of defense, apparently, and then said, "So the last thing was, I got to be friends with Elena, and I got my job, and then . . . I met Dillon."

"All in a year?"

"All in a year. But you know, Missus G. says our years, for Elena and me, are like dog years, seven in each one." I nodded. "I like this place, don't you? It's not really cooler in here, but it feels like it is, you know? And nobody can see you. I used to sit here and read sometimes."

"Why not now?"

"No." She lowered her voice. "I'm afraid, a little, of some of the boys who come here to drink. They come right in the day now, and you know, if you're by yourself you can get scared. . . ."

I nodded, thinking, But not of your boyfriend and his .45.

"What I figured was, writing to Dillon was just supposed to be a part of everything else."

"Of your program."

"Right."

"He understands everything, Miz . . . I mean, Annie. He understands how I feel. . . ."

It was getting dark, and in Texas, darkness *falls,* there's practically a sound to it. Arley needed to get herself home or she'd get in hot water. But suddenly I wanted to, had to, tell her about Rachael and Carlos. And if I didn't do it now, this moment, before I knew her better or thought better of it, the moment would disappear as quickly as the faint halo of light above the big cottonwood at the edge of the field.

"My sister was in love with a boy like Dillon once," I told her. "And we aren't the kind of people stuff like this happens to." I could feel, though not really see, the quick lift of her eyebrows. "I mean, not that you are. But my father was a doctor. Of course, your mother's a nurse . . . I mean . . ."

"I know what you mean," Arley said softly. "You can just tell it."

And I did. About the book-storage room and the time Carlos's five aunts came to my parents' apartment for dinner, and about the fight Carlos had in a campus bar with a boy he thought looked at Rachael and how the boy ended up with a concussion. "But it was like she didn't even care. She saw him hit that kid with a beer mug, and she didn't even care!" How cloddish, I thought. How utterly stupid! *She* understands; look what she did. . . .

Arley said, "What Dillon did . . . it seems like on TV to me. I don't rightly know how I would feel if I saw him with a gun in his hand. I try not to think about that, because he's so sweet in his letters."

"But you know what he did—"

"Annie, I know, of course I know, but a lot of boys do bad things. A lot of girls too. I could have done like that. I think a lot of kids who get a little attention from their parents, but not too much, they do bad things to get more."

"But you didn't get any attention, and you didn't do anything bad."

"Well, I did all that *good* stuff. It's the same thing. So everybody would—you know—notice me." She whipped her dark hair back and forth like a wave. "And think, what if I tried everything but I wasn't good at any of it? What if I was fat or slow and I couldn't make the team? I think that's what Dillon did. I mean, I think he tried to be good but he wasn't as smart or as big as—"

"Arley, the way he describes himself, he could do anything he wanted—build houses, move mountains—if he weren't . . ."

"But you don't believe that, do you? It says in magazines that boys brag all the time because they're insecure. If he really could do all that stuff he says, he wouldn't need me so bad. I'm just a fourteen-year-old kid!"

I felt the breath escape me with a rush that made me dizzy. He hadn't taken her in at all. She saw him clearly, with all the womanly wisdom *Seventeen* magazine could provide. "Arley," I said slowly, "you are a good person. And I believe you when you say that Dillon needs your love. But what will you get out of this, in the end?" She didn't answer right away. She stood up and headed for the car, brushing off her hands on her jeans.

Finally, she said, "I don't know."

"What about your life? Maybe you could get a scholarship with track. Go to college. What about your program? What's going to happen to all that?"

"Well," she said, glancing at the dashboard clock and looking out the window. "I don't think I would have to give up on myself to love someone else. Or even a lot of other people. Like, Dillon says his mama is real lonely. He says when his little brother, Philippe, was born, she really wanted a girl. And she's got a bad back, so she can't work—"

"His mama?"

"Yes, she wishes she had a daughter."

"What?"

"Well, she wishes she had—"

"I heard you," I snapped, exasperated. That was just what Arley needed, another steel magnolia to take care of. "Do you two get along?"

"I never met her. She might go see Dillon at Christmas, and then he's going to tell her about us." She turned to me. "But, Annie, no matter what else happens, look what I already have! If I didn't learn all my poems and do all that other stuff to improve myself, maybe he wouldn't even like me. He says he had lots of chances to write to other girls. But he never did. Except me. And he wanted to marry *me*. I wake up in the morning sometimes and think, I'm married. I'm a married woman. I can't believe it sometimes. My mother never even got married. You know? I'm already farther than my mama was. And the more I know Dillon, the, like, stronger I get. When somebody loves you the way he loves me, it's just like you have to live up to it. You want to make them proud of you. It's as though I was waiting all my life for somebody to be that proud of me. . . ."

It terrified her when I started to cry. To tell you the truth, it sort of terrified me. I'm not high-strung or even premenstrual. I don't cry, except over "Soldier in the Rain." But I put my head down on the steering wheel and I couldn't stop, I couldn't stop. In a couple of minutes, my head felt like I'd inhaled a public pool. Was it just the pure pity of this kid, who reminded me of . . . me, but not really. I'd never been anything like her, never been in such old shoes at such a young age. But had I ever been as young as she was right now, so ascendant with the glory of a situation that could serve as the model for a textbook called *Ten Rules for*

Fucking Up Your Life Permanently? Pathos and melodrama were the sausage and eggs of my professional life. In my personal life, I relished order and predictability. Was this some kind of germ for middle-aged chaos finally blooming into a full-fledged illness?

"Annie," Arley kept saying, patting my arm. "Are you sick? Do you think it was eating those onion rings? It's too hot for that kind of food. . . . Do you want me to call somebody?"

Finally, I got enough of my composure in both hands to hold the wheel and take Arley home. Then I charged through construction traps like . . . well, like a Texan, laying on the horn and swerving onto the shoulder until I got home, where I didn't even bother to use the garage, just tore open the door of our town house and jumped on Stuart, where he sat on the couch, separating sections of the *Times*.

"Is it my birthday?" he asked me, incredulous. I usually needed a glass of merlot and a half hour of arctic air from the vents before I could bear to be touched on a day like this. "Do I have a terminal illness I don't know about yet? Are you crying?"

"No." I burrowed my hands under his golf shirt and felt his bowed ribs and his flat belly with its hint of give. "I just love you. I love you because you're the same every day. I love you because you're my best friend."

"Anne," he whispered, "do you ever say the right thing at the right time? Huh?" But he pulled me down across his chest and ruffled my hair before he kissed me. "It doesn't matter. I'll take it."

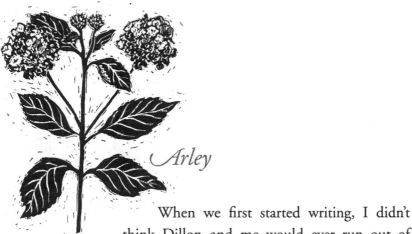

CHAPTER FOUR

Arley

When we first started writing, I didn't think Dillon and me would ever run out of things to tell each other. It was like there were things in me I'd been saving up a whole life to say, things I didn't even know I knew. I couldn't see him, so it was like practicing singing in the mirror. I didn't have to watch him scrunch up his face the way Elena did when I hit a clunker. I could say anything I wanted. He sort of had to pay attention. I mean, he couldn't go out and work on his motorcycle or something, or go out with another girl. It made me feel strong and really confident.

Those letters to him were my treat I saved up for when I had all my chores and my studying done. I really had to be alone in the house to go down into thoughts about Dillon. I couldn't think about him fully during the day, when I was so busy, or at track, when the pounding in my knees and my neck drove out every hope but thinking my way over the next hurdle. So I started to set aside little times, fifteen minutes before bed, when I could brush my hair out and have on my clean nightgown, light as paper on my skin. When I would look in the mirror at one of those times, I would be cloudy and pretty, the way you always look right before you go to bed, when nobody is even going to see you.

Dillon's letters to me I would read in school. There was only so much time in class you actually had to pay attention. And then I would start planning my answers. Late at night, I would stand out on the porch, hanging the dish towels out, and I'd be noticing the dark. There weren't many lights on that street—maybe because Avalon is the kind of place you leave when you grow up, so there were lots of old people on our block. And they go to bed early. I'd start thinking words about that dark, words I'd normally write about in my notebooks, for poems, stuff you could never say to another kid your age. But I could write all that to Dillon now. Like he was a journal too, my diary. I would keep copies sometimes, because they were like theme papers.

One of those nights, I wrote: "The lights are really all that separate you from everything else out there. I can hear the wind blowing down from the hill country, and it scares me. That same wind is blowing through all those rooms at the Alamo, where there's nobody lived there for a hundred years. And it's blowing down in canyons where somebody could be lying, a skeleton, and his people not even know where he is. I think you can get lonelier in Texas than anyplace on earth, and I used to think you could get lonelier in Avalon than any other place in Texas. But I guess it's probably the same anywhere in a little town. You can't imagine anyone feeling that way in Dallas."

Dillon wrote back and told me this thing about how his grandpa used to have a place way out in the far corner of nowhere. This was when his mama, Kate, was a little girl, and she used to complain about how lonely it was. But his grandpa would say there was all kinds of life you wouldn't notice in a lonely place. Bats and lizards. Even mesquite and gorse bushes. All kinds of life people didn't even see. Prison, Dillon wrote, was a lonely place too: "You wouldn't notice much in the way of human life in here. But I feel full of life, even in this place, when I get your letters." I would read those things, and every part of me would go soft. I would feel the breath flood into me like I once would have from seeing a surprise shining under a Christmas tree.

Then there would be sometimes when the mail was slow, or he missed a day or two, and then I couldn't think about anything else; I would start making deals with the school clock—like, if I looked up and more than five minutes had passed, that would mean I had a letter. If I looked up and it was less than five minutes, it would mean I should write to him again first. If I could better my time even by a tenth in wind sprints, there would be a letter. If I couldn't even beat Paula, then I would get punished, and I wouldn't get one. Those days were like not having enough breath to live on. But there was never a day bad enough I didn't want more of him, even if it meant more waiting.

Then one day I got a letter from Dillon that started out just like all the others, just like we were still in the middle of that conversation about how funny it is that you can feel trapped by too much space the same as you can by too little. No matter how I talked about all that emptiness, Dillon wrote, he thought I was a real Texan. "I think you like the loneliness a little bit, like I do. Yankees wouldn't understand, because they're all wimps. But I hope you don't like loneliness too much, because I think we ought to figure out when you can get on my visitors list and come and see me."

That made me so jumpy, I almost got sick to my stomach. I had to get up in social studies and go out to the bathroom. I mean, I was supposed to be *eighteen years old*. And it wasn't just that I knew a kid my age couldn't go up and see a grown man in

Solamente. It was that I knew, if he saw me, he would find out I was just a kid, and it would all be over. I never thought Dillon would have paid me much mind if he hadn't been stuck there. To this day, a part of me still believes that. What they say about prison is that you're supposed to get rehabilitated, which really means getting used to the world again. What I was thinking right then is that once he got used to the world outside prison, he would real quick find someone his own level. I knew that I was smart, smart for a kid my age. But I didn't know all the things I really would have known if I was eighteen. Like, I would have had a lot of other boyfriends, for one thing.

I needed Elena. Elena knew more than me when she was born, and she had those older sisters too, and even Gracie, bad as she was, didn't, like, disappear when she was twelve, the way Langtry did. But I was afraid to let Elena in on Dillon. First of all, I knew it would piss her off, the way it pissed her off that Connie loved Kevin. But it's also because of the way Elena sucks up all the attention from every situation she's in. She just has to stand there, and it's like there's a bonfire in the middle of the room. Everyone *has* to look. You don't ever notice this when you're with her, 'cause you're looking too, but you think about it later. It wasn't like I thought she would try to take Dillon away from me or anything—I guess I wasn't even sure, right then, how much I felt about him. I just thought Elena would see something or find out something about Dillon and me and it would ruin it for me. But it turned out I didn't give her enough credit. All the while, she was picking up pieces and making her own shape of what was going on, and she was getting madder and madder at me for keeping it to myself.

The night of the party, it would all blow up to heaven, and

something between me and Elena would change forever. If it hadn't changed, would she have pulled me back? Would I ever have ended up in that chaplain's office at Solamente River Prison?

It was just a couple of weeks before the party that Dillon asked if he could call me collect to talk some Saturday morning. "I just wish I had a face to put with your words. Or the sound of a voice to create a face to go with it. I'm sorry it has to be collect. But that's the only thing we can do here."

I was desperate then. There was no way in hell Dillon was going to be able to call me at my house. Mama didn't look at much, but she looked at the bills when she paid them like she was studying how to do a heart transplant. The very same night I got that letter, I went over to Elena's for dinner. Mrs. G. made taco pie, which I love, and so we were a long time just sitting there eating, her saying, "*Querida,* you have some more. You can see through you, Arley." Which is not true, by the way. I'm not even that thin for my height; people are surprised when they find out I weigh a hundred and forty.

We were going to do our math later in Elena's room, but she wanted to paint her toenails first. So I had to wait, even though I reckon by then I could feel the outline of that letter in my pocket, like it had edges that would bruise me if I moved around too much. I could never take my eyes off Elena when she polished her nails. She was like some kind of artist, getting each one of them little nails just right in one sure, practiced, even swoop. I'd have had it all over the floor, my fingers, and my feet, if I even ever tried it, which I never would. Finally, I thought I would totally explode if I didn't say something fast. So I just took the letter out and said, "You have to read this."

She kept on painting. But she looked at me with her mouth in a pout, like she wasn't even surprised. "You think I don't know about that?" she said, so soft I could tell she was angry, because Elena's normal voice is as loud as a cheerleader's.

"I know that you know."

"You didn't tell me."

"I told you I wrote. I figured you knew, anyhow, that he wrote back and stuff."

"Not how much."

"Well."

"So how much?"

"A lot. Almost every day." It felt unlucky, just saying that.

Elena slowly screwed the top back on her chocolate-colored polish. And then she opened the letter, holding her fingers flat the way she did whenever she touched anything, and so she wouldn't mess her fingernails.

She read a long time. I think she read so long because she was trying to make me twist. Which she did. She got to the bottom of page two and then went back and read something in the middle of page one. Finally, I said, "Elena. For God's sake . . . You never read anything for that long a time your whole life."

"Well, it's really good reading."

"Stop that."

"Don't you think it is?"

"Cut it out. You're being mean to me."

"I am not," she said, but she smiled, so I knew she was happy that I noticed. "This here's mostly about old Langtry, don't you think?"

To tell the truth, I *had* noticed that little thing.

Elena read it out loud: " 'Imagine a woman like you living so close to me all her life and I have never even met her. Of course, I do know your sister, Langtry. I don't mean this in any rough way at all, but everyone in South Texas knows that girl. I even spent some time with her one fine night a couple of summers ago. She wouldn't have been much older than you are now. And Lord, that girl can dance. We had them standing in a circle cheering at Chase's. Even the band was clapping. She can move, Langtry. But personally, I like the quieter type of woman—' "

"That's enough," I told her.

"It sure is," Elena said, starting to unscrew her nail polish again. I hate this about her. She can just leave a talk right there and not say another word, but you're losing your mind. I was miserable.

"Do you think he likes Lang?"

"Hard to imagine a boy with a dick wouldn't like Lang."

"Shut up."

"Well, Arley, holy shit. She advertises it."

I didn't like when people said that, but the fact is, that was true about my sister. Not that Elena really knew her. She'd seen Langtry exactly twice in the year and a half we'd been best friends, but one of those times Lang had on those lizardskin boots of hers that look like they were made from some kind of magic dragon— purple and red and golden. And Elena asked me how Lang could afford boots like that, which must cost, like, three hundred dollars. It made me feel stupid, because I couldn't answer. Langtry really never did move back home after Grandma died. I didn't even know what she did for her job, and I sure didn't know a thing about Ricky Nevadas's uncle back then.

"Come on," I said to Elena, "give me a break. Maybe he really likes Langtry and I should tell her to write to him."

"Well," Elena said, "I don't think Langtry would want much to do with him. I think he sounds like he's gay."

I sat down hard on the mushroom chair Elena had at the end

of her bed. "Cut it out!" she shouted. "You're going to make me smear on nine!"

"What do you mean, gay?"

"I mean all that talk about 'a woman like yourself' and stuff. Regular guys don't talk like that."

"How do you know?" I yelled back. "Dillon reads a lot. Who do we know except dumb high school boys?"

"I think he sounds like Mister Joybutt." She meant Mr. Jabeaut, who taught French and ran the drama club. It was Elena started the nickname, after she saw somebody in a movie called that. I thought it was nasty and small, even though Mr. Jabeaut could be a little too much sometimes and always wore a scarf around his neck, even in summer. But nasty as it was, it was also funny. In fact, I could feel the muscles by my mouth jumping the minute she said it, even though I was fit to be tied.

"Well," I said, "I don't think he sounds that way at all. Maybe I won't show you any more of his letters, if you don't care."

"I care," she said. "I just think he sounds like a big asshole. You know, I've read Connie's letters too—she don't know it—but old Kevin is just like his brother. He thinks the Spurs are just waiting for him to get out of jail so he can play point guard. Who do those LeGrande boys think they are?"

I didn't say anything, but deep inside, I had a tap of doubt, followed by an anger that closed over that doubt like a fist. "Look, you're my best friend. You're not my mother." She gave me that look that said, clear as day, Excuse me?

"Now, that's the truth. Your mother probably has some good advice about stuff like this. Why don't you ask her?" Elena said, being nasty.

"Elena, I know you think I haven't been telling you enough stuff. And I know I promised I'd tell you everything." It was true.

We were pledged, with a real pact. It sounds like a kid thing now, but we took it seriously; I still do. We swore major truth to tell each other our worst and best for all life and to honor each other's trust. So far, we'd never failed. We even had a code. In front of other people, Elena would signal me, "That's an ITH." It meant "in the house," or, as my French teacher would say, *"entre nous."* It would never go further than us. We wanted to swear in blood, but we'd had it drilled into us all our lives that you never, ever exchange big time bodily fluids with anybody, no matter how much you love the person, so we each chewed a piece of gum and then we switched them. Elena said we were "spit sisters." So that night, I said to her, "I know I'm wrong in keeping this inside. But I just feel weird, and you don't have to go off on me about it."

Elena looked me up and down. I looked her right back. I'm shy, but I don't like people making me drop my eyes; and this was big, so I sure wasn't going to do it right then. Finally, she looked at her pinkie toe.

"Okay," said Elena. "I don't think he likes Lang. I think he likes you. And I think he's also putting on more than he could really feel, since he never even saw you. But I can imagine how a man would get that way, sitting by himself."

"What about him calling collect? I mean, if I'm this big college girl and all, how can I say, Don't you dare call me?"

"Have him call you at my house."

"And your parents get the collect call? That's totally brilliant. Duh."

"They won't get the bill right away. We could think of something. Kevin calls Connie. We could just say it was that."

"Wouldn't Connie know?"

"Yeah."

"Would she tell?"

Elena started to laugh. "Yeah. Because my dad has a shit fit every time he sees one of those phone calls. Even if she pays him."

"So that won't work. What else?"

"Write and tell him you're living with your mother while you're getting a new apartment."

So that's what I did.

But one Saturday morning, my mama was right there when the phone rang. I picked it up. He sounded like the stage actor who came to school to read from Mark Twain. Just this sweet voice, low but not rough, not scary, with some big old fat accent. A real man's voice. "This is a collect call," the operator said, "from . . ."

"Dillon Thomas LeGrande. Ma'am."

And I said, "No one here by that name."

The operator's voice got all flat and pissed. "It's *from* him, honey. Not trying to get him."

"Oh, well," I said, trying to stretch the cord out into the living room from the kitchen. "I just can't accept that call. I just really can't. Now." Mama didn't even notice.

But he wouldn't let up! He said, "Operator, ask her again, please. Ask the party whether she will accept . . . this call from Dillon LeGrande." Like he was saying accept *him.* But I just had to say the same thing again. "Sorry . . ." And when I got off, and Mama kind of looked at me, I didn't even try to explain. I just said, "Wrong number, I guess." All I wanted to do was be alone so I could think over the way I could hear the breath come out of him, his very breath from his body against my ear. At the beginning, I was so flustered when I talked to Dillon, especially when I was with him, that I had to get away and remember him, word by word, to make him more real.

I felt like a fool. But Dillon somehow got a letter to me right that Monday, and he told me my voice sounded like hand bells. "I have to see you," he wrote. "I need to look at your eyes to see if you're real."

Well, I wrote him back a bunch of nonsense about my mother trying to buy her a new house, so that it really wasn't fair to put collect calls on her bill. That I didn't have a driver's license, because I didn't have a car—I said I couldn't afford one with paying for college and all. I offered to send him a picture of me (an old one—I had to say it was old!). It took a few days for him to write again. And he didn't even bring up the visit. I could have cried with relief. He just asked who my favorite poet was. "Obviously," he said, "my favorite is the Irishman Dylan Thomas, my namesake. He's my namesake whether he wants to be or not!"

My favorite poet was Sara Teasdale. I think I've outgrown her now. The truth is, I still love her, but I know she's sentimental and foolish. Back then, though, when Mrs. Murray gave this one talk about "Sara Teasdale, or Why Bad Poetry Is Written," I was shocked. I had to believe it was because Mrs. Murray never had the kind of feelings Sara Teasdale wrote about, which must have been so sad they were unbearable, because she killed herself.

In the next letter, I put in part of one of her poems. I was trying to get him to see that you didn't have to be with a person you cared about every minute to feel the person's love. It goes like this:

> It is enough for me by day
> To walk the same bright earth with him
> Enough that over us by night
> The same great roof of stars is dim.

I also told Dillon I didn't have very many friends. "I guess you can count all the Gutierrezes," I wrote. "And Paula Currain and

Cora Allen on the track team. And Luz, the other waitress on our shift at Taco." I told him about Mr. Justice too. "This old man, Ginny (that's the owner of Taco Haven) really hates having him come in, because he sits around humming and playing the air fiddle. She says he used to be a musician, but now he's just a crazy old drunk. Ginny says his name is Remy Justice (is Remy a French name, like LeGrande?), and that he's a woodsy, which means he lives out in the scrub someplace. I think it means he's homeless. But I like him. He calls me 'Miss Mowbray.' And the other day, you know what? He said he was going to make me a stile to prac- tice hurdling at home. I run track. (Did I tell you that?) I thought that was real nice. But Ginny said, 'You keep clear of that one, girl. He ain't a bad man. But he's crazier than a cootebray.' I think that's not too fair, though. Everybody has their troubles."

And then I stuck some stickers on it, bats and cactus, that I got at Oberly's. They were kind of juvenile, but I thought they would cheer him up, remind him of what he said about his grandpa's old ranch. He wrote back, just a card, saying that a true friend was rarer than a great steak, which I thought was kind of weird, and saying he'd really like that picture of me. So I sent him one then, the best one I had, which Elena took. I was in my track silks, but it wasn't the one they used later in the magazine. Both pictures showed I have nice legs—they're my best thing, except my hair—but they weren't revealing or anything.

And then that week started. The week that ended with Eric Dorey's party on Saturday, which led to my going to the prison the next Saturday. The week that changed everything.

What it was, was this. He didn't write back.

He didn't write back for two days, and so I waited until Mon- day. He didn't write by Wednesday, and so I figured the mail was just a little slow. By Friday, I was frantic.

We had our second practice of the week that day. At first it wasn't so bad. We just practiced coming out of the blocks. Coach had us watch Paula, because she had that real slingshot motion you try to get, how you just throw yourself forward without really standing up. We broke up to run our events. People think you *jump* over hurdles; after all, even the low hurdles look pretty high. But what you really do is you just run over them. Going over the hurdle is part of your stride. If you have the length in your legs, you get up your speed and you measure your steps and you sail over without stopping. You never stop getting a little sore from it, but I suppose it's like a dancer going up on her toes; it just gets to be what you do. I'm a pretty natural runner. That day, though I'm normally more nervous at a practice than at a meet, from trying to be perfect, I wasn't paying any mind to anything. I was what Coach Diaz used to call "in your body." Even when Coach had some of the older girls watch me, which would usually make me so self-conscious I'd miss my stride, I kept going. It was like I could hear an engine inside me, revving and whining, and all I had to do was follow that sound. When he called for wind sprints, I didn't count them like I used to; I just fell right in. I couldn't do enough: twenty yards, stop, and back—twenty yards, stop, and back. When I looked up, everybody else had gone in to change. Coach was standing there with his fingers hooked in his belt loops, grinning.

"Take five, Mowbray. Save some for next week. You're a steeplechaser," he said.

I got on the scale after practice, and I'd lost four pounds since morning.

Right then, right after my shower, I went out behind the practice facility, and I got out some of my special paper and wrote this note:

Dear Dillon,

I'm sure you're very busy with your own life, but it's been so long. Not that a week is a very long time, but it feels long. Letters are really a treat for me. It's like getting a present. But anyhow, if you don't want to write anymore, that's okay too. I will miss hearing from you.

Arley

What I really wanted to write was, Now that you saw my picture, do you think I'm ugly or something? Can you tell I'm only fourteen? Did I let too much show with that stupid poem? Are you sick of me? But I didn't say any of that. I did mail that letter second-day, even though I knew it was a waste of money because it would get there Monday, anyhow. And then I waited for a letter on Saturday.

No letter came.

That morning, I got a blank card out of my underpants drawer. I don't know when I bought it. It had a picture of a little river flowing into the sea, and underneath it said, "The biggest chance is just ahead. . . ." But I wrote on the inside:

Dear Dillon,

Probably by now you really think I'm just a pest. Maybe you're sick or really busy or dealing with a big crisis in your family. Or maybe you have a girlfriend now, and she doesn't want you writing to anyone else, even just as friends. I would like to know, but you don't have to tell me.

I looked up your name, LeGrande, in my French vocabulary. Not your name, really, but the parts of it, as words. And it means "the great" or "the biggest one" or "the most." The card I'm enclosing here is really a New

Year's card, but I was going to give it to you now, sort of in advance of the new year and your birthday. It reminded me of your name when I saw it because it says this year is going to be the biggest one yet. So if I don't get to talk to you again, at least you know somebody wishes that for you. I hope you get more than you ever hoped from this year, and from the rest of your life from now on.

> With love,
> Arlington Mowbray

And then I just went up and lay down on my bed. I couldn't even drink water. I was supposed to work a fill-in that day, and I did something I never did—I called Ginny and lied and said I was sick. I figured if I went to work I'd kill somebody by putting green chili sauce in their salad dressing or something.

Elena came over about two o'clock, pissed that she'd had to do my fill-in herself. I didn't even answer the door. Mama was at work. I could hear Elena yelling up the stairs and finally pounding up. Elena is little, but she can sound like a herd of buffalo. Now she even drives that way, loud and hard and fidgety, lots of big motions. She came into my room and said, "Y'all sick?"

"No," I said. "Or maybe yes. A little."

"You got your period?"

"No."

She sat down by me then, and she did one of those things that make me love her. She laid the back of her hand on my forehead, like I was her little girl, the way Mrs. G. still does to her, and she said, "You hot?"

"No."

"Well, you going to get up?"

"No."

"Arley, tell me," she said, and it was so much Elena's generous voice, the voice that made me go to her even when my coach would look at me like, Why are you two together, that I just started to cry, and I told her I thought I loved Dillon, and he hated me, how I lied about my age, how he must think I was ugly, and he only wanted someone to talk to but I practically told him I couldn't live without him. And Elena rocked me back and forth and said, You fool, beggars can't be choosers, that boy's lucky a girl like you would even write him no matter if you're six years old, you'd be better off loving Mr. Justice with the invisible fiddle or Cully the cook with his dreadlocks he never washed in five years; and though I didn't believe her, I still think of her holding me, and when I put that up against what happened that same night, I still feel like somebody snapped a flashbulb right in my face: I have to shut my eyes and look away. Elena and I made up, almost right away, and we'll always be friends; but after that night, nothing could ever be unsmudged and clear again. Elena says when I married Dillon, it stopped us being girls. But maybe it was really that night.

When I finally stopped crying, we went downstairs and got some peanut butter and water biscuits, and she said, "Let's us not go to the movies tonight. There's a party."

I told her I wasn't going anywhere. For one thing, I had to work on my "Three Poems by Poe" paper for quarter grades. For another, I was half sick to puking.

"Girl," she said, "you know you need a party. You don't need to be sitting around writing about the crow."

" 'The Raven,' " I said, "and the one about the kingdom by the sea, and then 'The Bells.' I like those, Ellie. You like Patty Loveless."

"You can't sing to them."

"Missus Murray showed us how you can sing every poem Emily Dickinson ever wrote to the tune of 'The Yellow Rose of Texas.'" And I started doing that: "Because I could not stop for death, he kindly stopped for me . . . ," and we started laughing, and I thought, Well, what the hell, I could get a poetry paper done in one night, anyhow, and I was just going to sit around making myself sick with worrying, so I said, "Whose party?"

"Eric Dorey's," she said. I kind of liked Eric; he sat by me in math. He told me once he was going to be a doctor, like his dad, and I believed he was already on the way to it, since his hands were so clean, they were practically wrinkly and faded out from washing.

"Birthday party?"

"Nope, a parents-are-in-Dallas-for-the-football-game party."

"Well," I said, "when?"

"Nine."

"Nine?" I yelled. "We never get back from the movies later than even nine-thirty. Where am I going to say I'm going that starts out at nine?"

"Well, Arley, let's think logically," said Elena in her teasing way. "Say we go out at seven, like we always do, and we just keep going—we get barbecue or something, then we get back on the bus and go to Eric's. It's right outside Angelus; they got a big ranch thing. I mean, how many times in your whole wide life has your mama been home when you got home on Saturday night?"

I thought. "Never."

"And when does she come home?"

"Bar time. Or morning. If she's working."

"And Cam, the wonder man—you think he'd notice if you came home at midnight and brought the Chicago Bulls with you?"

"No." I was laughing now. "Maybe the Spurs . . ."

"So there you have it, Arlington. Logic just like Mister Hogan taught me in math."

"Like Mister Hogan taught me and I taught you, you mean."

So I compromised. I worked on my paper an hour, reading over and over those lines about Edgar Allan Poe's lost love. This one library book said that Poe married his little cousin, who wasn't but thirteen or so. I had thought it was Elvis or somebody did that. But it said they were very happy, and he even liked his mother-in-law a lot. But that age-difference thing made me start thinking of Dillon again, and Elena had played all the old Lynyrd Skynyrd tapes in the house and was going through the medicine cabinets, reading all the labels on the bottles Mama had lifted from the hospital when people died and left their pills behind. Finally, she kind of whined, "You got a shirt I can wear? I'm not going all the way back home."

So we went in my room, and I put my Poe book back under the *P*s. Then we pulled out all my clothes and put them on the floor, and Elena ended up wearing my summer track day-camp silk tank on backward under my denim shirt, which left me nothing to wear but the rose-colored blouse I got for school pictures. With my jeans and the black-and-red boots Langtry left once and never came back for, I looked pretty good. I went to brush my teeth, and when I finally got back in the kitchen, there was Elena sitting on the table, talking to old Cam, which was kind of a shock.

"Arley," he just looked up and told me, "I'm coming to this party, why not?"

Well, he struck me dumb, I must say. Cam going out, except to hear music with that boy Jesse Hudson—who we called Dracula because he wore some cape thing—or to dance with the older girls at Chase's, was unheard of. Out with me, for God's sake, never; the river's likelier to run backward.

"This is just a party for ninth graders," I told him, shooting Elena the eye. Why would she want Cam around all night?

"It's not, though," Elena said. I thought, What in hell is the matter with her, she doesn't give Cam the time of day, and then I remembered that night she'd stared at my brother.

"Eric's a sophomore," Elena said. Which was true enough. Elena and me were in the high math—but only because I did both ours.

"Well, Cam," I said then, getting disgusted, "you could probably comb your hair for it. Or is that just an annual thing?"

"Arley, why don't you shove—" he began.

But Elena snapped at him, "Shut your mouth," and off he went like a puppy, and when he came back, Lord, had the boy cleaned up—a yellow shirt embroidered with an angel, and his best boots, and his hair in an Indian band. Him and Elena were talking about the BoDeans all the way to the bus stop, and then at Fat Boy's, Cam put this old band called The Drifters on the jukebox, and Elena got up and started dancing around. I ate half her barbecue. Cam ate two. Then we walked up Sam Houston and he lit a cigarette, and Elena said could she have one, and he put his hands around hers to protect the lighter from the wind. If I hadn't known better, I'd have thought he was coming on to her. We took the Cemetery bus to a stop about a two-block walk from Eric's. Cars were lined up nose-to-tail even there. Every time somebody else would spin around that drive, which was big, like the Texas houses on TV, the juterbirds would squawk out of the cedars that lined the driveway. It sounded like those cars didn't have but three mufflers among the fifty of them.

It took us a long time to find Eric in his own house. Kids were in every room, and every room had different music. It reminded me of the Care Fair at school when I was little: one room the cakewalk and one the black-light dance.

Finally, there was old Eric, stretched out in a lounge chair. There was a full container of Morton's salt and a bottle of Cuervo Reserva de La Familia. "That's rich, my brother," Cam said. "That costs."

"I never bought it," said Eric, with a moony old smile.

"Let me do one of them shooters," Elena said then. My heart started to twitch in my chest. I knew Cam and Dracula drank beer, but I never saw Elena do it. Still, she knew just how to make that little hollow on the back of her hand, between her thumb and her forefinger—they call it nature's saltbox—and Eric filled it up with salt and handed her a shot of tequila and held the lime for her. She threw her black hair back and sucked it all down and grabbed the lime and said, "Damn."

Then Cam said, "Damn, girl."

I just took off. There were some kids line dancing, and I like to do that. So I danced for a while. Then I went back outside. Elena was lying in the chaise, my brother sitting next to her. Eric was down on the patio blocks, but he didn't look sick, just asleep.

"How much of that you have?" I asked Elena.

"Six," she said. "No, five."

Eric sat right up then. It about scared me to death. "You want one, Arley?" He had me dead to rights. So I made a cup of my hand and sipped the salt, and then down went the tequila, and you know, I never thought it would taste like a cactus smells, but it does, like a cactus burning. My head went around once.

"That good?" asked Cam.

"Well, I guess."

"You don't have no more. You ain't but fourteen," he said.

Well, I thought, didn't you just watch me have it? For a second just then, I loved Cam again. It was like when we were little and I'd get extra chores for punishment, and he'd help me do them behind Mama's back. But even a girl like me, when you're the age I was that night, can have a wayward tendency—so the absolute wrong thing seems the only thing to do. Maybe I just felt fed up with being such a good girl, doing everything the right way, like using a ruler to draw a pencil line at the top of my theme papers to write my name so it wouldn't be crooked. What good had it all done me? Dillon hadn't even written back. So I poured me another shot and took a sip—Cam still watching—but that sip seemed to dive plumb down into my bowels, on top of the greasy pork I'd eaten, and I set the glass down on the ground carefully, the top of my head feeling like a hot stove. I walked into the hall and up some stairs, and there came Ricky Nevadas, dragging some girl along the hall; she had her arms around his neck like Virginia creeper. "Arley," he said, "this is Allison."

"Pleased," I said, and went into the bathroom. All the stuff in there was Eric's mama's stuff, and I used creamy mint skin cleanser to wash my wrists and my forehead. The smell was like my toothpaste. I was sure then that I wouldn't puke.

When I went down, everything was dark. For a minute, I thought I'd, like, gone to sleep and everyone'd gone home, but then I saw the shapes on the couches, so I kind of felt my way back toward the terrace, where I could see a big wheel of broken moonlight on the ground, shining through a roof trellis.

I got as far as the patio door.

What I saw stopped me dead in my tracks.

Elena was stretched out on that chaise, and Cam was on top of her, and they were kissing so hard their heads looked merged. Then his hand came up and grabbed the waist of her tights, and she lifted her hips to help him pull them down. Then she lay back down and opened her legs partway.

She was so beautiful. I had seen Elena undressed four hundred times, but only changing, or trying on dresses at Dalton's. Now I saw her the way a boy would see her, her belly this brown little hill that looked perfect as a vinyl doll. Cam laid his hand on her so light he could have been touching wet paint. "Look at you, girl," he said. Then he pulled her tights the rest of the way off and let them down on the side of the chaise longue and went to raise up the denim shirt. *My* denim shirt. She pushed his hand away. "Let me look, Elena," he said. "Just look." So she let him, and there was nothing underneath that little tank top but breasts practically silver in the moonlight where her tan left off. "Let me kiss you," Cam said, sounding like he had bread stuck in his throat.

"That's all," she told him, loud.

"That's all," he promised.

I swear I could feel it both ways, the way her brown nipple must have tasted, like a lozenge in his mouth, but at the same time, the way it felt to her. I put my hand up and squeezed my own breast. Scream, girl, I thought. Run. You must be some kind of damn pervert, looking at your own brother about to have actual sex with your best friend. But right then, Elena sort of started to sit up, and Cam said, "Honey, wait. This is good. Don't you like it?"

She said, "Well, I reckon I don't hate it. Here I am."

"You ever let a boy love you?"

"No way, José," said Elena. "I'm not getting no damn AIDS or cooties—"

"I want to love you, inside you."

"—or having no baby."

"I can pull—"

"No. You sit up now." But *she* wasn't sitting up, and when Cam reached down real fast and started to rub her, she just opened her legs a little wider so he could get his whole hand against her. His hand disappeared under her, just the white of his wrist showing.

"Touch me, then," Cam said.

"Touch your own self," said Elena. But she didn't kick him or roll away when he undid his silver buckle.

"No, girl. I need you," Cam said.

"Then put that away." He pulled up his underpants and she opened her legs all the way and let him center himself on her, as she started to buck her hips up and down a little. Cam groaned, putting his whole face on Elena's chest, and then she looked right over his head and saw me.

"Arley, you shit!" she yelled at me, and she was up off that chaise longue so fast it dumped old Cam on his butt.

"I'm sorry! I just got here!"

"Arley, you are sick, sick, sick," Elena was yelling, picking up her tights and jamming them into a ball.

"*I'm* sick!" I said then. "That's my goddamned brother there."

"Well, I ain't his sister."

"You're my friend!"

"Not anymore! What were you, jealous? Thinking about old pervert down in Solamente River?"

"What's going on?" Cam sounded like a busted cassette. He couldn't seem to get his belt buckle to shut. "Who's in Solamente River? In the army?"

"He's not in the army!" Elena screamed.

"Shut *up*!" I screamed even louder.

I turned around and ran away from them, tripping over some

guy and girl lying on the floor, falling to my knees and getting up running. Tears were coming down my face, but I had no idea where I was going. To catch the bus, I guess. To get away from the sight of them, because though I knew they hadn't done anything to me personally, I felt like both of them had betrayed me in the worst way they could.

I almost got knocked over by one of the cars when I pulled open the front door and ran out there, half blind from crying. This one bunch of guys in a pickup and this other guy in a big old blue antique car were jamming around Eric's parents' circle driveway like it was the Indy 500. From what I could see, there was a girl sort of half standing up on the hood of the car, holding on to the roof, and all the guys in the back of the pickup were standing up and yelling. The music was so loud from the bass cannon in the truck, it made my insides shake. Then this other guy pushed past me and ran for one of those pickup trucks that sit up on the big stunt wheels. "You sonofabitch!" He was laughing and yelling. "Wait'll I catch up to you." The guy in the passenger seat of the car sort of jumped up and leaned out, the way a dog does when it wants to catch the wind in its mouth.

I could hear Cam calling for me, and I turned to go back inside, and then I heard the crash. Not a crash. A big, hollow *whump* that was even sicker than metal against metal because you knew it was worse, much worse. Right away, people started to scream. I heard a girl crying, "No, no, no, no, no!"

"Arley!" Cam was all sweaty, his shirt snapped up with the snaps not matching. "What the hell is going on out here?"

"They were racing the cars around. . . ." Cam leaned over me, and I saw his face sort of heave and his eyes pop and then squint shut tight.

"Get back out on that patio," he told me, grabbing my arm so hard I had a bruise the next day. But I fought him, silently, trying to see over his head. . . . The door of that high-up truck was wide open, and the window was smeared and running with blood thick as syrup; you could see the barn through it, shining red.

I clawed at my brother's arm. "Cam! Somebody's hurt!"

"Some kid's just puked up is all—"

"No, Cam, look! It's not that!"

"Arley, I said get back on out there!" We both heard the sirens then, and Cam half dragged me back through the living room to the patio. Elena was out there, sort of huddled in my sweater, her makeup all smeared and running, and Eric was trying to push himself high enough on the back fence to see the front drive. I wanted to help him up, but Cam turned then and made us run; we took off out past the corral, where the horses were awake, whickering and plunging around, and back out past a mesquite brake into the easement of some old railroad tracks. I did puke then, puked as we ran up to the top of the embankment, where we could see Eric's driveway, and an ambulance there, and six blue squads, with their silver stars. "Some kid got sick is all. Jesus," Cam said. "That Eric, he's going to be shitsville Monday."

"You know something else happened. Somebody got cut."

"What happened?" Elena, her breath ragged, kept asking. "What the hell happened?"

"They were drunk is all. Come here, honey," Cam said to her, trying to put his arm around her.

"Let me fucking alone!" Elena snapped at him, stomping off through the broom grass. "I'm going home." We both just stared at her.

"Elena," Cam said, "I'm going to take you." He looked at me. "Both you all."

"Fuck you," Elena told him. I don't know why she was so damned mad at Cam; maybe just embarrassment running over on a boil, maybe because she was scared and she was in front of me. "You leave me alone."

And off she went in the dark. We could see her under the moon, coming down off the embankment, out past the next place over to the Doreys', and then way far off, where there were streetlights.

"What's that street?" I asked Cam.

"Kings Highway, I guess. Shit, Arley, I don't know where we are, but I know we can get to a bus. We ain't going nowhere near that house." There were kids all over down there, small as plastic soldiers; you couldn't tell one from the other, boy or girl, but we saw them fall back as an ambulance went howling out of there. Every light in the house was on, and police cars were threading their way into the driveway, and every so often a siren would go *whoop!* and kids would go running out of the way. A boy started up the hill right toward where we were, but a cop tripped him and grabbed his arm. Then he let his flashlight sweep the hillside. Cam jerked me down practically to my knees.

"Go on," Cam whispered, pushing me, when the light was past us.

We walked an hour. I had to stop every little while to puke some more. I tried to talk. My head felt broken in quarters.

"I'm never going to make a drunk," I told Cam. Cam didn't say one word. I tried again, telling him, "I'm sorry." But he didn't even look at me, and I wished more than anything else in the world that none of this had happened. But if it hadn't, I wouldn't have gone running Monday morning to send Dillon a postcard, practically begging him to let me come and see him.

Cam and me finally got on the bus up past the mall. Riding home, we passed Elena's—I tried to see in, to know if she was all right—and then we got out at the stop three blocks from our house. Cam went right off, walking fast ahead of me, and by the time I got inside he was gone in his room. I heard the door slam and the lock click. Mama wasn't home. I was crying by then. The heel was broken off my boot, and my head felt like I had a wet bathing cap tied on it. I got a piece of bread and the aspirin bottle, trying hard to remember every single thing I'd ever overheard about being drunk, and went upstairs to lie down on my bed. Then the phone rang. Cam picked it up, but I heard him swear and slam it right down. "No one there!" he yelled. Elena said, after we were speaking to each other again, that no, she never made one call.

I know it was her, though.

A few moments later, I heard a motorcycle roar up to the front of my house and stop. Just before I fell asleep, I heard its engine gun up again. I was so tired and low, I didn't even get up to look. I knew everything had changed. In fact, things I didn't even know about had changed, in terrible ways, things I had nothing at all to do with. They had an effect on me, though. If I had it to do over, I have to think I wouldn't do it the way I did. I'd have let it stop with Dillon right where it was. I would have been better off in most ways if I had. But I guess I wouldn't have been me. You don't get to recognize your destiny for what it is because it comes to you piece by piece. But once you've got it, it might be full of grief or easy and happy, but you know it's yours.

That night was for sure the end of something. And something else was starting, a change deep down. I was going toward something, and I couldn't see its shape, but I could tell there was no going back. It was like it was already in my mind, like a name on the tip of my tongue.

CHAPTER FIVE

Annie

I could blame the warden of Solamente River Prison for the fact that I became a home owner.

I still tease Arley that it's really she, not Ray Henry Southwynn, who's responsible for my enduring attachment to the money pit at 4040 Azalea Road. But she's onto me. In fact, she shoots it right back.

"It was the heat," she'll say, looking at me sideways and sly. "All that heat. Annie, New Yorkers can't handle *real* heat, you know?" I do. I know exactly what she means. But I'm still not at the stage where I can joke with Arley, woman-to-woman, about things like "heat." I suppose, despite everything, she's still a child to me.

After I visited Avalon, Stuart and I had the first good night we'd had in months. Looking back, I know it was only partly because of my contrition, and partly because Kim McGrory had just got a stay and a new date for the long sleep. When a client was about to die, Stuart had such jits that I could literally feel his skin jump away from me when I touched him. He didn't mean it. He was just long gone, into the body of the damned, into the mind of the guy planning a meal of fantail shrimp and peach cobbler and a smuggled airplane bottle of Johnnie Walker.

That night, though, Stuart was between crises. He had stacked up six months' worth of *Basketball Digests* (I would nag him: "You already know how those games came out, Stuart," and he would let his reading glasses slide down his nose and say, "It's the game, Annie, not the outcome"). But I distracted him, putting on one of his Brooks Brothers shirts over nothing, a costume Stuart could never bear for long, and initiating the kind of practiced, absorbing lovemaking two people who've been dance partners for years can perfect if they have the time. Then, though it was after ten, we got up to make coffee and watch *True Grit*. And when we fell asleep, not touching but in companionable heaps, I felt clean and exercised and lucky, like a stroked kitten.

When I woke up, Stuart was already gone. I was feeling so good, the way you do after you have had a satisfying night—when people come up to you on the street and ask you what kind of vitamins you take—that I left a message on Stuart's machine at work: "Who was that masked man? I wanted to thank him," and then turned to all the Ins in the In bin.

Estralita Gomez's excellent husband had violated the second restraining order—this time throwing a gallon of red paint through her front window, himself after it. Then a mother from Port Arthur, whose husband was doing time for beating her into a skull fracture with a full six-pack, had left three toddlers (how the hell did she get three toddlers?) at the shelter, with a note entrusting them to whoever could raise them better. Call Social, I scribbled. Call Jeanine.

Then I phoned my sister, listened to her voice mail: "This is Rachael Singer. . . . I know your financial dilemma can't wait, but neither can the person's on the other line, so I'll call you right back." I left a message I hoped would produce some guilt— something about not having heard the unrecorded voice of one's only sibling since Labor Day.

Finally, I got Lilia to track down Ray Henry Southwynn's phone number. He'd have been the one who denied LeGrande's request for a customary conjugal visit with his bride, and he'd be the one who could reverse that decision, no muss, no fuss. Ray Henry was sort of a friend—a decent guy who'd once been, God help us, a social worker in San Antonio. Affable and generous, he was a man who loved women (although never to the extent of offending his lady wife, Fleury) and considered all men guilty until proven otherwise. He was a welter of contradictions, a card-carrying Democrat who stated and believed to the marrow of his Methodist heart that every man Jack in Solamente River Prison was a deserving and justly impounded maggot. He did not like the governor. He did not like the death penalty and would never have worked at an institution where lethal injection—he called it "the poke"—was administered. Fleury served on the board of Women and Children First, sufficient reason for me to excuse myself from this Arley business if it got any further. But all things being equal, with our kind of clients, people aren't too white-gloved about the exact cursive letter of the law. I had hopes that as the abundantly proud father of two daughters (one, Miranda, a law student), Ray Henry might be sensitive to Arlington Mowbray's display of spirit if I told him about her. We could get this over with, no major holler, as he himself would say. Ray Henry had told me more than once, after a few beers at various Women and Children First shindigs, that he wanted his baby girls, including Melissa (who must have been about sixteen by now) to be any goddamned thing they wanted and better by half than any man, while still being good wives, obedient to the Lord's recommendations.

Well, Arley was trying, after a fashion, to do that.

One thing was for certain. Of all the prisons in all the hollows of all Texas—and my adopted state specialized in formal confinement facilities of all stripes—Solamente River was the best place for Arley's dearly beloved to be cooling his heels, because I could reason with the fellow who was standing between the young lovers. I could hear his thoughts on the matter without my blood pressure rising to stroke level. And perhaps I could get Arley out of her unsympathetic jam, and out of my dreams, quickly and easily, without having to resort to a writ of mandamus encouraging the justice system to follow its own stated rules and do what it should—which is more or less the only thing most law is about, anyhow. Despite the nagging sense that this jam was only the honeymoon period (as it were) of the great jam to come for Arley, I'd promised her my best. Besides, there was a principle involved.

"Ray Henry, ol' Ray, how's every single thing?" I said that morning, when I finally caught up with him on my third try at a call, testing out my own best excuse for a drawl. He loved this— the New York Jewish girl trying to redden her neck—and he recognized my voice right away.

"That's Warden Southwynn to you, Counselor," he replied gruffly.

"You mean . . . it's over between us?"

"I recall the distinct offer of a Corona? A Corona at your expense, for the last favor I did you, or my sweet bride did you, which I can't keep track of, being a man in my fifties burdened with all manner of distress."

"Do you mean overcrowded conditions, Ray? Or gum disease? Or what? And anyhow, Corona tastes like piss."

"It do, it do, Miz Singer. That's why you have the lime with it."

"How are the girls?"

"They are sunflowers."

"That's good."

"You called to ask about my daughters?"

"Ray Henry, I got a problem, and you are the only man on earth who can solve it."

He sighed. I could hear him open his drawer and take out something metallic to play with. The man was never still. "Tell me," he ordered after a moment, all business. It gave me a quiver, the way it always did, to be reminded that Ray Henry, no matter how affable, had a steel rod up his butt at the best of times, that he actually considered his job a public service. Maggots were not abused in his jail. But they were not treated, he liked to say, as if they'd gotten their application forms for prep school mixed up with their arrest warrants. By all accounts, the prisoners the majority of whom, I'd come to believe, were either engaged to, married to, or siblings of the majority of my clients—liked Ray Henry and considered him a fair guy.

"Ray Henry, you have a guest called Dillon LeGrande—" I began.

"Him and his kin. We've got a special rate for those *rivière* boys, a corporate rate. Pissants."

"Well, come on now. You know the situation. The girl he married has come to me with your denial of his request, and she—"

"I know what she wants. But more'n that, I know what

he wants. And I'm not going to lift my pinkie to see either of them gets it. Especially her. Which you should be thanking me for, Annie."

"I'm not going to say I don't know what you mean."

"Aren't you, then." It wasn't a question.

"Ray Henry, no. I've seen this girl. You've seen this girl—"

"Oh my, yes. I had to be present at the tender ceremony just the other day."

"But you didn't try to interfere with that."

"I don't interfere with the laws of the state of Texas, ma'am. And that little girl had her mother's legal permission to marry the maggot of her choice. And he's certainly over twenty-one, though he may have the mind of a bird."

"But she—"

"But she nothing, Annie. That little girl is as pretty as a storybook and she has brains in her head, and I'll tell you the truth— and this is not an official pronouncement, and if I ever hear you treating it as such, you will think a house has fell on you—but I wouldn't no more let that trash bop her than I'd let him bop my—"

"So that's it."

"What?" I heard a furious rattling in the background. Someone's paper clips were getting an aerobic workout.

"It's personal."

"Annie, it's not personal. And it has nothing to do with the fact that this little girl is even younger than my Melissa, though she is, and goddammit if that don't matter to me, even if it don't to her own mother. What it has to do with is that a conjugal visit will controvert correctional objectives in this case. This guy has boffed jailbait a hundred times."

"That doesn't concern us."

"Well, how about this? One of the girls Mister Dillon loved cut her wrists when her papa made her move with the family to get away from him. Your Mister LeGrande was sleeping in the house with her, coming in the window at night—"

"Jesus, are you kidding?" I breathed. I could have bitten my tongue.

"I'm not kidding. And some people say he put her up to it."

"The suicide attempt . . ."

"Yes."

"But, Ray Henry, this wasn't a criminal matter, this thing with the girl, if it even ever happened—"

"It did happen. But it has nothing to do with my decision. My concern is with the rehabilitative efforts on behalf of this inmate, who will not be served by it. It is asking for trouble, given his nature."

"He's been in real serious trouble, then?"

"He was probably born trouble. Most of his type are."

"But he's been on report, in repeated situations, for antisocial behavior within the . . . ?"

"Annie, don't start with me," he replied, almost gently, rattling what sounded like the chain on a desk light. "No. Dillon Maggot LeGrande has a clean record for his behavior. He is helpful and cooperative with efforts made toward his betterment."

"So you don't think the benefits of a loving and caring relationship . . . ?"

"I think that little girl comes into one of those trailers for the night, and we're going to have this guy and forty-seven other maggots howling at the moon for the next month. She wants to please her man, let her wait out the century. He keeps up like he is, he's going to get good time. I'm not going to be part of this thing now. It's denied. Right there in the denial, I speak to the issue of the minor child involved. In my esteemed opinion, it would be a crime."

"It would be a crime, Ray Henry, if they weren't married. Which they are, under the laws of the governance that pays your wages. You know I'm going to have to get crosswise of you on this."

"That's good Texas there, Annie. I don't give a damn if you do. We can support this denial hands tied, because we can get psychologists to bring in all manner of stuff in confidence. And the fact that our state honors the pioneer tradition of letting little girls get married, figuring if they're tall enough, they're old enough, cuts no ice with me."

"I think if this has to be a big show, it's you who's going to owe *me* a beer, Ray Henry. And maybe some cold shrimp too."

"Don't do it, Annie. For once in your life, pay attention to what's right instead of what's possible. I mean it. You know this isn't right for this child. And sure, I've seen a lot worse." I heard the drawer, and the conversation, slam shut. "But that don't mean I still don't want to see better once in a while."

I wanted to put my head down on my desk blotter and roll my forehead back and forth like a stamp on an ink pad. "What I know, Warden Southwynn, is my job. And my job is not to figure out whether people are correct in their wish to exercise the rights guaranteed to them under the law, but to see that they get the chance to exercise them. I'm not Solomon, Ray Henry."

"Well, I am, Annie. In this place. For these matters, I am."

"That must make it hard to sleep some nights, sir."

"It do. But I fight the impulse to toss and turn."

"See you in court, Ray Henry."

"You won't see me, missy. You know better than that. You'll see my legal representative, Lee Petty."

"Ah yes, Petty. Some people look like their dogs. Some people look like their names, huh?"

Ray was laughing now, but quickly sobered up. "I know Lee does his job." We shared an opinion on this particular member of the Justice Department counsel team, and both of us knew what it was, just as we knew the conversation had grown too dicey to share it.

"Well, I'm glad for you that he does. And I do mine."

"Well so."

"Love to Fleury."

"Will do." He was gone. I wanted to blame the hell out of him. I wanted the sense of unrighted wrong that usually helps me get my adrenaline flowing. But I didn't have it. Now I had another phone call to make. Yet I was reluctant, for some reason, to make it—to call Arley and even get started with the preparations we would need to make to go to court. They wouldn't be much, in any case, beyond a little coaching about speaking up and dressing as if she were ready to go out for Sunday supper with her church youth group. I fiddled around, making other, miserably postponed calls for other clients, making sure Matt had followed up on an arrest warrant—which would be equally ineffective as the restraining order, I was sure—for Estralita's op-art stalker of a husband. I debated whether I should give Matt or Patty the job of getting me a quick date with the Galleon County Judge who'd drawn the dog duty of hearing Solamente River prisoners' writs for the month.

After a few minutes of fuming, I sent Matt an E-mail, telling him the specifics of the pound of paper he'd have to drive to the clerk's office in Galleon County. The county was basically a cluster of one-stoplight towns that surrounded Solamente River Prison like the prefab neighborhoods that used to surround auto-manufacturing plants, except that the employment base was people who made license plates instead of cars. Matt would first have to phone Mr. Dillon LeGrande himself (I knew I should do this, but I didn't have the stomach for it) and make sure that our proposed lawsuit reflected his true intentions, because technically we had no evidence of those intentions beyond the copy of the letter to the warden Arley had given me in her folder. Then there was, of course, the writ of mandamus itself—*Ex rel. Dillon Thomas LeGrande* v. *Ray Henry Southwynn* and so on and so on—a slew of other motions, including the request for the waiver of court costs, with copies of that and everything else to everyone Matt could think of, starting with Counselor Petty and continuing up through the universe.

In the late afternoon, Patty came into my office and flopped into the leather judge's chair I'd liberated from a courtroom renovation site in Ballou County.

"Child abuse," she said.

"We're not for it," I agreed.

"I wish I smoked," Patty said.

"I eat to forget," I told her.

The case Patty was involved with had drained her, on and off, for two years; even for Women and Children First it was a real slam dunk. Mom and Dad were the kind of abusers who could have been trained by the junta in some South American prisoner-of-war camp, but the five kids had found a good stable home with Mom's ex-boyfriend. The boyfriend had just learned he was HIV-positive. The county's position was that there was no alternative but a foster placement. Our position was that we wanted the boyfriend to be certified as a foster parent, with a full-time attendant funded by the county. No one was going to adopt five troubled siblings. The county was worried about the children's "future." "What future? How about letting these kids have a little healthy present first?" Patty was mourning now.

"I think I should adopt them all, I can't stand this." I was very fond of Patty. She not only lacked the lizard hide of a lawyer, her skin didn't even have normal human thickness. Pain went right through. She was wrong for this work; but it was her dangerous compassion as much as her Notre Dame summa that had made me hire her. I did my best to comfort her, and when she left, I called my friend Jeanine.

"Let's go over to the clinic and get some medical attention," I suggested. "The clinic" was a trendy Tex-Mex café called something in Spanish that Stuart insisted meant "sad-eyed lady of the lowlands." It was a watering hole for young doctors; Jeanine and I liked to gaze at them, playing one of two favorite people-watching games. One was "Would you, could you . . . ?" and the other was "Too cute to be straight?"

The restaurant was located in the King William district, south of the city and near the river, where the great pillared homes of German cattle barons bloomed in the nineteenth century, moldered toward the end of the twentieth, and were now deep into the impasse between handsome young hoodlums raising hell and handsome young gay home owners gentrifying up a storm. I loved the King William neighborhood, which was also the location of my favorite tchotchke store, Tienda Corina. At Corina's storefront, once a gas station, I bought almost all my gifts for non-Texans, like little statues and pieces of silver jewelry commemorating November 2, All Souls' Day, the sacred Mexican Catholic Day of the Dead. My favorites were silver studs in the shape of tiny skulls, with turquoise eyes.

They nauseated Stuart, even after I explained that El Día de los Muertos was a happy day, when the departed got to come back and do the things they loved most in life. I had four or five little statues, made by Mexican artists, including a skeleton bride and groom. I'd wanted a skeleton mother cuddling her skeleton infant, but Stuart had stalked out of the store when I showed it to him.

"What gripes me isn't that you like this sick stuff," he'd said, when I told him I thought the Madonna-and-child skeletons were touching. "What gripes me is how you think my reaction to it is funny."

"Well, it's a big overreaction."

"You're just playing at being some kind of latent Catholic."

"I am not. I think it's a sort of lovely statement about . . . well, about the fact that your real immortality is the life you lived. Or something."

"Clearly a statement made by people who never saw a crime-scene photo."

Ah, my Stuart. Always there when you needed a curmudgeon.

I called Stuart and left a message, asking him to meet Jeanine and me for dinner and to bring Tarik—Jeanine had a crush on him. It was Wednesday night, a big going-out night in this part of town. The restaurant, Amor Ausente, was filling with a lazy mix of Hispanic and Anglo professionals, pulling off ties and wrinkled sports coats, plus the district's own artists and working-class folk—both of whom, Jeanine had pointed out, wore paint-spattered clothing, except the artists wore scarves too. The waiter, Luis, was our bud.

"You look not so happy, Anne," he told me, his skin shiny as a chestnut and, I imagined, as soft. He had to be, what, twenty-three?

"I'm absolutely perfect, Luis," I told him. Jeanine arrived

then. Her mood was no better than Patty's had been. "It's apparently *mi amiga* here who's in the dumps."

"Ah. What's the problem?"

"Children." Jeanine sighed. "The children whose children I have to find parents for, when I should be finding parents for the children who are giving birth to the other children."

"Would you like a margarita?" Luis asked sweetly.

"Actually, I would like a baby, Luis." She sighed. "I'd like to have a family of my own someday. And I'm never going to, at this rate. I'm just going to keep spending twenty-four hours a day making or unmaking families for other people and dating guys who had vasectomies before they got divorced. . . ."

"So you do want a margarita?"

"Luis," said Jeanine, "would you like to have a baby?"

What was in the air tonight? Was it the annual equinox for the overwound biological clocks of all thirty-something females? Jeanine was at least seven years younger than I and had often told me that her intake files were the original inspiration for the phrase "Just say no."

"You're kidding," I told her.

"No, really. I couldn't be more serious. How about it, Luis?"

"Okay," Luis agreed. "I get off at twelve. Can you wait that long?"

"Italian-Irish, like me, and Mexican—you know, fair and dark . . . ," Jeanine went on.

"Drinking and praying . . . ," said Luis.

"Fighting and singing . . . ," Jeanine agreed.

"And guilt," I put in. "Don't forget guilt."

"I'll get you just what you need," Luis interjected, and headed toward the bar.

"I really do want a baby," she said after Luis retreated. "The pediatrician thinks one of the best things about me is that I'm a 'career woman' who doesn't, in his words, want to 'nest.' Not that he didn't nest for twelve years and two sons with his ex-wife. And the cop is afraid that having children might be too much of a risk, given his line of work."

"I've heard that before."

"He says he sees too much."

"I've heard that before too. Why don't you adopt one of your babies?"

"Because I want the whole thing. Husband. House. Hanging up my diaphragm forever. Nine months of finishing my whole meal . . ." She paused, as if she'd just received my words by mail. "What do you mean, you've heard that before?"

My voice did one of those slide-guitar things with the vocal cords. "I . . . when Stuart and I talk about kids . . . well, he says he doesn't think that he could really handle—"

"I didn't know you and Stuart were even considering that. You love your life, Annie."

"I do. I do love our life."

"You never told me you wanted to have a baby. I just assumed . . ."

"You shouldn't assume."

"But you and Stuart . . ."

"It's not like we have to decide tomorrow or anything."

"Day after, though, right?" Jeanine pressed me. "You're . . . how old are you, Annie?"

"Jeez. I'm going to be forty, Jeanine. Happy now?"

The drinks arrived. "Well, I didn't mean anything." She took a sip of hers. "This is not a margarita. Luis!" she called softly. He turned from the bar. "You know, this is not a margarita."

"No," he said, his handsome, gentle face almost sad. "I decided a margarita was not enough for tonight. I decided I must choose the drinks tonight. A mission. This establishment most proudly offers thirty different blends of tequila. This is why the bartender is called Jesús not for nothing. You are in my hands."

Now, I love tequila. It's the only liquor that doesn't make me feel, before or during, as though I'm one step from phoning ralph. By the time Stuart arrived, there were eight shot glasses on the table between Jeanine and me, actually in kind of a nice pyramid. The residue at the bottom of some of them had dried to various tinctures of gold, from orange to flax, and one looked like some kind of psychotic child's science project—a chartreuse from outer space with a red dot, like a fertilized egg yolk, still floating on it.

"That's called a Martian Boob," Jeanine said.

"It's not." It seemed important to give Stuart correct information. I stood up for emphasis. "It's a Venetian Nipple." Stuart grinned with half his mouth, which always made me think he looked like Steve McQueen, and eased me back down into my chair.

"It looks pretty effective."

"Oh, it is," said Jeanine. "Join us."

Tarik came in then, dressed, as always, like a *GQ* model, in soft heather-colored slacks made of some kind of slightly iridescent material. How he could afford to dress this way on a death row lawyer's salary was beyond me. "Rich relations," Stuart suggested once.

"What kind of relations?" I had asked him. "A sugar daddy?"

"Or a sugar mama?" he'd retorted.

Neither of us had ever known Tarik, whose looks were as model perfect as his clothes, to date anyone, male, female, mineral, or vegetable.

The two of them sat down and ordered longnecks, and we got

some chips and salsa and a plate of bean burros to share. Stuart kept staring down into the neck of his beer bottle as if seeking an oracle, and I really didn't want to ask, I really didn't, but I finally had to say, "Honey, what's up?"

"It's Kim McGrory," he said.

"That's the guy who killed everyone after Thanksgiving dinner," Jeanine put in brightly.

"He's my client," Stuart said. "My client."

"He got a stay," Tarik explained. "A psychiatric evaluation—"

"He poisoned everyone, right?" Jeanine persisted. "Am I thinking of the right guy? He said it was botulism—"

"He didn't say it was botulism," Stuart explained weakly. "He didn't say anything. He was in the hospital for two weeks. Somebody poisoned that meat—"

"No, Stuart, I read about it," Jeanine said. "They said he was abusing his granddaughters, and what he took himself turned out to be an overdose of aspirin or something. He didn't really try to kill himself—"

"Well, Jeanine, I wouldn't ever presume to argue facts with the press. He did, however, really try to kill himself today."

"What?" I asked. "You just said he got a stay—"

"He doesn't really want a competency hearing. He doesn't want another psychiatric evaluation," Stuart continued softly. "His mother was in and out of institutions his whole life. She set fire to the house when he was six, and his grandmother got custody of him. But she made him live in a horse box—"

"These stories are all so touching." Jeanine smiled, toasting Tarik with her second Venetian Nipple. Stuart and Tarik shrugged, silent, their tension stiffening the very air around them. I could feel the friction between their despair and Jeanine's bleary wit. I sent her a mental E-mail: Flirt with Tarik now. Leave this alone.

She wouldn't, though. She was in the mood to pick at something. "The children in that family who died when Kim cooked dinner— I'm sure their stories were pretty bleak too."

"Actually, they were, Jeanine," Stuart said. "Abuse is a gift that keeps on giving, generation after generation."

"Well, he took care of that for future generations."

"You should have been his defense attorney, Jeanine," Stuart said thinly. "Kim's lawyer was such a moron, he just about said the same thing."

"He'd have to have been a moron to defend a guy who poisoned his whole family, not to mention the neighbors."

"But you know, Jeanine, because you are a well-informed citizen," Stuart went on, "Kim never confessed to any crime and was never really proven to have killed anybody. And now he actually might not need to get the poke, after all. Because he's probably taken care of the job himself."

"A huge loss to the commonwealth."

"Well, cheer up, Jeanine. Now he's in a coma. Nobody knows how long he was hanging from one of those rubber exercise bands in his cell. Folks tend not to notice prisoners on death row— especially when they're just hanging around like that, you know?"

"Stuart . . . ," I began, pleadingly.

"Oh, Anne, I don't have to listen to this bullshit—"

Jeanine cut in. "Why don't they spend money on trying to give kids a better start so they don't turn out to be serial killers, instead of trying to save—"

"Where's the cutoff? Which generation should we start with? Is thirteen too young? Is seventy too old?"

"You're such a tedious liberal, Stuart." Jeanine plonked her glass and her elbows down on the table, nearly upsetting our pyramid.

"You have such a strong, powerful sense of social justice for a social worker, Jeanine," he said.

"Shut up," I told them both. This spat wasn't helping my digestion. The congealing beans and tortilla chips looked as appealing as haggis, though I knew I should eat something. The tower of glasses winked and subdivided before my eyes.

Then all of a sudden, Stuart was banging open the door and gone.

"He'll be back," Tarik said.

"Maybe not," I said morosely. "I can hope for the best."

But I knew the only choice I had was to follow him out. To tell you the truth, though, I wouldn't have minded right then getting hold of Kim McGrory's exercise band and using it on him and Jeanine both. Tarik started to say that he'd get Jeanine home, but I assured him we'd just walk around the block and cool off. Outside, the night was what makes people put up with Texas— tropic, lush as a red fruit but without the wet dullness of summer. You didn't have to wear a sweater, but a little ribbon of cool from somewhere made you appreciate the fact. From the gloom of a deep gallery, someone was playing the old song "Por Un Amor" on a guitar. I took Stuart's arm, making noises about how everyone had had a hard day. Actually, even I had had a hard day, a circumstance I began to describe, when a wide-eyed look from Stuart simply shut me up. His mishegas was always worse than my mishegas. His was life; mine was usually quality of life. I always felt I had to apologize for that. Besides, though I wasn't drunk, the motion of my arms and legs didn't seem quite in synch. So I just stopped. And I looked up.

And there was this house.

It was a rambling red-brick Revival of Everything pile, with every cliché from a B horror movie well represented. "This place has more wings than a Saturday night in Buffalo," Stuart said, relaxing a little under the embrace of the sweet night air.

Whoever designed the house had really kitchen-sinked it. There were yards of crumbling gingerbread lattices over carved lintels, wrought-iron rails overgrown with trumpet vine that reached out from the arms of a huge, shedding pecan tree. The front garden looked like an EPA site; Stuart would later say he'd expected to find a car buried in the yard. A series of abused mailboxes of various vintages lined the front walk.

"Someone evidently went postal," Stuart said. I punched him on the shoulder. "Why do you have such bad friends?" he asked.

"I don't have bad friends," I replied. "Why do you have such bad manners?"

"She's just typical of . . . everybody, Anne. 'Why don't *they* spend money on children instead of convicted killers?' As if it were a genuine set of equal options—you know, just like adoption, not abortion."

"Stuart, she *is* typical of everybody. Everybody doesn't give a shit whether somebody who killed his whole family also has a sad history."

"Do you know just what this place looks like?" Stuart asked me, looking up at the house again and shrugging off my explanation like a wet shirt.

And I, feeling suddenly as though a question had just been answered by telegram, said, "Yes, exactly."

"It looks like the big old house in *It's a Wonderful Life*."

"Yes, it does. Exactly. Mary and George were coming home from the dance and they threw stones at the windows and the one who broke the first pane got his wish . . ." Stuart had already picked up a little rock. He had a good arm, from years of

high-stake lawyer's softball teams, but he came nowhere near any
of the six or seven thousand still-unbroken panes in that house.
He was picking up another stone when I said, "Now, wait. That's
not fair. I get to try first."

At first Stuart looked at me as though I weren't quite there. It
dawned on me that he hadn't fully entered into this re-creation of
the sacred Capra romantic moment; he was pissed, pissed like a
kid, and just felt like breaking something. Right then, the moon
shrugged a cloud and shone directly on a huge pair of eight-
paneled windows fronting what I realized I'd just decided would be
my bedroom. Stuart was a good sport; he grinned and handed me
his stone and reminded me to use my shoulder, not my wrist. And
I put it right through a pane that couldn't have been more than five
inches by five, which would later cost me nearly a hundred bucks
to replace, and I turned to Stuart and slapped my hands on my
thighs and said, "And that is how that is done. I get my wish."

I only got to gloat for a minute.

Stuart was gazing over my shoulder, alarmed.

"What?" I whispered, whirling around and almost colliding
with the lap of a big blond guy carrying a big pointed stake. My
forehead hit him at about waist level. I looked up and up, reaching
back blindly for Stuart's hand, before I realized with relief that the
guy probably wasn't really a hobo defending his jungle with . . . yes,
a sledgehammer. He was actually carrying a lettered sign. And wearing painter's overalls. And a feed cap. Just a big, blond Texas guy.

He said, "You shouldn't bust out the windows. It's not nice."

Is this, like, Lenny? I thought, and righted myself. "I'm sorry,"
I said quickly. "We were being foolish. We just . . . I'll gladly pay
for it."

The blond guy looked up at the overhang of the eaves. "I
don't know who you'd pay, ma'am. The owner . . ."

"Yes?"

"Well, she's dead, ma'am," he answered, beginning to pound a For Sale sign into one of the few unmailboxed spaces in the yard.

"Are you her son?" I asked stupidly, trying to piece things together.

"Nope. I just do a lot of repair work and stuff around the neighborhood. People have some beautiful gardens—I caretake a few of them. This lady had some nice plantings. You hate to see it all ruined. Somebody's going to spade all this up and put a damned hedge in here or something."

Still alert, but recovered, Stuart asked, "How long has this place been abandoned?"

"I don't know," said the blond man. "What? Five years? The old lady for sure still lived here when I was in college. Maybe it's more like eight or nine years. A house won't hold up long in this climate with nobody to mind it."

"Didn't she have . . . family?"

"Not that I ever saw. I guess somebody finally decided to sell it to one of those brokers who takes on vacant houses. It's really beautiful inside. And under here"—he pointed to the heap of mailboxes—"there's this gorgeous perennial garden." Even in the deepening dark, I could see his smile grow eager. "Hibiscus and cacti and . . . well, that's a Rio Grande abutilon, that orange flower. And see that tree with the trunk the same green as the branches? That's paloverde. Evening primrose all over. My house is two blocks away. Gardens are kind of a passion of mine, but even I don't have this nice a garden. Or the space for it."

"I could imagine having this garden," I said then. Stuart stared at me. "Well," I said, standing erect with some effort. "I think I'll buy this house. Stuart, don't you think I should buy this house? How much is it?"

"I don't know, ma'am. It might be . . . well, it can't be much. I was just out here this afternoon sort of doing the rounds and I ran into the real estate agent—he was on his way to his kid's soft-ball game—so I said I'd stick this in here for him. . . ."

"Real close neighborhood," Stuart muttered; unkindly, I thought.

"Judging by my house," the man went on, "I'd say . . . *maybe* sixty thousand. Or not even. It's . . . ah, it needs a lot."

"Well, we could—"

"We?" Stuart asked. "That's not what you said. You said *you* might buy this house."

"I meant *we*," I said. "Stuart, want to buy a house? With me?" I turned back, craning my neck to look eye-to-eye with the blond giant, and asked, "What sort of house is this?"

"This," he said, pushing back the brim of his denim baseball cap, "is a Queen Anne."

"See?" I said to Stuart. "There you have it!"

"See what, Anne?" he asked me.

"Well, look at the address. It's forty forty . . . what street is this?"

"Azalea Road."

"Forty forty Azalea Road. I'm going to be forty. *And* I broke the window. It's an omen. And . . . and . . . I was talking to the warden at Solamente River today, and he said—though I didn't agree with this—you don't have to do a thing just because you can. . . ."

"And your point?" Stuart asked, a little coldly.

"Well, by the same token, that means you shouldn't avoid do-ing a thing just because you . . . just because it's possible to think of all kinds of reasons that would stop you."

"Anne, we don't need a house. We haven't even decided whether we're going to get—"

"Stop. I want this house," I said. I felt like sitting down on the bottom step and bawling. "And I want to go back to Amor Ausente."

"I like that restaurant," said the blond man. "My name's Charley Wilder, by the way. My mother lives around here too. And one of my brothers. What do you guys do?"

"I'm a lawyer," Stuart said.

I said, "I'm a lawyer too."

"A pair of lawyers?" I could hear Stuart's scornful quiet snort, and I hoped this nice kid couldn't; Stuart could be so impatient with the slow speed of Texas geniality. "Now, the couple across the street are lawyers too. They're both men, though. . . ." Stuart snorted aloud then, but I had the odd feeling that the teasing had been deliberate, that the blond man had a firm grip on the reins. "And the guy who owns Amor Ausente lives right"—he took off his cap and, with his yellow hair springing free in lank curls—"right over there on the corner. The big adobe place."

"I never met him," I told Charley Wilder. "But we eat there all the time. And go for drinks." That was probably obvious.

"Ramón. He's a character. 'Lost Love,' " said the blond man. "That's what the name of the restaurant means. But you probably know the story. . . ."

I turned to Stuart. "I thought you said it was the sad lady of—"

"Anne, I just said that because you kept asking. You know more Spanish than I do. You know what *amor* means."

"But why did I believe you?"

The young man added, "This guy started the restaurant when his wife ran off with a cowboy—"

"He ate to forget," said Stuart.

"That's my line," I told him.

"Excuse me," Charley asked. "Should I leave the sign?"

"We'd probably just throw rocks at it," I told him.

"Or each other," Stuart added.

Charley pounded the sign in with a few sure blows. "I'll let you two work this one out," he said.

CHAPTER SIX

Arley

I had to work in the morning, though I was as sick as a dog eating grass. Elena breezed in right the same time as me, and she looked as if she'd spent the night at a beauty parlor, her hair all twisted up over one ear, her blush swept up just so over her cheekbones. She did stupid stuff the whole first hour, knocking two of my orders right off the pass-through window on purpose, splashing guck out of the bus tub on my uniform, laughing and talking in Spanish to the dishwasher, Eduardo, pointing over at me when she knew I could see. But I didn't pay her the compliment of noticing one thing.

I just told Cully the plates were greasy. I didn't let her get to me. Annie always says I'm self-possessed. After I got over thinking she meant that I had a demon in me, I kind of agreed. It must come from being alone so much, because after a certain amount of pushing, I just hit a point where nothing can touch me. It's like in running: you get to a place after a mile or so where you know you could just keep on going forever if it wasn't for the fact that it would eventually kill you.

That morning at work, it got to be kind of interesting, seeing Elena twist herself inside out trying to make me notice her tricks.

I just tried to forget last night and make myself think about what I was going to write to Dillon in my emergency postcard: "I'm coming to see you. If that's not okay, please write soon"? When it came to that, I didn't feel so self-possessed. But I tried to act as though I felt confident. It was a way I'd get accustomed to acting very soon, and with even less reason for confidence.

On my break, I went up to the phone booth on the corner of Alameda and Honora Streets—you couldn't see it from the restaurant—and called Connie G.

She said right away, "Arley. Oh, honey, are you okay?"

I held my breath. This is crazy, I thought. Unless Elena told her sister about Cam and all. I just said, real slowly, "I'm okay. I'm fine, Connie."

"I know you were there. Tina Secora's little sister Allie was telling me she saw you and Cam. And I know Elena likes that boy Eric. Or she did. Now I guess she won't be seeing him. . . ."

It was like the crazy wind, the one off the desert that Mrs. G. says used to make the Apaches kill their brothers in the night. I had no idea what she was talking about. Did she think it was such a big deal some kid got arrested for underage drinking? Then I remembered that truck's window, the eerie light on the top of the ambulance.

I had to ask her, though I didn't want to know.

"Did you see any of it?" Connie asked then.

I said, "Connie, I know what Elena thinks, but I didn't see a thing."

"Well, did she see any of it?"

"I . . . I guess . . . Did you ask her?"

"I didn't even know it happened until after she left for work."

"Oh."

"Does Elena know? Did Cam drive you two home?"

"We took the bus. . . ." I realized, then, she did mean the accident, whatever it was. Thank you, God, thank you, I thought, sagging against the cold glass of the booth, finally letting myself feel how chilled I was without my jacket, which I'd had to leave in the washing machine that morning—it was all over with throw-up. "I don't even know what kid it was."

"Girl, it was the Nevadas boy."

My stomach jumped. I remembered the sound of that bike in the night. "Ricky or Gary?"

"No, the other one, the cousin. Corty. He lives up by us."

"I don't even know Corty Nevadas. Did he go to the hospital? Or just the police station? How old is he?"

Connie was so silent, I thought the phone had gone out. "Arley," she said, so gently I knew that anything she said was going to make me cry. "Arley, they took him to the morgue, girl. His head was ripped almost off. . . ."

"What?"

"He was hanging out of the passenger side of that car, the Dorey kid's car, his daddy's classic Ford something-or-other. Some kid named Raiford got it out of the garage and he was driving around and around that circle driveway, and then some other kid—I don't know who, but it was on the news that he was just sixteen—opened the door of a pickup and it tore Corty Nevadas's head right—"

"Don't tell me any more!" I yelled at her. "Oh, poor Corty. Poor Eric. He's such a good boy. . . ."

"I know."

"And he was just drinking is all. Nothing but that. God, oh God. I have to tell Elena. . . . *You* call up and tell Elena, okay?"

"Why, Arley? What's the matter?"

"Nothing! Nothing! I just can't tell her is all, and I know she has no idea, or if she does, she's crazy, because she's running around in there laughing her head off—oh God, I didn't mean that. . . ."

"Arley, you all are too young for that kind of party."

"Yes!" I said. "Yes, we are!"

"Honey, why'd you call me?"

I was so tense, I had to hold on to the roots of my hair to stop the gnashing of the pain in my jaws. "I—uh—I wanted to know when you would go back out to Solamente River."

"Mmm, next Saturday."

"Do you stay over? At, like, a motel?"

"No, I come back. You only get an hour."

"Are you going to drive over there?"

"I don't have a car, Arley. And Gracie's is getting fixed. I'm taking the bus up. The Greyhound."

"Can I come with you?"

"It's a public bus."

"Oh, okay. Okay."

"I'm sorry, Arley, honey. Of course you can come with me. You mean to see Dillon really."

"I really want to, —want to," I said, realizing then how much I did. "Connie, just don't tell Elena I'm going. Don't tell her. I want to tell her myself."

"Okay," she said, softly. "So this is why he was asking all about you—"

"He asked about me?"

"He didn't ask me himself. He sent me a note with Kevin. He wanted to know *all* about you, were you serious about any man or anything. And I told Kevin . . . well, I didn't know how you felt."

"What?"

"I told Kevin I didn't think a guy Dillon's age should be all that interested in a little bitty girl in the ninth grade."

All the vinegar steeped into that pig sandwich from the night before came right back up my throat like a gully wash right then. I had to bend over and spit out the door, and I saw Mr. Justice, leaning on stop-and-go pole at the corner and looking at me. He started toward me, but I shut the door and shut my eyes and turned away. My legs were churning back and forth like they did when I didn't drink enough water before I ran. When I opened my eyes, he was walking the other way.

". . . though I guess you could say it wouldn't do anyone any harm. You can't do anything but talk, anyway," Connie was saying. "Plus this is about half my fault for telling you about him in the first place."

"You told him I was only fourteen?"

"What?"

"I gotta go, Connie," I said. "I'll call you tomorrow, okay? I . . . It's too hot out here." I threw the phone down and it didn't even go into the cradle, but I just left it hanging and ran back toward the restaurant like there was rats after me. It only took me about two minutes to get there, but I saw Elena burst out the door, her hair all down, crying, and she just about knocked me over, grabbing me around the waist. How'd Connie called her so fast? But I knew she had.

"I'm sorry," she sobbed. "I'm so sorry. I was mad at you. I was, like, getting back at you for keeping secrets from me. . . . I'm so sorry I was such a jerk with Cam. I'm . . . oh God, did you hear about Corty? Oh God, Arley . . . Eric Dorey's going to go to jail. It was his house . . ."

Then I was crying myself, hugging her hard, inhaling the way she smelled of vanilla and serrano peppers like it was oxygen from a canister, relieved at how strong and the same my best friend felt. But if I tell the truth, I was only half crying because of our fight and poor Corty Nevadas. I didn't give a damn if every kid in Bexar County got his head busted like a pumpkin right then. No, it was that I felt sure Dillon hated me for my lies, and I was never going to hear from him again, and I realized just how much my whole world had started to contract into smaller and smaller circles, like the narrow end of a fluted shell, and how, in the space left by that smallest of circles, with Dillon at the center, I could not move or turn away.

When we couldn't stop crying, even as we wiped the tables clean, Ginny Jack sensibly told us both to go home. Instead, we went and sat in Alamo Plaza and got piña colada snow cones; Elena actually helped me plan my emergency postcard, though she still didn't approve of Dillon and especially, as she put it, my "doggin' after him." What she suggested I write was really brilliant: "I know that you know what you know. And I'm sorry. But people a lot older than me have done things a lot more foolish for a lot less reason. I do not have very much experience, and someday you will be glad."

I asked her, "What do I mean by that?"

"It means you didn't sleep with another boy. He would want to be the first one."

"Ellie, I'm not going to sleep with him."

"You will someday. If you love him. I mean, like in five years."

"Are you going to . . . are you going to do it with Cam?"

She licked the white ice off her upper lip like a cat and pulled out her scrunchie band; her hair dropped down her back the way human hair never does except on TV—like a thundercloud bundle undone. "I don't know. I guess not. Because it might make you not want to be friends with me. But he is . . . hot."

"You almost . . ."

"I never did that much before, Arley."

"You looked like you knew what you were doing." Quick as a silverfish under the sinkboard, she dashed the leftover drops of the snow cone on my legs.

"You did see!"

"No! Not really!"

"You did! Major truth . . ."

"I saw some of it. What did you want me to do? Yell out, 'Hi, y'all'?"

"I wonder," Elena said, gathering her hair back up, "what it feels like to die." Her face was still streaked with clown drops from her mascaraed tears; but she didn't look sad when she said it. She looked excited, like she knew she should stop but didn't want to. We started to talk about Corty then, a kid neither of us had ever seen and now never would see, about how having your head just laid open like that must simply be like a power outage—one instant light, one instant nothing. "And then after," Elena said, "they say you look down and you see yourself rising up from your shattered body. . . ."

"It's making me sick to my stomach," I said. "I don't want to think about it."

"Do you think you can feel?" Elena asked me. "After you're dead? With your soul? Do you think he'll be there at his funeral, watching us all cry?"

I told her I didn't know. But I knew we were past the point of horror and guilt over the death and near the point of beginning to enjoy it—to relish our firsthand involvement with a notorious story, the kind of story kids would be telling at school for months or even years. People would ask us about it; we were there, after all. It makes me ashamed to think how we were.

135

The bus was late, and after a while we took off our waitress shoes and white stockings to let our legs tan. We were sitting on the edge of the big Republic fountain, the one with the golden lady hoisting up the eagle, when Elena suddenly hissed at me, "Arley, behind you! It's old nutso. Look what he's doing!"

It was Mr. Justice. In one hand he had that beat-up Spurs cap he always wore, and he was pretending to trail his other hand in the water; but what he was really doing was scooping up coins, coins people came and dropped in there. People on dates. Kids with their parents. You'd see them all the time. They'd stand with their backs to the fountain and flip a dime or a quarter up over their heads.

"Pretend you don't see him," Elena said, without moving her mouth, like a ventriloquist. But I couldn't pretend. Everything in me was so keyed up that day, so close to the surface, like a boil starting to roll.

I stood up and I said, "Mister Justice. It's Arley Mowbray. Don't do that, okay? It's not right." He looked at me, and his mouth opened and his eyes closed tight, like the sun hurt them.

Of course, I instantly regretted it—the way his face looked. He went so pale under his tan, the color of his cheeks looked like bad makeup. Just the way, in some photographs, you can see how a little kid will look when it's all grown up, you could see in that minute the way Mr. Justice must have looked once, when he was young, and drinking was something his body could just throw off—how he must have been handsome and slender and dark, with eyes the shade of blue jeans.

"I'm sorry," I said quickly. "I'm sorry. Here." I dug in my uniform pocket, grabbing a wad of dollars, quarters—my tip money. "Here. Take it."

"Are you crazy?" Elena yelled.

"I'm sorry." I started piling the money on the white marble lip of the fountain. "I'm sorry it embarrassed you and I'm sorry I saw it."

"Arley," said Mr. Justice, "I shouldn't have been doing it. I'm sick is all. I hate to have you see it."

"It's not your fault."

"You know," he said, not nuts at all but just slow and careful, "that it is."

"Please take the money," I begged him. He got up, the silver coins he'd dug out slurrying droplets as they slid back into the fountain pool.

"No, Arley," he said, drying off his hands. "I can't."

"Then you'll just ruin everything more!" I yelled at him. "First you tried to steal all those people's wishes—"

"Arley, are you crazy?" Elena screeched again, mystified.

"And now you want to make me ashamed because you don't have any money. It's not fair. So take it! Do me a favor!" I swept my tip money off the edge of the fountain onto the ground; and Elena grabbed me by the arm and we ran for the bus just pulling up, our white shoes thumping against our collarbones where we'd hung them by the laces. With his hands limp by his sides, Mr. Justice watched me go.

But when I was in the bus, safe behind the tinted windows, I saw him pick up those bills and the change and put them carefully into his jacket pocket. As the bus pulled away, he lifted his hat like he was sort of saluting me, and he smiled.

"That was practically your whole day you just gave him," Elena said.

"He's poor and he's sick and there's just . . . there's just too *much wrong* in the world," I told her, sobbing.

"You should have let him just take the money out of that fountain. The city gives it to them, anyhow."

"To who?"

"Poor people."

"But I couldn't. It would be a curse! I would never hear one word from Dillon again! Something terrible would happen—I mean, something else terrible! Like, death comes in threes, you know?"

Of course, I didn't believe any such thing. I was exhausted was all, on an ignition burn.

I was only fourteen. I have to remember that. I had never really thought about death in relation to a person young like me, until Corty. And to tell you the truth, not even then. What happened to Corty quickly became like a movie death, dramatic but distant. That afternoon in the park, as Elena and I ran for the two o'clock bus, ran from Mr. Justice and the tragedy of the previous night, we folded death into our pockets with our tights and hair nets. We put it out of sight within twelve hours, the way we put those singles and change in our uniform pockets and forgot, until closing, how heavy those pockets had become.

Of course, death *would* come in threes. I could not have known how soon, and how urgently, I would have to think about death, be asked about death. I would have no choice but to fold my warm hand over its cold one and accept it as real.

CHAPTER SEVEN

Annie

"It's truly hideous," said Jeanine.

"It's structurally quite sound," I replied.

"It's almost monumentally hideous, like a ruin or something," Jeanine went on. "This is big, Annie. This is really big, mistakewise."

It was a December morning, and we were standing on the sidewalk in front of 4040 Azalea Road. My closing on the house had been dated and slated with unseemly haste, as if the broker could hardly restrain himself from snagging this ever-so-fresh fish. A lawyer can't abide anyone else feeling that he's putting one over on her. Clue up, mister, I wanted to tell him whenever we met. I actually know how bad this house is, and I'm buying it anyway. This thing is personal, I wanted to explain. I just couldn't explain why.

In the weeks since the night of the broken glass (Stuart's term for our moonlit stroll into mortgageland), I'd had several garden-variety final-exam dreams and one episode of high-noon heart banging I could describe only as an anxiety attack. Eleventh-hour jitters. Pro forma. But I hadn't backed out, in part because I knew that Stuart, with an irritating air of superiority, kept expecting me to do just that. Four times with Jeanine, once with Patty, and even once with Arley, I'd driven past the house, trying to see it from an angle that would deliver me a sharp kick in the pants and send me back to my senses. It didn't happen. I'd see something else that bewitched me: a turreted tower fit to house a tiny princess (which in fact one day it would), a handmade, overgrown shrine in the backyard, a pebbled arch with "Santa Cecilia" shakily spelled out in bright bits of glass mosaic. Authority on all things Catholic, Jeanine told me Saint Cecilia invented the pipe organ. Surely the patron saint of piano teachers—one of whose number, I'd learned, the former owner had been. Had Santa Cecilia kept safe the surge of music through this house, even as the owner grew frail and bats snuggled in the attic? What I needed was the patron saint of plaster and landscaping, I complained. One night, on one of the rare occasions when he spoke of the house at all, Stuart warned me that this was a bad area for Jews. "The list of great Jewish carpenters is very short, Anne," he intoned. "Look what happened with the last one."

Stuart confined his involvement with the house to accompanying me on a single debris-removal expedition with a borrowed pickup, the day after I signed the loan papers. Standing in the foyer while I ran up and down the great solid spiral of staircase, he pointed out that the risers were so scarred, it looked as though the previous residents had used the hall to train racehorses. He hadn't even deigned to inspect "our" bedroom, and I was too proud to insist. He continued to maintain what I described to Jeanine as his "letting-Anne-learn-her-lesson stance."

Not once had he tried to dissuade me from buying the house, and not once had he offered to put up half the down payment. He never said he would not move into the house with me, but neither would he discuss moving plans. Whenever he caught sight of my sheaf of plat documents, inspection reports, and real estate offer forms, he did a reasonable imitation of a southern schoolmarm, pursing his lips and wagging his head in a display of silent disapproval. One day, he'd found an old book of Faulkner short stories at a rummage sale and left it on my bedside, with "A Rose for Emily" prominently marked by a piece of ribbon.

I threw that book at him. Enough was enough.

Just because buying a house had been an impulse that took Stuart by surprise—especially from straight-arrow Anne, his own predictable partner, the same woman who once thought having an aquarium would tie her down too much—I was on a path toward some future as a demented recluse, drifting from gable to gable in a nightgown of tattered lace, no matter what Stuart thought.

I figured Stuart would settle down about the house, and I didn't give a lot of thought to what would happen if he didn't. We lived around the subject, playing football in Garner Park against the district attorneys, shopping for birthday gifts for my nephews, buoyed up and blown along by the impatient current of our ordinary work lives. Kim McGrory had awakened from his coma, angry and aphasic, not at all happy to be alive. If it had been a sin to execute him before, it was now an obscenity—after all, Kim, once an ordinary downtrodden punk with lousy luck in lawyers, had become a brain-damaged man who couldn't speak on his own behalf. Stuart was busy gathering testimony on the evils that would emerge from further efforts to set Kim's big date. He was also preparing a brief in a new case, an appeal on behalf of Tyler Talley, the "Ready Get Set" killer, a nineteen-year-old football star and B student, poor as chalk, sentenced to death for the execution-style murder of two convenience-store clerks. Given those kinds of clients, he wouldn't have been around very much at even the best of times.

Between us, it wasn't, however, the best of times. On two lonely nights, Stuart had turned away, angry and soft, unable to make love to me, a circumstance unknown in his history. He'd blamed the heat and his chronic lack of sleep, but I could feel the stalemate between us nibbling at his confidence. Stuart had never come on like a stud; he was simply a man who really did prefer the company of women over men and really did think that sex was one of the things—along with basketball, steak tacos, and Marx Brothers movies—that human life offered as a compensation for the knowledge of death. Late one of those nights, as we lay in the dark, I with a whole batch of "never mind"s and "no big deal"s cooling on my lips, disclaimers I knew wouldn't lay one finger on his humiliation, he'd told me, "Every time, now, I think of this being procreation."

"Stuart, it isn't. I wouldn't do that to you."

"I know you wouldn't. What I mean is, I think of it as being linked with procreation, and the zest . . . the passion of it . . ."

I suddenly wanted to slap him. "Stuart, honey, you know that *was* the original intention of intercourse—"

"Stop it," he said, and I thought he was about to cry.

But I was wound too tight to stop. "Stop what?" I asked him. "Stop what? Stop myself from even thinking about anything I might want in my life? Stuart, this . . . phenomenon of yours isn't my fault."

"It's not your fault, but it's both our problem, Anne. I mean, are you happy here? For ten generally pretty terrific years, we've done this one thing really well. Plenty of three-pointers, you know? Plenty of memorable overtimes. Why does everything good have to change?"

142

"I guess because not everybody thinks that it's always good for everything to stay the same. Life is progressive."

"This is really progress, Anne."

From my point of view, the house, with all its entanglement and expense, meant a moratorium on the baby decision. The house would keep us plenty busy all by itself. Stuart, however, saw it as exactly the opposite—a goad, a challenge, an ultimatum. So the fears I had about the house, about affording it, about even wanting it at all, were things I couldn't share with my nearest. Instead, I'd sit sleepless in bed through light gusts of December hail, until the sharp, freshened smell of asphalt began to rise from the pavement below our apartment windows, the day already heating up before the sun even rose. Maybe Stuart was right. Maybe I wasn't exactly declaring my right to procreate. But a five-bedroom house was a much bigger deal than a twenty-gallon tank, some neon tetra, and a few black mollies. It meant putting down roots, big time.

But even all that didn't ruin the house for me. Every time I passed it, or parked my car and strolled from Amor Ausente through the dapple of overreaching branches up the street and around the corner, past vast hacienda-style stucco ranches and stout colonials to what would soon be my own front door, I felt like an explorer. Like the Meriwether Lewis of soon-to-be-forty single white females. I felt connected with something so large it might become unmanageable, and that was somehow heady. When I drove Arley past the house, and told her to squint her eyes and use her imagination a little to see how it might look someday, she breathed, "I don't have to pretend. It's just like a castle, Annie. It's the most beautiful house in the world."

I sort of felt like that too.

In broad daylight, however, that morning with Jeanine, it had

143

an almost sinister aspect, like some shopping-cart derelict intent on making a vile suggestion. I leaned against one rust-furred spoke of the iron fence, and the whole fence wobbled. Jeanine caught my arm.

"You seem to have your choice of mailboxes," she pointed out. And indeed, though we'd eliminated many of them, there were still a dozen or so, one in the shape of an old carriage. I hoped I might be able to fix that one up, and I had designs on a few of the others as flowerpots. Toeing one of the mailboxes aside, I struggled to get the palm-sized front-door key to tumble the sticky lock. The real estate agent had offered to meet me at the house for my first formal tour as owner; but I'd told him I'd do just fine on my own. Now I wondered whether I'd have to slink back to the office and ask for help even to get the door open. Jeanine asked me again whether Stuart was coming around. I was tempted to ignore her. Jeanine had a nose for trouble, and the fact that Stuart and I never fought, and never nicked one another in public, filled her with awe and vexation. "Isn't there a risk that this is going to ruin everything between you, Annie?" she asked with what sounded like some pretty ill-concealed pleasure.

"He'll be fine," I told her, still fumbling with the lock. "People change, Jeanine. You have to have some flexibility. You don't always want exactly the same things." I didn't doubt that Stuart would share the monthly bills for the house, though even my income from Women and Children First was more than adequate for the financing I needed, even given the thousands I had to build in for major remodeling. The price of the house itself was ridiculous—on the telephone, my father left messages: "Now, Anne, I don't mean to be offensive, but sixty thousand dollars for a five-bedroom house strains the imagination . . . are you sure this isn't a very dangerous neighborhood?" This from a man living in Manhattan, one of the murder capitals of the free world.

"You wouldn't do it if it would really put a big strain on you and Stuart, would you?" Jeanine pressed. Jeanine herself was so paranoid about any man she adored eventually dropping her that she used a backup system: she backed up the pediatrician with the state cop, Jack Becker, whom she'd met when she knocked down a few dozen construction cones on Highway 10 while rushing to one of her birth mothers in Kendall County.

"If I thought it would be such a big strain, I'd be more worried about me and Stuart than about the house," I told her, just as the door abruptly popped open and I stumbled into the foyer, banging my knee against the jamb.

"Think of your dignity, Annie. You're a woman of property now," Jeanine said, grabbing my elbow. We stared into the gloom of the huge lower hallway. Jeanine fumbled for a light switch; there was none either of us could see. My knee felt like a cap pistol had exploded inside it, and when I reached down to rub it, my hand came away bloody.

"Look," I said. "I'm bleeding."

Jeanine went back out onto the porch to look for help. As I plopped down on the bottom stair, cradling my knee, I heard her talking, her voice taking on certain telltale characteristics—the ones that always came out when a man was around. When she came back over the threshold with the blond giant who'd been planting the sign the night we first saw the house, I was only annoyed, not surprised. Jeanine had forgotten about my knee, forgotten about sharing my proud inspection of my crummy new mansion. She'd seen big shoulders and blond hair, high up, and it had immediately transformed her into Heather Locklear. Simple as that.

"Hi, Charley," I said.

"You know each other?" Jeanine was surprised. And a little disappointed. A small thrill of satisfaction rippled through me.

"This is my neighbor," I told Jeanine.

Charley helped me up. He was actually such a sweet-faced person. I was ashamed that I'd referred to him, to Stuart, as a "Hitler youth."

"I knew you were coming over here," he said. "I was getting coffee down at the corner when I saw you drive by. Of course, I didn't know there was going to be a first-aid emergency. But I wanted to offer my services."

Jeanine's thoughts were so loud, I was afraid Charley would hear them. I felt my cheeks heat up.

"You . . . huh?"

"Well, like I told you, I've landscaped a lot of these houses. And I do carpentry. Electrical. Everything, really. And I'm cheap." I couldn't meet Jeanine's eyes. Charley said, "Your leg is bleeding."

"It's just a scratch," Jeanine assured him cheerfully. "Where do you live, Charley?"

"Two streets over. I have a two-flat. It's been under construction for about ten years. But it has water. You could come over to my house and wash that knee," he told me. "And you should probably get a tetanus shot. This is Texas, you know; the germs never die."

"I know about germs," I chuffed. "We have germs where I grew up too. Why do people in Texas think they invented everything? Good and bad? No problem—I'll just wash it off here."

"There's no water," Charley said gently.

"How do you know?" I asked. "It's just turned off, the guy said."

"There hasn't been any water for years. You can see where the water leaked . . . well, it's probably better you don't look too close at that right now."

"So I need to call the water utility."

"Well, it wouldn't do any good to call the utility . . ."

"Why not?"

"Well, see, the pipes must have broken quite a while ago. . . ."

"So I need new pipes?"

"Right."

"I'm suing."

"Who?"

"Somebody."

"Well, might be cheaper just to fix the pipes."

"Do you know where to get cheap pipes?"

"There's no such thing as cheap pipes."

"I thought you said you knew how to do everything cheap."

"No, I said that *I* was cheap."

"But first I have to buy the pipes."

"Well, yeah. But I do know where I can get some faucets for you wholesale. They're tearing down this old house on Mariposa—"

"And you just sort of tiptoe over there in the dark, when you're supposed to be, what, watering the lawns in the moonlight . . . ?"

"You know, we recycle on principle in the King William district. A fireplace ends up a paved walk. Carport somehow just turns into a garden fence. We all believe that once it's here, it ought to stay."

"My mailboxes have sure stayed. So I can be a lawyer with expensive pipes and stolen faucets."

"Repeat to yourself: It's not stealing. It's *sharing*," said Charley. And I laughed.

After we locked the door and got back into my car, Jeanine said, "He's *muy* cute."

"Last time I checked, you already had a couple of nice big guys on the stringer," I told her. "Isn't that enough?"

"We're talking futures here, Anne. It never hurts to have a spare."

CHAPTER EIGHT

Arley

8477298372
Texas Department of Corrections
Solamente River, Texas

Dear Arley,

I have been in a terrible state of uncertainty. I'm sending this overnight mail, hang the expense, because I want you to know my thoughts before you decide whether to come and see me next week. I will leave that decision up to you. But you need to understand the facts about how I feel before you make it.

Dylan Thomas wrote, "Were vagueness enough and the sweet lies plenty/The hollow words could bear all suffering/And cure me of ills."

Trust an Irishman. (He is my favorite poet. In fact, my name is Dillon Thomas LeGrande, though I'm named after Mama, sort of, not after the poet. Dillion is her maiden name. I still think there can be connections that aren't intentional, though, don't you?)

Back to the matter in hand. I have been avoiding it because it is too painful. You did lie to me.

And even if you meant this to be a sweet lie, it has caused me to lose faith.

First, you quoted Sara Teasdale in that letter to me. I immediately went on cloud nine. It was almost as if you were trying to send me a message. I never read Sara Teasdale, but it was like she knew us. Right away, I started in writing a poem just for you.

Then, just a few days later, I happened to see the guest list for Saturday, and there was none other than "Constanza Gutierrez," visiting old Kevin for maybe the 150th time this year.

Well, I got a guard who's a kind of buddy, and anyhow, I wasn't asking to do nothing wrong, so I told him that if it was possible, could I come down for just a minute and give Connie a message for you from me. And also thank her, because it was, after all, Connie who got our relationship started. And he said, well, maybe, okay, and come that Saturday, I get walked down there, and there's Connie and old Kevin. Now, it was their first contact visit, and it was downright raw, they were smooching away like crazy, and him running his hands all over her. Anyhow, I says, "Connie?" And she looks up and smiles real big—which Kevin did not, because I think he wanted to get back to it—and she comes over to me, with the guard standing right there, and I said, "I just want to thank you, kind lady, for bringing Arlington into my life."

And Connie says, "Oh, she did write to you, then? She's a sweet girl. She's my sister Elena's best friend a long time. They go to Travis together." And I think, Travis? Last I heard, that was a high school up there in Avalon. And so I says, "Connie, don't you mean she used to go there? She's in college with you now, isn't she?" And Connie just shakes her head like I'm stupid and crazy and she says, "College? That little bitty girl ain't but a ninth grader."

Well, I couldn't say a thing. The guard took me back to my place, and I just lay down on that hard bunk. You let me believe very basic, simple things about you that were not true. Maybe it sounds corny coming from a man the world regards as a convicted felon, but I believe in honesty.

I didn't realize, until right then, how my feelings for you were changing. Getting deeper and deeper in a way that I never experienced before.

It took me days before I could even think about the whole thing in one piece, you know what I mean?

If you were older, this would not matter so much. If I was in my 30s and you were in your 20s, it would not be such a big deal. Rich men do it all the time. But once, I did go out with a girl who was only 17. And I was hardly 20 myself. And you'd'a thought her daddy was going to call out the Texas Rangers. He said I was nothing but a slinky skunk who wanted his girl for just one thing only, which was, in fact, not the case, though indeed she was very ready, willing, and able in that department.

I vowed to myself, then, that I would never make the same mistake twice. So should we go any further? I don't know. Once trust is broken, it is hard to mend it. Maybe we can be just friends, depending on how you define friendship. I need to go now. This has about worn me out.

Yr obedient servant,
Dillon Thomas LeGrande

.　　.　　.

Dear Dillon,

I'm sending this by overnight mail too, because I won't come to see you if those are your feelings. I guess the sight of me would only remind you that I really am only fourteen, and of how disappointed you are in me. I did not realize your feelings for me were growing stronger. I only knew that my feelings were growing so strong for you that there were nights I watched the moon cross the whole sky and go down without getting one single second of sleep. That whole week I didn't hear from you, I felt like I would stop eating and die. In fact, I did stop eating. (I lost three or four pounds.)

What happened, if you will think back, is that you just ASSUMED I was the same age as Connie. I should have corrected that idea right away. But I wasn't brave enough.

Why would a man of your age want to write to a kid in high school? I have never enjoyed talking to someone so much as I did with you. I knew that if I told you the truth, I would have to give all that up, and just go back to my boring life the way it was before.

Believe me, I did think about the future. But it all seemed so far away. By the time you got out, I would be 16 or or even older. Maybe things would be different then. If you did want to see me, I thought I could explain things to you then, even though, by then, you will be almost 30, or whatever.

I know I have no right to ask for your forgiveness. In fact, I don't expect to hear from you ever again.

So, I am going to say all the things I would have said if we went on. I'm going to wish you a happy birthday now, for December. My birthday is April 1. Elena says my middle name should be "Fool," as in "April Fool," because I've messed this up so much and made her mad and you mad and Connie mad too. Anyhow, I wish you the most happiness for your birthday. "Joie LeGrande." That would sort of be the way to say that in French, because your name means "The Biggest" or "The Most," doesn't it? Anyway, I want to send you congratulations for when you get out. Get a great job, find someone worthy of your love, and have a happy life.

Arley Mowbray

P.S. I know you probably already know this. But Dylan Thomas was Welsh.

.   .   .

8477298372
Texas Department of Corrections
Solamente River, Texas

Dearest Arley,

Happy birthday.

In advance for you, too.

But not because I won't be in touch with you at the time of your birthday. And afterward. And maybe for the rest of your life.

I guess that I got your letter and felt that something between us was being reborn.

Your letter was so full of maturity and decency I couldn't stay mad at you. I guess they don't make 14 year old girls like they used to. Or maybe you're just a remarkable person and you would be the same at any age.

I wish I could touch you so that I could express to you so many things I can't say in words. Like forgiveness. Your letter convinced me that your mistake was made out of a sincere desire to continue communicating with me. I felt more affection in that letter than I had felt in any of the others.

Maybe we only let our true feelings show when we feel we have nothing left to lose. I certainly have nothing left to lose, except you. And that I couldn't bear to lose.

Maybe the world would think what I'm going to say is ugly and wrong. But the world is a pretty cold examiner, to me. It doesn't make much room for people who have to do things their own way. So I'm just going to say it plain. I think I am falling in love with you. And I don't care if you are just a girl. You are a woman, too, in my mind and heart. My grandma wasn't but 13 when she married my grandfather, and they lived together for 60 years and had seven children, of which my mother, Kate, is the fifth one. When my grandma had her first baby, she told me, she was so young she hadn't even reached her full height yet. And she had never even been outside her mama's house over-night the night she went home with my grandpa, and him only 17. Before my grandma died, she said to me, "Half the time, that old man wasn't worth the powder to blow him to hell." And I said—I don't know, I was a kid—I says, like, why'd you stay so long if you were so mad? And she said, "The other half of the time is why."

I am many years beyond you, girl, but if we were on flat ground, equal and free, and it was the future, even the world might smile on you and me. I want the chance to see you in that future. Will you give it to me?

You must not think this is only the lonesomeness of a captive talking to you. I am not bad to look at. (See photo enclosed.) I've had my chances, even in here, to bind a woman to me. But I have not taken them. Arley, I was waiting for you. If you doubt that, read the poem I named after you and that I am placing in this letter.

Dillon

After I read that poem, the one he called after me, "Arlington," well, that was that.

That was that.

I knew it was a good poem, besides everything else. It meant that I was right about Dillon—despite all the hard times he had brought on himself, Dillon was an unusually sensitive person. Later on, when Annie read it out loud, I could see people react, and I was so proud.

When I read these words, when he called me "the place I am always moving toward," I just started to cry. I cried right through reading it five times, and by then I knew it by heart, though it normally takes you a long time to memorize something. It was about me, my own self, real and unique as the circles of my own fingerprints but drawn around by Dillon's love for me, like a heart around two names on a tree. That letter with the poem, the week before I went to see him for the first time, was the beginning of the part of our life together that no one else would know. Except Annie, and then only partly. And Elena, of course. But then, also only partly. I never showed Elena another one of those letters. I didn't want to share that part of my life with anyone else.

Because I was so young, back then, I had to rely on other people to get Dillon and me together. I mean, together in the sense of face-to-face. I started getting closer to Connie. Not to use her, but because she was going through the same thing with Dillon's brother. It was like we were kin, sisters-in-law or something, and so we had a special connection, even though she was a lot older.

Also, she was pretty immature. She still is, but at least she's not with Kevin LeGrande anymore. After his part in what happened, Kevin's going to be in Solamente River for a long, long time, and even Connie doesn't have enough patience, nor should she.

Anyhow, it was Connie who told me how Dillon had to put people on his list and give a reason why each one was included (he said I was a friend he'd met through his mother's church), so they could be approved in advance. Otherwise, they plain wouldn't let me in. And they wouldn't call ahead to tell me, either. They'd just stop me at the door. She told me I was going to get searched too, but just my purse and my pockets. It helped me not to get scared when she walked me through it, how it was going to feel when they locked those thick green steel doors behind you. How it would rob your breath, even though you knew you were going to get to walk right back out and go home after an hour went by.

The last few days before I went, I was so nuts I couldn't think about anything but Dillon. At home, I kept looking at his picture, which I had taped inside my French book, and trying hard to see what he really looked like. But the picture was a little far away. He was hunkered down next to a tree, like he was looking off into the distance. He had on normal clothes—I didn't know, back then, that people in prison wore jeans and T-shirts; I still thought you would wear striped pajamas or a surgeon's outfit or something. His legs were strong-looking. But I couldn't tell much about his face, and to tell you the truth, I couldn't even look at it that long. When I did, the longing and the awe in me got so sharp my insides ached and turned, the muscles clasping so tight I could sit up at night and feel a sore place, as if my period were about to come. I could be all alone, and still be as embarrassed as if fifty people were leaning over my shoulders and pointing and staring. It was as if Dillon himself could see me—as if he could look out of that picture and could tell just how my eyes licked over his jaw and his neck and the skin of his shoulder, where his shirt was pulled away a little, like a kid trying to catch every single drop of ice cream before it melted.

When I was in school, I didn't even dare open to the picture. Everyone'd see. They'd see my face flush and my eyes lock on a spot far away. See my thoughts materialize above my head in block print, strange thoughts, hot to the touch: awe is not too strong to describe it. I just couldn't take it all in—the oneness that Dillon seemed to want for him and me. Dillon was a man, a whole man, with strong muscles and perfect eyes and a history of griefs and jokes and books he'd read and songs he knew, and he was all mine, to know, to love, maybe even to touch. A whole other person. I wanted to know everything about him. I wanted to eat his past like a loaf of bread, so it would settle inside me too. Then I would be able to recall the first time he washed his car without a shirt on or listened to the oldies station from Lake Charles until the sun came up. I didn't just want to hear about these things; I wanted to have seen them. I wanted to really feel the first time he got a bee sting, the six months when he ate nothing except banana flakes, when he learned to walk in heeled boots without wobbling his ankles, the time he tried to patch his dog Donut's ripped-open leg after she tangled with a coyote. I wished I could have lain beside him the night his papa was burned, while he tried to block his ears so he wouldn't hear his mother's wails; when he was six and lost a tooth in school and cried because he didn't know baby teeth fell out and thought he'd done something wrong; and the first time he'd tried to impress a girl by swinging out on a mustang grapevine over the swimming cove at Grapetree Fork—that, actually, I didn't like to think about very much. But I guess if that memory had been offered, I'd have taken it too, because it was part of him and because much as you hate to think of the boy you love with someone else, one of the things that makes you want him most is that other girls do too. Then and before, plenty of girls would have wanted Dillon, no matter what he'd done. He was nothing if not pretty. It still makes Annie crazy when I say that. But I'm not going to stop saying it just because it bothers her.

At last, Saturday came. I was meeting Connie G. at the Greyhound, which meant taking two city buses downtown.

I had to leave early. That meant running right by my mama, which felt like running past a firing squad. There wasn't no excuse that would be good enough to get me out of my Saturday chores.

At first I thought she was just going to ignore me, and for once I was really happy about that.

She saw me, though.

"Where you going, girl?" Mama asked, soft and blurry, bent over her coffee like it was a flower and she the bee.

"I have to go out."

"Out where?"

"Just to meet a friend. I have to go right now."

"You get you back in here, Arlington. You know you have your things to do. You don't go noplace on a Saturday."

She didn't even look up. She sure didn't bother to get up.

"Bye now, Mama," I said, and I opened that door and ran, and I didn't stop until I came to the bus stop. I got on and paid the driver and sat down, and then I took another bus and got off at Alamo Station. Connie was standing there with her backpack slung over her shoulder. I paid again, and we sat down toward the back of the Greyhound, but not too close to the bathroom. Connie started to take out the presents she had got for Kevin

LeGrande. An electric razor. A box of Midnight mints. A deck of tarot cards.

I didn't have a thing. Not a thing. I looked at Connie and started to cry. "Are you always supposed to bring them something?"

"Well, it's not necessary. Not everybody does." She was just being nice. It made me feel even worse.

"I've been thinking about him so much, I forgot about . . . everything," I told her.

"Open your purse, there, girl," Connie told me, and I took out whatever I had: a pack of Beeman's, my new hairbrush, my wallet, my makeup bag, and my little book, *Poems of Storytelling and Adventure*, which I'd bought for my Poe paper and was using now to memorize "The Highwayman" so I could show off for Mrs. Murray. Connie held the hairbrush up to the cold light from the window and said, "There now. It was just like you planned this all out. They need these nice things in there." And then she picked up the book and set it on her lap. "Girl, you can't even tell this has been opened up. You just take my pen here and write in it something he'll always remember." I took the pen and wrote, "Dillon. I will always remember. Love, Arley M." And then I looked up at Connie, and she looked at me, and she shook her head side to side real slow, like she didn't quite believe me, and then pulled me down on her shoulder and rocked me and rocked me as if I were a five-year-old scared of a windstorm. I did just what that little kid would do. I fell asleep on Connie's arm, and I didn't wake up until the bus stopped at a pretty green park, which was not a park at all but the planted land that surrounded the maximum-security prison on all sides, the way one of those little felt skirts surrounds a Christmas tree.

It was just like Connie said. Big heavy women guards with hair cut shorter than most boys' used the palms of their hands to try to feel whether we had weapons (or bags of pills or pot, Connie told me later) in our pockets. Connie said the guards' hair was so short because they didn't want to risk prisoners grabbing hold of it. They felt up under my hair, too, and sort of pulled it out to its full length to see if I had anything stuffed in it. Then I did my braid back up.

Afterward, I waved good-bye to Connie and they put me on this little bench in a hall with doors at both ends. The doors had windows in them about the size of an envelope. One of the doors opened, and the guard led me into a narrower hall, with windows along one side. In front of every window, a bench was bolted to the floor. Some of the benches were empty. But on the rest of them, women were sitting, talking on telephones. When I got alongside, I could see that there was the exact same setup where the men were. They were all wearing black T-shirts and jeans, talking on phones at big scratched Plexiglas windows with crisscrossed wires embedded in the panes. One prisoner was pretty much the fattest person I'd ever seen. His rolls of flesh started under his chin and got bigger as they went down.

Then the guard stopped, and I saw him. My Dillon. He got up, quickly, and sort of glanced down, and then he smiled at me. It was a little boy's smile, sort of silly and embarrassed, and I thought then that I would never love anyone so deeply again. One thing is for sure—I'll never fall in love again at the same place in life I was then, the place where you don't know anything about love or sex but what you feel right at that moment, for the first time, for the first person.

He motioned for me to pick up the phone.

"Hey," he said. "Arlington. Arlington."

"It's me."

"It's you."

We smiled at each other like fools. I had to look away.

"Are you okay?" he asked.

"I'm fine." I felt my throat closing, could hardly get the words out.

"Thank you for those things." The guards had brought the book and the brush around to him before I came in.

"That's okay. They sure aren't much."

"They're sure nice to me. And you sure are pretty."

"So are you," I said, then I said, "I didn't mean that like it sounded."

"That's okay."

We sat there.

"We only have an hour," Dillon said then. "You get used to the idea that you don't have much time to waste. You skip the small talk." He motioned to me. "Lean closer." I did. "Put your hand up on the window." I did. He put his hand up on the other side, as if we were touching palm-to-palm. Our hands were exactly the same size; Dillon was pretty little for a man, though I could see he was strong. I couldn't feel anything, of course, but I imagined that the glass got hot, the way it would with a stove coil underneath.

"Arley," he asked. "Do you love me?"

I answered, "Yes."

"Am I the very first one you ever loved?"

What did he think? I was *fourteen*. Dillon told me, though, and I guess I already knew it, that plenty of girls my age had already done *everything*. He thought that maybe one of Mama's boyfriends had touched me, or worse. I told him that nothing like that had ever happened. He wanted to know what I'd done with boys, and I told him the truth. Not one thing. "People I knew," Dillon said, "didn't do much until they was in high school, at least. But I know, from personal experience—and excuse me for this, Arley—that Gracie Gutierrez was doing boys she wasn't but in seventh grade. Not me. At least not then. But I know those who had her. Connie's a good girl, though. I know she never slept with Kevin yet."

"Well, how could she? He's . . . he's in here."

"You'd be surprised, Arley."

"Aren't they always watching, though?"

"Not always. I mean, sometimes they look the other way in the visiting lounge. I'm sure some people have started families right in there." He laughed. But then he reddened, right up to under his eyes. "I'm sorry, Arley. I shouldn't talk this way in front of you."

"It's okay. I've heard it before."

"Okay. And you know what else? They let you have an overnight visit with the person if you get married. Even in here. They have a special place."

"A hotel?"

"No, honey. Not a hotel. It's like a house trailer or something—I ain't never seen it. A guy got married last month. You should have seen it in here that night. It went all around on the drums—that's like, you know, the gossip—that they was out there, the two of them, and the guys were going crazy. I mean, they was ready to climb the walls."

"Really?"

"Yeah."

"Imagine."

"A man misses such things, Arley. Some nights, it's all you can think about. They don't allow no flesh magazines in here or nothing. For that reason. Men in need of . . . pleasure can get pretty hard to control."

"Do they hit you?"

"Who?"

"The guards and stuff."

"No, not me. Not me, ever, honey. I just keep to my own business. I work in the library, and I work in the laundry. I don't do nothing. I just want to get myself delivered out of here."

"I sure want that for you too, Dillon."

He looked at me with those green eyes then. He didn't blink, like other people. He never seemed to. He could look at you forever; it could make you squirm if you didn't know him. I looked back at him, and the light seemed to go down in the rooms we were in, both his and mine, rooms that were white and plain as nothing. All I could see were his eyes. Surrounded by darkness.

" 'Do not go gentle into that good night,' " he said.

" 'Rage, rage, against the dying light,' " I said, trying to remember what I'd read.

" 'Rage, rage, against the dying *of the* light . . .' Say that Sara Teasdale thing. About just knowing you're in the wide world with him . . ."

"I can't. I don't know it all."

"Just say something, then. Say some poem you know."

"I don't know a whole one."

"It don't matter."

So I told him what I'd already learned of "The Highwayman." I recited all the parts about the highwayman came riding, riding, riding, up to the old inn door. He leaned forward. " 'One kiss, my bonny sweetheart,' " I said. My mouth was full of cotton. " 'I'm after a prize to-night, But I shall be back with the yellow gold before the morning light; Yet, if they press me sharply, and harry me through the day, Then look for me by moonlight, Watch for me by moonlight, I'll come to thee by moonlight—' "

"By moonlight," said Dillon.

" 'By moonlight, though hell should bar the way.' " I went right on to the part where Bess, the landlord's black-eyed daughter, shoots herself to warn the highwayman that the soldiers are looking to catch him and hang him.

"She killed herself?" Dillon breathed.

"She did," I said. We were both whispering. "She warned him with her death."

"He was an outlaw."

"A robber. But I don't think really a bad person."

"Did he kill people?"

"No, he just took whatever they had. It was probably rich people carrying bags of gold or something. This was before the American Revolution."

" 'One kiss, my bonny sweetheart . . .' "

"Right."

" 'I'm after . . .' "

" 'After a prize to-night.' " He nodded, as if he were a little kid about to fall asleep, and I kept on murmuring. " 'But I shall be back with . . .' "

"Arley," Dillon said, almost too gruff and soft to hear. "Do you love me?"

"I love you more than . . . I love you."

"Would you do that? To warn me?"

He meant would I shoot myself. My breakfast churned around in my stomach. I didn't know what to say. I did know what he wanted me to say. "I guess so," I told him. "If there wasn't any other way."

"Do you love me, Arley?" he asked again.

I don't know why I did it. You probably wouldn't think so from what I've done, but I'm pretty shy. I'm shy about my body.

Even changing for meets, I had a hard time in new dressing rooms with other girls. So what I did, well, I didn't think much about it. I followed the directions written in Dillon's eyes. I knew that any second a guard could come waltzing into Dillon's room—our hour was almost up—but it was like the scene in those gangster movies where you see people getting shot and the camera makes it so the blood comes blooming out of them really slow, like a scarf shook out, instead of how it would really be . . . a pop, a thing so fast you would hear it longer than you saw it.

I put the phone down. Without taking my eyes away from Dillon, I reached up and unlaced my braid and let my hair shake out. It felt good, like a warm towel coming down around my shoulders. It was so damned cold in there. Dillon's forehead creased and his lips drew back a little, like he was hurting. I didn't look away. I put my two hands on the bottom seam of my shirt and rolled it up. Under my shirt was one of those little tight T-shirts people wear for sports. I like them even better than sports bras; they don't cut you. I rolled the T-shirt up, too, and leaned my whole top, my warm skin, against that cold and smeary glass, my breath coming so fast I thought my heart would burst. I tried to act cool, like a woman, as if showing someone my Dixie-cup breasts was just about the most natural thing in the world to do. Back of my eyes, I could feel tears starting, like little pins stabbing. I was afraid and ashamed and excited and proud all at once. Dillon hung up his phone and put out his two hands, flat against the glass where my breasts were, as if he were holding them, holding me. Then for real I could feel the heat. I had to shut my eyes. When I opened them, I saw that he'd closed his eyes too. We stayed that way maybe a minute. No guard came. Dillon took his hands away the moment I let my shirt down.

He picked up his receiver. "You're beautiful, girl. You're

beautiful as a queen and as a statue. You're the landlord's black-eyed daughter."

"I love you," I said.

"Marry me, Arley," Dillon said.

I swallowed. I opened my mouth, and nothing came out. I shut my mouth and opened it again, and I said, "Okay."

I can see that girl now. See her sitting there, breath coming shallow and fast, trying to do her hair back up in a braid, her eyes big and dark as coffee in cups. I can see the guard come and sort of survey the room and give me a look that seemed to say he'd seen it all before, and then pull Dillon up, and me standing up and straining, after the door on his side closed, to see the white-blond top of his head as he was led down the hall. Reaching up with my hands, surprised to find tears on my face.

When I look back at that picture of me, left alone on one side of that dirty window, waiting for someone to unlock the door behind me and let me out, I think of a line from Carl Sandburg that I didn't read until a long time later.

I don't remember the whole poem.

But I remember one little part.

So far, it said. So fast. So far, so fast.

CHAPTER NINE

Annie

My sister Rachie was considering becoming a drive-by accountant. "People have been calling to cancel their appointments all month," she told me, her voice crackling on her car phone. "They're too busy. Their kid broke its collarbone. Or they have to shop for the holidays. I think I should just get one of those little red pickups, like the people who fix windshields. 'Have tax shelters, will travel.'" Her voice rose about fifty decibels. "Dammit, buddy, the idea is we take *turns* at the stop sign! This is incredible. People act like they just remembered that they're going to hold Christmas the same time as last year."

For the first time since we'd moved to Texas, Stuart and I weren't going home together for Christmas, and I was blue. Of course, we didn't actually celebrate it, but Christmas was the time most of our friends washed up in the city. There would be impromptu excursions to the half-price tickets booth for Broadway seats, and lots of dinners at smoky restaurants and in the half-demolished houses of couples in the remodeling period of their lives. More for the sake of sentiment than form, so that our folks could have the prodigals all to themselves, Stuart and I would sleep apart during the winter visit, in our old rooms, making silly, sweet hour-long phone calls to one another from Princess phones next to the beds we slept in before we'd ever imagined San Antonio, the law, or each other. At my parents', we'd exchange eight nights' worth of trinkets for Chanukah, no matter when it had actually fallen, and we'd light the menorah Rachael had made in her jewelry class in high school. On Christmas Eve, we'd all go out with Stuart's parents, his brother and his wife and their kids, for Chinese and then for old-time dancing at the Carillon. For sheer dance ability alone, Stuart had made me the envy of all my friends. Like his father before him, Stuart wasn't just an enthusiastic dancer, he was a good one; he could jitterbug, he could even tango, and he put to shame most of the men of my generation, who acted like they were giving blood if you expected them to stand up and bob their shoulders at a bar mitzvah. Those late nights of dancing at the Carillon, high above the snow-shrouded reaches of Central Park, were among the sweetest hours of my adult life.

Not going made it feel as though everything was changing between us, changing in a way I could have stopped, though only by stopping what I had begun to see as my own evolution. It's entirely possible, however, to feel very sad even while being very true to yourself.

We finally sat down together a few days before Stuart was to do the unthinkable—go home without me.

"All right," he said. "Truce time. Tell me what this is really about."

We're drifting, I wanted to cry. We don't see eye-to-eye on the most unnegotiable matter in a couple's life, and we can't talk about it. The house doesn't matter, I wanted to cry, the house is just a red herring! But I said, "Well, I can't afford to come."

"Anne," Stuart said, "I bought you a ticket. I mean, have mercy. The picture of you sitting alone scraping paint off the lintel post or the newel post or whatever at the House of Usher while all of us are going out—"

"Stop it! I can't stand it, either." But you're going to have to face this, Stuart, I wanted to say. *We* are going to have to face this and deal with it. "It's too much money—"

"It's four hundred bucks, Anne. Big deal."

"Four hundred bucks is three rooms of flooring refinished. And anyhow, I can't let you take me because I dug this hole myself and I have to get out of it myself. You don't approve of the house. You can't imagine what I've already spent on it, and you don't even want to know."

"Honey," he went on. "Come on. Let's go home and have a good time and forget all this shit for a while. Jesus, Anne, I need a break. The funding could really be in jeopardy this time." This was a threat every winter. "I've been working twenty-hour days—"

"I also have been working twenty-hour days, Stuart, plus trying to get a house in shape. For us."

"You didn't buy that house for us."

"I did, too."

"You bought it for you. You bought it to draw some kind of phony line in the sand. Time to be middle-aged! Time to be grown up and responsible! Well, I'm not buying into it, Anne. We had a good life together . . ."

"Nice how easily you put our life in the past . . ."

"I'm not going to argue with you. And I'm not going to go off feeling like I've abandoned this poor little puppy, because you're doing this to make a point, Anne. You're doing it because you're stubborn. I don't have a choice about going. My uncle and my aunt are going to be home, together, with my father, for what will probably be the last time in their lives."

I sighed loudly. It was childish, but not so childish as the way I really wanted to behave, which was to sit down on the floor and kick my feet. This was all my fault, and so I wanted to slap Stuart for it.

He frowned at me, "Okay, sigh, Annie. But it's my family. Family values, Anne. You know?" He took a red-and-white-striped ticket folder out of his sports coat pocket and slapped it on the kitchen counter. "Come home or don't. But I'm not going to be the villain here." He started to stalk off, and then he looked back. I'm sure I looked like a golden retriever, my face a pattern book of stubborn misery. He leaned over and kissed me, catching my lower lip softly between his teeth for an instant. "Never change, babe," he said.

At the last minute, I decided to drive him to the airport. I dressed up for it, deliberately putting on matching underwear, a shirt that was almost see-through, and silk pants that kept moving a smidge of a second after I stopped. We necked so much in the car that Stuart was sort of a groaning mess by the time we got to the airport. Delightfully mired in my own spite, my crotch thumping with unsatisfied arousal, I bid him a soppy and flushed farewell, with much protracted rubbing between our two trench coats.

I needed to go over to the King William neighborhood and give Charley Wilder a check for some fixtures, but I decided I couldn't face it right then. Giving Charley checks was like a weekend job, and these days, I wasn't sure whether to laugh or cry every time I saw him, which was three or four times a week, since one of us always seemed to have just one small thing to check out with the other. I had come to appreciate Charley: his general

calm, his attachment to the neighborhood, and his tender-
ness with me. He truly was the carpentry angel, taking care to
space out the written estimates of what it would cost to bring
4040 Azalea Road into public-health compliance—never mind
aesthetic beauty. But even his gently worded estimates were sick
and shocking. The house was a money sink, with an ever-circling
black drain.

The downstairs bathroom, for example, lacked plumbing, in
the twentieth-century sense of the word. The former owner had
evidently operated it for years with water carried from a mop sink
in an adjacent closet. By knocking out the wall between the bathroom and the closet, Charley explained, he could create one de-
cently functional room large enough for two adults to stand in
side by side. "Always important in a bathroom," I grumbled.

"You never know," he replied cheerfully.

"And why stop with the wall? Why don't you suggest we
knock the floor and ceiling out too?"

"Actually," he said, painstakingly removing his nearly ever-
present clean bandanna and retying it around his forehead, "we
really will need to do the ceiling eventually. . . ."

"What?"

"To put in a skylight. Any other kind of light you put in . . .
well, Anne, it's just not going to make any difference. It's going to
look like Madame Tussaud's in there, because of the way the eaves
overhang that window, and the size of the pecan tree outside."

"At least the tree is healthy."

"Yes," he said, as if talking to a very young child, "it is. And
once you remove the branches that are putting weight on the
eaves—since some of those branches are the size of young trees—
and it could cost a thousand dollars to take down each one of
them—"

"Jesus! I'll cut them down! Can't we just rent a chain saw?"

"We'll think of something," Charley told me comfortingly. He was, indeed, comforting altogether, a person nothing much seemed to flap. I was only now beginning to figure out exactly what it was precisely that Charley did all day and night, since he was always busy. From hints he'd dropped, I knew he did work on commission. He was restoring a tiny, ancient civic building, dry-walling a Habitat home on Saturdays, and he had a grant to design an orchid garden at the historical center. When we were together, no matter what part of town we'd invaded for one of Charley's salvage missions, he seemed to know everyone. One of the other things he did was maintain the landscaping for a couple of restaurants, like The September Garden, the funny old Chinese restaurant with rock bridges that Texans seemed to love just as much as tourists did. One of the perks of the job meant that Charley got meals there free; the proprietor always made a huge fuss over him.

A couple of days before Stuart left, I'd joined Charley there for what turned out to be a three-hour lunch, interesting enough to re-create on the phone for my sister. The things that fascinated Charley Wilder didn't fascinate me. I was a pavement-and-bright-lights person; as far as I was concerned, shrubs and ferns could keep their secrets.

What did beguile me was Charley's passion for the things he did. It was . . . not childlike, exactly, but endearingly new, as if he drew wonder from a solar battery that didn't have anything to do with money, which, I figured, he didn't have in abundance. I'd begun to look forward to his good-humored and various rambles. He was becoming, as I told my sister—who said, "Hmm"—an unlikely kind of pal.

That day at The September Garden, the subject was live oak

trees. There were two huge live oaks at the back of the restaurant's elaborate topiary and rock gardens. Under one, the restaurant had built an awninged bar. Under the other was a "bar" for children, featuring fruit smoothies and herbal iced teas. Children sat at their own bar while adults, just twenty yards away in clear sight, enjoyed their cocktails. "Just a couple of years ago, they were going to take those trees down," Charley told me. "The bars were my idea, really. A way to make use of the space without wasting those trees."

"They must be a hundred years old."

"Lot more than that. These trees might have been here when the Woodland Indians were here, maybe eight hundred years ago, maybe more. There's burial mounds in East Texas that have things in them that could be thirty thousand years old and that aren't from around here, like little masks with shells that came from the seashore in Florida."

"So were they nomads?"

"Traders, I think. I think they had, like, traveling salesmen."

"How do you know?"

"I don't *know*. It's just what I think."

"So you're saying these trees were alive when—"

"Not alive."

"They're not *dead*."

"I mean, the part of them that's alive now wasn't alive then." The waiter was hovering, and I asked for a menu, but Charley told me he never used a menu at The September Garden. The fun was in the whole ritual of offering and praise that accompanied every surprise lunch the chef prepared for him. "Unless," he said, "you're kosher."

"I'm not."

173

"I know you're Jewish."

"But I don't keep kosher. Anyhow, how do you know I'm Jewish?"

"You remind me of my aunt from New Jersey. I grew up spending summers with their family at the shore."

"The shore where?"

"The Jersey shore."

"I thought you were from here."

"I'm from here. But my folks got divorced when I was five. And all us kids spent all the summers out East. You sound like New Jersey."

"Well, New York. And Long Island."

"I'm a little rusty."

"Still, pretty good for a Texan." We sat there in a suddenly awkward silence. And then we both began at once, him to explain live-and-dead live oaks, me to ask about them. We looked into our glasses. That was one of the times I wondered how old Charley was. Twenty-five? Twenty-three?

"What I meant," he went on, inhaling, with obvious pleasure, the steam from the noodle bowl the waiter placed between us, "trees aren't really living things all through. If you take U.S. Ninety from here toward Uvalde and then head a few blocks west of the courthouse, there's this metal garage built right around a live oak tree. That tree must be three hundred years old. But the part of it that's living, right now, is all on the outside. If you could core deep into the heart of that tree and find the tiny piece of it that sprang up from an acorn centuries ago, that little, well, piece or strand of wood, that's dead. It might be perfectly preserved, but it's sure not living. The living parts of that tree are all on the outside. Maybe down one inch deep. Not very old at all. Not older than . . . than me."

"But as a whole, the tree is alive. . . ."

"A coral reef is alive, too, and kind of in the same way. See, it's always growing on the outside, but the remains of the life that came before are buried deep inside it. Like its memory. Of the past that isn't really happening anymore. So a tree really has generations—"

"Like a family."

"Exactly. Well, sort of exactly," Charley slid the bandanna off his head, carefully smoothed and refolded it, and laid it beside his plate. His thatch of wiry blond hair sprang up in a way that would have looked laughable except for the expression on his face: pure concentration. "The living part has to go through droughts and storms. It has to heal the wounds and live for itself. But under that live part, which is all we see, is the heartwood, the shape of all the previous generations of the . . . of that system's life."

He carefully retied his bandanna on his head. "It's sort of the way my father is inside me. All his bad ways and his good. He drank, and I don't. But that's inside me too. So is his father and *his* . . . and my mother and her ancestors. Even the branches are stories. But the tree is still one creature. It's not like a family made up of people. It might produce fruit from the sexual union with other trees, but those acorns must go on to become other trees." He paused to eat some noodles. "But even though it's an individual creature, it's not like an ancient person, either, because it's always producing that new skin, always finding a new way to reach up."

My noodles, chin high, drooped cooling from my chopsticks.

"This probably falls under the category of way more than you wanted to know, and it's probably boring—"

"It's not boring," I interrupted him. "I just . . . I don't know how to respond. It's not as though I ever thought about the comparisons between people and coral reefs and trees."

"That's what I think about all the time." Charley smiled. "Well, maybe not all the time."

The noodles dropped with a satisfying heat into my stomach, which seemed so ravenous it would jump me if I didn't pay attention to it. The taste of the spices was hot as well, but in a different way, like incense, or flowers burning. I had to put the chopsticks down and rummage for my fork, to get more in at each bite. The waiter brought two bowls of dumplings—one a mealy yellow, one tinted the paprika red of Greek Easter eggs—and salmon fried in a batter made of crushed almonds. "This isn't regular Chinese food," I remarked to Charley.

"The chef here is . . . real flamboyant. An artist. He's a good guy. Describes himself as a Cajun from Taiwan. Every few years, I build another couple of rooms on his house for the kids they've had in the interim."

"How long have you been doing this?"

"For him?"

"For anybody."

"I've, well, I've had my own business since I was seventeen, believe it or not. I started right out of high school. So twelve years, more than twelve years now."

"You said you went to college. . . ."

"Sure."

"But you had your own business . . . ?"

"I went to college a couple of times a week. Landscape architecture, other things." Charley offered me seconds of the pink dumplings, which I accepted, though the waistband of my jeans was beginning to cut the flesh. "You guys don't have kids, do you?"

"Me and Stuart?" I asked. Of course me and Stuart; who else could he mean? "We don't. Actually, we aren't married. Yet."

"Sure. Of course. I remember now. You just seem as though you're married."

"It shows, huh?"

"It's no big deal. Forget about it." Distracted for a moment by something off in his tone, I looked up; but his face was as still and placid as it was while he painted or broke down walls. "When are you getting married?" he asked then, with a smile that revealed a substantial overbite. He was cute. He was really cute, in that kind of obvious big-blond-guy way that had never quite made sense to me before.

"I'm not that sure we'll have children," I went on. I was feeling replete and drowsy, as ready for a nap as I would have felt at five in the afternoon after a lakeside six-pack picnic. I wanted to bundle the flannel shirt Charley had draped across the opposite chair into a pillow and fall asleep under the whisper of the oak leaves.

But that was when Charley told me that he had a daughter. "I felt a little ambivalent when I first found out," he said.

"Oh, me too," I agreed, missing a beat, still thinking we were discussing the pros and cons of having babies.

"Huh?"

"Uh, what did you say?"

He laughed at me. "That I was a little ambivalent when I found out we were pregnant"—my teeth hurt; I hate that usage—". . . not so much because of the baby as because of the timing."

"How did your wife feel?"

"She wasn't my wife; she still isn't. We didn't discuss anything much, Lakin and me."

"That's . . . the mother?"

"Yeah. We were together for about nine months, no pun intended."

"That wouldn't have been a pun."

"Well, no whatever intended."

"What does she do?"

"She's a football cheerleader."

I said, involuntarily, "Oh God."

"Well, it's not like Lakin was a stereotype. Really. But we just didn't have much in common beyond the obvious. . . ."

"And the obvious was what led to your situation."

"Yeah," he said. "Don't get the wrong impression. I wasn't just using Lakin because she was a . . . well, a vixen—though she was." My sluggish reverie snapped like the stem of a wineglass, leaving me rattled but bright alert and unaccountably furious. I sat up straighter. "We agreed that our relationship was a present, not a future. I think those things are possible—"

"Like limited-term employment?"

"If both people agree."

"So what happened?"

He actually blushed. "It seems . . . well, Lakin liked me. You know, she's a good person. And she had a really good singing voice, and we'd go to these places where she'd get up and do a turn with the band, and I really encouraged her in that. . . ."

"And so?"

"And so I treated her well."

"I see. You treated her well, so there was no future in it."

"I mean, I treated her well, and so she got the impression that . . . the communication between us—that is, the level of—"

"You don't have to say any more."

"No," said Charley, "I might as well finish it. Do you want that rice?" I shoved the bowl across to him. "She didn't tell me until she was four months pregnant, because she didn't want to jump the gun, you know, right away. We hadn't seen each other for a while by then, and it had always been a situation in which we were very careful. . . ."

Just a moment before, I'd been thinking of Charley as kind of a cad, and sweet Lakin, whom I imagined looking like a Texas version of Nicole Kidman, as a victim of her own charms. But suddenly the tables turned. Surely Charley, with all his talk of ecosystems and sexual unions, couldn't be such a dope about simple biology.

I watched him shoveling in his rice. I'd never seen anyone eat faster with chopsticks.

Maybe he could be such a dope.

"Do you think it's possible that you were the only one who was careful, Charley?" I asked.

"I considered that," he went on. "But Lakin was very sure, and she told me right up front, she didn't want children right away."

"And naturally you thought she was on the level. . . ."

"I had no reason not to."

"Maybe you were the first man who'd treated her like a real person, and she didn't want to let you go. Maybe she started out feeling one way, and things changed. Maybe that's why she waited four months to tell you she was . . . I mean, Charley, it doesn't take a reasonably intelligent person four months to figure out that she's pregnant."

"She wanted to be certain."

"She wanted to be abortionproof," I said flatly, simultaneously hearing myself, my jaded-bitch self, as I must have sounded to him. "She wanted you two to get married, I think."

"Well, that wasn't possible."

"Right."

"Nothing had changed. I mean, we had a friendship that was fun, but it wasn't intended to be a partnership. I didn't want that with Lakin. We didn't have . . ."

"What? Shared values?"

"No, we did have shared values. We still do."

"Well?"

"Well, we didn't have the makings of the lifelong conversation, and . . . well, this sounds ridiculous, but she didn't want kids. And I do. More than one. So I knew that we could enjoy each other for a while. . . ."

"But she had a kid, Charley. Your kid."

"She didn't want to. She didn't plan to—"

"So far as you know."

"So far as I know. She's a good mother, but that's not the same thing as wanting it, having it be something that's got to be part of your life no matter what. Which is more like how I feel."

"Are you in touch with the child?"

"Anne," said Charley, slowly setting down his chopsticks and pushing up his bandanna to reveal the band of white that neatly framed his gardener's tan. "I love my daughter. I support my daughter. I visit my daughter. Because I didn't have a lifelong relationship with her mother, at least of one kind, doesn't mean I don't want to have one with my daughter. I might have other children someday. I expect to. And I'll want to raise them with a woman I love. But she will always be my firstborn."

"What's her name?"

"Her name is Claude."

"Claude."

"It's Claude. Because Lakin's last name is Monet. You might think that sounds like a joke. Actually, I didn't think it up myself, but I like it now."

As I got up, he reached out in a kind of courtly, other-century way and guided my elbow. Stuffed and restless, I felt hanging in the air something in need of an apology, and I made a stab at one, which Charley waved away. I found myself wondering what had really gone on between Charley and Lakin, and I didn't mean their cheerful, dumb-sounding friendship.

What I was thinking about was . . . the obvious.

We didn't talk during the rest of the ride, and I left for the office as soon as the tire of his truck kissed the curb in front of my house. The rest of the day turned out to be a real pen-chewer, in which nothing got done.

After I described that lunch conversation to Rachael, who was threading her way through traffic while we talked on our respective cell phones, I decided to change the subject. I decided partly because her silence couldn't be accounted for simply by the vagaries of cellular phones. She was thinking about something.

"So anyhow, Rachie, part of why I'm not up there with you is the house. The repairs it needs before I can even camp in the living room are vast. They are titanic. They are immense."

"Colossal."

"Herculean."

"Brobdingnagian."

"The Patrick Ewing of remodeling."

"But everything's big in Texas, Annie."

"Yes. Except my bank account. I have no money, honey."

"But you do have your cute carpenter. . . ."

"Yup."

"Annie?" Rachael said suddenly, and in her tone was the unmistakable "Annie?" of our childhood, the sharp upward lilt that signaled a plate shift in one of our conversations, a new vein to be opened and mined. "Do you like him?"

"Who? Charley?"

"Yeah, him. I'm in my driveway now, Annie. Expect to hear the dulcet tones of your shrieking nephews momentarily. . . ."

"Of course I like him. I'm allowing him to further destroy my already nearly entirely destroyed house."

"You sound like a TV news anchor. A house can neither be created nor destroyed entirely. Destroyed *is* entirely."

"I miss you."

"I miss you too. But listen, do you like him?"

"You mean, *like* him? As in like to sleep with him?"

"Yeah."

"Jesus, Rachael, he's . . . he's, like, twenty-nine or something. And he's, like, this semiliterate longhair—"

"He didn't sound that way."

Involuntarily, I reached down beneath the silky pouch of my slacks. There was a pulse there, beating in my crotch. "You think I'm fooling around with the landscaper?"

"I think you took up a lot of time telling me about a lunch with a guy who does work for you. You took up eleven minutes. . . ."

"You timed it?"

"I was curious. And furthermore, you told me about it in a girl-guy way—where you say, 'Then he said and then I said and then he said . . .' "

"Come on, Rachie. That was just local color."

"Really?"

And then I asked her, "Rachie, do you ever think of Carlos?"

She didn't skip a beat. She didn't make that *phhht* noise that signals "Get out of here!" even over the phone.

She said, "I think of Carlos . . . well, not every day. Most days."

"And what do you think? When you think of him?"

"Annie, why do you care all of a sudden?"

"There's this kid," I said, and then I was telling her about Arley and about Dillon. And pretty soon I'd got back to my own apartment, too, and let myself in, still talking into my cell phone. Then we disconnected, but just long enough to get Diet Cokes and go to the bathroom—she in New Jersey, me in Texas—and settle down, Rachie still in her bathroom, the only place she could hide from her sons, me on our little half-moon balcony overlooking Summit School playground, where Chicano kids played shirt-and-skins in the cool evening, leaping like elongated demons in a shadow play against a fat mappler moon.

"What I could see about him didn't stop me from loving him," Rachael said. "And you know, Annie, I could see everything. It was that none of it seemed so bad to me."

"He did bad things?"

"But not to me." I could hear her sigh, hear the dull rattle of ice in her glass. "You think of your life as overlapping circles. You are one circle yourself. Your kids are another. At different times in your life, like when they're babies, their circle and your circle are almost . . . like a total eclipse of the moon. All the parts of your life touch all the parts of their lives. But with Carlos, there was only one small part of our circles that overlapped. We didn't have a common background, or friends or school to talk about. We didn't read the same books or see the same movies. It was only us. Only our love. Like a planet with air only we could breathe."

"But all that other stuff, all of that . . . everything else . . ."

"In the end, sure, everything else is what won out. What is the Japanese parable? A fish may love a bird, but where would they build a house? But the way I was with him, it was real. It was a whole life. But it wasn't one of those things you look back on after twenty years and ask, What was I thinking?"

"Well, what *were* you thinking?"

"I wasn't thinking, Annie. Maybe I was afraid of what I'd

come up with. I only knew that when he . . . when he was with me, when he was really with me—well, you know, inside me—it was like there was no surface on my body that wasn't him. It was like when I drew in breath, what I breathed in from him was no different from the breath already inside me. I smelled like him. When he moved his arm, I couldn't tell if it was my arm—"

"That's sex, Rachie. That's a sexual high, and it doesn't last—"

"No, it was more than that."

"What do you mean, more?"

"Well, more. A connection that was bigger than sex and bigger than . . . being friends. It was a real bond. But we could only express that connection one way. Through sex. But it wasn't all *from* sex. We didn't have all those other ways that allow people to link up and connect, to make a three-dimensional relationship."

"Would you do it again?"

She was quiet. She breathed in, long and slow, then out again, not quite a sigh. I could hear my nephews yelling in the background, yelling at each other murderously, ferociously, as if what they were fighting over was the last morsel of food in the cave instead of what it probably was, something like the channel changer. "Now?"

"Well, not necessarily now. But after."

"I could have, after. He called me a few times. Right after Don and I were married."

"What happened to him?"

"Well, he wasn't in the Department of Linguistics at Oxford, Annie. But he wasn't in San Quentin, either. He . . . he had this sort of dance bar with his uncle or his cousin or something. I remember the name of it was Sunset Alley. It was in Brooklyn, and one night I drove over there. . . ."

"You saw him again."

"I didn't go in."

"Why?"

"I knew what would happen. I knew that even if he was bald, or even if his hair smelled like Kools, and even if he was a hood and wore a leather jacket, he would still be that black-eyed kid. And we would still do the same thing. But it would be a wrong thing now. Something I couldn't blame on youth and hormones."

The moon had risen as Rachael and I talked, and it spread its light across my hands, coloring them ivory, graceful as polished bone. The silver of my right-hand ring, a cat's eye from Tienda Corina, was a black smudge. I could have gotten up and turned on the lights, invited in the customary business and bustle of a Friday night, slid in a CD, warmed up some pasta. But I sat, as the air lightened and cooled out of day into night, quietly, as if I and my sister were physically side by side in the sun room of our parents' apartment, our chairs drawn up to the window that looked down on the Mayflower Hotel, our feet wedged against the pane, coffee cups balanced on our stomachs. "The reason that I couldn't be with Carlos when I grew up didn't have anything to do with him or me, Annie," Rachael told me then. "It had to do with . . . context. We didn't have any context in the world. We'd have had to move to New Zealand or something. And even then . . . I live in my head, you know? Intellectual stuff matters to me. I would have wanted to make a living. I would have needed to."

"So all that does matter. It's real. And it turned out to be more important than what you had with him."

"Not really."

"How can you say that, Rachie? It's so . . . hopeless romantic coming from you."

"I really never put it to the test. But, Annie, I believe it's true.

It was like in *West Side Story*. We were right, and the world around us was wrong."

"Rachael, come on. I don't think of you as having these big, melodramatic—"

"They're just human emotions, Annie."

"But they're . . . well, they're the kind of emotions that can end up destroying you. Except for this one lapse, you don't do your life that way. Neither of us does. We're sensible."

"This *was* sensible. It was doing what my mind and body, mixed together, told me was the right thing to do. It just didn't match the rest of my life."

"Not even then?"

"Well, even then, I knew how I was going to turn out to be."

"Sort of . . . conventional?"

"Yeah." She was quiet for a moment. "Sounds like a skin disease, doesn't it?"

I sighed. I didn't know what to say. And then Rachael spoke again. "I just don't want you to have the impression that I didn't think about the way I got involved with Carlos, or that I wouldn't have done it if I had thought about it. You know? In fact, Annie, you know what?"

"No, what?"

"For a long time, for a longer time than you would ever imagine, I didn't have too much respect for the world. I felt that it would probably always be the kind of place where a boy who knew the things Carlos knew would never be allowed to be happy with a girl like me. I thought that was unfair. And, Annie?"

"Yeah?"

"Sometimes, I still do."

It was probably nine o'clock by the time I drove over to my house. I don't know what I expected to do there; it was just too oppressive to sit around and think of Rachael and how much I missed her, and of Stuart hunkering down in some SoHo bar with our old friends, all of them whooping it up and not thinking about me. From the car phone, I called Arley's house. The phone rang and rang. I could picture it where it sat, on the little red-painted hall table, ringing as if it were a live thing, shivering and summoning her. It was winter break, and she probably was out with Elena. I called Patty, remembering just before her phone rang that she had just left for New Jersey. Jeanine was spending the holidays with her parents in Key Biscayne—according to her, the only place that was more depressing to spend Christmas in than Texas.

I heard the music the instant I turned off the engine, but I figured it was coming from someone's TV, through an open window somewhere in the neighborhood. It was, after all, the night before Christmas Eve: families were gathering. And the music had that old-radio sound you associate with vintage movies. The closer I got to my door, however, the louder it got, and I realized it was coming from inside. Fear seized me, injecting a few seconds' adrenaline spurt, until I recognized the song. My mother sang it. I could hear her: "Keep that breathless charm . . ." That was it: "The Way You Look Tonight." Feeling like a fool, I knocked at the door. It was opened by the Ghost of Christmas Past—Charley, completely floured in plaster dust; even his hair was white.

"Anne!" He reached self-consciously for a rag and began wiping off his hands and face. We hadn't seen each other since lunch the previous week. "I didn't think y'all were in town. I thought I could get that ceiling down if I put in a couple of hours. . . . I've been working twenty-four–seven over there at the historical center—"

"It's okay, Charley. I don't care when you work here. I just didn't go home like I planned to. Stuart went."

"Aww, Anne. That's too bad."

"No, I'm okay. I just needed to . . . take care of some things around here. No big deal."

"When will he be back?"

"It's okay, Charley. I'm a big girl."

He eyed me. "Not so big."

"I'm mean I'm an old girl."

"How old?"

"What kind of question is that?"

"I reckon it's a pretty easy one."

"I'm forty, Charley."

"You don't look it."

I stepped inside, wishing I had brought a sweater. The place seemed to have conserved cold air within itself like a vault. It had to be warmer in Newfoundland. "Is there air-conditioning in here?" I asked Charley.

"Not yet, Anne. Actually, we need to talk about that. The wiring just isn't going to support the kind of current you'll need for central air, so if you end up wanting it, it's going to run a little more than we discussed. . . ."

"You should have a T-shirt that says that, Charley. 'That's going to run a little more.' Do you think you'll ever tell me, 'Hey, Anne, you're going to be spending a little less than you thought'?"

"It'll be the first time in the history of construction."

"And anyhow, why does everybody say, 'You don't look it'? Like it was this big compliment. Why does everybody think the best thing is to look younger than your real age?"

"I didn't say how much younger you look."

"Huh?"

"Well, you look younger than forty. But not that much. Maybe thirty-seven. No gray hair or anything."

"Gee, thanks, Charley. What a nice way to put it."

"You started it."

"In fact, I'm thirty-nine. I'm thirty-nine until next month."

"I had a hunch."

"You did?"

"Well, that night you and Stuart came to the house, you told him you wanted to buy it because of the address. . . ."

"I was drunk." I scanned the room—the chalky drifts of deconstructed ceiling, sagging doorframes, wall cracks as long and deep as the Nile. "I wish I were drunk now."

"Do you want a beer?" He had a six-pack of Lone Star longnecks in a little cooler. I accepted one, cracking off the cap on the lip of the iron mail slot just inside the door.

"I didn't know you could do that," Charley told me appreciatively.

"Charley," I asked him then, "what's that music? It sounds like one of those old Victrolas."

"It *is* an old Victrola." He led me back through the hall to what had once been the music room, where a vaulted ceiling of powder blue was frescoed with faded stars: Charley hoped to preserve it. The record player was in a polished cherrywood case. Charley had found it in someone's trash, rewired and refinished it. Now he picked up 78s wherever he could find them. "I like the way it sounds. Not that it sounds good, you know? It sounds like it's far away even when it's right here."

"Like a train whistle."

"Like that." He smiled at me, streaks of dust settling in the wide creases of his cheeks. "Want to hear another one? 'The Blue Skirt Waltz.' " I didn't know the song. "Old one. Maybe the twenties."

"How do you know those oldies?"

"I was the son of two music teachers. That's how I knew the

189

old lady who owned this house. She was a piano teacher, too. Do you like to dance?" Charley asked.

"I do. And what we do is, every Christmas Eve, we go dancing, my whole family. And Stuart's family. Up at this big beautiful place on the top floor of the Carillon Hotel. They have all these real trees inside there, decorated, you know, and it smells so good. . . ."

"It doesn't offend you?"

"What, Christmas trees?"

"Yeah. Lots of Jews feel like it's kind of shoved down everyone's throat."

"I did when I was a kid. I thought we got cheated, really. Like we got the difficult holiday, Passover, where you had to wash the same set of dishes three times a day for a week. And they got all the pretty lights. Now, though, I actually like Christmas Eve, because we're the only ones who don't have to worry about baking cookies and buying a million presents. . . ."

"Don't have to have Santa Claus come."

"You do, though. Do you have your daughter?"

"Not this year. We alternate. It's Lakin's turn. But that's okay. When I have her, she'll be four, and it should really be fun to see how she reacts. My mother's really sad, though, that Claude won't be here."

"Aren't you?"

"No point feelin' sad over what you can't change."

"I still do, though."

"Well," Charley said. And then he asked me, "Do you want to dance, Anne?" Now I knew that shirt was going to get plaster dust all over my perfect silky black pants if I came within three feet of Charley. But the thought of my slacks just fluttered past, like an envelope glanced at, then dropped from the surface of a long-awaited letter. I nodded and put up my arms.

"How come you can dance?" I asked him. "Guys don't dance."

"Well, my older sister taught me the ballroom stuff. That was because she was the prom queen but she couldn't get a date, so I had to take her. . . ."

"Her younger brother had to take her?"

"Yeah, she's pretty, but she's mean." Charley laughed. "Anyhow, I knew lots of guys who went to the cowboy bars and danced. In college. Just enjoying the music."

"But a waltz . . . are you sure you can waltz? Or just slow dance? I thought that being able to waltz skipped a generation."

"I guess I'm a throwback." Charley smiled and put his arm around my waist.

Oh God, I thought, don't let him be a good dancer.

But he was good.

Not like Stuart, but good. Charley didn't have the kind of sinuous bounce and squeak of a smaller, more supple man. He wouldn't have been one of the boys who studied the steps and then added his own touches. He just had a kind of plain, slightly lumbering grace. Filthy and reeking of turpentine, his jeans shot through at the knees, Charley folded his hand on the small of my back so that only the edge of his thumb touched me, the way my grandmother Esther had told me real gentlemen danced with a woman, so as not to wrinkle her dainty garments.

He didn't make me feel partnered so much as protected. I felt tiny and womanly, nearly lifted in his arms.

Charley's face was serious, almost grave, as we made neat boxes of waltz on the scarred wood floor of the music room. It occurred to me that Charley might be making some kind of pass at me. But he did nothing to pull me closer, nothing to disturb his concentration or the rhythm of our motion. When the song ended, he simply put on another record. And finally it was I who moved closer and put my head on his shoulder, and he reacted neither by tensing nor by grasping for more. Charley simply held me companionably, standing still as the record scratched to a stop.

Through the open window, we could hear the distant roar of the traffic on Kings Highway. From some store or other came the intermittent sound of recorded bells rising and fading so that, from one second to the next, you couldn't be sure you weren't imagining it. Then the breeze would come, and you'd hear it again. Someone had one of those electronic angels on their outside lights, I guess.

"Hideous noise," I said.

"Yeah," he agreed, still holding me. "But kids think it's beautiful. Claude thinks the music in department stores is like choirs of angels."

"Kids care more about the whole . . . feeling."

"That's the best thing about them. They're pretty grateful."

"You must be grateful, Charley. That you have Claude."

He sighed. "I am. I just wish I had gotten her another way."

"Well, you got her, at least. I don't know if I'll ever have a kid. Life's short, Charley."

"You know, Anne," he answered, slow and precise, taking time to let go of me long enough to shift me to arms' length. "People always say that. But, I think, life is long. Sometimes long enough." Charley turned and switched off the old Victrola. He carefully closed the cover. I just stood there. Slowly, it dawned on me that I was waiting for an invitation. I half-hoping it would not come. But when it didn't, I felt stung, disappointed.

"Well, you have . . . good holidays," I told Charley then. I waited for one beat more.

And I let myself out my front door.

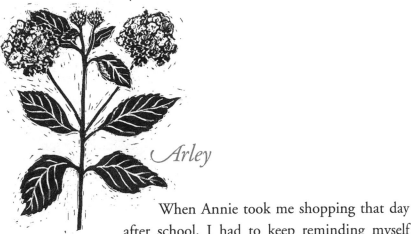

CHAPTER TEN

Arley

When Annie took me shopping that day after school, I had to keep reminding myself that I was already married and we weren't shopping for my wedding day. Because that was how it felt. It wasn't like it was the first time I ever went shopping or anything. Elena and I did a lot of shopping. We would go from store to store in the mall, putting together whole outfits, trying the pieces on, counting up how much they would cost all together. That was shopping.

But *this* was buying. It was a lot better.

I felt really foolish about it at first. The little I made at Taco Haven had to go for school clothes and mousse and stuff, necessities. I told Annie that. I couldn't really afford an outfit for court. But she said there was a special fund for cases like mine at Women and Children First, though it was mostly used for women who had to run away from husbands who beat them up, because sometimes they just left in the night with no suitcase or anything. Now I think the special fund was really Annie, though she still denies this and even asks me what did I think she used to make before she went into private practice, anyhow. She drove us over to Dillard's, and Annie told me what I had to get. I had to get clothes that made me look the way college girls look in *Seventeen.*

"Arley," Annie said, "I know you're a nice girl, but if you come in there wearing a crop top and jeans, with your navel showing, they're going to think . . . well, they're going to think you're exactly the kind of girl who'd marry a guy in prison." She sighed. "Which you're not. Though you did. . . . You know what I mean."

We turned right inside the door where they have the juniors section—all those white metal bins they try to make look like The Gap, with every different color and size of sweater or leggings rolled up like sausages. I immediately saw about twenty things I would have been happy if I had, but Annie wasn't too impressed. "This stuff is scuzzy," she said, fingering a waffle-fabric top (it was so cute, it was raspberry, and it had these little hooks and eyes all down the front). "It's not well made."

Over the years, I would get to know that this was Annie's favorite way of describing clothes, of which hers cost, like, three hundred dollars apiece. She sighed. "I'm no good at this. I only have one outfit." She's right about that, though I didn't know it then. Annie's outfits, except her jeans and boots, are all exactly the same, no matter what color they are—a little skirt, or a long skirt, and a sort of tunic top. She thinks these make her look taller and thinner, which is crazy. Annie isn't fat at all, but she will say right out that she thinks she looks like a turtle. One night much later, when we were having dinner at that Mexican place in the neighborhood, just her and me and Desi in her carry seat, Annie got a little drunk and said, "I look like Annette. You don't know who Annette Funicello is. But she's this actress from when I was little. She was really pretty, but no matter if she weighed fifty pounds, she was going to look fat because she had no neck and a lot of hair. And she was, like, five foot nothing." Which Annie also is, although she doesn't seem to know that she's lying when she tells Charley and other people that she is five foot two. Maybe it's just stretching the truth. I've got eight inches and twenty pounds on her, but she always acts bigger than me, like she did the night in the hospital, and not just because she is older.

That day in Dillard's, she steered me over to the women's department. I must have looked discouraged, because all the clothes looked like what Mrs. Murray would wear for parent conference day. We lit out of there real fast and went to sportswear. "This has always bugged me," Annie said, like she was a TV announcer or something. "I mean, sportswear is supposed to be for sports. It would be, like, tennis clothes, right? Or running clothes? And these are not sports clothes."

"It's like clothes you'd wear to work. If you worked for the telephone company," I explained.

She looked at me like she had glasses on she could see over. "You're right," she said.

In those days, I had exactly one skirt, which used to be Langtry's, so it was about a foot too short. I picked one off the rack. A stretchy one in persimmon. Annie said no, navy blue.

"Annie," I told her, "nobody in Texas wears navy blue. That's why there're so many of them here left."

We compromised on a gray skirt, a nice short flannel one, and two sweaters, both cotton, that you wore one over the other. They were just the color of washed-out denim, cloudy blue. Even if you washed them for years, it wouldn't make that much difference. I put them on, and Annie nodded. Then I saw this rose-colored blouse, it was silk and sort of gathered at the waist. It made me think of those old pictures of dance hall girls in Paris. Annie just watched me rubbing it against my hand, and finally she said, "You want that one?"

"I have to decide," I told her. "It's going to take me a few minutes."

What I would have done if it had been my money was take a walk. Maybe looked in a couple of other stores to see if I could find something pretty like it for half. Or slept on it. If I go back the next day and it's not there, that means it just wasn't meant to be. I've learned to live with this and cope with the disappointment, generally.

But Annie started tapping her foot. "Take them both," she finally said. I felt guilty about that blouse, and sometimes I still do. Because I just snatched it up, like I was some kind of kid from the reform school who never got new clothes. I still love it, though, but I've hardly worn it. And I wouldn't have let her get it if I'd known she was going to go on and get me other things.

"Thanks, Annie," I told her, but she brushed it away, saying it was money from the agency, anyhow, but I told her, "I still think I ought to say thanks. I guess I'll write the agency a letter."

Annie smiled at me then. "I'd just be the one who got it and had to answer it. And as far as that goes, we try not to remind the board of directors too often that we actually spend the money they raise. They'd probably ask me why you didn't learn how to make clothes for yourself in home ec class," she said.

I told her, "I didn't take home ec. It's not honors."

"Well, it wasn't honors when I was a kid, either, but most of my friends took it for the easy A," Annie told me. "And it was different then. Those home ec teachers assumed you'd be cooking and sewing for your whole family." She said then, "You know what? Stuart took home ec too. I thought it was so sexy, when I first met him, that he was such a feminist. But then he told me he did it just to meet girls." Annie laughed. "I'm grateful, though. He's a great cook."

"I guess I could have used them too." I sighed. "The cooking and cleaning part anyhow. My mama sure didn't seem to know too much about that stuff, or if she did, she didn't teach me. We just kind of made it up as we went along." She stared at me like I was nuts, then started to nod a little.

"Home ec applications for the nineties family," she said, soft like, to herself. She went on some more about Stuart then, that he was the only boy ever at Hoboken High to take sewing and that he worked for a tailor when he was in college and learned to alter his own pants. "And he once made me a wrap skirt, in about one hour, because I needed a black skirt. How do you like that?"

It sounded silly to me, to tell the truth.

"Didn't you think it was kind of girlish?" I asked her, not meaning anything by it, really interested.

"Arley, a man who can do woman things and not feel goofy about it is the kind of man you want to have."

"I guess I do, then."

"Huh?" she said, probably not meaning to sound the way she did.

"Well, like, Dillon writes poetry and all."

She sighed and turned away from me and started flipping through a rack of coats. "Do you have a coat?" she asked me.

"I have a jean jacket."

"Don't you have a real coat?"

"I don't really use one much. It doesn't get that cold, except that one winter, when I was about ten, and it snowed twice—"

"Well, pick something out," she told me. This was even harder than the skirts for me. There were so many. Some had a

197

lining you could zip out. I told Annie they cost more, but she
said it didn't matter, was I planning to spend every day of my life
in San Antonio—which, I had to say, I probably was. But she
asked me, what about college and everything? I tried on black
raincoats and blue ones. But I thought I looked like a crossing
guard. Finally, I found one I really loved. It was iridescent green,
like something in nature that would have wet wings, and it also
reminded me of Dillon's eyes, which, up close, had little golden
flecks in them, though I didn't mention that part to Annie. She
sighed all over again when I modeled that one for her. "You're going to look like the little mermaid," she said. But even she had to
admit it felt soft and pretty, and it didn't cost as much as some of
the others. It was London Fog, which Annie said would last until
I got so sick of it I'd give it to the AmVets (which was the kind of
place where I usually got my clothes, to tell you the truth). I
knew right then I would never give it away, and of course I won't,
unless I get too fat for it someday.

By lunchtime, we had bags of stuff—shoes and underwear
and this slip thing you didn't have to wear a bra with, which I
loved because I had kind of a little pot belly even then. And last
of all, a chenille robe with stars on it, which I didn't even need;
Annie said she wanted one like that when she was a little girl, but
she told me that her mother said chenille looked like Blanche
DuBois in *A Streetcar Named Desire* and wouldn't let her have it.
We were lugging more bags than I'd ever seen anybody carry except at Christmas, and I was starting to have this miserable feeling like it was wrong for a person, who was, after all, not going to
live or be young forever, to have all those clothes; but then I realized I was probably just hungry and tired from all the things we'd
seen.

We were sitting down in the restaurant at Dillard's, which is like a big greenhouse, eating Cajun chicken salad, when I brought up Dillon's poems again. "I didn't show you them at first," I told her, "I guess because they're so personal."

"Do you think he wrote them himself?" Annie asked me. I was kind of shocked that she'd think Dillon copied poems to give me; but then I sort of thought about it.

"I know he did," I finally told her.

"Why?"

"Because not all of them are that good," I told her, not meaning to put Dillon down. But Annie laughed, and I felt terrible. "I mean, they're good to me. But I know they're not, like, Dylan Thomas."

"Or William Butler Yeats."

"Or William Shakespeare."

"Or William Wordsworth."

"It's not fair. I don't know any more Williams," I said. "You probably do, because you went to college."

"And you will too. You'll learn all kinds of useless stuff." Then she said, "You know, you're really smart. I want to hear one of your poems."

"I can show one to you when you take me home."

"You don't know any by heart?"

"Well, I do," I said. "But I'd feel pretty stupid."

"How about Dillon's?"

Of course I knew his by heart, from reading them so often— I'd had them laminated at the school store to keep them from falling apart. I thought I would tell her the poem he wrote about my name: in some ways, that's still my favorite, because it came before everything else. But I didn't know if I could say it right out, there in a restaurant.

"Go on," said Annie. "I'm your lawyer. That means you can

tell me anything. In fact, you're supposed to tell me everything."
Right then, I thought of what "everything" could mean, like what
happened the first time I visited Dillon at the prison, and I guess I
just blushed harder. "I mean, you don't *have* to say it. I could read
it later. But it's just the same as singing to the radio in the car."

And so I did. I repeated, slowly, the way Mrs. Murray taught
me, the poem he wrote called "Arlington." I said it right down to
the tabletop, though. When I looked up, Annie's eyes were dark
and bright. "It's beautiful," she said. "It's very like you. It's also
good. Now I want to hear something you wrote."

And so I recited my poem called "To Dillon For Our Wedding Day."

> "Love is a season
> for the migrant
> heart to rest in.
>
> "Love is the wild
> wind the heart
> rides home on."

Annie just sat there for a long time when I was done. She finally
said, "That is really beautiful. Does your mother know you can do
that?" I didn't say anything. And then she asked me about my wedding day. I'd never told anybody about it. Elena knew, of course.
She would have been my maid of honor, after all, if Mrs. G. had let
her come—not that I blame Mrs. G. at all for that. I wouldn't let
Desiree go to a prison, even for somebody's wedding.

The truth is that my mama didn't want me to go that day, either. I could tell, even though she didn't say so. When I put the
permission paper in front of her, she didn't even put on her read-

ing glasses to sign. She just put her name down on it in one swoop, Rita B. Mowbray.

I told Annie that I'd asked her, Mama, what's the *B* for? My middle name, she said. I asked her what it was. She looked at me like she was looking at food caked on a plate. "It's Belle," she said. "It's Belle."

"That's pretty," I told her, slowly folding up the form and putting it in my pocket, with my birth certificate.

"It's shit," she told me. "It sounds like the name of a damned cow. Rita Belle."

"Whyn't you change it?" I asked her. I didn't think she would answer, this already being nearly the longest talk we ever had.

"You can't really change nothing," she said to me.

And then she got up and went into the bathroom, and I heard the shower go on. I started to cry. It was foolish. It wasn't like I thought she would come with me, or even tell me good wishes, but you always think people will change at the last minute, don't you? You always want to hope the best, even though you know that what you have already seen of people, day in and day out, night and morning, is the best they have to offer.

When Connie came, she had to honk about six times for me, and I still couldn't stop crying. Connie thought I was changing my mind, and it took a while to tell her no, that wasn't it at all, it was my mama. Then Connie started to cry too. She was driving Kate LeGrande's car. Here was the person who was supposed to be my mother-in-law by the end of the day, and I had never even met her. It was Connie called and asked to borrow the car, because Mr. and Mrs. G. wouldn't let Connie use theirs for such a purpose. I was a little hurt Kate wasn't coming to the wedding, either. I didn't even ask Connie why, whether Dillon's mother disapproved (I later found out she did; she thought I would be the ruin of Dillon, which, considering where he was already, seems kind of feeble) or whether she had one of her back spells (I later found out she had). Anyhow, Connie was having all this trouble shifting, going on about how she'd told Kate she knew all about driving a stick, though she'd never done it before in her life. "And I swear to God I thought I was going to grind the hell out of the gears just getting down that hill outside their house," Connie said. "But I made it. I was praying to Santa Caterina the whole time." It was only the second time Connie had ever met Kevin and Dillon's mom; the other time, she'd gone to their church just to meet Kate.

"What's she like?" I asked. The ride seemed awful long, and I was getting hyper. I'd never even been out on a date with a boy. Now here I was marrying a grown man! Here it was, the biggest, most important day of my life, and I couldn't even concentrate. I kept thinking how was it going to be to be married if we never even got to see each other? Would I tell people? Would I have to change my name legally for school and stuff?

"She's really little," Connie said. "And really nervous. The kind of woman my mother would call a nervous blond. She's got freckles. Doesn't look a thing like Dillon or Kevin. She started to cry during the service, and some big lady got up and sat down by her. I guess she starts thinking about the daddy or something. . . ."

I didn't know everything about Dillon's daddy's death, only that it had been horrible. He had been a welder, and a pipe at a refinery exploded. . . . "He took three days to die," Dillon told me on the phone. "It was such a goddamn shame. He was so goddamned careful, he wouldn't even let us stand in the shed when he was welding because he thought we might look at the spark and it would hurt our eyes. We would stand on each other's shoulders outside that dirty window and look in and see that sparkler shinin' blue as a star."

There had been a lawsuit, and some money. But Kate, Connie said, seemed to have spent it all on foolish land schemes with her brothers and her father. And then she married that Cajun, which took care of the last of it. And then the Cajun died, in a fight or something. That was why she was so out of heart all the time, and why it sometimes took her in church. (Mrs. G. did not agree with how sorry all the ladies at church felt for Kate; she said Kate Dillon was wetter than a sea urchin when it came to men, that she'd outlive ten of them and keep on drawing sap, but Connie and I thought that was mean.) Anyhow, when Connie first introduced herself, Kate acted like, Oh, do you know Kevin? "And we're practically engaged," Connie sniffed. And then, Connie said, Kate just kept trying to escape. She told Connie she had to get home and get her garden weeded and make lunch for Kier and Philippe. "I didn't really get anywhere with her," Connie sighed. "But today I told her I would give her all these free samples from my classes—all the ones for really white skin—if she'd let me borrow the car. She called me up to remind me to bring the samples with me. And she gave me some of these here prayer things from the church to give to Kevin. I'm sure he'll just love them."

We were both laughing a little by then. I felt much better. I said maybe, after I was married, we could go over and take Kate out to lunch someday, the two of us. "I guess," said Connie. "Let's get this over with first. You sure you want to go through with it? I mean, you could give it some more time. He ain't going nowhere, honey."

"I'm sure, Connie."

So Connie gave me the bag with Elena's homecoming dress in it, 'and I lay down on the backseat to change. It was the prettiest thing, I told Annie later, who reminded me that she'd seen the picture. It was almost yellow and almost white, like baby-duck down, and even though it was short on me, Connie said it looked beautiful. Then she said, "We got to get you a bouquet, girl." Just before we got into Solamente River, we stopped at a gas station that had a little store. Connie said they'd have flowers, but they didn't have anything except one chocolate rose in red tinfoil. We drove on a little farther, and I was crying again—I hadn't really stopped—until Connie pulled off on this little caliche road that was all busted into cracks like open seams, from the droughty weather, and picked a whole armload of lantanas. "I don't know why we didn't think of this before," she said. "We just see them all the time, and we don't remember that up North these would be considered flowers, girl."

While Annie and I were eating our lunch at Dillard's, I told her everything I remembered about the wedding. About the clerk's red plastic glasses that I kept staring at because they were one of those things you couldn't tell whether it was a joke or not. About what the warden said when he took a look at my birth certificate.

"What did he say?" Annie asked sharply.

"He said the ink wasn't even dry yet."

I told her about how it was to hold Dillon's hand—and I thought of his hand then, how warm and dry it was, soft as sand—and be able to smell him for the first time. He smelled like the wood chips we used to have in second grade for the class hamsters, that smell that always reminded you of being clean and little and safe. And his skin wasn't all zits like most boys, because he wasn't a boy, after all, but it was almost golden, except for the big dark rings under his eyes. In fact, all he said to me was, "I didn't get much sleep last night, honey." I couldn't even look at him. I thought my heart would blow out of my chest like a piñata bursting with spirals of colored foil and cut-out diamonds. I kept trying to steal glances at him as he stood straight and easy next to me, but my love for him was so large, it was almost like his face would be too bright for my eyes.

It was December 6, the only wedding day I would ever have, the anniversary of it something we would celebrate every year, and I couldn't even look at the man I was giving my whole life to. I could hear the chain around his feet slide and clank when he shifted position. They didn't have his hands cuffed, though. I kept wondering if I'd be able to say "I do" when the time came. But by that moment, the air around me was as loud as the inside of a shell pressed over my ear. Connie had to nudge me. And then we didn't have a ring, not for me or for him. Connie made this disgusted face and pulled off her moon spirals. Dillon slipped one over my fourth finger, left hand, but we couldn't get the other one to fit any finger of his except the first joint of his pinkie. "That's okay," he told me, right next to my cheek. "It's the new style."

The whole thing took, like, ten minutes. The chaplain was ready to do the whole long ceremony, but the warden said no, do the short version. When the chaplain said, "Kiss the bride now, boy," the warden had a big coughing attack. Dillon was a real gentleman. I know he probably wanted to crush me. But Dillon just put his hand on my back as though we were going to dance at the senior prom, that hot, light hand I could feel on my back long after he was led away. And he just brushed my lips with his. Connie said she had to give him credit. A convict would normally jump all over you, she said.

But I can still feel that kiss, like a mirror of all his kisses, his lips open and wet or closed and parched. I can't see his face anymore, but I can feel his mouth and smell it, and it wasn't until just recently, when I had to go to the clinic for strep, that I realized what he tasted like at first—like those wooden paddles doctors use to press your tongue down. After the doctor left the room, I took one of those tongue depressors out of its jar and slipped it in my pocket, and on the way home on the bus, though my throat felt like a road made of busted glass and my head ached from fever, I held it against my nose.

I didn't tell Annie that, then or ever. And I never told her what happened the first time I visited Dillon, what happened as I sat on the other side of the bulletproof window, the few seconds I thought of as our real moment of becoming married. Despite what happened, we were man and wife, Dillon and me. You can feel guilty and filthy and regretful as sin, and your own life something you want to turn your face from seeing. But even then, there are some things you can't dishonor by giving them away.

CHAPTER ELEVEN

Annie

The Solamente County Courthouse was a Florentine fancy, a leftover from an oil boom long since extinguished. It bloomed in the middle of the tired town like an orchid in a field of broom grass. Arley couldn't take her eyes off the ascending mosaic of black and white tiles in the domed atrium. "It makes me dizzy, Annie," she told me, grasping a rail and leaning backward. "It's like church."

"If it makes you dizzy, don't look at it," I told her, more sharply than I had intended. The last thing I wanted was for Arley to stagger into court looking like some gum-chewing pothead from the flats. I gave her a last once-over. We'd succeeded. In her silk blouse and gray flannel skirt, she looked a little older than she really was. The touch of lipstick and mascara only made her prettier, not tartish, and enhanced the sedate quality that came to Arley naturally. She'd tied her hair back gently into a French braid intertwined with cherry-colored ribbon. She'd told me gravely, in the car, that she was going to teach me how to do a French braid, to bring my mop under control in damp weather. The only thing that worried me was the cowboy boots; but Arley would not be moved on them, not even by the tempting pair of leather T-strap flats I'd bought for her. No, she'd worn those boots on her wedding day, and she'd wear them in court.

Well, it was Texas, after all.

We huddled on one of the mahogany benches that lined the hall, and I walked Arley through the things we'd agreed she would say: that she comprehended the seriousness of her husband's mistakes but believed he was working hard to repent of them, that though she realized she was a very young woman chronologically, she had carried out the responsibilities of a household from a very young age. In fact, I hoped Arley would never have to say a word to the judge, Harriet Clay, beyond "Yes, ma'am."

The clerk called, "LeGrande versus the Texas Department of Corrections and Ray Henry Southwynn," and we took our seats. Ray Henry looked good—Fleury had told me not long before that he'd taken up running three times a week, to siphon off some of that restless energy—but he was attended by weasely Polyester Petty, his counsel, who somehow embodied every cliché a cheap script about a bad lawyer could offer, from darting eyes to wide-spaced, gray little teeth. He grimaced at me. Ray Henry telegraphed me a look that on any other day might have embodied a wink. I leaned over to pat Arley's hand. She was straining like a greyhound—even her fingers were rigid—and when I looked back, there was Dillon, loosely manacled, being led into court by a bailiff.

I had never seen him clearly before, even in a mug shot. Arley's two pictures of him were indistinct, the main impressions being of his fair coloring and his small size. In the wedding-day Polaroid, though Arley beamed straight into the camera, Dillon's head was turned, almost out of profile, a chin line distinct and strong as a check mark the only really clear feature. Now I saw that planed chin, and the tanned hollows below broad cheekbones, wide-set green eyes bright as peridot, set wide apart, and a nose that was almost funny, straight, sharp, elfin. His hair was white blond, thick, as long as prison would allow, and when he turned to Arley with a lazy half smile that lifted one cheek, I tried to remember having seen a more physically beautiful man, but I couldn't. He looked like the bronze of the Coppini cowboy—weary yet erect and clean, childlike, ironic, and tender. Beside me, I could feel Arley's attention surge out of her like a thing that had mass, like a javelin. She did not move, but her lips parted; her breath came in soft, small sighs. The rapture on her was like a vapor. I had to shake my head.

The judge stomped out and took her seat without ceremony, quicker than the clerk could call a rise—we all bobbed up and down like jumping jacks. One of the first black women to sit on the bench in Texas, Harriet Clay was now the only one; and though well over sixty, she continued to sit her ground not so much out of a sense of mission but, as she once told *Texas Woman* magazine, "because I'm the benchmark." She had Ann Richards hair, a pair of slippery pince-nez, and an attitude that did not invite nonsense. "I have reviewed these documents," Judge Clay told us, "and I am very interested in knowing just what the nature of the conflict is herein, because what I'm seeing here seems to be a whole lot of conflicting emotion and a little bit of law." She motioned to me, with an upraised palm, like a minister advising a congregation that it was time to rise from the pews.

I told her simply that our motion spoke for itself. "My client and Mister LeGrande are legally married under the laws and provisions of the state of Texas, Your Honor. Here is a certified copy of their marriage certificate, along with the permission of the client's mother for her daughter, as a minor, to marry Mister LeGrande, and here is Mister LeGrande's request for his conjugal visit with his wife, as well as the warden's summary denial of that request, an ordinary one under the law and one granted"—I quickly consulted my notes—"a hundred and sixty times in the past year at Texas penal institutions, with only a single disruptive incident"—I paused to gaze at Lawyer Petty—"created when a spouse who'd been a guard employed at the institution where her husband was incarcerated attempted to help that man escape. It was an unsuccessful attempt. There were no injuries—"

"And husband and wife now share a landlord," Judge Clay finished for me.

"Yes, Your Honor. Well, not quite, but close enough."

"And Mister Petty? What's your position here?"

"My client, Raymond H. Southwynn," Petty began, "is, Your Honor, entrusted with the rehabilitative efforts on behalf of all inmates in Solamente River Correctional Institution. In this endeavor, he is responsible not just for the welfare of said inmates but for the interest of all the residents of Solamente County and, indeed, the state of—"

"We are aware"—the judge sighed—"of the scope of Mister Southwynn's obligations to the government."

"Reports from various social service agencies and the institution's examining psychiatrist may not seem to reveal a current pattern of antisocial behavior," Petty went on, handing the clerk a sheaf of documents, with copies for me as well. "In fact, his adjustment to his current life pattern has been going quite well. However, we do have two pieces of very critical information here, Your Honor. Very critical." Judge Clay looked down over her spectacles and raised her eyebrows. "One, a report dated October, just over six years ago, a complaint involving an allegation of forcible rape of a minor, a young woman aged fifteen at that time—a charge that indicates a prior pattern of abuse—"

I was out of my seat a little more energetically than was probably necessary.

"Your Honor, excuse me. Mister Petty knows full well that Dillon LeGrande has been convicted of armed robbery at a filling station. And that is all. He has no prior record of any kind of criminal activity at all. Mister Petty knows that his charge of sexual assault was dismissed, that this was, in fact, a romance between two young people, and that Mister LeGrande was, himself, barely twenty years old at the time."

Petty continued: "We also have here copies of letters provided us by the family of the young woman, who now lives in Corpus, letters from Mister LeGrande that suggest what we fully believe to be harmful . . ."

The judge looked from one of us to the other. "Do these letters refer to or illuminate any substantiated incidents of assault, abuse, or violent behavior?"

Petty and I answered "Yes" and "No" at exactly the same moment. I'd seen them, and they were regular adolescent sexual rantings about the things Dillon longed to do to Rebecca Rae, how he longed for her to lie quiet and still while he stripped her . . .

Well, she had been only fifteen.

But Dillon had been all of twenty.

That didn't sit well with me. It just didn't. No matter how I tried to get around it, it creeped me out, the age difference between them. What he'd written was even creepier: "If we were both dead, we'd be flying free together . . . ," though a dozen popular songs said worse. It was a stretch to construe such foolishness as provoking a suicide pact. Wasn't it? My protectiveness toward Arley was working overtime. I looked at my client's husband. He was just a green roughneck kid from Texas. That was all. I needed to believe that.

211

"Given these circumstances, and others, and especially given the tender age of the minor child involved here, it is entirely appropriate for Warden Southwynn to deny a conjugal visit between this young girl and this much older and very hardened man," Petty went on. Judge Clay glanced at Dillon, who was sitting, straight and head bowed, in his seat, fiddling with a callus on his thumb, like an altar boy during the sermon. "Indeed, we can be thankful that this is Warden Southwynn's—"

"Ray Henry?"

"Your Honor?"

"Want to add to this?"

"That about covers it. Least, what I'm allowed to say, ma'am."

"Are you certain that this denial reflects institutional objectives and not some personal bias?"

"Beyond a doubt, Your Honor."

"Miss Singer?"

"Warden Southwynn and counsel know very well that this denial has been based on an offense to the warden's sensibilities and that this is not a reason contemplated by the law, Your Honor. I mean, we don't know who Dillon LeGrande dated in high school, either, or whether he always remembered to open the passenger-side door for her. . . ." I was going too far, and Judge Clay's mouth, quickly bunching in disapproval, confirmed it. "In any case, I think it is clear from the correspondence between Arlington and Dillon that theirs is a very loving and indeed a creative relationship." I hadn't meant to, but I suddenly added, "Which is beneficial and supportive to them both. As they are lonely." What in hell was I talking about? "With the court's permission, I will read, briefly, from one of Dillon LeGrande's poems for his wife. . . ." Nobody stopped me.

And so I read it, from the embossed and laminated piece of

stationery on which Arley had carefully used a calligraphy pen to copy out:

Arlington

In some dumb wisdom your mama named
you, not after a person, but after a place.

Darling, you are all the lonely hometowns
in Texas, brown and sun-burnt, a little wild,

a little sad. You are the high meadow
streaked with shadows of quick-moving clouds.

You are that narrow valley outside of town
where flowers bloom after a few drops of rain.

You are the place I am always moving toward,
the yellow light that spills from open

doorways, a darkened bedroom
with a dress thrown over the chair.

Dillon Thomas LeGrande

There was no sound in the courtroom save the whicker of the ceiling fan. Then a child, outside on the lawn, yelled, "You're out! You're out!" and Petty cleared his throat and whined, "I'm sure none of us expected a dramatic reading. . . ."

I glanced around the room. Dillon had raised his head, his perfect forehead furrowed by a single earnest line, and was peering, not boldly but with some intensity, at Judge Clay's face. She dropped her eyes, suddenly flustered. I heard Ray Henry breathe, "Sweet bleeding Jesus," and saw that Arley had tears in her eyes.

213

Judge Clay stood up as abruptly as she'd entered and told us, "I'm going to have a look at this, and I'll get right back to y'all, okay?" while the clerk helplessly called for all of us to rise. The door of her chambers whished shut behind the judge's bustling back.

Suddenly I had to get out of that courtroom, out of the crossfire of Arley's and Dillon's locked gaze as the bailiff helped Dillon to his feet. Down the hall was a washroom casually used by all the attorneys: custom was to yell a greeting upon opening the door, in case of a gender conflict. I locked the door behind me and inspected my face in the smeared mirror—my cheeks were as round and flushed as pomegranates. I looked as though I were running a fever. For some reason, Stuart's voice kept jangling around my head, his Jersey voice I so loved, over the phone when we were apart for work, and even on those few occasions when we'd had a fight, or a conflict of plans, and gone our separate ways for a weekend. "Annie, I love ya!" he would say. "I'm your biggest fan. I'm rooting for you!"

I'm rooting for you.

I soaked a paper towel, folded it, and pressed it against my face; it felt as though my skin might ignite the coarse pad. When I came back out into the hall, Ray Henry was holding the door of the courtroom ajar. He jerked his head at me, and I slipped under his arm and took my place as the judge stomped back up onto the bench.

"Counsel," she said, and Petty and I stood. "I have reviewed this material. And I have made a decision regarding this petition, and I will share several observations on that matter before I present you with that decision. I have had three marriages and six children. It is my experience and my sense of the world that bad marriages are made every day but that we in positions of authority seem to care most about the consequences of those marriages where the people involved are people without money or resources."

She lowered her glasses and addressed Arley, who had popped up and stood beside me. "Young woman, this is a mistake. Though I fervently hope that I am wrong in this case and that your marriage prospers, statistically and realistically I know that I am not. This relationship may be the one that puts the lie to those statistics, but I see nothing here that would indicate a belief in that being the case."

To Petty, Judge Clay said, "Sir, I must say to you that I indeed believe that Warden Southwynn may be right about his fears and misgivings. He may be right, but he is not within the law. If this court had its way, there would be no Missus LeGrande except this boy's mama. But it is not for this court, nor for the Texas Department of Corrections or its officers, to decide who is to be married to whom and when." She sighed. "Accordingly, Miss Singer, please prepare an order reflecting the fact that this court will require Mister Southwynn and that department to permit a conjugal visit between Mister LeGrande and his wife, as instructed and provided for by the laws of this state, which shall be signed and delivered in accordance with . . . procedure. I wish you all a good day." She paused. "And good luck."

Dillon had leaned back in his wooden chair and hooked his fingers into the loops of his jeans as best as his cuffed hands would allow. I saw the look on his face then, the flicker of malice in that somnolent grin; and I wanted to grab Arley's arm and run, or plead with Ray Henry to have the man trumped into solitary, or injured, or gelded. . . . Arley's strong arms were around my waist; she was hugging me and whispering, "Oh, Annie, thank you thank you thank you. . . ." And the bailiff was whisking Dil-

215

lon away. I thought, again, helplessly, of Rebecca. She was married now, a young mother. I'd looked up her phone number. I could have called her. I could still . . .

Unable even to look at Arley's radiant face, I shuffled my mess of paper into my case and tromped downstairs, borrowed a typewriter from someone's vacant office, and filled out the order, Arley all but jumping up and down at my side.

Then we went outside and sat under the live oak trees in the courthouse square, next to two old men in baseball caps who were playing chess. Without asking, I bought lemonades for both of us. Arley took hers silently, nodding her thanks, watching my face, tugging at her skirt, and brushing the end of her braid across her lips, a parody filmstrip of all her little nervous gestures. Finally, she said, "Annie, we won. Are you mad at me?"

I couldn't even answer her. I just shook my head, not trusting my lips to deliver the merest civility. I was angry—with Arley, yes; and myself; and Texas—for reasons I could not begin to name. But especially I was angry at the boy with the mesmerizing eyes, like a cheap copy of an August birthstone, who had said not one single word to me, and made not one single inappropriate gesture, but had managed to make himself my enemy.

CHAPTER TWELVE

Arley

I was in my room with Elena when Annie called to tell me that we had our big date.

It was Saturday morning, and I thought the phone might be Dillon, so I about flew down those stairs to grab it. We had this system worked out now with my mama: I paid her a sum from my wages every week to cover exactly one fifteen-minute phone call on Saturdays.

But that day, Elena heard me gasp, and she came running after me. I was jumping up and down like I was crossing the asphalt lot to the swimming pool at high noon on the Fourth of July.

Covering the mouthpiece, I squealed out to Elena, "Guess what? Guess what? I got me my wedding night!"

It was set for January 16, which happened to be Annie's fortieth birthday. I would get to go in with Dillon at six in the evening and come out again at six in the morning. I was supposed to eat beforehand, though there would be Coke and chips in the trailer.

"I don't particularly want to spend my birthday driving you to Solamente River for what will probably be the rudest awakening of your life," she said. But then her voice got softer. It sounded as though she'd dropped the phone for a moment, and then she said, "I'm sorry, Arley. I have a big mouth. I don't know what's wrong with me. I . . . I'm worried about you. But it's your life."

I was still reacting to the idea of her driving me to Solamente River. I hadn't thought that was part of what a lawyer did. "You don't have to take me," I told her. "I'll just go by bus like I did before. Or Connie will drive me, if she's going."

"It's a Friday," she said. "Doesn't she usually go on weekends?"

I hadn't thought of that.

"And another thing," Annie went on. "Do you really want to make that ride down there alone? Do you have any idea how you're going to feel when the guards strip-search you? When they do a body-cavity search? They aren't going to let Connie go in with you for that."

"Body cavity?"

"Arley. Honey. I can't tell you to grow up, because that's not possible for you. And it's also not your fault. But your husband is a convicted felon! They have to make sure you're not bringing in . . . what the other convicted felons' wives bring in. Bags of smack. Razor blades and zip guns. Stuff he could use to kill guards later on and escape. Stuff he could use to kill you and then kill himself, not that he would. Awful shit like that is the *reason* some of those people get married. They think that nobody's ever thought of it before. You know, Arley?"

One kiss, my bonny sweetheart, I thought. A goose walked over my grave. My ribs seemed to wriggle under my skin. But this was Dillon. Dillon wouldn't hurt a hair of my head. Hadn't he told me that all the other inmates had the worst hatred for people who harmed the weak—the wife beaters and the ones they called "short eyes," the child molesters, who had "eyes" for short people, that is, children. Regular prisoners wouldn't even eat around people like that.

"I know," I said to Annie. "I guess I know. And it's not true for Dillon."

"Well, you'd better know, Arley. This isn't going to be the high school prom. Now, are you absolutely sure you want . . . ?"

I thought of the window in the prison's visiting rooms.

"Oh yes," I said. I wasn't at all sure. "Tell me about the body cavity. Like, an X ray?"

I could hear Annie coughing. It sounded like she was choking on hot coffee, like she did sometimes. She could never wait for it to cool off. "No, Arley. They will put on plastic gloves and search your vagina. And your anus."

"My anus?" I asked.

"Arley," said Annie. "Look it up in the dictionary."

Elena was sitting on the living room floor, watching me. She'd turned one ear my way. She'd busted an eardrum jamming a pen into her right ear when she was little, and I think her hearing wasn't all that perfect on that side. It made her look like she didn't quite believe you, which was the way she looked right then. But when I said the word "anus," she fell right over on her back, laughing. I thought she would crack her skull. Then she started pointing to the butt of her jeans. Anus, I thought. Oh Jesus Christ. I had to twine the phone cord around me to turn away from the door into the living room. I almost pulled the plug out of the wall. Elena was practically holding her breath to hear what I'd say next.

"And you'll need to bring condoms, Arley—" Annie went on.

"But we're married, Annie. You're not . . . you don't have to when you're married." That much I knew.

"Arley, listen," Annie told me. "Do you want to walk out of that prison pregnant at the age of fourteen? Do you have signed proof that Dillon is free of HIV or any other STD?" She sounded like grownups do when they spell out words little kids aren't supposed to understand.

"Actually, I do," I said, triumphantly. "And so do you." Dillon's medical history had been included with our court petition. He was clean as spring water. Didn't even have tooth decay.

Annie went silent. "Well," she grumbled after a moment. "That was almost a month ago."

Did she think Dillon was having sex in prison? And him married? With the female guards? Annie knew Dillon wasn't gay. Well, I guessed she did. . . . "I'm not worried about that, Annie," I said.

Was he? With men? I'd never even considered it. I wanted to hang up the phone so bad. I felt like my bladder was about to let go like a water balloon hitting the concrete. I finally told Annie that I had to call her back, and me and Elena went upstairs.

My mind was running around like a gerbil on a wheel. I knew what was right for me to do, and what I wanted, and yet to tell the truth, I *was* scared. I'd been thinking that the conjugal visit would take, like, months and months to get set up, even though Annie had asked that compliance be granted forthwith. I thought I'd probably be fifteen or older by the time I was Dillon's wife in the physical way. In fact, I'd just been dreaming around school with Connie G.'s silver moon spiral ring on my hand, sometimes just stopping in the middle of the hall, with kids foaming around me like a smelly, noisy river, standing there with my book bag dangling from my hand and papers and gum wrappers sliding down out of it, thinking, Arlington Mowbray, you are *married*. You are a married woman. You could walk right up to Mrs. Murray and say, "My husband was saying the other day on the tele-phone . . ." I could go to the doctor and write down, "Mrs. Dil-lon T. LeGrande," although I hadn't decided for sure whether I was going to use "Mowbray" for my middle name. I kind of liked it, and I never did have a middle name.

What Elena and I'd been doing when the phone rang was go-ing through all my papers, like my school records and my blood donor's card and my National High School Track Association membership badge, and trying to decide whether I should change my name on all of them or keep things a secret from school, Dil-lon being where he was and all. As we sifted through all the things in my jewelry box, we started talking about the wedding, and we'd both ended up with tears on our faces. I'd been crying so much the last month I could have needed salt pills. Of course, I hated the fact that Elena didn't get to be my maid of honor, and she did too. After we got back up on my bed, she said, "Looks like I won't be with you on the most important day of your life this time, either," and she smiled like a little fox.

I told her to stop it. "Listen," I said. "You have to walk me through this. Even if we get really embarrassed. What he's going to do and what I'm going to do."

"You know," Elena said, looking away suddenly. "You know all that."

"I don't, is what," I told her, jerking her around so she faced me. Just then, the door banged open downstairs. We both knew it was stupid Cam, but we froze, anyhow. And then we started laughing. Like little kids in the haunted house.

"I haven't done . . . it all," Elena said. "The farthest I ever did was, you know, with your brother. . . . Did you know, they didn't even call charges on Eric Dorey, him being so clean and all. Proba-bly because his parents shipped him off to military school . . ."

"They did?"

"That's what I heard. Or they moved—"

"And you are changing the subject," I reminded her.

"Well, Arley, all I know is, if you lay there and kiss the boy enough, it just happens. I only know one person real well who's gone all the way, and that's my sister Grace, and she says you just sort of fall right into it. You don't even notice when you take your clothes off."

"Who takes them off? Him or you?"

"I don't know."

"Ellie, I was counting on you for this!"

"We could call Gracie."

"And her knowing then what I'm doing! What about Connie?"

"Connie ain't never done it."

"She's got to have done more than we have."

"What are you worried about, like, the most?"

"I'm not worried about it hurting. Track makes you so you can take pain. I'm worried about being . . . ashamed."

"Well, it's not like you're fat."

"Fat?"

"Well, if you're fat, I always thought you'd be worrying about laying in the right position so he didn't see your rolls or whatever. You're . . . perfect, so you don't have to think about that. I never thought about that, when I did things. You just sort of lay there, and they act like you gave them a check for a million bucks or something."

"Do you . . . really like it?"

"Well," Elena said, scooping up her cloud of black hair, "I must say I like it. It's, well, you know how it feels when you touch . . . ?"

I knew what she meant right away. But I'd never done that, either. Not even by accident? Elena wanted to know. No, I told her,

222

though of course I'd had physical feelings. Particularly since I'd seen Dillon face-to-face. My dreams were so out of control, I woke up sweating. Elena had begun sorting through my papers again, and she came up with my bride poem. I hadn't showed it to her before, but I figured it was okay to do now. I was pretty proud of it, and it wasn't like showing her letters. She read it soft, out loud.

"Every bride

holds the future
in her mind
on her wedding night.

Here is the future
I want—enough
time to grow

ordinary and dull,
evenings
that settle

like moths,
you and I
on the porch stairs

in the dark, the glow
of your cigarette,
the smell of the first drops

of rain in the dust,
nothing to look forward to
but tomorrow

and the day
after that."

She sort of sighed when she was finished reading it. "That all you want?" she asked me.

"What?"

"Just sitting on some dumb porch?"

"I . . . I don't know. It would be enough, I guess."

"It's pretty, Arley. But you know, I thought, with all your brains and stuff, you'd want so much more than that. Some excitement. You know—college, the city. Whatever."

"I couldn't go to college anyhow, Ellie."

"Because?"

"I don't have the money."

But she started me thinking of all that was going to go by me because of the choice I made, and I felt shabby about it.

"You'd get a scholarship, Arley."

"Maybe. Maybe I still can." But maybe that was one of the things that was already over for me. Maybe over before it began. "You know, Elena, just being married to him is a whole lot more than I already had. It's all I really want." Was I telling the truth? I thought. Was it really all I wanted? It was all I could see, or think of, or plead for, from the shadows in the corners of my room at night. It must have been true. It *was*. We sat there together, quietly, side by side. It's one of the times I can remember exactly, though it seems long ago.

On the afternoon before our wedding night, I started sitting out on the porch steps an hour before Annie said she'd be there, thinking about those things. I'd been up since dawn, never really slept. Called myself in to school, telling them my mama was at work, which was true, though I wondered whether I was going to get a detention anyhow. Talked on the phone to Elena while I made a casserole to put in the fridge for Mama and Cam. Left all the salt out of some pie crust, and you know, that really ruins it, even though it's just half a teaspoonful. I took it over and gave it to Arrowhead, Gary Nevadas's dog. Then I folded laundry and did ahead work in my math book. Showered, then redid my hair four times, because pieces kept squirreling out of my braid. My fingers felt like pork sausages. I was wearing my court skirt and blouse, because Dillon had written that when he saw me in it, he couldn't wait to get his hands on me. When I thought that, of course, I right away thought of his hands on me. My crotch jumped, and at the same time my teeth started to chatter. I'd try to put it out of my mind.

That afternoon, while I was waiting outside, who came up the road but Mr. Justice. Ginny Jack had been pretty stern about keeping him out of Taco Haven lately, and when he did come in to eat, she had Luz wait on him rather than me, though she knew we were friends. So it had been a while since I'd seen him.

"Girl," he said, when he was almost in front of our house, "you all dressed up. I've never seen you so pretty."

"I'm going off," I said. "How are you, Mister Justice?"

"On the move, Arlington," he said. "I'm on the move." He didn't look so good, to tell you the truth. Skinnier than normal, even for him. Not shaved. I could smell him from the sidewalk too, that malty smell even fairly clean people have when they're drinking.

He looked down at his boots and then put his hands in the holey pockets of his old jeans. "You been practicing your hurdling?"

"Some," I said. Hell, I hadn't. Not at home. And just after

school wasn't enough if you wanted to keep your speed and your conditioning. I was thinking of giving up the team altogether, what with the amount of time I spent on Dillon, plus my homework and my job and Mama's stuff. "But you know, Coach used to say I could make all-conference for spring. If I keep up."

"You ought to keep up," Mr. Justice said. "If you do something real well, you ought to hug it close."

"I'm married, Mister Justice," I said all of a sudden.

Search me, why I said that.

He looked down at the end of the street, squinting into the late sun. Then he said, "I know."

"You know?"

"I hear a lot of things. People love to talk. Guy like me is fairly invisible." That didn't sound like a crazy person. He smiled at me, crinkling up his faded blue eyes. I smiled back at him. "I hear that your man is in prison too. That's not all bad. Not always. Some good people end up there, Arlington, through nothing but foolishness. But most people who end up there deserve to. I hope your man is one of the first kind."

"He is."

"You're so young, girl," he said. "But there's this way you can tell if what you want is what you should have, no matter what age you are."

That scared me a little. It crossed my mind again, what people said about him being crazy. I looked around. There wasn't a soul on the street but us. Not even a car. So I asked him. "How?"

"You think about five years on. Five years on from this minute. And then you wait to feel it, right here." He put his hand on his stomach. "It don't have to be what you think is good for you. You'll feel it here."

226

"How?"

"Well, I don't know." He smiled, and I saw his teeth still looked pretty. Maybe they were fakes. "I lost the hang of feeling it a long time ago. But I remember it was true."

Annie's black Camry came wheeling around the corner from Church onto Jean-Marie. "I have to go now, sir," I told Mr. Justice.

"Well," he said, "best wishes. Better make you a wedding gift, when I get my hands on some wood that's wanting to be something."

"You don't have to do that."

"How's your brother?" My brother? Well, Mr. Justice had been the town drunk since God was a boy, after all. He probably didn't really know who Cam was.

"I guess he's okay. He plays the guitar."

"Any good at it?"

"He's real good. And he plays the fiddle too." Mr. Justice shoved his feed cap back on his head.

"Blue norther coming," he said softly. "Cold tonight." He shivered. "Fiddle. Fiddle, huh? Well. He's blond, though, isn't he?"

Well, Mr. Justice was pickled.

"Who the hell is that?" Annie asked me. She'd come jumping out of the car, talking before she hit the ground. She had four picnic box lunches and four cups of coffee—like her and me were a school bus full of people or something. Thank God Mama was pulling a double shift. I knew she knew about where I was going. But she hadn't said a word.

Annie looked . . . odd. I was used to seeing her in suits, mauve or navy or brown. She was wearing a turquoise crop-top sweater over a flowery skirt and cowboy boots. Bright-blue cowboy boots with turquoise lizards on them. She looked down at them the moment she got out of the car. "My birthday present from Stuart," she said. "I think they're cool."

"They're nice," I said. "Hela-nice."

"Hela?"

"Kids say that."

"Oh. Well, I like them. They make me feel like I'm not a hundred and fifty years old. Which I am."

"Annie, you're not old."

"Arley, I'm forty years old today and I'm not married, and you're fourteen years old and you are married, and I'm driving you to your wedding visit at a goddamned prison, and . . . what a world, huh?"

"Are you and Stuart getting married?"

"I think so. No, maybe we are. You know, his work is pretty demanding—trying to save people who are on death row."

"Would he do that for Dillon?"

She stared at me. "Dillon's . . . Dillon's not in any danger of capital punishment, Arley. He's . . . he's basically a short-timer."

"If he ever did anything . . . really bad . . ." My brain was taking off for Saturn from the stress.

"Let's hope that never happens," Annie said, and buckled my seat belt like I was three. Which I liked, I must admit. "I guess Stuart and I will get married. But I still don't know about having kids. And he's pretty sure."

"Oh," I told her. "I don't think he should pressure you."

She shot her eyes over at me and smiled. She doesn't have a Texas face, Annie. But I noticed that moment how pretty she really was. How her eyes were brown, but not almost black like mine, a gentler brown, with red in it, like a winter leaf, and they turned up at the corners, which makes her look like she's laughing even when she isn't. "*He's* not pressuring *me*, Arley. *I'm* pressuring *him*. Stuart doesn't really think he'd be that happy as a father. I'm the one who wants a baby. I think I do, that is. Some days."

"I didn't think you could . . ."

"What?"

Might as well. I was half in the muck now. "I didn't think you could have a baby after you had the . . . after menopause."

She did laugh then. "Arley, I haven't had menopause. Women don't have menopause until, well, most of them until they're in their fifties. Plenty of women, particularly women who have careers, have babies well into their forties."

"I'm sorry," I said. "You know I didn't mean anything by it. I just figured, forty and all . . ."

"Arley, forty's old, but not that old. Not for some things. Now, if I wanted to become a ballerina . . ." We pulled away from the front of my house, the house I'd lived in until all those things that happened to you ran together into one linear groove you thought of as your life. A high school girl, I thought as we started off, and I'll come back tomorrow a woman. But we weren't in that car fifteen minutes before I fell asleep, and then Annie was shaking my shoulder. We were at a gas station just outside Solamente River, and she wanted to know if I wanted to clean up before we went on. I walked into that bathroom, which was so blue—ceiling and walls and tile floor—that I swear it was what made me throw up my breakfast cereal. I washed my mouth with soap, and my hands. I put more mascara on.

We kept on driving. Annie was talking fast now, the way I later learned New Yorkers talk: about how first intercourse could be painful, and often the woman didn't have an orgasm the first time, and how Dillon probably hadn't been with a woman in a while and he might be rough, and how we should go slowly, and how it would be good to be aware that the prison staff was going to be checking on us periodically, probably through a one-way window, and how changing my mind, even now, would be okay, it would not mean an invalidation of the order for my visit, we could reschedule it, and how I needed to be aware that first inter-course often led to a painful condition known as honeymoon sci-atica, an infection of the bladder, and if that happened, I wasn't supposed to worry about it, just tell her and we'd get some antibi-otic cream. . . . She sounded like the health lecture in sixth grade, and I wanted to clap my hands over my ears and sing Reba songs real loud to shut her out, but I didn't dare. She was only trying to be kind, even though I couldn't take it all in and it didn't much matter, anyhow.

And then we were there. Annie was speaking to the woman guard, a little one this time, saying, in her tough-chick law-yer voice, "My client is a minor child, and I wish to accom-pany her. . . ."

"That's not possible," the guard said. Didn't even look at Annie. Just shoved a clipboard at me with a paper to sign, though Annie grabbed it up and read it before I did. The guard motioned me through the metal detector, and Annie reached out and put one hand on the woman's arm.

"Please," she said. "Please. Look at her. Just let me come with her as far as the search. Please." The guard looked at Annie, and at Annie's blue boots. Then she nodded her head to one side and let Annie pass.

They would have done worse to me if Annie hadn't been there. I know it. As it was, being in the hospital with Desi was a breeze after all the embarrassment I endured in that little room.

Caring for Annie was something I never really thought about until those minutes. It was something I assumed she knew—that I respected her, that I was grateful. But what she did when the matron searched me was take my big rose-colored shirt and hold it around my shoulders while the gloved hand moved around below, not hurting, just shaming me. She put my head on her shoulder while they combed their fingers through my hair, and she told me this long joke about a guy who had a flat tire in Brooklyn who kept going from house to house asking to borrow a car jack, finally getting so disgusted and aggravated at the last house that when the owner opened the front door, the guy with the flat tire just said, "Keep your fucking jack."

After I was dressed, she took two packages out of her purse. One of them held a few sanitary napkins, some A&D ointment, and a little package of condoms. "I was afraid you wouldn't get the latex kind, Arley," she said. "The other kind doesn't prevent diseases as well. The rest is for . . . afterward." In fact, I gulped when she said that. I had forgotten to bring the condoms I'd had to beg Connie G. to go into Oberly's and buy for me. They were in a bag right in the middle of the kitchen table, like a sandwich. Oh God, I thought. Oh my God. But I struggled to smile, and Annie helped me open the other package. In it was a Japanese nightgown, silk embroidered all over with clouds. "Like the dream you told Dillon about, Arley. In your letter. Your colored wagons." I started to cry then. And hugged her. "Be happy, Arley. I'll be here tomorrow when you are ready to come home."

"You don't have to do that."

"I want to." Annie was biting her lip. I could see she was crying too. "Here," she said. "Your hair's all messed up." I pulled one of my red ribbons out of my pocket and Annie helped me put it in my braid. The guard was polishing the front of her badge with a piece of tissue paper, not looking at us. Then Annie had nothing left to do. She picked up her purse.

I said to her, "I love you."

She really cried then. Like the day in the car. A few weeks ago, that was all. Finally, she said, "I love you too."

The matron and a guard with a rifle walked me over the back grounds to the trailers. There were three. Behind a fence, about fifty yards away, a few inmates were working on patching a piece of fence. Why would they do that? I thought, crazy like. It would be something on the order of digging your own grave. They all stopped and looked at us walking, and one of them said something real loud in Spanish that sounded almost like a coyote yipping in the dark. I heard the guard cock the rifle as the matron opened the steel trailer door with a key from her ring. He pointed the gun at the door while I walked through. And inside, there was Dillon.

He was sitting on a nice clean couch just like a regular person, wearing a beautiful green chamois shirt, without leg irons or anything. I ran right into his arms. And from his arms, I listened to him agree to all the rules, about voluntarily opening the door to a knock every two hours throughout the night, about emergency procedures. And then I heard the door close, and then lock, from the outside. We were alone.

For all that came and went and was built and shattered after that, I would not have had it any different. Dillon held my face in his two hands and said to me, "There's this part in the Bible. About looking for your loved one's face and coming forth to meet her. It says, I have found thee. I have found thee. You're here, Arley. You're mine." He kissed me then, and he picked me up and set me on the couch and got us Cokes and turned on the radio. We sat down beside one another and Dillon smoked two cigarettes, and he just stroked my hair over and over, and every time I'd start to say something, he'd say, "Just wait, honey. Just a minute." And then, when I was about to start getting nervous he was out of love with me already from waiting too long, he pointed to the radio, and the guy was saying, "This one here's for Arley and Dillon. On their honeymoon night. You be good, y'all. And you be good to each other." I just couldn't believe it, that somehow he'd got someone on the outside to call and make this request for us, for right that time. It was "And I Will Always Love You," the Dolly and Vince version, the good version, not that whiny old Whitney thing. While it was playing, Dillon laid me down on the couch and kissed me and lay on top of me, and when the song was almost over, the deejay broke in and said, "Let's do that one more time, folks. You only get one honeymoon night, now." And they played it all over again.

It was like Elena said. I'll give her that. When my mouth opened, and Dillon put his tongue inside, just a little at first, and then more of it, it wasn't sick and it wasn't gross. It was like drinking at a fountain when you were so thirsty you couldn't imagine you ever thought of anything else in your life but water. Dillon didn't even try to touch me through my clothes. He just reached behind me and, with just one hand, unhooked my bra faster than I could have done it myself and lifted my shirt over my head the way I do for Desi. "Arms up," I say to her. 'Course, he didn't say that to me. But I put my arms up that way, and then I was half naked, cuddled under his shirt. We lay there that way for a moment, and then he started to talk, slowly. "Don't be afraid, Arley. I'm your husband, and I love you with all my heart. And I won't do nothing to hurt you. And anything you don't want, you just say stop, and I swear I will stop." He pulled my skirt down and my stockings, never making me get up, never making me feel any of those things I'd been afraid of, like big and clumsy and ashamed. And then I was all the way naked, lying under him. A couple of centimeters, I thought, a couple of wisps of cloth, and his body would be full against mine. So much was going on, I had to force myself to concentrate: on the muscles in his legs tightening and letting go, on the slight scrape of his chin against my chin, our mouths by now practically inside one another. A kissing chin, Elena called it later, what I had the next morning, a place below my lips buffed raw by Dillon's beard, which must have grown back stubbly overnight.

Dillon leaned back then and stood up, and I shut my eyes, and my arms snapped down over my body like a pocketknife closing. "I got to look at you, Arley," Dillon said. I heard him opening his zipper, heard the *shush* of his clothes falling.

"No," I said. "No way. We don't know each other well enough."

"Don't know each other well enough? Honey, I'm your husband."

"Doesn't mean I know you." I couldn't figure out what to do. That couch felt bigger than a basketball court. I didn't know whether to roll over or curl up in a ball. The radio was playing "You Never Can Tell," and the fabric under my face, its plaid of yellow and red, suddenly seemed as loud as the song. But Dillon lifted me up—I still wouldn't open my eyes—and kept me right beside him while he opened the couch into a sofa bed, and then I lay down and he lifted the sheet and put it over me. Through my eyelids, I could see the light change, and so I kind of looked. The light from the guard tower was sweeping and gliding, and now it was the only light in the room. It swept over Dillon, who had nothing left on, and I took in my breath. He was so beautiful, I had to shut my eyes again. But I'd seen his dick standing up full

234

and purple against his belly—not like I'd imagined, though, but really straight up.

No way is this going to work, I thought, sweat breaking out on my wrists. This sure as hell can't work, because if he tries to put that thing in me, it's not going to bend, and it's going to sprain or I'm going to get bad hurt, one of the two. But then I figured he'd know, so I just opened my arms, and he lay down with me. I put my mouth against his shoulder. He tasted like the mouth guard I used to wear playing field hockey—like clean rubber, pliant and smooth. He told me that he wanted to kiss me down there, and I begged him not to. I couldn't imagine him wanting to, even, though I'd heard plenty of boys did it. "Don't be scared," he said. "I'll touch you first, just a little, and if you don't like it, we'll stop for a while." And he ran his hand down my belly and laid his finger flat against me, rubbing at first gently, then a little faster. It doesn't sound very beautiful, but I can only describe it as a sting. And before I knew it, I was turning my body to follow his hand, making sounds like I was straining to breathe. "Arley," Dillon said, "are you crying, honey? Are you afraid?"

I didn't think I'd be able to talk, but I said, into his shoulder, "I'm not crying." He started to rub on me again, little slow scrubbing, and this time I tried not to make the noise, but it kept coming.

"I'm sorry," I gasped.

"Don't be sorry, Arley," Dillon told me. "It means I'm pleasing you. It's good." He put his mouth on my throat, then on my left breast, and I flashed on the sight of Cam and Elena. This was it. And happening to me. To Arley Mowbray, who never even let a boy kiss her except Curtis Melby in second grade. I opened my eyes and peeked down, at Dillon's blond head swiveling away, at my breast rippling, and then I shut my eyes and stopped making pictures in my mind at all, and wherever he went with his mouth on me, my brain went to that part and called out for me to come over, and there I stayed. "I'm going to kiss you now, honey, suck on you a little." And though I didn't really want him to, I let him. It didn't seem so strange, after all, by then.

I watched the guard-tower light sweep, sweep, searching like an eye, and felt Dillon's mouth tugging, his tongue inside me, nerve explosions like little darts across and up and down, feeling things done to me I never imagined you could even let happen, much less describe to yourself at the same time. And then there was the knock at the door.

I pulled the sheet up over my head, and Dillon jerked his jeans up over his hips and went to open the door.

A big hefty man in a green uniform was standing there, his hands in his pockets. He was the same man I'd seen in court. He wore no gun. "I am here to check on your welfare, Mister LeGrande, and that of Missus LeGrande, as required. . . ."

"She's fine, Mister Southwynn," Dillon said, his voice reedy and nasty. "She ain't no different from how she was when the other folks left. I've done nothing to change her."

"Sorry to disturb you. Beats us looking through the observation window, though, don't it, Dillon?" the warden asked softly.

Dillon waited a moment and then said, "I reckon."

"Please sit up, Missus LeGrande." I poked my head out, with my eyes closed tight. "Are you all right? Do you need anything?" The warden's voice was tired and kind.

"I'm fine," I said. And then the door clicked shut. Dillon came back, and we lay there side by side.

"Touch me," he said. "Bring me back to life." Of course, I'd never touched a boy, but I figured it would be okay so long as I didn't look. "I'll guide your hand," he told me, and he wrapped my hand in his. It was hotter than the rest of him, and soft, so soft, soft as rose petals, really. I don't know how they can call it hard. It felt like its own thing, like it was living, moving; it filled under my hand and Dillon's as he pushed roughly up and down.

"Don't hurt . . . yourself," I told him.

"Honey, it don't hurt," he told me. "A man can take a lot of friction." And all of a sudden he stopped, and sucked his breath in, and rolled away and said, "I want to make love to you now, my wife. Is that okay?" I just nodded my head up and down. He rolled his leg back onto me, his silky hairs tickling and brushing my thigh. And then I remembered.

"We have to use the . . . things," I said, sitting up, my hair springing out of my braid all at once. "We have to."

Dillon sighed. There was a loudspeaker announcement outside; I couldn't make out the words. Then the lonesome sound of a whistle. Night call, Dillon murmured. Recreation was over, and it was time for a cell check. This is prison, I thought. This is prison. Jesus Christ. I wanted Annie. I reached for Dillon's hand. "Arley," he said, sharper, rubbing my palm as if it were stained. "I don't have any diseases or . . . anything."

"I know."

"It's not as nice with one of those. You can't feel everything. I want to fill you, girl."

"I can't get pregnant."

"Are you sure?" he asked. "Then what are you worried about?"

"I mean, I can't, I won't, I don't want to get pregnant. Not tonight. Not now."

"You're a married woman."

"I'm fourteen, Dillon. And I live at home and I have no

money at all. And my mama would kill me deader than Elvis. No fooling."

"You don't have to stay there. You could live with *my* mama." We both went silent. "Well, okay, maybe not. You could go on the state."

"I won't do that."

"Why not? You're just a kid. And just 'til I get out."

"I won't be a welfare mother. Like in the magazines. No."

He got the condoms out of the box. "Let me put it inside you first. Once. So it's really me who goes into you the first time." I lay back. "Open your legs, honey. Open for me." He kissed me soft. I felt it, like someone at a door. Pushing, blind. He steadied it, with his hand. "Arley, honey, this will hurt some." His face was hot, his cheek hot against my cold one. The red ribbon I'd used to lace in my French braid snaked over my shoulder and caught in my mouth. Dillon nudged it away, then took it in his hand and slowly wrapped it around one finger.

"Just do it," I told him. And he did. Like a needle as thick as a knife, for an instant. I dug my fingers into his shoulders and he yelped, and then the pain started to melt and my muscles to melt, too, and he started to rock me, and while it didn't exactly feel normal, it was working. I am fucking, I thought. Me. Arley. My God. "I would wait for you, honey," Dillon said through clenched teeth. "But I can't."

"Get it, then!" I told him. He ripped the packet open with his teeth and fumbled to slip the condom on. It didn't feel any different to me, except his body changed as it got more serious for him. He skimmed over in sweat, cool as a porpoise, and bucked and arched, almost like I wasn't even there. Then he shook drops off his hair and stared down at me.

"You get the number of the truck that hit me?" he asked. When he got up, he looked like he'd been in a fight. "Arley, Arley, Arley," he said. "Now you're mine." I started to get up too. But Dillon motioned me over, raking through his pale hair until it stood on end, funny. "Now I have you, I'm not done with you yet." He came back with a cigarette, and he stroked my belly while he smoked it, and then we did it again.

I had to use the bathroom after that. There was a toilet and a sink with some towels behind a screen. It was open at the top. I guess they assume that if you can make love with someone, you also can pee in front of him, but I had no idea how I was going to manage to go in front of Dillon. "I have to go to the bathroom," I told him. "Can you go outside and wait? I'm too embarrassed."

"Honey," he said, laughing, "we all are locked in here. You think they want me and you to get up and walk on out of here and catch the bus to Laredo?" Of course, he was right. "I won't pay no mind," Dillon said. "I understand. In here, you got to use the toilet in your cell with the bars open out there. I like to had me a locked bowel for two months. A person likes his privacy. What I'll do, I'll turn the radio up loud." So I pulled on my shirt and stood up. And then I saw the blood. Not a little bit, like Elena and Annie said. Rivers and splotches and maps of Argentina made of blood.

"Dillon," I said weakly. "Look here."

"Oh, for Pete's sake," he said. "Shoot. Did you bring anything?"

"What do you mean? Like, a transfusion?"

"No, I mean, like . . . pads."

"Actually, I . . . yeah." I thought of Annie's packages. "But . . ."

He went behind the screen and wet a washcloth with warm

water and told me to lay down. He washed me gently, and then he played the radio high so I could pee. The bleeding was just on the surface. It didn't last. We ate chips, and we sang along to Brooks and Dunn; one of the guards came back to check us, and I put on my nightgown with the clouds, and Dillon smoked and clapped when I modeled it for him. Then I sat cross-legged on the bed and read all of "The Highwayman" to him, looking up and repeating the parts I knew by heart. He applauded at the end of that too. "My wife the poet," he said. "That ain't nearly as good as 'Every Bride,' Arley."

"It is so. It's totally better. He's famous."

"Arley, listen. You write like an adult. No joke. I know about these things, Arley. I'm a big reader, from way, way before us. And you really write. You should go to college someday and be a famous poet."

"So should you."

"It looks like I'm going to the school of hard knocks, girl."

"Not forever, though."

"No, baby, maybe not forever." He looked so sad then, I got up and sat on his lap. He pulled off my nightgown and unbuttoned his shirt, and we sat with our chests pressed together, his nipples standing up rosy just like mine, his breastbone as hairless and soft as a girl's, though packed tight with his muscles. His skin was fair, almost golden, and mine's dark. We looked like complementary fabrics, pretty. You were supposed to like men with hair all over their chests, but I liked Dillon's smoothness. Eric has a furry chest—not that I've ever seen him really undressed. You can see a curl of his hair over the neck of his T-shirt, though, and feel the crackle of hair against a dress shirt when you press against him. It's not that I think it's unattractive. But when I look at men in magazines, it's always the smooth ones that catch my eye and make me wonder how their skin would feel on mine. Even months later, when it was torment to think about that night, I could still blush remembering what I did then. And I could still get wild on it, so wild that, though such thoughts shouldn't even have possessed me, given the shape I was in, I would have to roll on my own hand in the dark, and I'd end up crying.

I raised up now like I was on the vaulting horse, and reached with my hand and put Dillon inside me, and I felt him grow and fill me until it was really frightening. By then, between my legs felt like I'd been peeled. But after a moment, the pain gave way to that purring sting. You knew you had to get rid of it or die. Every few minutes, Dillon would start to move faster, and the sting would fade away, and I all but got mad at him. "Wait!" I told him. "Stay just how you are for a minute, okay?" And I balanced myself on my long, strong, track-cured legs and rode him until I wouldn't have cared if the guard came in and poured himself a Coke right then. I wouldn't have stopped. "Get the condom," I told Dillon, panting. "Get it."

"Arley, we already done it twice. I don't have enough spit in me left to make a baby chicken, much less a real baby."

"Get it anyhow," I told him. "Annie said for us to use them."

"Annie." He spit it out, disgusted, stopping altogether. "Annie ain't your husband."

"Come on, Dillon," I said, wanting the stinging to begin again. "Come on." But instead, he took me by the hips and pumped me slowly, his green eyes looking light-to-light into mine, his lips a firm line, almost angry. He'd draw away from me so long, I thought he would never move into me again, and then he'd ease back in, staying a long time, pulling away again. I

241

should have stopped him. But pretty soon, there was no me left to stop him. That spreading hot sting was the center of the world; it was all that was, and all that mattered, and fucking was all I ever wanted to do, then or ever again. It drew all my reason down into it, and splashed that reason over until it drowned, and I was holding my breath and biting on Dillon's lower lip and pounding on Dillon's shoulders, crying, "Please, please, please, please," until I fell forward, fighting for air, feeling my insides jumping and dancing all on their own, my hair falling across his back and mine like a tent, big enough to hide us both.

It was horrible that we had to wake up in the morning. I wanted it to be the night before. I wanted to brush my teeth. Dillon looked terrible, like an old man, in that faded-out wrinkly T-shirt we found under the couch. His eyes were hollows of madness, like it says in "The Highwayman." "You're going to leave me," he kept saying.

"I never will," I kept saying back, as the sun rose up, making the inside of that little trailer, so golden and homey the night before, look dirty and tired. When I finally put my skirt back on, didn't blood gush again and seep all over the back of it. Then Warden Southwynn knocked to bring me out, and I was crying and wouldn't come. A guard came, and when I heard them put the leg irons around Dillon's feet, I started to cry even harder, so I could hardly kiss him good-bye, and finally the warden went and got Annie. She brought a blanket from the car, so when I had to walk between the buildings again, past those prisoners watching me with swivel eyes, that blanket was wrapped around me, hiding me down to the tops of my shoes. Annie walked right beside me, feeling to me bigger than Dillon, bigger than the guard, bigger even than the prison, walking me right out the door, out the gate, and into the backseat of her car, where I lay down and fell asleep and slept curled up all the way home, just sometimes waking to make sure I could see the back of Annie's head and to wonder, in a haze, why I could feel my heart beating in the bottom of my stomach.

A Sound of Bells

I'll always remember our first night
together, you so flushed and shy,
me knowing what I know but
scared too because you are the first one

I loved. We poured our loneliness
into each other and filled the emptiness
and dark corners of this place with joy.
Seeing you naked made me feel so tender.

I think of your long straight back,
your strong legs, see your hair on the pillow,
your dark eyes close, and say your name
over and over. Arlington. It is the sound of bells.

Dillon Thomas LeGrande

The Terrain of Love

I thought love would be something so large
and bright I could not contain it, like an armful
of exploding firecrackers. I see now

that the terrain of love is small scale. There
are the fine golden hairs on the backs
of your hands, your voice as it thickens

when you say my name, your thumb
on the pulse in my throat, the day we first
stood together, not touching, just knowing.

Arlington Mowbray LeGrande

CHAPTER THIRTEEN

Annie

I loved the terrier quality Stuart had. He thought he was such a tough guy.

I think it was the reason he was a death row lawyer.

After all, death is the biggest adversary. It's bigger than the cruel blank corporation. Bigger than racism, even bigger than malpractice. Death's the biggest bully of all, and it gives a five-foot-nine guy from Hoboken a definite swagger potential, being the one who beats death back. But for Stuart, there was even more to it. He could make cutting remarks about the mothers-of-many who were my clients at Women and Children First—telling me that the quid pro quo for legal services should be getting spayed—but could always find compassion for the most heinous criminal on death row. No one got there by choice, Stuart said. No one chose to be evil. The Talley kid's father died in Vietnam, and his mother's crack dealer boyfriend beat her senseless in front of him. Kim McGrory was five when his grandma locked him in the barn and had a stroke the same night. It took four days for the police to find the child.

"See?" Stuart would ask people, "See what I mean?" He could understand voters supporting the death penalty in the abstract—

but specifically? Up close? How could you? The pity and pain and rage were just too great. He didn't even see it as a liberal-conservative split. It was humans against the inhumane. Stuart played sports with more intensity than skill, followed the major leagues with the reverence of a boy who got his first pair of thick glasses in fourth grade. But his job was really Stuart's World Cup, his U.S. Open, and his Final Four.

On Valentine's Day night, which would be the last of our best times together, Stuart was retelling the stirring tale of Trevor Bentley, who helped himself to the same dozen kids' lunches every day for three years, until one day Stuart decided that it had to end.

He was up to the climax of the story, the part in which Stuart faced the bully—who had grown, over the years, to the size of Mean Joe Green—at the New Jersey version of the O.K. Corral. As he described the epic battle, I played my customary part, which involved teasing him to the brink of anger.

"It's probably me, Stuart, but I can never quite picture a gangster named Trevor," I chimed in, meanwhile taking advantage of Stuart's rapture to rob him of choice morsels from his plate of mu-shu beef.

"Anne," Stuart said, "you weren't there." I remember him tossing his chopsticks, both of them, into the air and catching them stylishly with one hand, then grinning in triumph. We each had our own chopsticks, and Stuart groused if I used his, which, he said, were perfectly weighted for the toss. He actually practiced doing this. It was juggling as a form of punctuation. "And his twin was even uglier and meaner. His twin ate raw sheep."

"What was his twin's name? Grace?"

"It was . . . Tristram," Stuart told me, very softly.

"Ahhhhh."

"Anne, for your information, Tristram was a knight of the Round Table . . ."

"So was Percival . . ."

"It was actually Tristram who finally beat the shit out of me . . ."

"Stuart, you never told me that part . . ."

The phone rang.

I told him not to answer it. I was sure it would be some urgent errand that would separate us: exculpatory evidence found, a stay reversed. It was a lot worse. When Stuart came back out to the terrace, he looked as though he'd lost ten pounds.

"What happened?" I asked. "Who died?"

"The Texas Defense Center," he told me softly.

The call had come from Stuart's boss, Mike Akers, a death row veteran with a flair for good publicity who'd managed to talk a Texas media gazillionaire with a tender liberal conscience into funding the center for the past five years.

Now the mogul was dead. And tonight, before the grass had even started to grow on his grave, his wife had simply snapped the string. She was a Broadway star; her charity was AIDS. The center could last until the end of the year, at most. Probably not that long.

I sat on Stuart's lap, and he combed my hair with his fingers.

We'd always known this day could come. Post-conviction lawyers in capital cases lived out of the career equivalent of wheeled suitcases. They always had to be ready to roll. Lots of them shuttled among the big death row states—the current favorite now was Florida, where, one of Stuart's former colleagues told him, there was "a kinder, gentler police state." The old joke was that if it weren't for weather, no one would do death row advocacy at all.

That night, I didn't know what to say to Stuart. Wild possibilities chased each other through my head: We could . . . start a private practice. Stuart could join the public defender's office. He could become the classy criminal-defense litigator some large firms carried for showy pro bono work. The likeliest possibility was the one I liked thinking about least—that we would have to move. That I would have to sell the house.

If we stayed together.

When Stuart suggested we wander over to what he now devoutly called "your neighborhood" and visit the clinic, I agreed, with a certain relief. Some knots just won't undo themselves without tequila. In the car, we did something we hadn't done for years. We held hands, and after a while, Stuart pulled me across so he could put his arm around my shoulders as he drove.

Amor Ausente was crowded with *turistas* fleeing the North for some pre-spring relief, and the tables were filled with couples. Valentine's Day. Stuart's news had made me forget—not that we actually observed greeting-card holidays. Since Charley had told me the backstory of the place, I kept an eye out for the melancholy owner, and sure enough, he was stationed at a window, ignoring the clink of glass and the laughter behind him, gazing mournfully out at Kings Highway as if he expected to see a damsel on a big wild horse appear over the crest of a hill. Luis found us an outdoor umbrella table and brought us margaritas, and we amused ourselves trying to make up stories about the other diners. We were good at this.

"Now, they," Stuart told me, sotto voce, inclining his head at a well-clad fiftyish couple engaged in intense though quiet verbal warfare, "they're illicit lovers, though they haven't, shall we say, done the do-si-do in about . . . six months. He's married. His wife's in a wheelchair—"

"Stuart!"

"Well, she is, and Female B, who will hereinafter be referred to as the Other Woman, has just found out that Couple A has bought a house on Cape Cod and they're going there tomorrow to spend the Presidents' Day week with their grandchildren. . . ."

"And isn't this just going to be one more thing to be decided in the property settlement? And how can he stand to be away from her for so long?"

"And why doesn't she understand that it's all part of the plan, honey. The wife is going to love the house back East so much, she'll want to stay there, and that will mean they'll have so much more time together—"

"Time together? They were supposed to be married by now! Like, five years ago!"

"Don't start on that now! You know what I'm dealing with! She wants to ruin me, and you want to ruin me too. I'll be dead before I'm sixty. . . ."

"Okay, okay," I said. "Enough of that." But even a little of the game had warmed both of us to the core. We played the couples game for a reason, because most of the people we saw just didn't look as happy . . . as *present* . . . as Stuart and I knew we still looked together, even after ten years—and maybe they never had. We laughed more. We just laughed more.

"Let's take a walk," Stuart suggested after we polished off our meal and the tables began to fill up. "They're as thick as mayflies in here tonight." He motioned for the check.

"Everybody's with their sweethearts."

"Yep. Guys who probably haven't taken their wives to dinner since this same night last year . . ."

"If you don't take her out on Valentine's Day, you'll hear about it the rest of the year . . ."

"Did I take you out last year?"

We both laughed. "I don't remember!"

A couple rushed past us, the man hurriedly shaking out his key ring. "Now they can barely wait to get started," Stuart said. "His place or hers . . . whichever's closer . . ."

"No," I said, looking after them. "They're parents. They have to get home for the sitter . . ."

"What a drag. Just imagine having to be home by a certain time," he said.

"I wasn't thinking of it that way," I told him then, realizing suddenly it was true.

"What do you mean?" He was genuinely puzzled.

"It's just . . . you always think of things from the point of view of your being the kid, not the adult."

"Annie, you're nuts."

"No, you do. You identify more with the kid."

"And you don't?"

"No. I could see . . . you know, getting a sitter once in a while. I've had twenty years of going out for dinner and drinks, you know?"

"So you picture yourself sitting home rocking the cradle. Correcting Junior's math papers. . . ."

"Sort of. Sometimes."

"Anne, you'd be bored stupid inside two weeks."

"Not really."

"You'd be calling up Patty and offering to do a termination hearing . . ."

"No, I wouldn't . . ."

"You'd be watching Court TV and talking to the screen . . ."

"Cut it out!"

"Well, Anne. I think you tend to romanticize things."

"Honey, I think you do, too," I said, thinking of the tears in his eyes on the night of the broken glass, the night he learned that Kim McGrory was near death. "They're just different things."

Stuart smiled wearily. "You could be right." We stood on the street outside Amor Ausente for a moment, listening to the restaurant's fountain. A fluted brass column about eight feet high shot water down into a series of shell-shaped bowls that got larger and thicker toward the bottom. In landing, the water made a series of little tones, like music.

"Charley built that," I told Stuart.

"Charley the carpenter?" he asked. "I thought he was basically a paint-and-paper kind of guy."

"No, he's a landscaper and a landlord and a . . ."

"And a land rover . . ."

"I want to make a wish, Stuart," I told him, "but I only have a penny. I want to make a dime wish, though."

He reached into his pocket and gave me a shiny dime, and I held it high and dropped it into the bottom-most bowl. I stood there, screwing my eyes shut tight, clenching my fists.

"What's the matter?" Stuart asked.

"I'm wishing," I said.

"Looks painful."

"I'm almost there," I said, and I wished hard. I wished for . . . family happiness. I figured that covered everything. When I opened my eyes, Stuart was shaking his head and grinning. "You're one crazy chick," he said. "Let's go see if Mother Bates is sitting up in the front parlor at your house."

A light was, in fact, burning in one window at 4040 Azalea Road. Charley was gone, but now he left a light on every night at my request. I wanted my house to take on the look of being lived

in as soon as possible. In the dimness, the house did its best
boasting. It looked magnificent, and from my window a tongue
of lace curtain billowed in the breeze like a beckoning. We're a
pair, I thought then, my house and me. I'd reached the age when
low light was going to be my best friend as well. Stuart and I
leaned on the fence, and I told him all about the progress of the
renovation: in a few weeks, once the plumbing and electricity inside were at least at the level of a primitive Scout camp, Charley
would start planting for summer. He would "liberate" native
species from all his gardens and step-gardens. That last sweet explanation had been a symphony to my ears—finally, something
that wasn't going to cost me a little more.

"Ah, Stuart," I told him, gesturing up at the portico. "This is
my dowry, not to mention my retirement condo and everything
else I ever hoped to buy or own. My little piece of the rock."

"Annie," he said then, "I have a present for you." He took out
a flat, round package, shaped like a mirrored compact. It had an
acrylic resin dome with the slender image of a skeleton Madonna
in the center. Dressed in rags made of Spanish moss, the fragile
skeleton was ringed by a wreath of chiles pequins sculpted into
the shape of flowers.

"Oh, Stuart," I breathed, in frank amazement.

"It's really sick, Annie," he told me cheerfully. "You should
love it."

"I do, I do, and I can't believe you gave it to me. . . ."

"Huh? I'm a sentimental guy, baby."

"I mean, I know you don't like it. Stuart, you don't tend to
give people things you . . . don't think are good for them."

"Well," he replied, after a long beat, "then you should probably have this too."

It wasn't a diamond. It was a pearl, set in the hollow of two arabesques of gold, like wings.

"It's an engagement ring, Annie," Stuart said. "It's Valentine's Day. Don't think I forgot. It's the day you get engaged. It's not like any other engagement ring, because you're not like any other woman. I want us to be engaged. But it won't be an engagement like any other, because we already live, as they say, under common law, as husband and wife. But I'd also like it to be as short an engagement as possible. Like, until the weekend."

"It's gorgeous. It's wonderful," I told him, meaning it, holding my hand up under the streetlamp to watch the moon-colored light slip and slide on the surface of the pearl. "Is it a real pearl?"

"Oh Jesus, Anne."

"I didn't mean it that way. I meant, you know . . ."

"Actually, yes, it is real. And it's from Texas. Right from here."

"I love it. And I love you for it. But, Stuart, is this really the time for this? We didn't count on the job change and everything, and this leaky old joint. . . ."

"Well, Anne . . ." Stuart put his hands in his chino pockets and inclined his head to take in the blue-jean sky, the witchly stoop of the pecan tree over my porch. "This here's Texas. And I guess this here's our house too." I had my arms around his neck before I had a chance to reflect. "I can always get some kind of county job here. And if that doesn't work out, we'll just peddle the place. . . ." My heart bumped, once, hard. "Or I'll do private practice. There's lots of options."

"But you don't want other options, Stuart. You want what you want."

He bit his lower lip. "I . . . do. But, well, I love you too, Anne."

"And as far as marriage, what about . . ."

"I've researched this, don't worry. Basically, it's a simple act. I say I do. Then, if you're not up to it, I say that you do too."

"I do," I said into his neck. He was so sweet. He smelled, anachronistically, of Lilac Vegetal, as familiar a smell to me as Rachie's Opium, which breathed from every closet in her house. "I really do."

"You mean what about a baby, though, don't you?" he said.

"Well, I haven't changed my mind. I mean, honey, I haven't made up my mind. I might want a child. I might very well want a child."

"And so?"

"Stuart?"

"So we'll have a kid."

"Are you serious, Stuart?"

"Annie, look. I'm not kidding, if that's what you think. I don't think I'm really father material. I don't know if I want to have a child, and I don't know if I can do it. But I'm also not going to count on the fact that once we're married, my excessive physical charms and intellectual probity will dissuade you from sharing your life with anybody but me. Though that's probably what I want."

"This doesn't sound very hopeful, Stuart."

"Well, you didn't let me finish. But then, you never let me finish."

"I'm sorry."

"What I was going to say is, I'm not sure I'm up to it, but if I'm ever going to be up to it, I'm going to be up to it now, with you."

"Stuart . . ."

"Because I want to be your husband more than I don't want to be a father. And it isn't like I don't want to be a father. I'm sure I would make very cute offspring."

"I'm not so sure," I dithered. "I mean, we've taken chances and nothing has happened. . . ."

"Baby, you ain't taken the kind of chances I intend to take with you."

"Seriously, Stuart."

"Seriously, Anne. The body has a head, you know? *We* haven't really tried to make a child. I think maybe you have to want to. . . ."

"Sure, Stuart. Like all those people in Rwanda or Biafra . . ."

"Well, I don't know. Jeez, Anne, don't put me in the position of reassuring you on something I don't want—"

"You didn't say you didn't want it. You said you weren't sure you wanted it."

"And you aren't sure *you* want it. So we're in the same boat."

I knew we weren't. Not really.

"You got a key to this thing?" Stuart asked me, using the sleeve of his shirt to polish the brass "4040" worked into the iron gate of the house.

"I do," I said, and Stuart carried me over the threshold.

"My God," he said, looking around after setting me on my feet. "Where's Morticia? Where's Lurch?"

"It's a lot better than the last time you saw it, Stuart."

"Well, the bats are outside for the night at least, I guess."

I sighed. There *were* bats, but if I told Stuart this, it would really spoil the mood, which was taking on that soft-focus quality that preceded lovemaking. Each time we'd touch—bumping hips or grazing arms as we negotiated the hallway—there was a growing awareness, a physical intention.

"Now come on. You look at this," I told Stuart, leading him into the library, where Charley had smoothed a dropcloth under the ceiling of stars and planets. He'd begun restoring the gilt; I reached up and showed Stuart where the constellations, faithfully rendered, began at the edge of the domed ceiling.

"Anne," he said after a while, fighting laughter. "You're glowing in the dark."

In the tiny bathroom mirror, I saw what he meant. My hair and even my eyelashes were dusted with a sifting of gold leaf. "I guess he hasn't got it exactly . . . fixed, yet, or something," I said.

"I think it's pretty. I think you should keep it this way. It goes with the house." He kissed the back of my neck, and slid his hands up under my sweater, neatly unhooking my bra with a practiced flick. He worked my breasts with both hands, increasing pressure from his thighs behind me as I leaned against the sink, pulling my sweater away and nuzzling and sucking on my neck and shoulders, nearly to the point that it nettled, pleasurably. I leaned back against him, feeling for a point of pressure, of contact.

"I want us to be naked, Stuart," I said. "Let's go to bed."

"You don't have a bed, Anne."

"Then here. Now."

I unzipped my jeans and let them drop and listened as Stuart, behind me, rustled out of his own clothes. He reached around to open me, but I pushed his hand away. "I'm ready," I said. "I'm all ready."

As he made love to me, I watched my own face in the mirror, watched my lips part and grow plump with the sexual rush, the gold in my hair and on my chin catching the intermittent gusts of street light that entered the room—first hidden, then revealed by wind swaying a branch on the pecan tree. Stuart's head and face were lost behind me in the shadows. In the bronze gloom of that mirror, I could have been a ghost myself, with my ghostly lover. The pulse of Stuart inside me became deeper, more rhythmic. . . . I thought of trying to wait, to tease myself and make it better, but I was already too far gone, and I crumpled against him gratefully, holding my breath, reaching down between us as if to seal us together. Then, as I finished, Stuart gripped my arms with both hands, and then pulled back abruptly, coming, awkwardly, hot against my cool bare backbone.

"What?" I asked. "What's happened? What's wrong?"

"I'm sorry. Force of habit," he told me, breathing in gasps. "Remembered we didn't have any birth control . . ."

"Oh Stuart," I cried, suddenly furious. "We just agreed we were getting married, what do a few months matter . . . ?" Unceremoniously, I stepped around him and left him, pants down, in the dark bathroom.

"Wait, baby." He followed me into the library, and curled up next to me where I'd thrown myself down on Charley's painter's cloth. I noticed a similar cloth, draped over the old Victrola in the corner. I thought of that night at Christmas, of our dance. "We didn't agree to have kids right now, Annie. Tonight." Stuart sounded peevish to me, tiresome.

"Well, I probably wouldn't have got pregnant anyhow. I'm probably sterile."

"Well, then we won't have one. Or we'll adopt."

"At a time like this, Stuart, having just practiced college-boy sex on me, you're supposed to reassure me, not think logically."

"Okay," he said. "Well, then I'll tell you something really sappy. I'm sorry." I was silent. "Okay?" he persisted. "Should I say the three most beautiful words in the English language?"

I started to smile against my will.

"I was wrong."

"Okay, okay." I nodded. "It's not that big a deal."

"You know, when I was buying that ring," Stuart said, "I was thinking, you know, what if I'm already too late?"

"Too late?"

"Like, what if she doesn't say yes?"

"Stuart, come on . . ."

"No, Anne, it's not, that's the thing. I never thought it was a given. I'm lucky, Annie. I'm a lucky guy is all."

"You're not the only one."

"What?" Stuart sat up, spiking his hair with one hand. "And all this time, I thought I was the only one! Isn't that what all this means to you?"

"Stuart," I said, "you can be such a doof. Cut it out."

"Well, I'm not all that good at this stuff. It's not something I've practiced. I just . . . wanted you . . . to know. Now can we plan the wedding?"

"I'm the girl. Aren't I supposed to say that?"

Throughout that long and good night, we talked and dozed. We agreed on a wedding in April—Stuart wanted his anniversary to be in the cruelest month. I thought I might have enough money by then to buy a fancy suit, at least at a vintage store. Charley could get the yard cleaned up so that we could have an outdoor tent here. And by then the house itself would probably be more or less habitable— or so I thought, though it did not turn out to be in anything near move-in condition until the end of the summer. Sometime during that night, we woke up and made love again (a not-so-common phenomenon after ten years, but then, neither was an engagement).

"Stuart," I asked him when we finished. "Are you scared? About this marriage? And about me? I mean, you're the one who says all life is timing. What if we passed our moment and we didn't know?"

"Then we'll get divorced, Anne. We're both lawyers, and neither of us has any property"—I glanced up at the moldering ceiling, and Stuart followed my eyes—"of course, besides Castle Dracula here, and honey, I'll stipulate to that exclusion, for real, so it would be easy. Our parents would be happier, because it would be more respectable to get married so we could actually get a divorce like decent people instead of just—"

"I'm not kidding."

"Okay."

"It's a big chance. The way we've lived—it's just so . . . like we were still college kids. . . ."

"And was that a bad thing, Anne?"

"It'll be a big change is all." I sighed. "Well, fortune favors the brave."

"Who said that?"

"Shakespeare."

Why did I want to cry? It wasn't like we didn't goof this way all the time. But now, this night, this night of our afterthought engagement.

Stuart was quiet for a beat. And then he said, "Annie, I'm lying here with you, in this ruin, agreeing to become a husband and maybe a father, even given my bad demographics and my advanced age, so I must be pretty brave."

"You make me sound like Omaha Beach, Stuart."

"Never change, babe." He sighed and wrapped himself in a clean corner of the dropcloth to go back to sleep. I got myself dressed and went back to sleep too.

The following morning, Charley found us there. As he shared his breakfast of tortillas and coffee with us, Stuart kept nudging me. "Aren't you going to tell him?" he asked.

"Tell him what? That we stayed over?"

Stuart motioned toward my ring, and I all but jumped, recalling with a shock what the pearl on my ring finger meant. "Look," I told Charley then. "We're engaged."

"That's a beautiful piece," Charley said, his hand lifting my fingers, gently, for an instant, as if he were a knight about to kiss my hand.

"You mean Annie or the ring?" Stuart laughed. Charley smiled thinly, with just a hint of a head shake. Stuart didn't notice, but I did.

"Congratulations, y'all," he said then. "They say pearls bring tears, but this one's going to bring happiness, I guess." I knew that I didn't mistake a certain heaviness in his voice, though. And I felt odd myself. It took me a couple of days, but I finally figured out that what I was feeling in front of Charley was embarrassment. As though I'd done something behind his back, somehow, or the little pearl on my hand had somehow ruined our great collaboration on the house in a way I couldn't really name. It was stupid; Stuart and I had always been together. But I deliberately kept away from the house for the next few weeks, though I found myself driving by sometimes, at night, to see if Charley's truck was parked at the curb.

And then, one night early in March, our apartment buzzer rang, and a small voice I no longer recognized on first hearing asked for Anne Singer. When I opened our door, there was Arley, carrying her soft green raincoat and a striped bag with a Tasmanian devil screened on it. "Hello," Arley told me. "I was wondering if I might get some phone numbers from you."

"Phone numbers of . . . ?"

"Of places, I guess. Places I can go. I'm pregnant, Annie, and my sister Langtry is moving back in to help Mama. . . ."

"To help Mama? What's that got to do with your being pregnant, Arley?"

"Well, 'cause my mama threw me out."

CHAPTER FOURTEEN

Arley

To tell the truth, although he's a good person, Stuart hated me being there. Not just because I was such a kid back then—though having a teenager around couldn't have been too much fun for a guy as tired and nervous as Stuart was all the time. What really drove him nuts was how Annie and I were. I think he was jealous.

Around me, Annie sort of acted like a big girlfriend. When I showed up at her house, I expected her to say something like, "Well, we better talk with Dillon and your mom about this . . ." the way most adults would, so that you'd think they all signed some promise never to give in to you too easy. She didn't, though. She just made me some food and started hanging my stuff in the coat closet. And later, when I heard her on the phone with Mama, Annie was saying, "You're all heart, Rita. You're all heart. . . . You sure *don't* deserve this. . . . Actually, to hell with you. Yeah, well, I'd do a better job of it. . . ." It upset me so much, I just turned over on the sofa, where I was going to sleep that first night, and put the pillow over my ears.

I was glad she said it, though. Mama deserved every word.

I always knew Mama was selfish, but I did not think that her first reaction to my being pregnant would be to say right out that I wouldn't be much use to her very long, and a baby would be no use to her at all. She told me right then that Lang had been wanting to move back in anyhow, and that she'd take care of Cam and other stuff for Mama. She gave me until the following Friday. Said she considered that generous, considering what I'd done. No shit. No fooling. Since that time, for sure, I've learned some things about psychology, so I know that this is probably what happened to her. When her own mother found out that Mama was pregnant, she probably just showed her the door. I loved my grandma Amelia, but I don't think she would have put up with a pregnant girl, especially since Mama wasn't married. In Grandma's day, there was the scandal involved, I guess. But also, Grandma didn't much like taking care of her own stuff. She always needed somebody around, Mama or Lang or somebody. Plus, I remember the story she told once, of when Mama's little sister got her high school diploma, how Debbie Lynn thought she was really smart until she woke up next day and found all her suitcases packed and on the front porch. "She had her a degree and it was time she used it," Grandma said.

I didn't know anything back then, though, about why people did things. And even if I had, it wouldn't have made it any easier hearing my mama just tell me to get on out of the house I'd lived in all my life. It wasn't like she was angry about it. She didn't act mad. She just said I was grown up enough to have a child, so I was grown up enough to go my own way. I asked her where I was going to go. She said she didn't know, but she reckoned I was smart enough to figure something out. She did suggest I call Elena's parents, though—as if I would have told them, when I hadn't even but taken the stick test that afternoon.

I hadn't even told Dillon yet.

I don't know what I'd have done without Annie. The way Annie acted was as if I gave her this big present by showing up on her doorstep like a cat in the rain. What else could I have done? Gone to a shelter or something? I didn't want to take that risk for the baby. Even though the baby wasn't but a speck yet, she was real to me.

In fact, though Annie kept saying "it" would be "pretty easy at this stage," I didn't even realize at first that "it" meant having an abortion. As soon as I did figure it out, I told Annie right away I was keeping this baby. I give her credit; she just took it in her stride. She's had a lot of experience with unwed mothers—which I wasn't, of course. But I was as good as.

Stuart was under a lot of stress then. His job was going to end. He was probably worried about what was going to happen with him and Annie, even though they'd just got engaged. So the big attitude toward me was likely enough a case of getting mad about one thing but acting mad about something else. How he acted was like he was jealous of Annie and me.

And she did make a fuss.

Right from the first, she changed my doctor and insisted I go to hers. She took off work to go get me signed up for Medicaid, and she brought the papers to the hospital for Mama to sign to make me an emancipated minor. Annie explained that it would protect me from Mama ever getting her hands on my property, in case I ever got any. Annie got me a whole bunch more new clothes, because almost right away, I couldn't zip my jeans. And when I started bleeding in my third month, she wouldn't let me get up even to cook my own dinner—though, afterward, I cooked everybody's and I did the laundry, except Stuart's because he didn't like how I ironed. While I was having spotting, Annie would leave me these little lunches, with fruit ("Raw food, Arley, you have to have raw food six times a day") and sandwiches, right by the bed for the whole two weeks, until the doctor said I could get up. She got a universal remote so I could run the stereo and the TV at the same time.

When I quit bleeding, I could have gone back to school. But not to my school. I was supposed to go to a special program school, for at-risk kids, but I refused. We went there for one hour, and it was all these really bad kids with supreme BTH and straight razors, and I was afraid they'd hurt the baby. So Annie arranged for me to get a tutor. The tutor didn't show up, though. (Texas is really not that great on education.)

Annie got exasperated then and said she should sue Travis High, the Alamo Heights School District, the school board, and the whole fucking state of Texas. I didn't want her to, though. I didn't want to call that much attention to myself. Then Annie decided to "home school" me, which basically meant I would school myself, because Annie was mostly always at work. I thought this was going to do the trick. Mrs. Murray sent me assignments every day on the fax machine at Women and Children First, and she even came over to see me a bunch of times. Mr. Hogan sent my math, too, at first. But then he seemed to lose interest in me—maybe because he used to be a DEA agent and here I was, more or less expelled for being married to a convict.

The more they ignored me, the madder Annie got. She started having huge ambitions for me. I was going to keep up with my work and take the GED and pass it . . . this year! I was going to tell the school board to go fuck themselves. She bought this used laptop for me from Stuart's friend Tarik and she got me hooked up to the Internet. She got somebody to give her a copy of the "goals and expectations" for twelfth graders in Texas, and she more or less showed it to me and said, Here, you can do all that, can't you? I didn't want to say a word to her, because I knew she really believed in me, but I was scared to death. When I saw stuff like "basic principles of geometry" and "major events in U.S. history," I panicked, because that stuff wasn't 'til junior year! One day, Annie had this psychologist come and IQ test me, and I got 129, which Annie said was almost a genius. She said if the public education system here wasn't so bad, I'd already be a genius, which made her mad. The next day, she suggested maybe I should take it over again, but I said no, thanks, almost a genius was good enough. I was already getting hives on my arms from worrying about the test, the baby, Dillon, and everything else.

At first, Annie was going to borrow all the lesson plans from public school and teach me the same way I would have learned at Travis. But she got bored of that right away. What she ended up doing was getting me a whole bunch of books each week from the public library—books about the invention of time and about the Civil War and about the tsars in Russia. If I didn't understand the books, or they were too hard, she would go get me a novel about the same thing. Like, she got me the novel *Andersonville* about the Civil War, which I really related to, because it was about prison and a teenager in love and the importance of lots of fresh water. Annie didn't care that I didn't know all the names of the battles or anything; in fact, she would say, "Just read those things, because you won't realize how much you got out of some of them until you're grown up."

The worst part for me was geography. I still think that Switzerland ought to be in Scandinavia instead of Europe, and if it wasn't for all those maps I got on-line, I'd still think it was. I started looking up stuff on the Net about twenty times a day, and then talking to other kids, some really far away, like in Illinois. That was so much fun it took off some of the stress.

So did our dance breaks.

Annie was this killer dancer; she could even do this mechanical-person stuff like Madonna, and she taught me how to do the jitterbug, which is what kids her age used to do along with regular dancing. A couple of times a week, we'd end up putting all these CDs on the twenty-five-CD changer of Stuart's—everything, from the old Michael Jackson and Aretha stuff Annie had to Reba and Coolio—and we'd dance around the little L from the kitchen into the living room, laughing so hard that the first time I got morning sickness (and I didn't even get it until my fourth month, and then it was at night; Annie called it "evening sickness"), I thought I'd made myself puke from all that laughing and jiggling. You wouldn't think you could have so much fun with an adult, though I've always sort of liked adults.

Sometimes Stuart would come in and smile at us. But mostly, he'd come in and say, "A little less volume, please? I have to make a few phone calls here about a man's life . . . ?" We'd start laughing even more then, not at Stuart, but at how bad we were. I felt pretty guilty about it, but not enough to stop laughing.

Not that Stuart was ever there that much. You'd have thought that if your office was closing, you'd figure you could take it easy a little, but of course, it wasn't like that for Stuart and Tarik and those guys. They had to do even more than they did before, because every brief or whatever they filed and every hearing they got before every judge meant one more guy on death row in Huntsville might get another chance. At first, in what became my room, Stuart's papers were laid out all over the place. It used to be Stuart and Annie's study. What Stuart finally did was scoop them all up and load them in copy-paper boxes and take them to his office. "Don't worry about it," Annie said.

But it didn't take a genius to notice how disruptive I was to the way they had their apartment, just from nothing but sitting there. I'd be lying in my room at night, reading or writing letters to Dillon, or poetry, or talking on the phone to Elena. All of a sudden, I'd hear Stuart getting mad. He didn't yell or anything, but he'd start saying, "Anne! Anne! Come on, Anne!"—like hitting a wall over and over with your open palm. It would make me jump, especially knowing that some of it was about me. I would hear them talking about moving, about selling Annie's totally beautiful house on Azalea Road. "But I couldn't *give* it away right now, Stuart," I heard Annie say one night, in a little voice that made me want to bite Stuart for making her sound that way. "It's *worse* than it was when I bought it." Stuart said something cranky, and Annie went on, "It isn't Charley's fault at all, Stuart. He's only one guy, and for what I pay him, he's probably losing money every day he works there."

My phone calls, especially those from Dillon, which were collect, also drove Stuart nuts. Dillon got mad one time when he overheard Stuart say, "Excuse me, Arlington, but that is a collect call, and you've been on there seventeen minutes."

"He got him a stopwatch?" Dillon asked.

"Shush," I told him, but Stuart thought I was talking to him, and he sort of stomped off.

Annie came by in a minute.

"Don't worry," she whispered. "You can't stay on too long, but don't worry about Stuart. He doesn't like guys in prison unless they're serial killers on death row."

I got off then, but I was sad, because Dillon and I had a lot to talk about. First, we talked about how the hell it had happened, after Dillon had assured me he was all drained out. "Must have been one super-sperm left," Dillon told me. "We LeGrandes are bulls, they say. Didn't my daddy have three sons?" We talked about other stuff, too. Whether I would get to come to see him more often. What we would name it if it was a boy (Ian, after Dillon's father, whose name was John; Dillon thought "Ian" was Gaelic for "John," and I didn't have the heart to tell him that "Sean" was what he really meant to say). He didn't care what we would name it if it was a girl, except he sort of wanted to call it Kate after his mama. I said nix to that right away: maybe I was already getting crabby, but I didn't want either of our mothers hanging their vibrations on our child. He didn't fight me on it, that or his terrific idea that the baby and I should go live with his mama in exchange for me "helping her out." I could see right off where that would go. Though I never imagined what would happen with Annie and me, I knew I trusted Annie more than I trusted anyone else right then, even Dillon, especially after I was pregnant. It was as if the seed inside me was like a weight that anchored me right down to the ground—if I were ever going to do anything flighty and irresponsible, I wasn't going to do it anymore. Like, I had called right away and made a prenatal appointment; in fact, it was because the nurse called back when I was at work that Mama found out in the first place.

Dillon felt closer to me, he said. Because of that, the first few weeks were sort of like a dream of bliss. Even before I knew I was pregnant, we were both missing each other so badly, it almost felt like a pleasure. Dillon wrote me what is still my favorite poem of his, or maybe anybody's.

What's True

The hardest thing is to say what's true. You
aren't the first or the only, but girl, when I think

of how you came to me, how your long dark hair
fell across my face, your skin rippled under

my hands, water-soft and water-cool, I am washed
clean, like Jesus said, and it seems to me
that if this is all I ever have, it is enough.

It was so sad; I should have noticed then what he was thinking. I certainly knew him well enough. When I look back on the
poem now, it's all there, isn't it? Just like he knew there wasn't going to be more joy ahead for him and he was trying to get used to
the idea that he'd already had the best time of his life.

Why didn't I catch it? Because life was opening up more for
me than it had before? Just as Dillon's must have felt as though it
was shrinking? It was all new. I had Dillon, and living at Annie's
was like being on vacation. Plus, I was excited about the baby.
One time, Dillon even had to tell me to pay him a little attention
on the phone and quit going on so much about the baby, the
baby, the baby. He'd told me that they'd taken him out of the library because he was spending too much time working on other
prisoners' lawsuits for better food and stuff instead of putting the
books away and cleaning up like he was supposed to. He got sent
back to the laundry, but he said he liked that because a couple of
times a week a supply truck would come with new sheets or de-
tergent or other supplies and, while the door was open, he had
what he called "a clear look at unobstructed air and sky, just like a
picture in a frame."

As for me, the more time went by, the more distracted I was by
learning all about the baby. It seemed to be all I could write about
to Dillon in my letters. "Our baby is now one and a half inches
long," I wrote him at the end of my second month, when nobody

but Annie still knew. "It already has a heartbeat, though the doctor says I won't be able to hear it for a few more weeks. I look exactly the same, maybe even thinner! Or maybe my weight's just in different places. Guess I won't be getting stretch marks. Except for on these really big boobs—actually not really big, but about like a normal girl would have, because I didn't have too much there before!" It took a lot for me to write that, but that's how husbands and wives talk to each other. I felt very . . . passionate during the early weeks of being pregnant, before I got sick. My lips were pink and swollen like a magazine model's and my hair got even thicker, and curled a little for the first time in its life. Guys were always looking at me at work. I got asked out ten times (finally! Now, when I totally couldn't!) and all I could think about at night was Dillon touching me. I would wake up sweating and shaking, and I'd know I'd been making love in my dreams. One of those nights when I couldn't sleep, I wrote him a poem called "Wind."

Wind

This love sucks at me
like the Texas wind
that wants my clothes
that unbraids

my hair. It plucks
here and there
with strong fingers
pulls at the cords

of my wrists til
like a harp they

ache and sing.
This love teases

unravels and loosens
til untucked
and love-struck
I open to you.

What I realized later, of course, was that all those "struck"s and "tuck"s sounded like . . . "fuck." And so that probably wasn't an entirely nice thing to do to Dillon, with him all alone there. He didn't react very well to it. In fact, he got kind of ugly. "You showing those big boobs to anyone else, girl?" he asked me, and it purely irritated me.

As if I'd have done that.

And it bugged me, how Dillon would bring everything about me right back around to himself.

Like when Annie started to bring me college catalogues that she had sitting around her office to motivate her other clients to go to school and make something of themselves. They were from everyplace the University of Houston, Louisiana State, Georgia Tech, the University of Virginia. When I asked her to, Connie G. sent me some material about her corrective cosmetics courses, and I thought about that again, too. It would be pretty nice to be able to make a good living that way after the baby was born and Dillon and me were on our own. In one of the course pamphlets, there was even a little part about how some people used the skills you learned to do elaborate makeup for special effects in movies. When I wrote Dillon about that part, he was like, "Go, girl! We'll head out to Hollywood and

I'll get a job as an actor! You can have me as your kept man until I get my big break!"

He could have done it, you know. He had the looks. But why did he just think of him, not us?

Maybe most men are that way, and think of themselves first off, because they're raised by mamas who let them get away with anything, the way my mama did with Cam. Or maybe it's the other way around, and they were raised so cold that they don't think as much of themselves as they should, which makes them greedy, afraid they might miss something in their lives if they don't push ahead of you in line. Not Charley, of course. Charley's so sweet, he's practically better than any girl to talk to. But Charley's not your usual guy.

Then again, Dillon wasn't totally wrong. It was like he could see through me, like he knew things were starting to take hold in my mind that didn't have anything to do with him. I was ashamed of those things, and didn't tell him, but I think he knew anyhow.

The first time it happened was when Annie and Stuart got these special-fare passes to go home to New York for one weekend, to celebrate their being engaged. Annie got all flustered. She didn't want me to stay alone, though I'd spent almost my whole life home alone already. When I finally convinced her I didn't have to go with them (Stuart was pretty relieved, I can tell you that), she insisted I have Paula or Elena stay over. Annie likes Elena but thinks she's wild, which she is, though not in a really bad way. Of course, anybody with good brains would think, hey, who could be a bad influence on a girl already had her first sex experience in a trailer at a prison? But Annie doesn't think like that, bless her heart. Anyhow, she was on the phone with Mrs. Gutierrez, saying things like, Yes, I think she is completely trustworthy, but I don't like to leave her in case of some kind of medical emergency. . . . Yes, I think they'd be better off at your house, but if you will check on them by phone, it's only two nights; and finally, Mrs. G. agreed that Elena could stay with me at Annie and Stuart's.

I started thinking, lying there half asleep, that what was so interesting to me about the phone conversation I overheard was that this was how it would be to have a full-time mother. A mother checking up on you and trying to keep you out of trouble. Here I was, fixing to be a mother myself, and finally having this fed-up-jeez-enough-already-don't-treat-me-like-an-infant feeling that normal kids have all the time, and sort of liking it, and sort of regretting that I was already way past it. And it just hit me for part of a second: maybe I'd be better off if it was just my baby and me. Or just even me. I'm not going to tell you I ever considered giving Desi up for adoption, especially after I laid eyes on her. But it did strike me that the very reason I was getting taken care of by Annie—because of marrying Dillon—also sort of let me be a kid for the first time in my fourteen years of life.

I couldn't wait to see Elena alone. Now that I lived in San Antonio, though we still talked on the phone all the time, I worked days at Taco Haven, because I wasn't in school. And we didn't get together as much at each other's houses. I was pretty shy about my situation, pretty sure Mrs. G. would hate me. Elena was really happy for me about living at Annie's and Annie teaching me at home—she just thought I had got fed up with being Mama's slave and got the hell out. She was kind of like, all right, girl! Though she had asked me about sixty-four questions about Dillon's and my sex, she had no idea about the baby.

I wanted to be alone with her to tell her.

The first big hurdle was getting Annie out the door. Two

times, she asked me to show her where the extra house keys were. She asked me to show her the list of phone numbers. And then she was going to call up and get Jeanine to come over and check on us, when Stuart finally got all impatient and said, "For Christ's sake, Anne. We're going to miss the plane. . . ."

"I want to make sure she's okay. . . ."

"Jesus. The kid's been on her own practically all her life anyhow. You're acting like she was raised at Miss Bennett's Finishing School . . ."

I never heard Annie say one bad word to Stuart until that moment. But she turned to him, right in front of Elena, and she said, "You shut your mouth, Stuart."

Stuart looked down and didn't say a word.

But then he muttered, "Sorry, Arley. I'm sorry." And Annie kissed me and they left.

Elena let out a big whoop. It turned out she had big news for me, too.

When Annie and Stuart were gone, she got right down to it. First, she said, she was going to sleep with Ricky Nevadas. The very next night, right there, in Annie's apartment. We were going to throw a party. Ricky Nevadas was eighteen—it seemed like every girl around Avalon or even San Antonio had to get Ricky out of her system at some point or another—and he was going to get some of his friends to come, and one of them who was twenty-one was going to get a keg of beer. . . . I stopped that talk right there. First of all, it would have been a fine way to thank Annie and Stuart, by having an underage drinking party in their house. Second of all, it was aces up we'd get caught. "Ellie, they are *lawyers*," I told her. Elena didn't know that if you have even one felony conviction, you can never practice law, and that if you get one after that, you could get disbarred. I started telling her off—didn't she even remember that night at Eric Dorey's? What was she thinking? She finally backed off the party idea, but she still thought it was only fair that she could have Ricky over so they could be alone.

I didn't have much ground to stand on there.

"You did it, after all," Elena said.

"I'm married," I answered. "And you don't even love Ricky."

"I love him that way."

"Elena, every girl in South Texas loves him that way. What about you weren't going to give it away until you were sure, and all that? What if you get pregnant?" She still wasn't convinced. Then I asked her what was I supposed to do while they were bouncing away in the bedroom? Watch the TGIF sitcoms? She couldn't think of an answer to that. "It's not fair, though," she pouted. "At this rate, I'm going to be a virgin when I'm a senior."

We were hungry, so we threw out all the chicken liver pâté and hummus and other junk Annie had left for me, and made a big mess of frijoles and rice, with lots of Cholula sauce. Finally, Elena perked up and asked if I could guess her other surprise. I tried a couple of things: Her mama was going to take her to see her relatives in Puerto Rico. No. She was going to get a car next year. No. She was going to go out for freshman attendant on prom court.

"Close," Elena said. "But better. One more guess." She'd brought a couple of those little airline bottles of wine she stole out of her father's workshop, and she offered me some, but I wouldn't take any. I was getting aggravated, so she just burst out with it: Last Saturday, with nobody, not her mother or father or me or anybody knowing, she had gone down to the fairgrounds and tried out for Flower Princess for the Fiesta de San Antonio in June. There were three hundred girls there, some of them already in college. And she was picked! One of only seven girls!

I screamed. I couldn't believe it.

When you grow up here, you think the fiesta princesses are like movie stars or something. They're always in the newspaper or passing out roses in Dalton's the Saturday before Mother's Day or giving trophies to college boys in big football games and stuff. On the first day of the fiesta (which is this superhuge thing, like a giant carnival, for a whole week), each one of the princesses got her own float; each float is a different color, and her dress and the flowers and everything match. I don't know who paid for everything, I guess the town did, though I know Mr. G. pretended to go nutty after he found out that the girl's family had to buy the dress (he was actually very proud; for years afterward, Gracie G. would call the arrangement of Elena's princess pictures on the living room wall the "Shrine of Santa Maria de Vaca"). On the last night of the festival, all the princesses were guests of honor at this big ball; Elena said I could come as one of her sisters.

Elena was going to be the Bougainvillea Princess, the red one. "That was always my favorite one!" I said, and I really did mean it. Of course you'd immediately like something involving your best friend the best, although I had always sort of favored the Primrose Princess, because when I was little, I thought her big yellow skirt looked like Cinderella's.

Elena smiled a tiny secret smile, not at all braggy. "It's so cool," she said. "I still can't believe it."

"When did you find out?"

"Last night! When Annie was on the phone with my mom, we already knew! And I was, like, dying to tell you!"

"What did you have to do to get it?"

"Well, I just had to walk around in different clothes—a dress, and jeans with some cowboy boots . . ."

"How do you know how to do it?"

"You just pick up this pamphlet at the . . . well, all over the place. You can get them at the museum."

This didn't sound like the Elena I knew. "What were you doing at the museum, El? Putting the T-rex together?"

"No."

"What?"

"I was there with Brin Dennison."

"Oh," I said. "She's nice." She really was nice. And really popular. She could sing and dance. Brin'd been Juliet *and* Marian the Librarian in the school shows, and she was only a sophomore. What was Elena doing hanging around with a sophomore? And *that* kind of sophomore? I loved Elena, but she wasn't the drama club kind of person. Then I got another surprise.

"I'm in variety show with her," Elena said. "I . . . tried out. And I got in the Stevie Nicks number and the *West Side Story* number. Brin is in both of those too. So we're together."

"Doing what?"

"Dancing."

"You can dance?"

"Arley, you know I can dance."

"I mean, I know you can dance. I didn't know you could *dance* dance."

"Well, I don't know if I'm so hot at it. But I can move. And you know, I gotta do something other than go to the mall and Taco Haven. By myself. I guess all your studying and being on track and everything rubbed off on me. You were a good influence." Well, I could have said something then—like, what kind of influence had she been on me? Here I was, the pregnant ex–track star. But I couldn't say anything. I just felt so bad.

At least I wasn't just paranoid; it really was what I'd been afraid of. Brin Dennison was her new best friend. I knew Elena wouldn't admit it, but that was purely what she was saying. Brin was closer to her than me now, and it had happened, like, that fast. It was like Mrs. G. said: everything happened in dog years. I swallowed hard so I wouldn't cry.

"When did you start all this?"

She shrugged. "Like, a month ago. Or a little more. After you moved here. Arley, come on. It's no big wup. I just . . . you're always thinking about Dillon, or writing to Dillon, or sending a package to Dillon—"

"He's my husband, Ellie!"

"Well, I don't have a husband! I'm fifteen years old!"

We sat there, quiet. We both looked out the window at the boys playing basketball in the playground.

"You were the one couldn't wait to grow up, so we could get our own apartment and everything," I said bitterly.

"I didn't mean to really fucking go and do it," Ellie snapped.

She drank down a whole glass of her airline wine. Then she started in on her favorite subject of all time: "I don't want to fight, Arley. We're still best friends, okay? Let's not ruin this time we have together. We don't get that much time. Now, I gotta know. Tell me once more exactly how it felt. When he stuck it in the first time, did it hurt right away? All at once?" I was a little grossed out by how fascinated she was. Still I remembered how I had felt the night before my wedding, quizzing Elena about every sexual thing I could think of. I tried to tell her as best I could. She finished the first little bottle of wine and pulled out another one.

"I'm not driving!" she said brightly, and added, "No one's going to know if you have one drink, Miss Goody Pure Married Sex Lady."

I told her then about the baby. She about died.

I never saw a thing sober Elena up so fast. She even called Ricky Nevadas and told him not to come over, that there was an urgent personal situation. Damn, she kept saying. Goddamn, goddamn, goddamn. Arley, damn. Finally, she asked me, "Are you going to get rid of it?"

"Of course not. I'm married."

"You can still get an abortion if you're married."

"I don't know if you can or not," I lied.

"You can."

"Well, even if I can, I don't want to. I want to have this baby. I mean, I guess I always wanted to have a baby. Maybe not this young. But maybe this is how it's meant to be."

"Are you scared?"

"Of what?"

"Of it hurting, for chrissakes."

"Yeah."

"Yeah, and . . . ?"

"I'm more scared of what happens after it's born. Like, what do I do?"

"How to take care of it?"

"No. I have books about that. I mean, what do I do, to live? I don't want to go on the state, and I don't know where I can live, and even with good behavior, it's going to be two years or something before Dillon even comes up for parole."

"You'll figure out something. Annie'll help you."

But there was more to it than that. What I was really, deep down worried about was what kind of mother I could possibly

281

be—because if there was a gene for bad parenthood, I surely must have it, having had one parent who wasn't ever there and one who didn't want to be. I wished I could ask Mama if there'd been a time, even a short time, when she'd rejoiced over the thought of having me, when she couldn't wait to see how I would look or what talents I might have. If I had known then about why Mama went traveling when she was a girl, why we got those names we got, I guess I wouldn't have troubled myself looking for diamonds in a cereal box, for I would have understood that Cam and I and even Langtry were just means to an end. But maybe all babies are. What matters is what the end is.

From the dream I started having again just before Desi was born, the old dream about colored wagons, I assumed I was like all the teen mothers I read about in magazines. I thought having a baby would make me feel important and grown up, that it would transform my life into something more significant. That I was having a baby so that I'd have something to love that couldn't leave me. Like a living teddy bear to dress up and play with.

All that was true, in a way. I didn't ever have anything reliable to love in my life, not completely, until Dillon. But that love had already changed me totally, inside and out, giving me everything where I thought there was never going to be anything much. I had no idea about Annie and me, or getting to know Charley and Jeanine and all, or how anything that started out so far outside the only world you ever knew could come to be so much a part of the inside, in such a short time. And of all the things I didn't reckon on being so important, I didn't reckon most on Desi.

I thought that eventually Dillon and I would have a little place, maybe someday even own us a house the way his daddy had. And we would both have jobs. I thought that having a baby, though it would be hard for us to afford, would be exciting and fun and a living proof of our love. Desi was an idea to me, then, a nice idea, like in the poems I wrote about marriage and being a couple when I never knew anything about marriage except making love. How could I have imagined a baby as a person? And for all I knew about babies, how could I have expected that knowing a person who couldn't even talk would teach me more about everything in the world than all the talking everybody else in my life had done all put together? And I certainly couldn't imagine anything like that back that night, alone in the apartment with Elena, because even though I was sitting there telling her all about my worries and my big news—it was way bigger news than hers, after all, even though it sort of felt like something to be guilty about instead of celebrating—I was really thinking about how it would be to be the Bougainvillea Princess.

It just came to me, right then.

I could have been the Bougainvillea Princess myself. I could have even been the Primrose Princess. My mind just never included it until it was too late. I mean, I had all these ideas about having good speech and getting good grades and being an athlete, but I never had any dreams about just fun stuff. My mama never said I was a pretty princess who could dress all up in a tulip skirt and ride on a float so covered with buttermilk flowers it smelled like a pole boat floating down the river of heaven. She didn't tell me, and you don't know if you don't know.

I wanted to bawl like a fool. Here I was, married to the handsomest man I ever saw and carrying his child and living with a good friend in a nice place, and I was mooning about never being able to be a flower princess. How could it be that I was growing up backward?

But that was just the beginning of what was happening to me. Did Dillon feel it, far away in his cell in Block C in Solamente

River? Did he wake up all restless and wonder where was his wife, his Arley, in her dreams if not in her body? Did he feel he was losing me, that he would have to win me crazy like if he couldn't hold me with his love? No, I don't think he really did. But I can't deny that I was changing. During those months I was pregnant with Desi, I wasn't just growing fat as a heifer; I was growing, growing, growing in my mind. Annie was making me grow, challenging me. Now I look back, you'd best believe I'm glad I felt uncertain about so much. It might have made the things that happened easier to bear, in the sense of my being prepared. It was probably my destiny turning over another card is all.

But I still worry. I still wonder.

The fiesta was in June, so I was pretty far along pregnant. I wrote Dillon all about the fiesta. Elena hadn't had anything to eat but fruit smoothies for five days. She wanted to lose five pounds. "And she's already thin!" I wrote Dillon. "I'm going to look so fat and ugly next to the other girls." I thought that might hurt his feelings, though, him having been the one who got me this way, so I added that most people, including guys, seemed to notice me a lot more, and hardly any of them could tell I was pregnant.

I guess that was stupid. Maybe I *did* want to make him a little jealous.

In the weeks leading up to the fiesta, a couple of really big things had happened to me. I took my GED, and I passed. Annie was so excited she sprang this big surprise on me: she took me to New York. That was the second big thing.

Now, how can I tell this? I hadn't ever even seen the airport. In fact, all I knew of even Texas was Galveston, and the part of Dallas you could see from watching the football game on TV. From our valley, where Avalon was, the whole world was like a medieval map with just Florence and China, or whatever, on it and then all these other big shapes and drawings of waves and sea monsters. I was on a map with only three points: my house; San Antonio, where Annie's and school and work were; and Solamente River, where Dillon was, where I'd said my marriage words and left my blood on a fold-up couch covered with yellow and red fabric, in a trailer next to a field stitched all around by a fence topped with razor-sharp steel ribbon.

I don't think I slept for two hours the whole three days I was in New York. Annie couldn't keep me inside her girlfriend Penny's apartment on Twenty-third Street. I wanted to go outside before it was even light and walk around, see all the groceries, with their big bins of flowers and fruit, opening up, the people walking dogs, hear the endless rhythm of horns honking that never died away, even in the middle of the night. Then we stayed at Annie's sister's house, and I met her two boys, both littler than me. Annie and I took the train with Rachael to the city to see *Carousel*. It was the most beautiful night of my life.

I think Annie chose that show not because she got a good deal on the tickets but because of Billy Bigelow being a bad boy who hit the girl he loved and left her pregnant when he died. I think she wanted me to see similarities, and I did—but I'll tell you, I wanted her to see similarities too. And I think she did. I think she saw how you can be helpless not to love somebody. At the end, when Billy came to see his little girl graduating, I cried so hard Rachael and Annie thought I was going to be sick, and they wanted me to go right home. But I wanted to go to the restaurant they promised me, and have a cream tea, and when they said I was getting hysterical, it made me get even more that way. "I want to see stuff!" I cried out. "This is my last chance!"

"Your eyes are bigger than your stomach," Rachael told me gently.

"I don't think any goddamn thing on earth could be bigger than my stomach!" I yelled back, and then I felt terrible, and Annie did too. Embarrassed by this Texas hick kid she brought to show her family, like I was some kind of big-eyed thing in a box from Peru. She started shaking her head at me, but Rachael smoothed it all over.

"Annie, she's got the jits is all," Rachael said. "It feels so strange when you're that pregnant . . . You feel like you're drowning in your own body." She got the cream tea packaged all up in a big box, and we took it home and ate it sitting on Rachael's deck, and Rachael told me how it would feel to be on my own at college and how there was plenty of what she called "federal money" for girls with babies who were smart. "I don't mean the babies have to be smart," she said. "That's not a requirement." When I told Rachael that I was pretty sure I couldn't make it outside Texas, she reassured me. "You can grow up ignorant about the world even if your father is a rich doctor from New York, Arley. People from up here don't have any special corner on being smart; they just act like they do."

That's how nice she was to me, a stranger, just because Annie loved me.

Coming home was a time for me to be lost and gone in thought. At night, I would feel like I wanted to cry, and I'd pray for my mind to fold up like one of those little origami pocketbooks and stay down nice and flat and tight the way it used to be. But it was all over the place, thinking about New York and junior college and maybe running track again—because Mary Slaney was even better, after she had her baby, and so was Jackie Joyner-Kersee—and hoping the baby would be a girl instead of the son Dillon wanted so bad. For the first time, as I covered pages of that beautiful recycled paper with poems and ideas for Dillon, I felt as though I was lying to him: that even though I kept saying it, he *wasn't* the only dream in the world for me, like I was for him. I still loved him, that was never a question, but I didn't think I could explain the changes in me that weren't obvious to the eye until we got some real time together.

The two times Annie drove me to Solamente River while I was pregnant, Dillon and I didn't hardly talk at all. He just rolled his hands and his mouth over me as best we could in a room full of derelicts and girl derelicts doing the same thing, him trying to hold back, but rubbing my breasts with his wrists while he held my face and kissed me. I wasn't comfortable with the whole scene. I was very conscious of him, physically, but a part of me was sitting back inside, high up on the hill of my motherhood, watching Dillon and me panting and smooching in that dirty room and thinking, No, no. Just like Annie was thinking. I could almost feel her, those times, out there in the foyer, smacking her gum and checking her watch. She didn't like Dillon and Dillon didn't like her. He called her my "jailer," because she had so many things for me to do on the weekends, when I wasn't working: going with Charley to pick out plants for the house, shopping for furniture for Azalea Road, listening to lectures and parenthood classes given by the people at Jeanine's agency who counseled the pregnant girls who were giving up their babies for adoption—all of which interfered with seeing Dillon. In six months, I could have another conjugal visit, and I sort of pinned my hopes on that, knowing that if Dillon and I were really together, our love would fall into place again. Meanwhile, I talked and wrote to him about my everyday life, and about hoping for my apartment.

Getting a place of my own, even if it was just a room in a rooming house, was starting to be this huge thing. After his one client got the poke and was buried, Stuart was really depressed. He was applying for jobs in Florida and in New York, and he kept

asking Annie if she was applying for jobs, too, but she wasn't doing anything I could see. It was obviously not a time for a couple
to have to put up with the stress and responsibility of another
person around the house. So Annie and Jeanine started talking
about me having one of those little one-bedrooms they give the
birth mothers who are working with the agency.

Jeanine is really a character. She has what Annie calls a generous interpretation of things. Jeanine would say, "I mean, there are
circumstances under which you would consider an adoption plan
for the baby, right?" And I'd answer, Yeah, like if I got hit by a
bus, but she would put her finger to her lips and go on, "So, technically, you are one of those people who could be served by this
available subsidized housing." We all knew it was just for the
short term, anyhow. No matter what the far-off future would
hold, Annie was going to move into Azalea Road sooner or later,
at least for a while. A couple of times, I asked her, if she was going
to go off to another job in another state, why did she keep making so many improvements on the house, and her eyes all filled
up with tears. "Sometimes, I think I want to stay here, at least for
now," she said.

Annie and Stuart were supposed to get married, by summer at
the latest, but I didn't know if Annie was going to go through
with it. Busy as I was with work and studying, I couldn't pretend
I was comfortable with the idea that Annie would leave. When
she would talk about these fantasies about us living at Azalea
Road and my going to college, I really liked that. It was getting so
when I thought of the future, I thought of Annie and my child
instead of my husband.

Dillon probably wasn't too happy that I didn't write so much
about our love but about other things: like about the leather-

bound set of books Annie got me for my fifteenth birthday, her favorites when she was a girl, like *To Kill a Mockingbird* and *A Tree Grows in Brooklyn*, all stories about girls in tough circumstances. Maybe it felt to him like I was bragging. Or maybe it made him think that his gift to me, his poem about his cell and the agony of not being free, wasn't much compared with those books. I had told him I loved the poem, that it was beautiful, but scary. But then I babbled right on about the cactus garden in a big pottery bowl painted with moons and stars that I got from Charley.

I remember I wrote, "Maybe we'll have it in our house someday. If cactus live that long."

And then I got the phone call from Mama.

Dillon would have never known about it, except we were having our weekly talk at the time. We hadn't been on but about five minutes when all of a sudden this operator broke in and said, "Got an emergency call for y'all from Rita B. Mowbray."

Well, I thought, sure enough, Cam's dead in a car wreck, otherwise why would she call me? But I said to Dillon, "Bet she can't live without me being her maid."

Dillon said, real quick, "Well, honey, maybe you should go on and live at home until the baby comes. I think you ought to be with your own. Blood is blood." It seemed strange to me at the time, but afterward I realized that he just wanted to get me away from Annie.

I told him, "Okay, honey, I guess I'll think about it."

The operator said, "Y'all going to hang up or not?"

So we did.

And Mama came on. "Arley," she said. "I need you to come on out here."

"Come home?" I asked her. "Why?"

"Just you come on out here . . ." It sounded like she was covering the phone for a moment; ". . . on Wednesday. For supper."

"Supper?"

Mama laughed. "Yeah, girl, supper." Then she hung up. Wasn't but a minute we talked, and I thought, well, there went my phone call with Dillon for the whole week . . . for nothing.

But it wasn't just for that week, though I couldn't have known that then. I didn't know that the days ahead would be so busy, with the festival coming and all, that, for the first time, I'd forget to write Dillon.

He'd never get a letter from me again.

That time he ignored me, at the beginning, when he wouldn't write me, I almost went crazy. Did he go crazy, waiting, too? Did he have time to listen to unsaid things, meanings underneath words, and decide that they were telling him to act? Do those things go out, over the wind or the telephone wires, on their own special frequency, between people whose ears are tuned to the slightest change in one another? Dillon had always believed in signs.

Anyhow, a couple of nights later, Annie drove me out to Mama's.

Right away, when I went inside, I could see things were different. In place of the old chipped-up pine table we ate at for a thousand years, there was this light, wrought-iron set that looked like it ought to be out on a patio in a house in France. Somebody, probably Lang, had put magazine covers in those pop-together plastic frames and hung them all over. I must admit, they looked fresh. The dumb old curtains I hated so much, but had washed and ironed so many times they were the color of old oatmeal, those were gone, replaced by miniblinds. Mint green, pulled tight against the sun. Mama thought sun faded everything. She and

Lang were sitting in the living room with *Oprah!* on, having a smoke.

"You did a lot of stuff," I said, to start things off.

"Wait till you see," Lang said, out of the dark of the room. "We're redoing the whole upstairs, with fabric drapes on the walls and stuff." Their faces as played up by the faint light from the TV were so similar in shape that I could have mistaken one for the other if I hadn't known it was my sister's voice. I didn't know how long it had been since I'd seen Langtry—a year?—but when she stood up, I saw she was thinner and more like Mama, more set, somehow, like a rubber figure; even her hair had that orangey color Mama called strawberry blond. "Girl," she said, "you're as fat as a pig!"

"I'm going to have a baby, Lang."

"I heard! I heard congratulations are in order, for my baby sister's baby!" Mama and Lang about died laughing then. Lang was getting out a plate from the fridge with sandwiches made of pita bread and cucumbers and cream cheese, and some applesauce in a bowl. "You living with Dillon LeGrande's people now, up in Welfare?"

It hit me then, and I had to sit down. They hadn't talked about my baby or my marriage for one second before I came into that room. They had this whole life of theirs going on, buying a set of soda chairs and a dining room table and some picture frames, and I was just this fly on the edge of it that came buzzing in, and they didn't pay me no more advance notice than they would if that fly had come buzzing up Jean-Marie Street past the Nevadases' house before it got to our door. Mama hadn't even told Lang where I was living, or what I was doing, or anything else except why she let Lang come home. My head started to ache like it did sometimes when I skinned my hair back too tight. "Where's Cam?" I asked. Neither one of them answered. Mama

291

said something, half to Lang and half to Oprah, about how she'd kick that man's ass over the moon for him, he tried that trick on her, and finally, I asked again, "Where's Cam? He dead?"

"He's at work," Mama said. "He quit school. He left you a letter." There was an envelope lying on the table, which I split open with my fingernail. "Arley," it said. "Hi. Where are you? We could have lunch. Yr. Brother, Cameron Mowbray." Touching, I thought. But after a second, I thought better of it. It wasn't so bad. Lang was sitting at the table, chomping on one of those sandwiches, and she motioned for me to sit down. Mama said she was going to slip out of her work clothes.

"He's one pretty man," Lang said.

"Cam?"

"Dillon LeGrande."

"Well, thank you."

"Why, did you make him up, honey?"

"No, I mean thank you for saying that."

"You all legally married and all that, huh?"

"Yes."

"He couldn't never get me, not like he wanted," Lang said, looking past me, out the window in the door behind me. "He got some, but not what he wanted."

"You? What?"

"When we were together. You know we were."

"No."

"Well, it don't matter, does it? Times change, and people change. I'm seeing a banker from Dallas. He's, like, forty! Mama's all jealous. We're going to take us a cruise. Mama wants to go. . . ." And then Mama was back in the room, laying down a folder in front of me with a stack of papers inside.

"Here," she said. "You sign these."

I couldn't even make out what it was, the light was so bad in the kitchen. Neither one of them made a move to flip a switch. "What is this, Mama?"

"It's insurance. Don't you mind. It's all paid up."

"Insurance? An insurance policy?" I thought she was going to give me something for me and the baby, to help us get a start. How I could have, heaven knows, but for a second I thought it was going to be like one of those holiday shows where people who never really revealed their true feelings were all of a sudden talking and laughing and speaking truths they'd wanted to share for twenty years and more.

But then my mama, my real mama, started to talk again.

"I took out these policies on y'all when you were babies, and I paid into them every year until they were all paid up. Yours just came finished, so if you just sign it, I can redeem it."

"Redeem it?"

"I can get the money. I got to be setting something aside for when I retire. And I want to do me some traveling."

"The cruise?"

"How do you know about that?" Mama's eyes were like minnows squirting away from a dropped rock—to the left and to the right.

"Lang said," I told her, and she sat down and started pulling the cucumber out of her sandwich and nibbling around the edges. But I still didn't entirely get it. I asked her, "Is the money for the baby and me?"

Mama just looked at me. "Did you pay for it?"

"You said it was a policy in my name."

"It was a policy on your life, girl. If you died when you was little, I'd have got something for it then. But since you didn't, I get my money now."

"Didn't you want me to come home?"

"What?"

"Come home, here. With you."

"I ain't got room for no baby here, Arley. I'm counting out the days, Lang and me, till Cam gets on his own." She looked up at me then and smiled that bright, big-joke smile of hers. "Anyhow, I hear y'all moving to the mansion district with that lawyer. Hear she's got that big rich house with two galleries and all."

"How'd you know about Annie's house?"

"Never you mind. I got me my sources." And I never did know and I still don't know what those sources were. But Mama wasn't above anything. After what happened that night at the cabin, I don't put anything past her. "So," Mama said, like we'd all had a nice, big meal together and finished our business. "You want to just sign this here, and how's that baby doing? My first grandchild, huh? And me not forty years old?" I could tell it was a big effort for her, and I almost wanted to make her keep it up, to make her hover, there, with that pen in her hand, forced to ask questions a normal mother would ask of her child, forced to pretend an interest she didn't even understand, much less feel, all so I wouldn't turn around and walk out of that fucking hole and slam the door without signing the paper.

I did finally sign it.

And I didn't even ask to use the phone. I walked next door, to old lady Jewell's, and used the phone there to call up Annie. When Annie came, I didn't tell her a thing, though I have to suppose she figured everything out pretty quickly. As we were driving home, it hit me that I never said good-bye to my sister, though I didn't realize then how it could be the last time you would see someone and you'd think it was like any ordinary good-bye. I never believed for one instant anything Lang tried to lay on me about her and Dillon being a big thing years ago. And I still don't. Lang was just like some kind of buzzard, wanting to claim whatever was lying there and then act all protective, like it was hers to start with. I still don't know, and I probably won't know my whole life, what happened in my attic room, before the blood was smeared on the billowed fabric walls . . . or about any of the other nights . . . I don't want to know.

I had deliberately requested a vacation day because I wanted to look good, for the last night of the fiesta. But by the middle of the morning, things weren't going so hot—though hot is what it was, steeping and boiling breath-robbing heat, and I was like this big furnace. I could sweat sitting still. When I stood naked in front of the bathroom mirror, you could see my belly shift and pulse like in *Alien*. It kind of scared me, it was stretched so tight, and yet in clothes, I just looked a little fatter. For real, though, I couldn't find anything to wear for Elena's big dance night, and I was fit to be tied. Finally, Annie came banging on the door and said, "For Christ's sake, Arley, let somebody else use the bathroom for one minute." But when I came out, and she could see I'd been crying, she put off her Saturday appointments and took me shopping for a dress, down in the Mexican market.

We went in and out of all these little shops, trying on stuff and getting really silly. One woman rolled her eyes and said something about *"su hija"* and *"embarazada,"* which I knew didn't mean "embarrassed," like it sounded, but "pregnant."

Annie said, "She's not my daughter. And she's not pregnant. She's very sensitive about being overweight." I hadn't thought Annie knew that much Spanish!

We cracked up then. The poor lady. But that was the store

where we finally got this beautiful, cream-colored floating thing made of Mexican lace, with its sort of shawl that you could hook up and make into big sleeves. It was when we were leaving with it that we passed this hair salon not far from Taco Haven that I'd always wanted to go in because it was so space-age and stuff, with countertops done up in foil with holograms. We stopped for a moment, and I said to Annie, "I want to get this here hair cut."

She said, "Arley. Jesus. Not your beautiful hair." Well, it was just the wrong thing for her to have said, because I was in there asking about it in five seconds, and then we were sitting down at a little tortilla shop, eating tortillas with cinnamon and butter and waiting for my appointment, and then I was in the chair, and this Hispanic girl like six feet tall was yelling for someone to go get a Polaroid and take pictures of my hair before she cut it, and asking me, "Are you sure, are you sure?"

When I walked out of there, I was carrying a bag of my own hair, which felt heavy as my track clothes used to feel after a meet. About a foot was cut off, which still left me with really long hair, well below my shoulders. But it all sort of lifted up and fluffed out and curled and had no weight to it at all. When I looked in the mirror, wearing that new dress and new hair, I looked like a woman, instead of a fattened-up little girl in a braid. Even Stuart, passing through the living room that night to get clean clothes, whistled at me and said, *"Muy linda!"*

When I weighed myself before I got dressed, I was five pounds lighter.

Just before I left, I got a FedEx package from Dillon, which wasn't so strange; he sometimes got so impatient to get a letter or a poem to me, or, once, the picture of him in the baseball uniform for the prison team, that he overnighted them. This one, however, I barely had time to open, because I was going right out

the door with Elena's dad, who hadn't seen me since I was married and was sort of standing there swallowing his tongue while
he talked to Stuart. It made me laugh, to tell you the truth, like
they were both nervous fathers before a big date. What was in the
envelope was this cream-colored card, like one of those cards you
return to someone who's getting married, saying whether you can
come or you can't, and a long, long strand of ribbon—really not
one strand but several, braided together, in four or five shades of
red. I turned over the card. Written on it, in ink, was "One kiss,
my bonny sweetheart."

For a moment, I thought he'd intended it for me to wear to
the dance, but hell, he didn't even know I was going. And then I
remembered the landlord's black-eyed daughter, plaiting a dark-
red love knot into her long black hair, and I thought with a kind
of stab right in my heart, What would Dillon think? It was gone,
most of it, all those waves of hair he bathed in when we made
love. There was not enough of it left to loosen and let down in
the casement. It was a regular girl's hairstyle, like Annie said,
bouncing and behaving. I didn't know what I would tell him, but
there was no thinking about it right then—a crowd of thoughts
of Dillon, all alone under those searching light-eyes at Solamente
River, was the last thing I wanted to carry with me to the fiesta.
So I just laid that letter down. I still have the ribbon.

The dance was held in a big pavilion right by the river, which
had sort of been tented over so it could be air conditioned. It was
a neat feeling, like being inside and outside at the same time, and
all the princesses' floats were pulled up like spokes in a wheel
around the outside. Colored wagons, I thought right away. That's
what they were, fragrant and insubstantial as clouds, so that even
up close you could hardly see the wire under the pillows of the
flowers. Elena came running up to me, and she looked like a

model or an actress; I thought right then, Maybe that's what she'll be, like Selena or something. Maybe this float of hers will be her first ride to glory. "You cut your hair!" she screamed. "You cut your hair, Arley Mowbray!"

She introduced me to all the other princesses, and while they were posing for pictures, I danced with Ricky Nevadas, and let me tell you, the boy was made to be put in a tuxedo. Ricky's nothing but a bike mechanic, but he looks like a Calvin ad for sure, when he's clean, and he was clean that night. He was on his best behavior, and I was teasing his head off about him being the handsome prince. "Just don't kiss me, Arley, girl"—he laughed— "or I will turn back into a pumpkin."

"A frog, Ricky. You'll turn back into a frog."

We were laughing so much I didn't see Eric Dorey come up until he cut in on us. He cut in, just like boys did at country club dances in Annie's old Nancy Drew books, which I read last summer when Desi kept me up all night cutting teeth. I couldn't even tell who he was for sure. He'd been away a long time, months by then, at the military school in Killeen where his folks sent him after the accident. And he had changed so much, the way boys do when they're in high school. Eric Dorey hadn't been taller than me before, but now he was big and lean and long, over six feet, and his voice was so down deep, I couldn't even see the sandy-haired squirt he used to be in algebra class.

"That you, Eric?" I said to him.

But he must have been thinking the same thing. I blushed inside when I saw how he was looking at me, like he was exploring my whole body, approving but curious too, wondering what was going on.

"I'm pregnant," I told him, while we sort of stood there and kid slow-danced, with my arms around his neck. "I'm six months, almost."

"Aww, Arley," he said, soft, looking away, like I'd told him I had cancer or something.

"No, it's okay. I'm married." Why didn't I tell him who my husband was, right then? Or where he was? I didn't tell him, and he didn't ask. We danced right through that song and the next, and then Elena came swooping down like a bright-red parrot and danced him away, and then he came back. What didn't we talk about! School, and how he loved the away part and hated the military part, though his daddy had been an air force man. How he wanted to be a scientist, or maybe a doctor, and work with burn victims, how he'd been in this mentor program with a cell biologist who cultured new human skin from leftover bits taken after surgery and it was all so amazing. . . . I told him about how I might do the corrective cosmetics thing, like Connie, and get a job right after junior college. He didn't seem to like that much, though I saw it as being helpful to handicapped people in the same way what he was talking about was.

"You're too good for that, Arley," he said, mad like. "You're too smart to be a cosmetics girl."

"It isn't just that."

"Well, whatever it is, you're too smart for that. You should be a . . . scientist. Or a teacher or a writer or something. Or a big athlete—"

"I'm big, all right," I said, pointing to my stomach, and right then, the baby turned and sort of kicked out and rolled between us. Eric leapt like a scalded cat.

"Is it all right?" he asked. I just laughed at him.

"Of course it's all right. It's alive, you know, Eric."

"It's aliiiiivvvve!" he sort of hooted out, and I saw he was really still a high school kid, though a good person, like he always was. He held me more carefully after that, and I started to have those crotch-tightening feelings, the kind you have when you want someone touching you who isn't, and I was ashamed as hell and sort of broke away from him, though he hung around me all night while Elena was getting her flowers and being in the grand march and so on. And when it got late, and little boys were starting to run around and pull bunches of the flowers off the princess floats, no matter how hard the Jaycee guys tried to chase them away, it was Eric drove me back to Annie's, talking the whole time about could I write to him, because he was going to have to do one more year at the military school before he went to college. . . .

I think we saw the police car at the same time.

The first thing I thought was, something happened to Annie. I started going crazy, and my mind started saying to me, oh no, oh God, some fuckhead cracko husband of one of her lousy clients had bushwhacked her in front of her own house and killed her and I'll never see her again, and she'll never see my baby—but almost immediately, I thought, That's stupid. There isn't even an ambulance out there, the way there was at Eric's house when Corty got killed. There wasn't anything but that one squad car. I knew, for sure, it meant something bad. Something about Dillon and me. It never even occurred to me that the car could have been there for people who lived in any other of the six apartments in the building.

I started to jump out of the car, but before I did, I turned around all of a sudden and kissed Eric really hard, not like boyfriends-girlfriends, not with our mouths open, but hard, like you'd do to say good-bye to someone putting you on a ship for a long journey, which was what I was going on. And then I ran, as

300

best I could, up the stairs, ripping one boot right through my beautiful lace dress—we had to cut it off, later, and hem it—and Annie was running out into the hall, her hair all sticking up, and her and Stuart both touching me all over and asking, "Are you all right? Are you all right?"

The police had come for me at the fairgrounds, but I'd already left for home.

He'd broke out, my husband. He'd broke out of prison and killed a man.

It had all happened a few hours before, along about when I got the FedEx, before the dance. But it took a while for the police to connect Dillon with me, or to figure Dillon might try to come to me, and then more time to figure out where I actually was. It was four of them, Annie said. Kevin LeGrande. That Indian kid who was in the robbery. And this guy who used to be a dental student. He was in for selling drugs, and he never got as far as the fence before he got shot. Someone saw them, I guess, and called out, and this guy panicked and ran. He wasn't hurt bad, though. He was the one told the officials at Solamente River how they planned it, mainly him and Dillon, if his word was to be believed.

What they did was start an electrical fire in the laundry, and then when the supply driver came in from the truck to check out the smoke, they knocked him out real quick, using a phone receiver they had hidden in a sock. Then they drove away in his truck, wearing his clothes, toting his ID. Outside the gates, they ditched that laundry van. Kevin told the police later it didn't go fast enough.

The man who got killed was a federal marshal. He wasn't even on duty. He just heard the bulletin on his radio when he was coming home from the Wal-Mart. He saw Dillon and Kevin hot-wiring a car in a parking lot, and he went over. What Kevin said was that the Indian guy, Spirito, jumped out of the backseat so fast you could hardly see it was a person and barreled into that poor man's midsection with his head, and then one of them got hold of his gun, one of those new plastic laser-type police guns that looks like a toy. The marshal had three grown kids.

I don't think any of us slept that night.

Sometime during the night, Annie answered the phone, and I picked it up at the same time on the extension in my bedroom. I should have hung up. But then I heard the voice, and I realized it was the same man from our wedding at the prison, the one who came in to check Dillon and me in the trailer. I remembered him, because he seemed so mad at Dillon and so sad for me.

"Ray," Annie said, like her heart was breaking.

"Lot of beneficial effect on LaMaggot from this close and supportive relationship you described . . ."

"Ray Henry, do you think that I ever wanted this?"

"I think you could have listened to me, Anne. I think you could have just once trusted the fact that I had a sneaky feeling about this all along, and not even a smart New York lawyer . . ."

"Don't. Don't. That's cheap."

"I know." The warden sighed. "I know." He stopped, and I almost hung up then, I would have, but they'd have heard the click. "Anne, the police have to know if this bird told the little girl anything. Anything she knows . . ."

"She doesn't know a thing, Ray Henry. I swear on my life."

"Because if she does . . ."

"She'd have told me, Ray . . ."

"Okay. Okay. Anne, I knew that marshal. I knew his wife. A finer man . . ."

"Please, Ray Henry . . . Please. I know I have to hear it. I de-

serve it. . . ." She started to make little noises, almost puppy
noises. My own eyes filled. Oh, Annie.

"Don't cry, Anne. Don't cry now. No one's blaming you."

"I blame myself."

"Just ask Arlington again. Anything. Okay?"

"Okay."

She hung up. I hung up.

When the police caught up with Kevin the next morning at
his mother's, they called us right away. Kevin said he never imagined anything would get out of hand the way it did. He said he
was filled with shame. He should have just done his time and
been out in a year, and not listened to Dillon. He should never
have listened to Dillon, who always got him in trouble, he said.

When they caught him, Kevin had that gun right there
with him.

But he said it was Dillon did the shooting.

So far as I know, no one ever saw Spirito again. He's still on
the Most Wanted list. Jack Becker, Jeanine's boyfriend who's a
cop, and that one lady from the FBI, said Spirito was the smartest
of all of them. She said Spirito was probably speaking Spanish by
nightfall, and he's probably speaking Spanish today.

Dillon was smart too. He could have crossed over the border
to Mexico too that same night, and he probably did, because we
know he tried later. If he had, he could have disappeared and
never come back. He didn't come back because he was too stupid
to lose himself in Mexico. He came back because he wanted
something else even more than his freedom. Or so I guess.

That night, I wanted to go out and climb on Annie's lap and
have her rock me like I was a child. But I couldn't. I was going to
be a mother myself; my kid days were over. And, worse than that,
I was so ashamed. I'd already caused Annie more trouble in a few

months than I'd ever caused anyone else in my whole life. And me not even hers.

Maybe, if I had let Annie comfort me, I'd have remembered about the card I got by FedEx. I'd have given it to the police. I know I would have, not that it would have done a stick of good. But it wasn't until a few nights later that I even remembered the card. I found it tucked between the pages of the book I'd been reading. I picked it up and held it to my cheek, where it seemed to burn, like a brand. Then I put it back. It's probably there still.

Cell Dreams

Late at night: I am dreaming, something wild
pushes me along like a pebble in the path
of a dust devil, something unbroken in me—
or too much broken, crazed they say. My life
is a walk through an electrical storm—each hair
stands up, each cell is charged with this current;
there is nothing behind me and nothing ahead.

Later: cheap whiskey redemption scalds my throat,
brings peace in the night.

Later yet: headlights (now I'm dreaming
of you) and a thousand miles of highways, the night
juiced up with music—lonely cowboys, angel girls,
and death, a 2:00 A.M. country preacher,
testifying, rocking in the spirit (we have to),
stop at the motel, tear back the sheets, tumble
and tangle together, call out, "Oh
Lord!" while above us stars burn
holes in the black night.

Dillon Thomas LeGrande

CHAPTER FIFTEEN

Annie

Once we got her into the apartment, the reporters found themselves on a cold trail. They could still bother me, but after a while even they wearied of sitting in the outer office, chatting with Lilia while she washed the philodendron, and they didn't show up anymore.

Then they tried to pursue other avenues to the "truth."

After all, it was a pretty swell little story—the desperate outlaw and his pregnant child bride. What really drove Dillon's odyssey into legend, besides the way he anointed himself with his new name, was unfortunately a testament to my consummate skill as an advocate—no shit, no fooling, as Arley would say: it was the poetry some pinhead found read into the record of the lovers' court proceeding.

I hit the roof when I found out that the story of Arley and Dillon's lawsuit, and the poem, had made the nightly national news.

That was just the beginning. It got worse, as these things tend to do. A San Antonio anchorwoman received a neatly chronological file of Arley's and Dillon's poems. At fifteen years old and eight months pregnant, Arlington Mowbray LeGrande had the signal distinction of seeing her poetry appear in *People* magazine, next to a photo of her in her track silks, legs up to heaven, braid snaking down over one shoulder like a patent-leather python, looking far too saucy and worldly to be Arley at all. Every time something surfaced with Dillon, until the night of the fire and even long afterward, the poetry was part of it. Some loon even set "What's True" to music, including some of his own lyrics about the hell in a lonely cell, which only served to point up how talented *Dillon* actually was. And of course, every time there was a new chapter in the legend of "The Highwayman," there was another spate of Arley photos—stolen ones of her pregnant, sitting on my back balcony, of her and Elena at the fiesta, but always, and especially, her track photo.

Her comment the first time she saw it, by the way, was typical: "I love that picture! I never saw it. Was it yearbook? It's better than the other one. Can I get a copy?"

The *People* headline read "Good Girls and Bad Boys" and it pretended to examine the facts of several cases of the recent past. But mostly it focused on Arley, and on the kind of social milieu, not to mention the kind of legal counsel, that would bless the entry of a young teenager into a maximum-security prison to have sex with a man twice her age. Everyone at Women and Children First had a copy or two. The board members were, to a woman and a man, deeply thrilled, I'm sure. Ray Henry sent me a tear sheet, with a note on a prison letterhead, requesting my autograph. I never replied.

Stuart bought me a gift that month: a Smith & Wesson nine-millimeter compact with a plastic grip and, according to the literature, "a metal slide and fixed sights."

"What am I supposed to do with this?" I asked him, horrified.

"You know, our life together has given me the chance to say

things I really appreciate the chance to get to say," Stuart replied. "Like this: Annie, get your gun. If this loon is laying for you and thinks you're the one keeping his bride away from him, you will thank me for carrying a heavier purse for the next few days, until they get him."

"Stuart, I couldn't fire a gun to—"

"Save your life?"

So off we went with Jeanine's sweet cop boyfriend, Jack, to the range the following Saturday. Turns out, I am a very good shot—something I, too, have to admit I never imagined saying.

It was a swell month all around: the first month Dillon was on the run, the first month Arley looked really vastly pregnant, the hottest single month in a star-studded cavalcade of hot months in the history of a hot state. Utilities conked with eerie prescience on just those streets where thugs were strolling past electronically alarmed liquor stores. Old people melted in stucco slums, and my office racked up a lifetime tally of spousal-abuse injunctions. There was no downtime and scant rest, but my whole being was focused on Arley's welfare.

As the days passed, the best efforts of the state police and the FBI turned up no clue whatever to the whereabouts of Dillon and his buddy Samuel Sanchez, aka Spirito. It turned out that Spirito had been trucked over to Solamente only a month earlier, after his conviction in connection with a knife fight at the boys' farm where he'd spent quiet days among the alfalfa since the robbery with the LeGrandes. When Dillon didn't show up at my house, or Rita's, or at the First State Bank of Texas, early publicity began to wane, only to be stoked up again by the poetry, but Arley, grieving and huge, was largely untouched. I couldn't keep her from watching the ten o'clock news, and her face was a textbook of guilt and panic as she did, playing and replaying the video tapes we made, freezing them on Dillon's image from booking photos. She was worried—she told me exactly once, and I went bananas, which I'm still sorry for—that someone would hurt Dillon before he got a chance to explain.

I didn't want her out of my sight. Arley's getting her "own place" seemed a ridiculous risk now. But Jeanine and Stuart convinced me that she'd actually be safer from Dillon in one of the apartments set aside for birth mothers by Jeanine's agency, Casa de Niños. Because the circumstances under which young women surrendered babies were often rough, the apartments secured by the agency with private and public funds were frequently shifted from complex to complex, and no one except the social workers and adoptive parents were given the address. The day Jeanine took me over to The Terrace—which, she pointed out persuasively, was only six minutes by car from my own front door—it looked so familiar I couldn't believe I'd never been there: behind similar apartment facades, I'd iced dozens of swollen eyes for my clients. The inevitable decline of those facades was visible in the trappings of cheap newness, the brave teal-colored shutters and window boxes, at The Terrace. It looked great, but it was like clothing from Fashion Bug—glamorous on the racks, washing up shapeless in a few months. In a year, these little boxes would look just like the buildings over on Alameda, where it seemed like half my clients lived, the grass worn bald by kid herds, doors slack as broken jaws. But by then, I comforted myself, Arley would be out of there, living, somehow, with me on Azalea Road, or in Florida, or somewhere at college—though she was far too young for college—or, at any rate, not here.

Worried as I was, and miserable as Arley was over Dillon, the few weeks she spent at The Terrace were probably the most peaceful time of her life. Another child her age would have been intimidated, indeed overwhelmed, by the work and care required. For Arley, it was unprecedented leisure, a beach picnic. When I look at Donnie, my nephew—he's the age now that Arley was then—I can't get the images to line up. Donnie's an ordinary slothful middle schooler. He has to be reminded to brush his teeth and change the sheets on his bed every couple of months. He and my brother-in-law routinely go to swords' point over a science project, and then Don spends a whole night gluing little silver sugar balls on a Styrofoam globe to represent the structure of the atom or something while his son sleeps on the couch. But for Arley, the interlude at The Terrace was the first time in her entire life she'd been responsible only for herself. Even while she lived with Stuart and me, Arley was the dictionary definition of conscientious. She did all the laundry; we never had to sweep or dust. I used to point out to Stuart how having her there actually lightened our load considerably, and basically for the price of her food. (He didn't agree—Arley, he said, made him feel "invaded.")

Seeing the joy with which she encountered her little apartment, one morning at dawn when we moved her over there, under the watchful aegis of an unmarked city squad car, was a witness to me. I felt both grateful and guilty, which, given my personality, often amount to the same thing. The decor was sheer eighties tack—"new earth tones" from top to bottom. But Arley loved the nubbly pumpkin-colored sofa, which made me itch just thinking about it, and she lovingly unpacked her poetry books, her leather-bound volumes, and all the tchotchkes she'd bought at Goodwill: a china zebra, a rainbow piñata for above the baby's bassinet, a lamp in the shape of a Conestoga wagon. She bustled about, round as a hen, a child playing house. Though I checked on her by phone twice a day and saw her almost daily too, she loved being alone—alone, but no longer Rita Mowbray's indentured servant. I found myself thinking of Arley's wedding picture, which she kept next to her bed in a heart-shaped frame made of pounded tin that Elena had given "them" for their wedding. It was a beautiful thing, especially given how their still-girlish tastes seemed to run to objects with decals of kittens or rock singers. I thought of Arley in that picture, wearing Elena's homecoming dress and the red-and-black cowboy boots she had to give up wearing after her feet swelled in the second trimester, and the ragged jacket she insisted on draping over her shoulders because, she told me later, it was something blue. She'd been smiling in that picture as though she were leaving the pavilion with an Oscar clutched in her fist. Despite the way I felt about Dillon LeGrande's influence on her life, whenever I saw that picture, I remember, I wished, for Arley's sake, that I could reverse the swoop of the clock hands with my fingertip—give her back the joy, however illusory, she enjoyed when Dillon was mostly a concept, safely tucked away in Solamente River Prison, along with the excitement of her first self-centered moments, moments nobody ever deserved more. Nonetheless, with every day I was more sure that Arley was better off with him gone—I knew nothing of the notes, or of her fear and helpless feeling of responsibility for what Dillon had done. It seemed unlikely Dillon would be heard from again, at least if he was as bright as he seemed.

I'd encouraged Charley, by then, to give up on making Azalea Road look spruced up for a wedding and simply get it ready to be lived in. I made ruthless choices: did I want tables and chairs or central air? (Central air, definitely.) By the time Arley, Stuart, and I moved in—I still thought it would be possible for Stuart to find work in Texas, maybe as a lobbyist—we would have a clean, cool, well-lighted space with practically nothing in it.

Because we wanted to speed up the moving-in date, or so I

told myself, I'd started going to the house to help Charley. When I talked about Arley and my fears, he did what no man had ever done with me. He simply listened. The questions he asked were real questions. He didn't give me advice. He didn't tell me not to worry. He just listened. He encouraged me to bring Arley along, and sometimes, I did.

Working with Charley in those days, days stiff with tension on all other fronts, gave me a peaceful pleasure. We'd stand side by side, him high on a ladder, me below, slapping on old-fashioned whitewash Charley had mixed. Sometimes we'd stand there, painting, for hours—and once we realized that the compounds in the paint wouldn't harm the baby, Arley helped, too. With the swoosh and scratch of the big flat brushes the only sound under the candied melodies from the old phonograph, it wasn't difficult to feel we'd drifted into a different century, a benign past in which we were a family, for whom preparing our homestead was life's most urgent priority.

Then there came that one cicada-loud afternoon when I, swooshing away on an upstairs bedroom wall, overheard Arley laughing so loud I had to go out to see what had happened.

Charley had been planting sago palms in one of the series of interlocking circle gardens in the front yard, and he was trying to keep Arley from helping him. "The fruit around the seed and the seed itself are both poisonous," he'd been telling her. "You don't want to eat this, Arley. People end up with things like Parkinson's twenty years later if they eat one of these things."

"Charley, why in the hell do you think I would eat one?"

"Well, you might, by mistake, and you're pregnant. . . ."

"I don't have brain damage from being pregnant! I don't *eat* things by mistake."

Charley noticed me then.

"Look, Annie!" he announced. "It's like having real dinosaurs in your yard! These plants watched tyrannosaurus rex walk around . . . well, not these, exactly—"

"Oh gee," Arley put in. "I'm glad you said that, because otherwise I would have thought that these here very plants were a few million years old."

Charley took my wrist and pulled me closer. "Let's ignore her," he told me. "You're supposed to ignore kids. . . . See, there's a male sago palm and a female sago palm. When they're little, they look mostly the same. When they grow up, they look different. Like male and female people. The female here, her leaves will spread out more, open, like a giant daisy; but the male's will have this sort of dome shape on top, like an open umbrella. When they're pollinated, the females produce the bright-red seeds. . . ." Charley had taken my hand, using it as a pointer to lead me through the various parts of the plant; and suddenly our faces were very close together, and I was inhaling the salt-and-chalk smell of Charley, and I knew he was aware of my inhaling it.

We both looked up, embarrassed, and Arley, not quite sure what it was she'd seen, suddenly evaporated back into the shadows of the front porch. That night, I had a dream about Charley and me making love. I woke up, sure I'd cried out, sure I'd woken Stuart, and I couldn't get back to sleep. I thought it was the heat, or a sign of the emotional and hormonal changes to come. Then, just two nights later, I had another version of the same dream.

We fell into a routine, during that vigilant and yet languid time of heat. Arley's doctor visits. My office and field days. Work on the house. The occasional night out for me with Jeanine and Patty, often with Arley along. The even more occasional night out for Stuart and me, during those few hours he could steal from the last convulsive days of effort by the expiring defense center on behalf of its condemned. Half the time, I remember, I felt as though I were asleep, my actions and reactions taking place outside me, without my direction. I had to remind myself that it was Arley, not I, who was pregnant.

I took Arley to Lamaze classes. The plump and shiny young matrons there seemed to make it a kind of parlor game, attempting to figure out whether I was Arley's mom or something more salacious. After the breakout hit the news, though, you could see recognition light up their faces, serially, week by week, and you could tell who'd read the newspaper, who'd seen CNN. I knew Arley must have noticed their whispering, the none-too-careful attention they gave to seeming not to pay attention to her. But she was all quiet grace, keeping her eyes on me, asking for her pillow, getting ready to practice breathing during transition. Her every small gesture of dignity made me more and more proud.

I knew her tension had to be consuming. But when the police called, she betrayed little. She never asked for the phone. She'd only raise her eyebrows. "Nothing," I'd say. And Arley would walk away.

Between Arley and the house, I'd begun living paycheck to paycheck, as I hadn't done since law school. There was the Evenflo car seat I laid out fifty-nine dollars for after Arley sheepishly showed me the one she'd been given by the lady who ran the rummage at Mater Christi, which looked as though it had already survived a crash. There was the nursery furniture we bought accidentally at SuperBaby when we were supposed to be out buying canned tomatoes to finish making gumbo. Maternity jeans and nursing bras—do you know how much those things cost, just because they know they have you cornered? I had to let Stuart think I was sending money to OxFam, buying Italian shoes, hiring

Leonardo da Vinci to restore the woodwork at Azalea Road. Even Jeanine, whose heart has been pierced by lost love or compassion so many times I'm surprised it doesn't leak, couldn't understand why I teared up when I described giving Arley her shimmering green raincoat, and why it touched me so much that she kept it hung on the wire she'd strung across one wall to dry her water-colors, as if it were a piece of art to be admired. Arley's eager grati-tude had no manipulation in it, and she didn't pretend not to be thrilled by everything I gave her and everything we did. Not even the wan faces of my clients, nor their toddlers with wide brown eyes like night creatures clinging to their mothers' knees, had ever roused such protectiveness in me. Compared with my peers' overfed and sullen teenagers, for whom love was no more than interference, she was like some kind of air fern, reared from nothing, thriving by accident.

On Arley's due date, we went for an ultrasound. The physi-cian's assistant, one of those breezy Donna Reed types in porno-graphically revealing white slacks, reported a tiny baby, with possible intrauterine growth retardation. That was common among young teens—they barely ate enough to keep themselves alive, after all, she told us. Anyway, she breezed on, missing the date was no big deal: the "real young ones" often got "their dates mixed up."

"Well, she couldn't have got her dates mixed up," I told her. "She only had sex one time." Even as air hit the words, and before the knowing smile, I realized what a chump Donna Reed must think I was. To her, Arley would have looked like everyone's worst nightmare—a tenth-grade Lolita. It took both hands to hold my tongue while she explained that "Doctor" was due for vacation week after next, so she would call the hospital and schedule an induction for the following Thursday, if nothing "popped" before then.

Pop.

God.

That was Friday.

On Saturday, against my better judgment, I called Arley's mother about possible complications with the baby. Rita was all compassion. "I expect she'll have her a time," she said. "I know I surely did. Trouble into trouble, I say." Rita worked at the very hospital where Arley was to be induced, if it came to that. Was she working that day or night? I wanted to know. Would she be able to come and be with Arley during some of her labor? "No, no, I'm sorry to say. Thursday, that's my night out. I reckon it'll be late before I'm home. I'll call you, how about? And you can tell me what's what." I was furious, but what had I expected? It would break Arley's heart that her mama wouldn't even come to comfort her as she gave birth, I was sure. But Rita would be something less than no use. A cat was more devoted.

Then on Sunday, so that one day should not pass without some painful event, Stuart asked me out for a drink. "Pencil me in, babe," he told me. I was suspicious.

At Amor Ausente, among interns cheering or bemoaning the residency offers they'd all received that day, Stuart told me about his own offer. The law firm in Florida had come through with a good one. Stuart was going to be able to go on doing at least most of what he'd done in Texas, but for paying customers and, with the firm's backing, a fair number of those who couldn't pay. They'd double his salary.

"I'm happy for you," I said, then wondered, how must *that* sound? "I mean, I'm happy. But Florida . . . ?"

"Well, Anne." Stuart sighed. "The offers here and in New York were just too . . . just ordinary litigation work. Interesting, but I can't do that right now. I'm not ready to be a civilian yet. The work can really make a difference, Anne; it's not a time to give up. . . ."

The work, I thought. Not "my work." The work. Like a preexisting condition.

"When do they want you to start?"

"Next week."

"Next *week*, Stuart? You expect me to resign my job and . . . and move to Florida next week?"

"No, Anne. I don't. You can have all the time you need for . . . whatever you need it for."

"What's that supposed to mean?"

"Just what I said."

"Stuart, we didn't meet yesterday. I know when you're pissing about something."

"It's nothing. It's just . . . Jesus, Anne, you've been so tender in your concern for my career. . . ."

"Well, I've had a few things on my plate. In case you haven't noticed, Arley's about to have a baby. And I took my last bit of vacation for next week to help her! So I can't even get time off to come with you and help you get your stuff settled. . . ."

"I didn't expect you to," he said. "At least, not now. But Jesus, Anne. Arley. Arley. Arley. Just what do you expect will happen with this kid? Not to mention with her kid . . . Do you think she's going to go on living off you?"

"She's not living off me, Stuart."

"Well, living off you or off Jeanine, or whatever. What I mean is, do you think you're going to be some happy family unit after she has this baby? That she isn't going to find someone even worse for her than the excellent Mister LeGrande? And as fast as she can?"

"She isn't like that, Stuart. And even if she did, I'm her friend. I'm her lawyer. I'm not her mother."

"You're more involved with Arley's life than you are with ours."

"I'm not. It's just been a series of crises, is all."

"I've been having a crisis of my own, Anne."

Right, I thought, shaking the ice in my drink. But your crises are chosen. Crisis is your line. You got into your line because you knew, somehow, somewhere, it would never give you time or space to get your teeth into anything more extended than the World Series. It's all a big game, Stuart. A big, meaningful, life-and-death game. The death warrants will keep on coming, like clay pigeons, and you'll always try to shoot them down. If not here, in Florida. If not in Florida, in Utah. I thought of my house, thought of Charley's hand guiding Arley in the gentle, patient sweep of the whitewash brush.

"I know how much of a strain you've been under," I said carefully.

"I don't know if you do."

"Well, I don't know if you appreciate my feelings with regard to all that's happened, either."

"I know that you're having some kind of overheated mommy lust for this kid—"

Suddenly furious, I said, "I am not. Stuart, I am not."

"It's completely obvious. You're over there with her and Plant Man every day and night, nesting your brains out—"

"What? What a lousy thing to say!"

"As if seven years at Women and Children First had never happened, or taught you anything about these women . . ."

"Stuart, are your clients poster children for wise choices and moderate behavior?"

"Not to mention that you have no time in your life left for anything except her and the house, so what would happen if you did have your dream come true and we had a baby? I'd probably see you on weekends, if you could squeeze me in—"

"It's *you* who's always so busy, Stuart. Your eight-day weeks. Your thirty-hour days. And I was supposed to be ready to be there for you whenever you got the time—"

"Anne, stop it," said Stuart. "This is lousy."

It was.

We sat there in silence.

And we spent most of the week in silence, Stuart tearfully packing his boxes with those things he couldn't part from even for the few weeks he'd spend holed up in the bachelor studio his new firm would provide in Miami—his Nolan Ryan signed ball, his running shoes on their stretching rack, the two Sinatra *Duets* CDs. Without ever actually saying so, we talked as if I'd follow him for a visit almost immediately—when at least I had Arley sorted out—to search for a job of my own. And, Stuart said once, it was entirely possible that Florida wouldn't work out, that he'd be back in a few months. We didn't say anything about our wedding. We didn't say anything much.

Early on the morning Stuart was to leave, Arley called me, sobbing. "I don't want you to miss Stuart on account of me!" I hushed her. It wasn't only her, I told her, realizing the truth of it as I said it. It was a whole world of my own, a world outside the consuming demands of my work, which had somehow opened, by chance, and embraced me: My house. Arley. And Charley Wilder. I couldn't ignore the fact that I didn't want to leave behind Charley's loony, beguiling anecdotes about paint and architecture and social history and plants. I'd asked him a few nights before what his degree was in, and he'd taken a while to ponder before he'd announced, "You know, I don't think I have an entire one. But I probably have three-quarters of one in English, almost all of one in graphic design, and another one almost done in horticulture." A few moments later, he'd added, "I guess I already knew what my work was going to be. You know what they say: you can lead a whore to culture, but you can't make her think."

No other human being could have elicited a laugh from me with that rank old sexist line.

My little world didn't, however, do much to lessen the velocity of my tears on the way to the airport. Stuart looked a little perplexed; it wasn't good-bye forever, after all. We'd spent plenty of days and nights apart in our life together. Still, we never really talked about our good-bye at the airport that day and what it might have meant. Stuart kissed me and got out of the car. But then, I remember, he leaned back in through the window. "Never change, babe," he said, his face the sweet and serious Jewish monk's face I loved so entirely it was as if we were siblings, reared on one stalk. It seemed unthinkable that Stuart and I could ever really be apart.

Our whole personal library of pre- and perinuptial fights suddenly seemed inconsequential. All the way home, I was besieged by images of regret and abandonment. I'd be lost without Stuart. I already was.

Then I thought, I'll go and see Charley. But immediately thought, how could you, Anne?

It didn't matter, in any case.

When I got home, Jack Becker was in front of my house with one Carla Merrill, agent of the Federal Bureau of Investigation.

It soon became clear that Langtry Mowbray, a white female, aged twenty-one years, had disappeared from her mother's locked house in Avalon, Texas, leaving behind all her earthly goods, so far as anyone could tell, except a pair of multicolored cowboy boots. A blood-drenched nightgown was found trampled on the ground below the second-story window of the bedroom now hers, once Arley's. There was blood on the walls of the room and on the open window, but not on the metal extension ladder that lay among the chile pequin bushes. Langtry's mother, Rita Mowbray, had been at work at Texas Christian Hospital when whatever took place at the house took place. Ms. Mowbray was quite calm. Her greatest anxiety was the ladder, which she was careful to explain was not hers, and to insist that it be removed before it ruined her shrubbery.

"Where is Arley?" I asked Jack, trying to restrain a scream. "Where is Arley right now?"

"She's in her apartment," Jack said. "And we have a unit on her, front and back."

"Would she have a way of knowing?"

"I can't read her mind, honey," Jack Becker said. "If she's watching TV, she knows."

I grabbed my purse to turn and run right back down the walk.

But the FBI agent broke in: "We need to talk to Missus LeGrande."

"Not tonight."

"Miss Singer, this is a homicide investigation—"

"She's having a baby at six o'clock in the morning! She's fifteen years old!"

"If she's been in contact with her husband—"

"She hasn't been in contact with her husband or anyone but me!" I pleaded with Jack. "You know it's true, Jack. Her own mother doesn't even know where she is. . . ."

"That is true," he agreed.

"I'm not saying you don't need to talk with her. But this kid has been through so much. A few hours—"

"Can mean a cold trail," Carla Merrill assured me.

"This is a terrible idea for her physical health, Miss Merrill," I said then, scrambling for my lawyer gears, settling down. "As you know, a girl this young is at considerable risk."

They stood there, both of them, staring at the curb. Then Carla Merrill said, "Well . . ."

I knew then that they'd give Arley one last night of peace. Jack agreed to keep in constant phone contact with me—I'd stay at Arley's apartment. But as I went to gather up my briefcase and my overnight bag from my apartment, Merrill touched my arm and looked me in the eye.

"You know, it's just possible that this has nothing to do with Dillon LeGrande," she said. Langtry, she went on, had no short-age of unsavory pals: she was apparently a successful call girl, with a real following among minor-league Hispanic hoodlums.

But there was one thing. Merrill hesitated.

"What? What? Tell me right now."

It just couldn't get out to the media; she'd have to rely on me for that.

I wanted to smack her one. But then she finally told me.

There'd been something found at the scene: a cream-colored card with letters cut from magazines to spell out a single line: "What?" I asked. "What line?" She told me: "Wait for me by moonlight."

Right then I couldn't have known the significance of that par-ticular bit of poetry. I thought the card found at Rita's house, with its spooky line, was one of a kind. But of course it was not.

Arley

If there is a hell, I'm going to it, because most of what I remember feeling when I finally found out about Lang was that her disappearing, however it happened, screwed up my first few months with Desi. After all, Langtry had no use for me, and I hadn't really known her except for a few hours every few months since I was a little girl. I was so sick and frazzled after Desi was born, and then finding out about Lang, that I couldn't even nurse Desi properly at first. And all the while, Annie kept acting like the Nazis were coming to break into the secret annex. She carried her ugly little gun everywhere and got me shuttled off to the cabin at light speed, even before I was supposed to leave the hospital.

At first I didn't really think what happened to Lang had anything to do with Dillon. And I certainly didn't know anything about any card at my mama's house. Or I would have told. I really would have. About my card with the red ribbons. About the card Dillon sent me. And about the card I found.

It sounds horrible, and ridiculous, but I didn't really think it was important. Not right then. Not by the time I got into the hospital just the next morning and the birth was starting and all.

I thought it could have been a prank. I was pretty sure Dillon never told anyone about the things we did, or the things we said.

But he could have.

He could have told Kevin.

And in my heart I did suspect that Dillon was the one who'd sent our poetry to that TV anchorwoman in San Antonio. He would have liked the attention.

But that morning, the day before Desi was born, I was outside getting my own mail. Mostly, I just got mail that said "Occupant," but I was looking for a CD I'd ordered through a special offer from the Ameristar Music Library. The guy said it would be there in three days, and here it had been six. I went flipping through the envelopes, looking for something in cardboard, and then I saw it.

It was a shiny black envelope. Like a fancy wedding invitation or one of those You're-Turning-Thirty birthday cards. No stamp on it.

I opened it. There was a card inside. It didn't look like the card I got FedEx'd on fiesta night. It was just a plain white file card, and the words on it were cut out of some book. Very tiny. It said: "Then look for me by moonlight."

It scared me so bad I dropped it right there by the mailboxes and went running back inside. Then I was afraid to go back down and get it. If it was from Dillon, then he knew where I was. But nobody was supposed to know where I was, and Jeanine's apartments were, like, sealed from the telephone directory and everything. Nobody but the birth parents knew where in the city they were.

And what did it mean? Was I going to see Dillon? My heart felt like it was starting to expand. With the baby, I could barely breathe anyhow. I thought I'd pass out, standing there by the breakfast bar. Where was Dillon? Was he telling me he was coming for me and for our baby? Coming to rush us off to Mexico? I didn't want to go to Mexico. I didn't want to have my baby in some old house with some old car sitting out in front of it. I didn't want to have my baby without Annie. On the other hand, I wanted to be with him, at least for a little while. At least for a night. To look in his eyes. To touch him and make love. To see whether he really hurt that man, or if, as I suspected, it was all Kevin and that Indian, with Dillon craving only his freedom.

How had he found me, I wondered. Someone would have had to see me come over, that first night, to know I was here at all. . . . It didn't make sense. He wasn't a ghost, even though I sometimes thought of him that way. He was just a person. He couldn't be in two places at once. . . . I didn't know whether to be excited or terrified.

If I'd known about Lang then, I'd have been scared to death.

But not much was making sense to me at that time. I was addled by my body. Even my brain seemed to float.

They say you don't recall labor—or you wouldn't ever go through it again willingly. But I remember every instant of Desiree's birth. It's before and after I don't recall. Hardly anything from the month before and not much of the whole month after, my first month at the cabin, when Annie was practically living there and I was asleep half the time. The birth, though, that was beautiful, though Annie would not say the same thing, particularly the shape she's in right now. At the time, she kept comparing the physical part of it, especially hooking the IV lines up for the induction, to what happened to Stuart's clients on death row, which was sort of weird. She even thought having to go to the hospital at six A.M. was horrible—like getting guys up at midnight to execute them.

She was a nervous wreck the night before we went to the hospital. I thought it was because she'd dropped Stuart off at the airport and was depressed.

But it was really because she was so afraid.

That's why she just kept babbling. Talking about death row. It didn't do much for my frame of mind.

"Think about it, Arley." She made us some macaroni and picked up the plates to rinse them before I could even finish mine. "Think about dinner dishes from your last meal—now, there's a concept, huh? Say they're all cleared away. What are you going to do for the night? Watch old *Mary Tyler Moore* shows? You could never sleep. No hope for that. And no hope for anything else, no room to maneuver, no way to back off and change the course, no reprieve, nothing to do but hang around. Like we're hanging around tonight. No! God! I didn't mean it that way at all! I'm just babbling . . . I'm sorry."

"Annie, chill," I told her. "Come on! I think you're more scared than I am."

"I'm sure I'm more scared than you are."

By that time, I'd almost forgotten the card by the downstairs mailbox. I guess it was swept up or something. I was so worn out, I slept like a baby that night. But Annie was up, checking the windows, fiddling with the phone. She wouldn't let me touch the TV. "The sound will drive me nuts," she grumbled. What I didn't know then was that she was keeping me away from TV news, especially those little breaks they like to do when something happens in a juicy case like Dillon's. Since I didn't know anything about what had gone on at Mama's house (though I did think that Annie got a strange number of phone calls at my apartment, even for her), I just believed she was all wired up over me going to have the baby and Stuart leaving, coming so close on each other.

Later, Annie told me she'd watched the parkway all night long like it was a movie. Every time she heard a rustle in the live oak outside my window, she'd turn, expecting what she called Dillon's "green glass" eyes. All night long, police cruisers glided around the apartment house, she said later, surfacing unexpectedly like sharks. She'd wondered, all alone, whether she should have brought me to the hospital that very night, whether Dillon would jump us when she brought me outside in the morning. And she'd kept thinking about what would happen if he did and wanted to take me. Would I go? Would I run right to him, without a backward glance? She had no idea how strong my commitment was to my baby. And neither of us had any idea how strong my commitment was to her, to Annie herself. So, until she heard the dawn birds, she didn't relax. And she never let me know.

About five in the morning, I woke up when I heard the door of my apartment open and close. I got up and slipped into my clothes, which I'd set out the night before, and looked out the window. Annie was talking to somebody in a police car. I knew it was a police car because Charley had showed me how to spot unmarkeds: four-doors with big tires. The phone rang then. I picked it up, and it was the hospital. They told me that the induction had to be rescheduled and they would call me later in the day with more information.

Dr. Carroll was overbooked. They were sorry.

They didn't sound sorry.

I started to cry.

Annie unlocked the door and came back in. When she saw me, she dropped her purse with a big *thunk*—it had her gun in it—and yelled, "Where is he?"

I looked up at her and shrank back on my couch. "Who?"

"Dillon! Is he here?"

"Annie," I said, shocked out of my tears. "There's no one here but me." Breath rushed back into my chest, hurting as if I'd run a mile of hurdles.

"What's the matter, then, honey? Are you scared?"

"No. But the hospital called. They said I can't have the baby."

She almost laughed. "It's a little late for that, I think. What did they really say?"

"They said they were . . . filled. There was no bed for me. So they would just do the induction next week or something."

"But you know that's a mistake, honey. I talked with Doctor Carroll yesterday."

"I know! I told them that! I asked to talk to Doctor Carroll, but they said he was busy. They said to call back later."

Annie stood there puffing.

She later told me that she was thinking maybe she could fire her gun, after all, take it into the lobby of Texas Christian Hospital and just open up. And then she grabbed up the phone and told me to go in the other room. I heard some of what she was saying, though, even through the door.

". . . a misunderstanding . . . Arlington LeGrande was to be admitted this morning. . . . In jeopardy, yes, and not just because of problems with the baby. . . . Oh, yes you do. . . . It had better not be because of that. . . . Yes, we will. Oh, no, do not misunderstand me. We will be there in approximately half an hour for this procedure."

Annie opened the bedroom door. "Get your duffel bag, Arley." I got my duffel bag. It was all packed. She was still on the telephone.

"Listen, you poor soul," she said. "I am Anne D. Singer, Arlington LeGrande's attorney. At a regularly scheduled prenatal ap-

pointment last week, I witnessed the decision to induce labor so as
not to jeopardize a pregnancy in which a young woman in fragile
health is past her due date and in which the fetus has demon-
strated some evidence of distress. I confirmed this situation by
telephone yesterday with Doctor Carroll. . . . No, it doesn't matter
a goddamn what has happened since yesterday. . . . Sorry, no,
here's the situation: As Arlington LeGrande's attending physician,
who has been responsible for her prenatal care since the eighth
week of her pregnancy, only Doctor Carroll can make the decision
to postpone this birth—despite the anxiety and emotional damage already caused my client by the nature and timing of the new
decision—for reasons that I can only surmise are medically suspect. But you tell him now that if he makes that choice, given that
any other physician would be very reluctant to assume Arlington's
care at this stage, and any harm result to Arlington LeGrande or
her baby because of what might appear to be a decision motivated
by expedience and reasons other than her medical well-being and
that of her unborn child, you can certainly expect that he and
Texas Christian Hospital will be called to answer for this harm in a
legal proceeding of serious proportions."

She waited. I guess she was on hold. "Turn out the lights, Arley," she said.

"Why's there a police car downstairs?"

"How did you know it's a police car?"

"I know. Everybody knows what those cars look like."

"Well, they're just checking, you know. They do that all the
time."

"Are you sure?"

"I'm sure. They're checking up on you, you know. They know
that Dillon would realize it's around the time when the baby

would be—yes, I understand." She was back on the phone. "No, there will be no inconvenience to my client in that regard. I'm sure you will make every effort to see Missus LeGrande to her room promptly."

That police car followed us the whole way. Once we got there, we didn't even wait five minutes. There were a few police in uniforms in the lobby. "There are always police in city hospitals," Annie said. "You should see Bellevue."

The medical technician came to take blood samples from me right when we got off the elevator. "Keep walking," the tech said. "Maybe you can get things happening on your own that way. Worked for me." I was in my room in under ten minutes. The nurse came right away. *"Sientes bien, mi hija?"* she asked me sweetly.

"I don't speak Spanish," I told her, trying not to sound like I was smart-mouthed. "I'm not Hispanic. I just look it."

It made Annie mad that they assumed I *had* to be Mexican, since I was a young girl and had no man. But the way it turned out, this nurse, Shelley, didn't even know who I was or what had happened with Dillon. She wasn't the type to pay attention to the news, not that any of this would have made Annie get less angry. By that point, she was ready to blow sky-high.

"Well, I never miss the chance to try out my Spanish," said the nurse, and she asked Annie, "Will you be with Missus LeGrande? Are you responsible for medical decisions?"

"I'm her lawyer, and I'm her friend, so yes. Her husband can't . . . be present."

"I see," Shelley said.

The nurses took my clothes and I showered. Annie stayed right there with me. I didn't mind. They gave me this cotton gown stamped all over with red stars. I found out later it came from the pediatrics ward and that they gave it to me because they thought I might like it better. I think that was a nice thing to do. As they were hooking up all the tubes and the baby's heart monitor, Annie took off and went for coffee. When she came back, I just for, like, tradition's sake, decided I should ask her to call my mama.

But Annie answered, "I already tried. I couldn't reach her."

Well. That was that. To keep from feeling sad, I watched Shelley and another nurse fiddle with dials and knobs.

"See?" Shelley said, pointing to the line of liquid light. "That's the baby's heart rate: one-sixty, one-thirty, one-forty, one-eighty. Can't tell if it's a boy or a girl. It's all over the place." All of a sudden, I felt the baby unfurl and stretch.

"It moved," I said, "the baby." It was only then I realized it. After months of gymnastics, the baby had hardly moved at all in . . . well, I didn't remember how long. I just hadn't noticed.

"Doesn't the baby move all the time, honey?" Shelley asked.

"No, not hardly ever," I told her. "Not for days and days. Is that okay?" I saw Annie and the nurses look at each other. The nurse who was not Shelley went out into the hall. Then Dr. Carroll came in—he was so clean!—and shook hands with Annie. She'd been his patient for years, but they didn't look very friendly right now.

"Doctor," Shelley told him, "Missus LeGrande isn't feeling very much movement."

"Maybe not much room left to move, I suspect? Well, that's why we're here."

"Okay," I said.

"Anne," Dr. Carroll said then, softly. "My daughter is a lawyer too. And she says that the primary rule of law is that you never go after a mosquito with a cannon, because you usually miss."

"You don't know what she's going through, or what she's going to have to go through," Annie said.

"In fact, there was no intent to upset or discourage Arlington this morning. It *was* a misunderstanding. And it would have been corrected within a very few minutes even if you hadn't—"

"She didn't know that. I didn't know that."

"But I did," he said firmly. "No patient's status with Medicaid nor any other events in her life have any bearing on my individual treatment of that patient. Surely, in your work, you practice the same standard."

"All my clients have the same status," Annie said. "Except her."

Dr. Carroll smiled. "I know this is a time of real stress for you. I know that as your physician and as your friend." He turned to me. "Shall we have this baby?"

"Yes, please," I said.

They left Annie and me alone for a while. Even Shelley left. I was just supposed to contract. The induction would be slow and gradual. "People say that you get harder labor with Pitocin, but it's just not true," Shelley told us when she returned. "You'll go just the same way as anyone else." As she hipped open the door, there came an animal howl from down the corridor. "Another citizen of the republic," she said, smiling. I gripped Annie's hand. That lady sounded like she was dying, not having a baby. She sounded like a horror movie.

I had to take my mind off it. "Let's watch TV," I told Annie. "Let's watch the *Today* show."

Annie said, "No. You have to concentrate." Now I know why she did that. But then I thought it was pretty unfair—after all, I was the one who was having a baby.

Plus I was starving. "I reckon they won't let me eat, huh?"

"No."

"I'm so hungry I could eat Saint Augustine grass."

"Well, hurry up and have a baby, then."

"Maybe I should try to sleep."

"Good idea."

She was the one who fell asleep, though. She closed her eyes and relaxed her grip on my hand, and in about one second she was gone, her head just leaning against the mountain of my belly. It was weird; I could see it get all hard, like the sides of a volcano, whenever a contraction came. They didn't even hurt. The sun was coming up, and the slats of the blinds made bars across Annie's face. She was moaning in her sleep. When Shelley came in and checked me, Annie didn't even move. "There's a policeman out there," Shelley said.

"It's because I'm a movie star," I whispered. I can't believe I said that. She could tell I was goofing around.

"I didn't know!" Shelley replied. It was like she actually believed me. But by the next time she came back in, I figured she knew exactly who I was, because she shook her finger at me, like "bad girl," and said, "You poor little thing. You ain't but a child yourself. I bet you wish he was here, huh?"

"I guess so. And I . . . I keep thinking about where he is right now and if he can feel what's happening to me. . . ." Something about those words woke Annie up. She told me to stop getting overexcited.

"I'm not overexcited!" I told her, but I was. I wanted Shelley to know I wasn't some gangster girl. "Those other boys who broke out . . . Dillon's not really like that."

Shelley left the room. Annie and I looked at each other. The contractions were coming closer together now and lasting longer. They were real labor pains. "I know I'm going to have to raise this baby all by myself," I told Annie, all of a sudden.

"You don't know that."

"Well, I know that after . . . what Dillon did, even if he didn't actually do it himself, I know we can't ever be together anymore. He can't be with the baby or me. He's going to go back to prison. Maybe he'll be like one of those people Stuart helps."

"That depends," Annie said, real slowly, like she was trying to ask me something instead of tell me something.

"You know it doesn't, Annie. You know they'd think of him as a murderer."

"Arley, you're having a baby—let's not talk about this now."

"I know all that stuff. But if I say I don't love him . . . if I don't love him anymore, if I'm not what he is, then I never loved him."

"You didn't know what you didn't know."

"You have to take the person for better or for worse. That's how it is. You're not supposed to just take them for their best." I tried to find words. "We made a person, Annie. And if I don't love the boy I made a person with, then I really am a fool like they all probably think. So I have to believe there was something in him that night that is gone now—or that everybody is mistaken about what he did." It was starting to really hurt. "I'm going to take deep, cleansing breaths. You're supposed to go without meds as long as you can."

"Arley," Annie said, "God made drugs for times like these."

"Innnnnnn. And ouuuuuuut . . ." I didn't want to take any drugs. Dr. Carroll said eighty percent of women didn't need anything at all.

Annie went downstairs for more coffee. Before she left, she

opened the blinds. It suddenly looked like it was going to storm, the clouds lowering and gray. When she got back and put her hand on my forehead, I smelled popcorn, which pissed me off a lot. "You ate good stuff!" I said. "And I'm starving!" She went into the little airplane-sized washroom and washed her hands. Shelley came in and examined me, told me I was halfway there.

"It hurts some," I told her. "Actually, it hurts pretty wicked."

"Do you want to sit in the whirlpool?"

"Will it hurt the baby?"

"I wouldn't suggest it if it would," Shelley said.

Sitting in the tub didn't do one damn thing to change the pain. It felt good in other ways, though. Like, I felt lighter. I could breathe. I think I fell asleep for a minute. I had a dream, about a swimming baby. A kind of baby mermaid. When I woke up, I couldn't remember how Annie spelled her first name. So I called her.

"With an *e*," she shouted back from outside the door of the whirlpool room. "The right way."

Shelley helped me dry off and gave me a scrunchie for my hair. "Things are going to move faster now," she said.

Annie rubbed my back, the way they tell husbands to do in class. I wanted to hunch over, clench my teeth, fight the pain. You weren't supposed to do that. You were supposed to ride on it, like a surfer on the waves. But I couldn't keep ahead of it. "I can't do this, Annie. I'm not old enough," I told her.

"You can, you have to. Look at my face: I promise I won't let anyone hurt you."

"Ever?"

"Ever."

"Breathe, blow," I said, trying to relax, and then this terrible thing happened. My legs, which had been paining like a pulled tendon—they all of a sudden were gone. "I can't feel my legs!"

Annie jammed her thumb on the red button. Shelley came running, but she said it was just some nerve depression or something. "There ain't nothing worse than labor," she sort of sang to me.

"I need a shot—"

"Just a little longer."

"No, now!" shouted Annie. I screamed when another contraction gripped me, this one like a knife in the base of my spine. I could smell my own sweat, and it didn't smell like me at all. It smelled like metal, like a piece of machinery that was on fire. I hollered again for Annie. It didn't seem like even a second since the last pain, and here I was having another one. I was going to rip apart and bleed to death, I knew it. I'd never felt anything like it, not a cramp, not a headache, not even the time I broke my ankle, and they say that's the sheerest pain there is. Annie took my face and tried to center it. But I was thrashing my head like a wild horse. I reached up and grabbed Annie's wrists and pulled them down.

"Get the damn doctor!"

"I don't want to leave you!"

"Get him, or I'm going to die right now!"

She ran. I grabbed the sheet in both hands and tried to rip it, though I couldn't. The pain in my back was so big, I couldn't imagine I would live through it. The only bigger thing was the feeling of wanting to push the baby—which I now hated—out of me forever. And that feeling was the biggest feeling you'll ever have on this earth. No other way to describe it. It simply towered over you. And so I began to push and grunt, and I felt spit coming out of my mouth, and I screamed, "Annie! Mama! Mama!"

And Annie came running in like the devil was chasing her,

and right behind her was Dr. Carroll, and he whipped up the
sheet and said, "Okay, okay, we've got a head crowning down
here . . . couple more pushes, Arley. Don't waste it. . . ."

"I was calling you—" I said to Annie, reaching for her hand.

"I heard you calling. Arley, honey, I tried to reach her. I don't
think she's here."

"I wasn't calling *her*," I said. The pain was coming again. The
rough and ripping pain that had nothing to do with my body at
all, pain that didn't even know I was there.

"I heard you call—"

"I was calling *you*, Annie. Annieeee!" I screamed. And out she
came. Blue-red and glisteny and looking like some special effect
from a sci-fi movie, a huge head, and arms and legs the size of a
man's fingers, but folded, the way you fold a shirt to pack it.
From her middle rose a huge grouty thing like a dragon's wing;
I'd forgotten all about the umbilical cord. I thought she had
something terribly wrong with her, and I almost screamed. But
then Annie was laughing and crying at the same time, and I knew
she would know if there were anything wrong. So I tried to reach
down for my baby, but she was so slippery that Shelley the nurse
had to kind of trap her in this towel, like you do a catfish.

"She is a beautiful child. She's a gift," said Dr. Carroll. "I
mean that, Arley. She's very pretty." He went to cut the cord, but
I stopped him. "Annie," I said. I remembered from the birthing
classes. The husband did that, to make him feel part of the baby's
life. I couldn't think of anything else to do for Annie. "Please let
Annie cut it for me."

Annie started wiping her eyes with the heels of her hands. "Arley, my hands are shaking too much."

"No," I said. "You have to." The pain was all gone: the
pain-of-the-cosmos pain. I felt ripped, though, which I was. The

baby wasn't tiny, like they said. If this was intrauterine growth retardation, I'm glad I caught it, because otherwise I'd still have her
stuck in me. She was really big, like one of those life-sized baby
dolls. I found out later that they make mistakes with ultrasound
all the time, and then just say, "Oh, that's interesting."

"Annie, look at the baby! Look!" She was turning her head,
left and right, blood glistening in her thick hair like bright jam,
and was sort of experimenting with opening her arms, the way
you see butterflies do when they dry their wings right after getting out of the cocoon. Shelley began to dab at her with the
towel, while Annie cut the cord. I swear I didn't even feel myself
push out the placenta. I just couldn't believe the size of her feet. I
couldn't believe that her palm already had lines, a heart line and a
life line. That somewhere inside her was a stomach, lungs the size
of butter beans, ovaries with little pin eggs in them that would
someday be able to make another one like her. I couldn't believe
I'd created a human being. I felt like minor royalty, like a duchess.
I wanted to jump up and sing.

By the time the doctor was done sewing me, they had her all
wiped off so that she looked almost like a real baby-book baby.
You could see that her hair, which had looked black with all
the goo, was really white blond, like little frills of cake icing. Dillon's hair.

"She's beautiful, Arley," Annie said, as Shelley passed the baby,
wrapped in a blanket, over to her. "Her Apgar scores were great.
She's really fine! Look, she has a little tiny cleft in her chin."

Uh-oh, I thought.

"I don't think that's such a good thing on a girl," I said weakly.
"Let me see her." But you couldn't hardly tell when you looked.
The cleft, right then, looked just like a little dimple. It would get
bigger, of course, but by then it would be part of Desi, and I

would forget that I'd ever believed any nonsense about a cleft not being a beautiful thing on any child, especially a girl baby.

The baby opened her eyes and looked straight at me. They will tell you newborns can't see, but I'm sure Desi could. She looked right at me, and I recognized her. She was the baby from the dream I'd had in the whirlpool tub. She was a person I'd known all my life. I said, not even thinking of the other people in the room, "I didn't know it would be you!"

There was food then, and Patty, Annie's friend from work, came over with champagne, and I even had a little of it.

Then, later, Jeanine brought a little goddess book on a chain from Tienda de Carina, to hang above the baby's crib, and told me that October 29 was a very magical day, part of Annie's favorite festival, Día de los Muertos, *and* the ancient feast of Persephone. Annie'd told me all about it, and now Persephone was my favorite story. She gets kidnapped by Hades, the god of the underworld, who rose up in his black chariot from beneath the wildflowers. Hades finally made a deal with Persephone's mom, Demeter, so Persephone would have to go back and spend half the year with him—and that was how winter got started.

I don't think Persephone minded going back that much, the way I recalled it. It was sort of a Beauty and the Beast type of relationship. But having all that magic surround Desiree's birth was a good thing. Even if some of it was dark magic, Jeanine pointed out, none of it was evil magic, and dark magic can be powerful. I told Jeanine I thought Desi was my little Halloween treat. Jeanine, who has seven brothers and sisters, said the trick would come later on, and don't you forget it. But Annie just kept chirping around the room like we'd won the big game or something; I loved seeing her so happy. It almost made me forget Dillon, to be honest, until Shelley came back to drop off the birth certificate forms. "You don't have to fill these out right now," she said. "Don't even think about 'em."

But I said, "No. I'm ready."

Quietly, Annie brought me a pen from her purse, and she and Jeanine watched as I wrote out her name: *Desiree Anne LeGrande*.

Mother: Arlington Mowbray LeGrande.

Father: Dillon Thomas LeGrande.

"That's for you," I told Annie, pointing. I didn't know that Anne was the commonest middle name on earth. "I always wanted a middle name myself. This is almost as good." She just nodded, with her lips pressed together.

But Jeanine asked me, "Why did you pick Desiree? Did Dillon like it? Is it a character in a book?"

"It means something."

"Desire? Like, the streetcar named Desire?"

"Well, no. It means 'want.' Like *Je désire la plume,* would mean 'I want the pen.' In French. And with LeGrande, it means 'wanted very much.' Which is how I wanted her. I don't ever want her to think, because of the kind of start she got, that she wasn't wanted. Right, Annie?" I said.

But she didn't answer. She had her back to me and was looking out the window at the hard rain that had begun to fall.

CHAPTER SEVENTEEN

Annie

I'd have loved to have taken Jeanine up on her offer to go out for drinks, in honor of the baby's birth, that night when we left the hospital. I would have, too, if it hadn't been for the dread. I was so keyed up that I smelled.

I'd talked with Carla Merrill twice during Arley's labor. The FBI agent had spent an enlightening hour with Kate LeGrande at her house, during which Kate expressed surprise that the law would want to know about all those times Dillon had called her or asked about the whereabouts of his wife. She assumed that since her son was a fugitive, the police already knew about his phone calls. "Don't they keep track of stuff like that? And the girl, I don't even know her," Kate had told the FBI agent. "I don't think she's really . . . our kind." Not once in the hour Carla Merrill spent with her did Kate LeGrande get up from the sofa, turn off the TV, or offer the agent so much as a glass of water. She did explain that she had not eaten or slept, "that I can really remember," for the past several years, and work was "out of the question, because of my nerves." Disability checks and the late Tom LeGrande's Social Security were hardly enough to live on, "and

341

since the boys left, we've had a lot worse time. You know," Kate confided, "the state didn't do a thing to replace the money the boys brought in. Dillon and Kevin were real good workers." Carla Merrill hadn't known whether to laugh or cry at the idea of income replacement for imprisoned offspring. The most unsettling thing was just outside the back door. It was the skeleton of some kind of huge bird—a gull or a hawk—lying in the dust next to an overturned tin bucket, with a length of light chain still around its neck.

No one seemed to know the whereabouts of the littlest LeGrande. Kate had to ask his older brother, "It a school day?"

The big teenager, Kier LeGrande, not visibly hurrying to either school or a job himself, sat at the kitchen table, rolling a log pile of unfiltered cigarettes. He only shrugged and said he had no idea where Philippe was . . . hadn't seen him for days.

The bloody spoor Dillon seemed destined to leave throughout South Texas appeared to trouble the LeGrandes less than his choice in women. "We weren't brought up to marry no little kids in grade school, ma'am," Kier told Carla Merrill. "My mama's right. People who do that aren't our kind."

Carla Merrill had no idea what he meant.

I suggested some options: Episcopalians? The downwardly mobile? Close relatives of spree killers? Merrill wasn't amused, and it was really no time even for gallows humor. A certain kind of bad family will do everything but rent bikes to backpedal on their commitment and distance themselves from their wrongdoer. Suddenly, the apple of mom's eye is someone she can't quite remember ever having met.

This bizarre conversation with Carla had a fuguelike quality. I understood now what people meant when they said, borrowing from medical lingo, that they were "in shock." For some reason, the cyclone force of Dillon's capacity for havoc had not really hit me until the previous afternoon. Perhaps I'd lived too long with Stuart. Shooting a marshal during a getaway seemed almost a logical thing to do, despite how haunted I'd been by the photo I'd seen of that man's blasted face, his eyes wide open in immortal surprise. What had happened to Arley's sister somehow upped the ante: With the kind of manhunt reserved for cop killers in full cry, Dillon seemed to have felt confident climbing right up, like an outlaw Romeo, to his bride's window and, finding Lang in her stead, done God knows what. He seemed to think himself as mythical, beyond human. I could not divert my imagination from Lang's nightgown, how it must have looked, crumpled under the window like a monstrous hibiscus. Had he taken her body with him? Buried her? Kept her alive, hostage?

Apprised of her son's possible role in this outrage, Kate LeGrande had commented, "My goodness. I didn't think he even knew that Arley's sister."

Rita, her eldest missing and presumed dead, her youngest about to give birth to the child of a psychopath on the loose, her house on Jean-Marie Street now draped in yellow plastic tape, swarming with detectives and FBI sifting the soil and photographing the facade, had gone off to work.

Since I had my gun, I supposed Jeanine and I would be safe enough among the friendly faces at Amor Ausente. Sure, it was just minutes away; we could have walked there. But once we got outside the hospital, my nerve failed. I hadn't handled my gun in many weeks, except to shift it from purse to medicine cabinet and back again. Until the last crowd-packed days before he left, Stuart had been the one to take it out and clean it, lovingly oiling and swabbing the barrel with the little kit he'd purchased, probably imagining himself shooting it out on the high plains with John

Wesley Hardin. I had no idea how I would begin to take care of it on my own. Perhaps Charley would know. Or Tarik. Certainly Jack Becker could teach me. Being a gunslinger was much more demanding than it looked in Arnold Schwarzenegger movies. Before we parted in the hospital parking lot, I told Jeanine that Dillon would have time to dismember both Arley and me in leisurely fashion before I could even load the damned thing. Then Jeanine left, and I looked up at the window where I knew that Arley, blissfully ignorant of her sister's fate, slept under guard, with strict rules written into her chart forbidding any television except for movie cassettes. No matter what the precautions, it wouldn't take long before some chucklehead turned on the news. But I wanted Arley to have as much unsullied time as possible, getting to know her little earth angel, the baby named to commemorate the first Mowbray woman in history who, despite an avalanche of adverse circumstances, considered herself lucky to have a child.

I'd never seen a prettier newborn than Desiree. But I'd never seen a prettier man than Dillon, either. What might you have been, Dillon? I wondered. If you still had a future, you'd have a chance to spend time retooling your life with your beautiful daughter. Something almost like a savor of pity passed through me. Under another star, couldn't the man who'd written those poems have made a worthy life for himself? Look what Arley had done, cooking herself up a value system and a personality structure from things she most certainly didn't find around the house, and then sticking to them despite her own worst judgment.

It should not have surprised me that my car, piloted by a conspiratory hand, wound up in front of my house on Azalea Road.

I'd been looking forward to a shower and bed, and then back

to the hospital in the morning, to face the task of telling Arley about her sister.

But once I was there, I knew. The night wouldn't be complete unless I could tell Charley about Desiree. I didn't even consider my spiky hair and the wings of sweat under the collar of my blouse. His truck was in front, but I had to wind my way through the whole place, calling, before I found him upstairs in my bedroom.

There was a bed in there, a bed the size of Utah, though clearly made before anyone except actual kings used the term "king-sized."

"Hey," Charley said.

"Hey yourself."

"This is a really old bed," I said.

"Really old, and really big."

"I didn't know they had beds like that then," I said, running my fingers across scuffs and dabs left over from an apparent attempt to paint it blue. It was a beautiful piece of furniture, with four curved posts topped with smooth orbs the size of softballs.

"Must have been for a really big person," Charley said. "Or two really big people." He turned to me. "Hi, Annie. You look like you been rode hard and put away wet."

"Aren't you going to ask me if Arley's okay?"

"You wouldn't be here if Arley wasn't okay."

"Aren't you going to ask about the baby?"

He smiled broadly, looking up from the peg he was gently pounding into one of the sideboards. "Tell me all about the baby," he said.

"She's perfect."

"Ahhh . . . she."

"Yes," I said, "and I am pretty terrific also, although not too

345

calm. . . ." He held out his arms, and I walked into them, pillowing my head on his chest. The top of my head fit just under his chin, as I had imagined it would. "I haven't slept in thirty hours, Charley. I'm, as they say, packing a piece. I'm probably being followed by a killer who thinks I'm keeping his wife from—"

"I heard about that."

"And I just helped a fifteen-year-old give birth to an eight-pound baby girl."

"Named?"

"Desiree."

"Ahh. No, Desiree Anne."

"How did you know?"

"Just a hunch."

"She told you."

"Arley loves you, Anne," Charley said, pulling off his bandanna. "She's lucky to have you." I lifted my face and we kissed, adjusted and kissed again, our mouths encountering each other like old friends learning that nothing much had changed since the last time they were together.

"And there is," I said, into Charley's half-open mouth, "this one other thing."

"Which is?"

"Which is you, Charley. What am I going to do about you?"

"Do you want a beer?"

"Uh, sure. But wait a minute. I just kissed you. Do you think this is a good idea?"

"Well, I don't think it's one of the things you have to worry about."

"You don't?" I cried, standing back from him. "You don't?"

"No, I don't," Charley said, and then he made a sort of bow, and a flourish with his hammer. "And now a historic first! Anne, this gorgeous bed isn't going to cost you a little more! It's going to cost you a little less! It's going to cost you—and this is the only time you'll ever hear me say this, Anne—nothing!"

"Charley, be serious."

"I am serious. It's not going to cost a thing."

"I don't mean about that." I fit myself back into his arms, and he let his wrists slide slowly and softly down my back. "Okay, I'll bite. How come this gorgeous bed is going to cost me nothing?"

"I got it from a family down the street who were throwing it out. Couldn't bear the memories of their mother's last illness in it. . . ."

"Right *in* it? And what was it, bubonic plague?"

"She died of old age. Peacefully. And the mattress was new the year before."

"Well, thank goodness for that! What about those sheets?"

"Those were an extra set. But they're probably as old as the bed. Hand stitched. Like it?"

"It's beautiful."

"Well, I thought it belonged here."

"Thank you, Charley."

He kissed me again then, a longer, more confident kiss, a kiss with intentions. We rocked together, nearly losing our balance, turning our faces this way and that to get deeper. I felt Charley reach down and free my blouse, his hand sliding gently underneath to cup my breast. We sat down on the bed. Then he unbuttoned his shirt, and I noticed what looked like a tangled squirrels' nest made of glossy green leaves flung over the carved headboard. "Funeral flowers thrown in as a bonus?" I asked.

"It's mistletoe."

"Witchcraft?"

"No, you know. At Christmas, people hang mistletoe in the hall, and whoever stands under it gets a kiss."

"Charley, I do know that much about Christmas. But this isn't Christmas."

"I know."

"And if somebody was going to be kissed under that mistletoe, the somebody would have to be lying down."

"Right. That was my idea."

"But you didn't even know I was going to come here tonight."

"I knew—well, I hoped—you'd come here eventually. It didn't have to be tonight." We lay down, and he kissed me again, balletically removing my jeans, my bra, even my socks. He drew the hand-stitched sheet, water cool, up over my hips. I reached to open his belt.

"Charley," I said, "this isn't something we should do."

"Okay," he said.

"Okay?"

"I thought you and I had the same feelings, or I wouldn't have let you kiss me."

"Let *me* kiss *you?* You were the one who kissed me! Don't get the impression this was all my idea. . . ."

"You don't want this?"

"I . . . yes, I do. But I'm . . . I'm marrying Stuart."

"You are," he said. "Are you."

"I am. I think. He . . . he agreed. He said he'd have a child, if that was what I had to have." Charley kissed me again, more urgently, stroked my belly, and gently dipped his fingers into me, one by one. It was disconcerting. It took my mind off things. "But, Charley, he doesn't really want to get married . . . he just doesn't want to lose me . . ."

"I wouldn't want to lose you."

"And he doesn't want kids. He just agreed to it."

"You don't have to want to, to be good at it."

"But you said—you had to want it more than . . ."

"I said that for me, it had to be the thing you wanted more than anything else. Not for everybody."

"Do you want more children?"

"More than anything. When I find a woman I want more than anything."

"You mean me? But, Charley, I'm forty. I don't know if I have time to have more than one baby. . . ."

"We don't have to have all the babies. Just one. Or two."

"Charley, I'm so much older. . . ."

"That's supposed to be a good deal for a woman."

"But . . ."

"It means I'll be able to keep up with you."

"It's nuts."

"Do you want to sit up and talk, Anne?"

"Not really."

We settled back down, and I opened my eyes to take in Charley's work-chiseled body, the reddish tufts on his chest, the lathe-turned muscles of his legs as he removed his pants. Naked, he rolled his leg between mine, and helplessly, I began to chafe myself against him, vibrating, tightening.

"Listen," I said then.

Charley sighed.

"Wait. Just please listen. Arley had a baby tonight, which was mostly a terrible mistake. But also, somehow, something that makes everything else in the world feel . . . possible. You know?"

A life warrant, I thought.

But I didn't say it. I kissed Charley and said nothing.

"Annie," Charley whispered, "I know. I know."

"And we don't have any birth control."

"I didn't think we needed any."

"You mean, we're going to just . . . ?"

"Just hope for the best."

"But I'm not like that! I've spent my whole life dealing with what's left over from reckless behavior. That's what I do. *I'm* not reckless, Charley."

"I'm not reckless, either, Annie. I'm not irresponsible and I'm not a kid. If I make you pregnant tonight, I'll be a good father. And if you'll let me, a good husband too."

"Husband? *Husband?*"

As it happened, I did not get pregnant, not then. Though not from lack of trying.

Just as well: I wouldn't have known who the father was. Stuart had left for Florida only three days before. Three days in which so much had transpired—so much that was outside our life together—that our life together felt distant.

My God—I hadn't even told Stuart about Desi.

Charley was up before me, whistling, brushing his teeth with a brush he got out of the downstairs bathroom. What else did he keep here that I had never noticed? I sat cross-legged on the bed, trying to get my mind around things, trying to rationalize what looked sleazy in the morning light. I had, after all, never even seen the inside of this man's house! What if it was as bad as his rattletrap truck? What if he had no house at all and was just screwing me for a place to stay?

I got up, kissed Charley good-bye, went back to my apart-

ment, and burst into tears. I left a message on Rachael's answering machine, telling her in sister code—in case a nephew should
press the button—what I'd done. I was glad Rachael wasn't there,
not because I didn't think she'd treat me gently—I knew she
would—but because I was ashamed. Still crying, I began scrubbing counters, and when the phone rang, I almost didn't pick
up, thinking it would be Charley or Stuart. But it wasn't either
of them. It was Jeanine, who said she'd been looking for me
everywhere.

"You have to move Arley," she told me.

"Well, the house should be ready in a few months, maybe less.
Charley's really working at it, and he's getting help. . . ."

Charley.

Charley kneeling on the bed. Pulling me to him, my legs a
wishbone.

"It has to be sooner than that."

"Well, with the help he's getting—"

"It has to be tonight."

"Jeanine!"

"It has to be."

"Jeanine, Arley gave birth eight hours ago."

"Okay, tomorrow."

"What are you talking about?"

"A couple of things. None of which means I don't love you, or
Arley, or even Arley's baby."

"Cut to the chase, Jeanine."

"Jack thinks, and I think, and the agency thinks—"

"Now we're getting somewhere. . . ."

"Cut that out, Annie. Just listen."

"Okay. I'm sorry."

Jack and Jeanine and her adoption agency, it turned out,

thought a couple of things. They thought Arley might not be safe at the apartment, even though, technically, no one was supposed to know she lived there and, theoretically at least, Dillon didn't know it, either. But there were other risks to consider. Like the safety of the other birth mothers and their children, for one. The fact that Jeanine no longer had any justification, however fragile, for giving Arley shelter at The Terrace—since she clearly was not going to offer Desiree for an adoption placement—was another. Not to mention, and Jeanine didn't, the fact that she shouldn't have housed Arley at The Terrace in the first place.

I understood. But I had no idea where to turn.

"Now, don't worry," Jeanine was saying. "I'm sure we can sort something out."

"She'll just have to come to my place," I told her flatly.

"That's not a good idea. You know it isn't. You know he's got to know exactly where you live."

"We could take her to her mother's. I hear she's got an empty room."

"Nice, Anne."

"Well, a hotel, then. If the police are so concerned about her, how about a hotel? In, say, Vancouver?"

"We'll think of something."

"I should be over there right now. She's going to see a TV any minute. Or a newspaper."

"I don't think she's going to be thinking about TV or newspapers this morning."

"Someone's going to tell her."

"Well, why don't you go over there, then? What are you doing?"

"I'm cleaning the counters."

"Why?"

I started to cry again and fought a serious urge to tell Jeanine everything. Fortunately, she spoke before I could. "I'll come over in a little while, and we'll figure it out."

That day, I did see the inside of Charley Wilder's house. It was clean, basic. Well, primitive. Arley and the baby slept in the bedroom little Claude usually used, where a futon on the floor looked up on a ceiling of mother and baby frogs on lily pads. Charley and I slept atop the quilt on his bed, which had a headboard he'd made himself from a slab of petrified wood.

Not that anyone slept much. Thin wails from newborn Desi, the new calculus between Charley and me, the undercurrent of unease and threat . . . we all acted like transients laid over in a bus depot, our slumber shallow and tense. Charley and I didn't make love. It would have been unseemly.

But in the morning, Jeanine came with good news. Her father was a minister, who'd once mentored a wealthy parishioner's son back home after he'd run away. In gratitude, the man, a rancher named Mallory, had given Jeanine's dad keys to one of his three vacation homes, a hunting cabin in the hill country. He'd also given him carte blanche about using it. Jeanine's dad had called his friend and told him about Arley. And Mallory said the child was welcome.

"It has everything she needs, and it's clean, and there are good neighbors in the fancy houses right up on the ridge," Jeanine said. "And nobody could find it. Even my dad can't find it half the time, and he used to take us out there all the time when we were kids."

"Will she be safe there, Jeanine?" I asked.

"She'll be fine. It's only about a half hour from here, you know, by Uvalde. Jack's parents live out near there, in the woods."

"What about wildlife? Coyotes and stuff?"

"She's not going to be bothered by coyotes, Anne. And the only wildlife in those woods are quail and people who live in those little tar-paper shanties . . ."

"What? Which people?"

"Like, hippies, Anne. Guys who want to be like Thoreau. Except not as . . . successful."

"What if they're dangerous?"

"Anne, the biggest danger to Arley right now is her own husband."

That was a fact. But the cabin turned out to be a miracle; it redeemed Jeanine entirely for ejecting Arley from The Terrace. She and I drove out there, with a trunk full of baby supplies.

Then, I had to go back to the hospital. I couldn't postpone telling Arley the truth any longer.

She was nursing. Awkwardly, but gamely, she kept readjusting the baby's head, which was round and rosy as an Indian River grapefruit. Arley beamed at me. "She's got the right idea but the wrong area. She's not good at geography either."

"Arley."

She heard it in my voice. And she shut down. The peculiar flatness she seemed able to summon at will took over, as it seemed always to do when she sensed bad news on the way.

"Dillon, right?"

"Honey, we aren't sure."

"Did he rob somebody or something?"

"Arley, look at me."

She looked up. Her lips were deliberately firm; but a wince, a momentary request for mercy, crossed her face at the lines of her eyes. "What?"

"Your sister, Langtry. She's . . . she's gone, Arley."

"You mean, she disappeared? Because that's no big deal, Annie, Langtry was always one to take off. . . ."

"She didn't take off. They think someone took her. Kidnapped her. She was in her room . . ."

"My room."

"Arley."

"Okay."

"She was in her room and the police think it's possible someone broke in and . . . there was blood on the wall. . . ."

"Hurt her?"

"They think someone must have hurt her."

"Killed her?"

"We don't know for sure; she could have just been hurt. It might not even be her blood. They're testing the samples now. . . ."

"They think Dillon did it."

"It's possible."

"They think he was looking for me."

"Don't be afraid," I said quickly, moving to put my arms around her.

"I'm not afraid!" she cried, pushing my arms back, holding Desi close to her chest. "I'm not *afraid*!! It just makes me sick is all! It's fixing to make me hate my baby, and I love my baby! No . . . !" She went on fiercely, as I tried again to touch her.

"You're going to be okay, Arley. We're going to take you to a safe place . . ."

"I have my apartment."

"That's the thing. The police think, and Jeanine thinks, that you won't be safe there, if this is as bad as it seems."

"Annie," she said softly, suddenly just a child. "That's my own place. . . . please . . . you tell them . . ."

"There's a pretty cabin in the woods, Arley. You'll be safe there until the house is all ready. Charley says it will be real soon." I was talking to her as though she were three, and I was embarrassed by the Mister Rogers lilt in my voice. "There's a porch swing, and a yard to walk in with the baby."

"I don't care."

"What?"

"I mean, I'm grateful. It just doesn't matter."

"So we have to go. As soon as the FBI agent gets a chance to talk to you."

"I don't know a single thing. There's nothing to talk to me about."

"She still has to talk to you."

"You mean we have to leave today?"

"Yes, Arley."

"I just had a baby! I'm all . . . sore! What if the baby gets sick?"

"Doctor Carroll says she'll be just fine. And so will you. You're young and strong. . . ."

"Well, I don't believe Dillon did *any* of this stuff. And if he did, he's just . . . he's evil. He's a punk and a liar. And he'll never see our baby, never." Arley raised her head, and I could see her forehead glistened with sweat. "Annie, do you think she's okay?"

"Langtry?"

"No. Desiree. My baby."

"Arley, sweetie, she's absolutely okay. She's perfect."

"Do you think she's . . . bad inside?"

"Arley, no. No! How people are born . . . what their parents are like, that doesn't matter. It's how you're raised that makes you what you are."

"Oh, great," she said. "That really cheers me up."

"You'll be a good mother, Arley."

356

"How would you feel, if you were me? Annie?"

"I don't know," I said, and I didn't.

When Carla Merrill arrived, I listened in silence while she asked Arley the rote questions. To all of them, she answered simply, "No, ma'am." When Merrill asked if she wanted to phone her mother, she answered, "No, ma'am." Her dumb show fooled me. I never would have suspected she was anything except shocked and hurting. I never would have suspected secrets.

She liked the cabin. She admired the soft oak-plank floor, noticed that there was a window air conditioner, bright banks of windows, and even a little screened sleeping porch where she could take the Portacrib and her rocker on days when the heat allowed her some respite. "That'll help some," she said. "I appreciate all this, Jeanine."

Charley, Jeanine, and I carried in Arley's few things. But just as Jeanine was about to go for groceries, Arley spoke up. She said, "I need my stile."

"Your what?" I asked her.

"My hurdle, for practicing. I left it at Mama's."

"We can get it," I suggested, hesitantly.

"No," Arley replied quickly. "I don't want to go back there."

"You wouldn't have to; one of us could pick it up."

"No. That's okay. No, thank you, I mean. I don't want anyone to go there."

"I'll make you a new one," Charley offered. "You won't be running hurdles for a while."

"The doctor said two weeks for exercise."

"I think you need a little more time than—" I began.

"No!" Arley said fiercely. "Two weeks! I want to stay in shape. I don't want having the baby to be the end of . . . everything. Of everything else."

I shushed her. Charley and I exchanged looks over her head.

Jeanine came back with staples—milk, bread, pinto beans. "Just in case. I'm beginning to remember how this place can feel like the far corner of nowhere," she said.

"I think that's what's called for now," I assured her. We looked around. Nothing stirred. The cabin was set in a small stand of cedar, in keeping with the Texan preoccupation with shade, surrounded by fields of waist-high Johnson grass nobody'd bothered to cut, hot and coarse against the unprotected thigh.

When it became clear that Arley was tired, Charley got up to leave. I was going to stay with Arley, but I didn't want to see him go.

I followed him onto the porch. "The other night . . ." I began.

"Just let it alone for a while, Annie," he answered. "We don't have to name it right this minute. I think, in time, it will be easy to tell. You have bigger fish to fry right now." Then he left.

I tried to let it alone.

And it got easier. The baby's needs gave time its own circumscribed rhythm. Even at work, I never felt far from Arley or Desi; but everything else in my life receded, became muffled. Even after I showered, my hands smelled of Desi's baby powder. After a while, both Arley and I started using the baby oil and soap, too; and the whole place smelled like a nursery.

It was quiet there at the cabin. Quiet in the day and silent at night.

I worked unaccustomed eight-hour days. On weekends, we were mostly alone. When we saw the tall grass bow and part, hundreds of yards away, we knew hunters were crossing the fields.

But that happened only a few times. Once in a while, we'd glimpse tiny figures on ATVs, buzzing up the flanks of the ridge like angry insects. That meant the owners of the lush houses were out on a country holiday. A couple of times, I saw an older man in boots and much-patched jeans, carrying a backpack, hiking along the main road a couple of miles from the cabin. I'd wave. He'd raise his Spurs cap. But I had no idea whether he was a neighbor or a vacationer. There were intermittent visits from Jack and other police officers, and sometimes I'd glimpse unmarked squads drawn back under the shade trees on the wooded road.

The commute to work was easy if I left early enough. Every other night or so, Charley would show up very late and stay, throwing his sleeping bag down on the floor. A few times a week, I'd invent for Arley's benefit urgent night field calls, and meet Charley at Azalea Road.

His smell, his voice, the calluses on his palms became part of my emotional clothing. Daily, our being together seemed less novelty, more context. The sense of crisis might have hastened things between us. I am sure it did not idealize them.

From the office, I'd phone Stuart, getting his answering machine as often as not. His new job was keeping him madly busy, and he sounded excited. But it didn't erase my guilt.

Each night before I closed my eyes, I would promise myself, I'll think this through tomorrow.

But truthfully, I was too exhausted to think anything much. Arley had so much to learn, tasks for which even raising herself hadn't prepared her. At first we took turns getting up at night with Desi, and then we simply parked her on the bed between us, so I could roll the baby over like a sweet-smelling larva in her receiving blanket and help settle her on her mother's breast, sometimes without even waking Arley.

"Why's she get up every five minutes?" Arley would wail. For brief moments, she'd sound annoyingly like an ordinary teenager, and I'd wonder how much of my affection for her was based on her deceptive maturity. Arley would lie on her stomach on the floor, studying Desi, who was wailing and cycling on her squeak-and-rattle Pooh bear quilt. "What do you want, girl? I changed you and I fed you and I rocked you, and I'm like to die on my feet here."

When I look back, I see how fatigued I really was. I'd settle down with a notebook to make lists and a pen to chew, hoping to sort things out even in an artificial way, and then the baby's inconsolable night wails would drive every other urgency away. Then there was the two-week period when it seemed Arley's milk had dried up, and *she* was inconsolable. Or maybe things were so distorted, they would have been no clearer had I been in peak shape. Could I leave Arley on her own and join Stuart? Get him to come back? Pack up a teenager and her baby and head for Florida, all the while keeping an eye peeled for her marauding next of kin? Stay here, playing house with a guy who hadn't even been born on the day Kennedy was shot? It all felt like a kind of illness from which I kept expecting to recover momentarily. If I'd been more myself—more Annie-as-I-knew-her—I might have read Arley's reticence about Dillon more clearly. Perhaps I could have spared her the eventual hell she went through. For the first time, she seemed unwilling to talk to me about him. Should I have simply declared Azalea Road open for business? Even though we would have had little beyond two beds and a couch, plus a couple of barstools for a kitchen that had no running water? I guess I should have. And yet reason told me Arley was safer where she was.

The word from the police was that Dillon had vanished into

Mexico. Either that, Jack told me, or he'd left all his flesh-and-blood qualities (footprints, hair, fingerprints, even visibility) back in his cell at Solamente River.

Then the stickups started.

Some were little, some were big.

A liquor store robbed of two hundred dollars in register receipts by a drop-dead-handsome young man who distracted the clerk by telling her that someone was trying to break in by the back door. The clerk never felt threatened; but she did remember the robber's astonishing green eyes and his cap with the armadillo embroidered on it—she had one like it, and they talked about it after he got all the cash stuffed into an inside pocket. "I'm not even going to show you my gun, honey," the young man told the clerk. "Just enough you know I've got one. No need to get ugly." And then he slipped away, like smoke.

His aftershave, the woman said, was lavender.

"The younger men don't use that kind much anymore," she said. "It was kind of old-fashioned."

Arley acted decidedly uninterested in the newspaper account of it. In fact, at one point she jumped up, took Desi outside, and sat with her in the rocker, singing.

Two weeks later, there was a very cordial armed robbery of an armored car picking up the receipts one rainy, moonless night outside the Red Ryder dance bar in Shadowland. The two guards had curled up for an hour's nap in the cab and were awakened, fuddled, by a light shower of what they thought was hail on the windshield. When one reached out to check, he looked straight into the muzzle of a handgun pointed at him by a small masked figure, all in black, who climbed down slowly from the roof of the vehicle. Another armed man, a light-skinned blond who made no attempt at all to hide his face, politely helped the other driver out of the car, handcuffed the pair together, and removed a single canvas bag of currency totaling about twenty-five thousand dollars. "He could have took ten times that," one of the drivers told a TV interviewer. "But he said he didn't need so much. He said he liked to travel light and keep on moving. Hit the highway. He was actually a pretty nice young guy. The other guy, the really little one, didn't talk or anything." The truckdriver's partner couldn't say for sure whether the unmasked man was Dillon LeGrande.

"The weather was bad," he pointed out, "and I'm not at my best when I first wake up and all."

Capture of the suspects was imminent, authorities said. But from what Jack Becker managed to gather from behind the scenes, and what Carla Merrill admitted to me during one of our several conversations, it was no more imminent than world peace.

Half a dozen times each day and night, cars with what Arley correctly identified as "that police look" slipped past the cabin, tooling up into the ranch of quiet resort homes on the ridge, waiting and watching. We got to the point where we barely noticed them.

That rainy night and the odd shower aside, it was a droughty season, desert dry and desert hot. The browned tall grass and agarita waved luxuriantly in places where the cattle or the county hadn't caught up enough to crop it. Cut grass lay bundled in fields too, soaked in five minutes and dried back into fuel in an hour. The humidity stayed low. And it would stay that way until January, when the baked ground sucked up the little rain that fell and looked just as parched afterward. And so the fire could have started the way a thousand Texas wildfires start every year. A cigarette butt. A lightning strike.

People thought that, at first.

One late afternoon when Desiree was about eight weeks old, I came into the cabin and found Arley frantically swabbing a spreading brown pool around the old Mr. Coffee that the owner kept in the kitchen. "I can't do this," she told me, red-faced. "This is the second time I've made this mess."

"It's in wrong or something." I opened the swing-out well in the unit's housing. She had stuffed a nice handful of beans in there. "Arley, these beans aren't ground. You have to grind them."

"We always used instant at home," she said sullenly. "I never saw anything like that before."

"What about at the restaurant?" Why was I needling her?

"They just got the *ground* kind there. I thought this would make the *bean* kind. I'm not retarded."

"Where did you get it, anyhow? Is it this guy's? He's got to have a coffee grinder, then."

She was sweating, her hair greasy, and she turned to me, hands on hips, with as close to a belligerent attitude as Arley would ever display to me. "Well, you brought the damn stuff! I know you meant it for a nice present, but look! I poured it all over the floor!"

"What present?"

"Jeez, Anne. The *coffee*. You know, the coffee?"

"I didn't bring this coffee."

She stared at me. "I found it on the porch."

"Charley must have brought it."

"It was just there when I hung out the baby's things to dry."

"Charley probably forgot and just got beans. Honey, take it easy. I'll have it ground at the store when I go home, and I'll bring it back to you. I didn't even know you drank coffee, Arley."

"Well, I do! All kids in Texas drink coffee! And now I'm going to have to drink it twice as much if I'm going to stay up all night every night of my life."

I sent her for a nap. And of course, I forgot all about the coffee beans. I found them in the trunk of my car the following spring, when, late for court, I blew a tire going over a curb. I never even asked Charley about them.

The flowers were another story. Just before Christmas, a bouquet of lantana and Indian paintbrush, tied with red ribbon, showed up on the front steps of the cabin. "They're kind of like from my wedding," Arley told me, her voice husky with fear and something else, almost a dreary elation.

"Arley, who do you think these are from?"

"I don't know. Maybe Charley? Maybe they're for you?"

"Maybe. But he'd have told me. . . ."

"Yeah, I'm totally sure he'd have told you."

"What do you mean by that?"

She turned away from me, with a sniff. I felt like a fool, then, for trying to keep the extent of Charley and me from her, and because I felt foolish, I got angry.

"Listen, Arley. Let's not worry about me. Have you heard anything else about Dillon, or from him?"

"No." But she hesitated, a hesitation no one else would have noticed.

"Have you?"

"No."

"Swear."

"Let me alone, Anne."

"This is serious, Arley."

"Don't you think I know that? Don't you think I know what he's done, or what they all say he did? You think I want him to come here?"

"I don't know. Do you?"

"No."

"I know that feelings are powerful, passion is powerful—"

"I said *no!*" she screamed. "Now what else can I say? Do you think I'm so stupid all I care about is sex? Do you think that's all I think about? What about you?"

"Me? Why am I in this?"

It was our first genuine fight. We've had others since, but not many, and never so loud. Arley shouted at me, red-faced: Shut up, she said, just shut up; she couldn't take any more bullshit questions, from me or the police or Elena; she was worn out with the baby and everything else, and she wished she'd never met Dillon or me, and she just wanted to be left alone to run her own life, and she didn't need me or my money . . . and of course, deeply mature individual that I am, I yelled right back—lovely things about where she might be if it weren't for my help and what had her own mother done for her—and then the baby woke up and started to cry and I stalked out of there and drove home, sobbing.

When I got there, there were already three messages on the answering machine: "Annie, I'm so sorry, Annie. I do owe you everything and I know that I was an awful bitch, but the thing is, I can't stand talking about him anymore; it just hurts too much. . . ." *Beep.* "Annie, it's me again. Like I said, I'm really sorry, and I guess this was all my fault. I know you just want the best for me, but I really don't know. Annie, are you there and just not picking up the phone? Which is okay, really. I would understand." *Beep.* "Annie, I'm better now, but I'm still sorry, and you're right, but didn't you ever know you were being really stupid about something, and then someone keeps reminding you how stupid you are, and you just have to defend it, anyhow? Just, like, to keep your pride? Probably you never did. . . ."

Of course, I felt like a nickel-plated shit, and I drove right back out there, beating myself up the whole while: No, I'd never done anything stupid, nothing like sleeping with the carpenter and neglecting even to mention that fact to my loyal and trusting companion of eleven years, whose ring I still wore on my hand.

At the cabin, Arley and I bathed Desi in a tin tub on the porch. Warm water soothed Desi, then and now; she's still a little porpoise. But that night, she actually fell asleep while Arley was dripping water from a squeezed cloth onto her blond tufts. We hated to move her, to dress her. The sunset turned Desi's bathwater pink and her body a deep rose. Her tiny toes floated like foam. She started to fuss when Arley diapered her, and suddenly seemed ready to combust. But I took her, and she caught her breath and sighed herself to sleep, light as flannel, on my shoulder, making me feel all maternal and proud.

Then we all sat on the little glider that took up half of the tiny railed front porch, and I told Arley everything she already knew.

"You know that Charley . . . ," I began. "You know that Charley and I are, uh, close. . . ."

"I know he's in love with you."

"Well, me too. Maybe."

"I know that too."

"Okay. But I've been with Stuart for eleven years. And I love Stuart very much. I mean, we had hoped to be married by now, really. And I just don't know if I want that anymore." I felt the tears start behind my eyes.

We sat there, pushing against the floorboards with our feet, in synchrony.

"I don't want you to believe that I haven't considered Stuart's feelings, or that this thing with Charley was just an . . . an impulse I'll regret later on. I think it might be . . . a change for me in the way I've lived my life."

"You mean you thought it over."

"Yes."

"Just not very long."

"That's right. But no matter how bad I feel about some of the *effects* of what I've done, I don't feel bad about—what I've done."

"Ahh." Arley looked up at the sherbet rim of light above the ridge. "I know what you mean."

"You're just a kid," I said. "I haven't even told my sister this yet."

"That's different," Arley said.

"I haven't told Stuart."

"Well," she said, "I'm sure he knows."

"What?"

"If he doesn't know it's Charley, he knows it's something, and you have to help him figure it out. People always know when the other person starts to change." She leaned over and stroked the ball of Desi's feet, watching her toes bend like a dancer *en pointe*. An unfamiliar car rattled past the opening of the dirt road, and Arley flinched. Was she thinking of Dillon, feeling for the sorcery of their connection, wondering if it still held true?

"How do you feel when you think of breaking up with Stuart?" she asked.

"Sad. Afraid."

"How do you feel when you think of leaving here? Of leaving Charley? And . . . us?"

"I don't think about that."

"I think you should go see Stuart," she said. "Don't you think you should?"

I knew I should; I said that I would. After Christmas.

Stuart couldn't go home for Christmas because of the new job, and since I'd been to New York just months before, I used the excuse of Desiree being too small to travel and Arley having no one else, and I spent my holiday in San Antonio. Charley gave me strict orders not to show up at my house for the two days before Christmas Eve, and I complied, though there were suspicious conversations on the telephone at the cabin several times when I was there, replete with smothered snickers and whispers, Arley then insisting, "It was just some salesman or something. . . ."

But on Christmas Eve, Jeanine and Arley arrived at my office with Desi, nestled in her car-seat shell, a Santa cap the size of a child's sweat sock on her head.

"We're here to pick you up," Arley said. "No arguments."

"My car's here," I said.

"No it isn't," Arley answered. "We've taken care of that."

"Put yourself in our control, Anne," Jeanine told me, steering me through my office door and closing it firmly.

There are twenty-eight casements at Azalea Road, and Charley had lit a candle in each one. For the thirty-two-paned bay window, he had fashioned a menorah from a huge potted cholla, each of eight cactus arms adorned with an oil candle in a fragile foil cup. Inside, courtesy of Charley's pal at The September Garden, was a Chinese feast laid out on the library floor, across three yards of snowy linen tablecloth, with chopsticks for ten. Patty Flanagan joined us for a while, and Tarik came with a girlfriend—a Filipino beauty who must have weighed eighty-five pounds soaking. Jeanine brought the pediatrician, but he left early. When his shift ended at eleven, Jack Becker and his partner, a cute black kid named Pedro, who couldn't take his long-lashed eyes off Arley, showed up to help us eat the leftovers. Arley gave me a journal to record my dreams, its cover embossed with cows jumping over the moon. I gave Arley a camera, a saucer bouncer for Desiree—her whole body, at that point, would have fit through one of the openings for the legs—and a basket full of lotions, potions, and soaps, all lavender, Arley's favorite scent. After midnight, Arley and Desi fell asleep on the library floor, curled on the Amish quilt Jeanine had given me. Since the water in the downstairs bath had needed to be disconnected temporarily, for the third time, Charley and I brushed our teeth with champagne and peed in the yard, and then we lay down upstairs, where the nubs of fat white candles still burned bravely on the sills.

"I'm . . . going to Miami in a couple of weeks," I told him, deciding at that moment that, indeed, I was. "I need to see Stuart and to talk all this over with him."

"That's going to hurt," Charley said.

"I know. But until I do, I don't think that I—that we—can go forward."

"I have a present for you," he said then.

"Besides the festival of lights?"

"Yeah. But I'm pretty sure it's in bad taste. And I don't want you to think . . . well, what I want you to know is this, Anne. I bought this for you a while ago, and I wanted you to have it even if you left. And if you decide to do that, I still want you to have it."

The ring was silver, a skeleton mermaid fashioned so that her own graceful hands lovingly held the flukes of her long tail. "It's a Day of the Dead symbol for fertility," Charley said. "Not . . . that kind of ring. Not a promise. Just a love ring. I want you to have all the love you want, Anne. And here, I hope." He slid it onto my finger, and I curled, speechless, against his warm chest. Lucky me, I thought. How had so many unlikely ingredients simmered up such a kettle of turmoil in just one year, since Stuart and I had thrown our wish rocks through the windows of Azalea Road? It was even stranger to tell than to live. And where, in all of it, was the late Anne Singer, she of sound mind?

"Will you look out for Arley while I'm gone?" I asked Charley.

"You know I will. She can stay at my place."

"She won't do that. She'd think it was an inconvenience to you."

"Then I'll go out there every day. And I'll do some work at night. You know I work best then, anyway. Then I'll go back to sleep. Remember the night I was putting up the sign—"

I thought my heart would divide neatly in two on me . . . But all I said was, "I remember. Oh Charley, it worked. My wish on the broken window."

"You didn't know that then."

"Maybe I did. Just not in my head. Otherwise, why did I buy this dump?"

"It was a pretty obvious way to get my attention."

I put my head on his shoulder. So I knew Arley would be safe, even if Charley would be exhausted. But even as I made plane reservations, I dithered. It was a terrible time to leave. Desiree was now blatantly colicky. Arley was thin and pale. But with Charley and Jeanine making daily visits and phone calls, and with Jack Becker's assurance that his state police cruiser prowled past the cabin twice a shift, I felt reassured.

On the day before I left, Patty visited my office. "You're going to look for a new job, aren't you?" she asked.

"I'm not sure."

"You don't have to say that. I know you are."

"I'm really not sure, Patty. I don't much like Florida."

"But who could bear to give up Stuart?" She smiled.

Who, I thought, indeed?

"I just know you're going to move," she told me, mooning around my office, rearranging my pens and my files. "How am I going to stand it here without you? Who's going to make up the annual list of the worst names for babies born out of wedlock?"

I made arrangements for Jeanine to drive me to the airport—I didn't think it was right for Charley to take me. The night before I left, I stayed with Arley at the cabin. And I called my sister.

"Remember the goyish carpenter?" I asked.

"Did he sue you?" she snapped back.

"No. It's worse than that."

"Did he make a pass at Arley?"

"Cold."

"At you?"

"Uh . . . you're getting warmer."

"You made a pass at him!" The triumph in her voice subsumed all concern for an instant—we are, after all, sisters. But she quickly righted herself, asking necessary questions, making comforting noises. "Are you sure he'll be . . . stimulating enough?" she asked.

"He's pretty stimulating."

"You know what I mean, Anne."

"He's not like Stuart. And with him, I'm not like . . . that. It's different. The parts with words aren't as fast. But the parts without words go deeper."

"I want you to promise not to beat yourself up," Rachael told me finally. "This is not a bank robbery, Anne. This is not murder."

"We've done that here," I said. "Why couldn't Stuart have

found a job in Utah? They have the death penalty. And you can have more than one spouse. . . ."

"I think Stuart would mind."

"Charley wouldn't."

"Anne."

"I know. I'm kidding. But what I mean is, so far as I can tell, what he wants is . . . to make me happy. That's what he wants most."

She paused so long I thought we'd disconnected. And then she said, "Well, that's not everything. But it's . . . it's plenty. And maybe," she added, her voice gathering speed with the kind of snottiness you can get only from a sibling, "maybe Stuart moved to Florida because he wanted to get away from you, Anne. Maybe you can't quit because he already fired you."

"Oh Rachael. You're so comforting."

"Well, Annie. I love Stuart." She paused. "But you're my sister. It's your happiness I want most."

Arley was waiting outside when I hung up. She patted my arm, and we sat on the steps, inhaling the dry, scentless air, a prescription for perfect respiration, a sort of distillation of everything good about Texas. Then Desiree piped up, and we both went inside. I headed for Desi's crib, but Arley said, "She's in my room again. It's easier."

Desi lay next to Arley's bed in a cradle I had never seen. It was, in fact, not quite a cradle but something more substantial, a sort of big sledlike crib with curved ribs and shallow rockers, winged at the ends like runners.

"Where did you get that?" I asked, marveling.

"The . . . the thrift shop in Uvalde. Charley took me the other day."

"How could you have afforded it, Arley? It must have cost—"

"It wasn't so much."

"It looks like it's handmade."

"It is."

"What kind of wood?"

"It's mesquite. Charley says it's mesquite."

I could hardly imagine that. Mesquite is a thorny little red-brown twisted tree—the kind of thing you expect to see in old movies with Charlton Heston playing a biblical prophet. Even in bloom, a mesquite never looked quite finished to me, not in the way a maple tree looks finished, no matter what season. But this baby bed was made of mesquite subjected to some kind of alchemy. Its colors rippled from the tan of hill soil to mauve to the ruddy shade of potter's clay we saw in our tire ruts along Ocatilla Creek. And the way it felt . . . It felt like the skin under Desi's chin. "Well, it's absolutely beautiful. Does Desi like it?"

"She loves it. She sleeps better. A little better." Arley looked up at me. "You're going in the morning."

"Only for two days."

She looked past me, up at the thickets on the ridge. "I'll be fine. We'll be fine."

"You have all the phone numbers."

"Ten thousand numbers."

"And Charley will come every day."

"He's threatening to sleep on the floor, Annie, you got him so worried."

"I know I'm being ridiculous. But I do worry about you. . . ."

"You wasted so much time on me, you don't want to give up now, huh?"

"Yep." I hugged her and scooped Desi up out of that satiny bed to kiss her head. "You got a great deal on this bed, Arley. I'm going to have you buy our house furniture."

"Hmm," she said, and hugged me back. Then she added, "You know, Annie, I called my mama a couple of weeks ago."

"You did?"

"Yep. I thought she'd want to know at least something about the baby. And I wanted to say I was sorry about Langtry. I wanted to ask her if she knew more. I didn't think I'd do it. But I did. It was like . . . I had to."

"That was good of you. No matter what she said, honey, it was a good thing for your soul that you did it."

"She didn't surprise me any."

"I can tell you don't mean she didn't have any more news."

"Right. I mean, she didn't surprise me the way she acted toward me."

"Well, she is how she is."

"She just asked about where I was, was I staying in a fancy hotel, like the police said. Was I even in Texas. And then she said she reckoned we all had trouble deep down in our blood, and why'd I have to go and mix it with more trouble and pass it on." We both looked down at Desiree, her sleeping mouth at work on one of her dimpled knuckles. "She's the worst person I ever knew, Annie."

"She's hardly the worst person, Arley. There's plenty worse she could have inflicted on you." I said that, but I didn't know if I believed it.

"No," Arley said. "She's the worst because she doesn't even care enough to hurt you."

I stopped by Azalea Road in the morning to kiss Charley good-bye. I didn't want to talk about my trip, so when I took my mouth off his, I accused him of sweet subterfuge. "Thrift shop, indeed," I told him. "That crib was made by some genius, Charley. You must have called in some favor to get that."

"Which crib?"

"The crib. The crib Arley says you got for her at a thrift shop."

"She told you we got it at a thrift shop?"

"Yeah, sure. The thrift shop in Uvalde."

"I told her not to tell you that."

"What?"

"I don't want you to worry about this, Anne."

"What? What the fuck am I not supposed to worry about?"

"I'm taking care of it."

"What?"

"Arley found that crib on the porch one morning. She didn't know where it came from."

"It was like the flowers."

"The flowers?"

I chewed my lip. "Nothing. Forget it. You're saying Arley didn't tell anyone about the crib. Not the detectives. Not anyone."

"No."

"No? No? Did you go along with a kid who was dumb enough to fall in love with a psychopath? Charley, get out of my way. I have to change these reservations—" I picked up my duffel bag.

"Anne, I want you to go ahead and see Stuart. It's wrong not to. We have to go ahead with our lives. Stuart too."

"He's out there, Charley. Dillon's waiting for me to leave."

"Anne, Dillon LeGrande is only a person. There's no evidence he's anywhere near here—"

"Then who left a baby cradle on the step of what is essentially a safe house? A place nobody even knows exists, supposedly, except the owner and Jeanine and her dad and the police . . ."

"I don't know, Anne, but think a little. Dillon might have worked for a carpenter for a couple of years, but he's hardly out there working in the woodshop between armored-truck heists."

"So maybe he stole it."

375

"Yes, a guy on the FBI's Ten Most Wanted list taking out time to knock over country antique stores run by little old ladies with blue rinses . . ."

"Well? Is that impossible? Maybe the little old ladies aren't around to tell anymore. Maybe they're buried in shallow graves in those good ol' Texas piney woods, Charley. Look what happened to Arley's sister."

"Anne, slow down a minute. I can tell you why Arley didn't tell the police." I stopped and set my duffel bag down on the tiled floor. "She didn't want them to take the crib. She didn't want them to lock it up and put powder on it to check for fingerprints and destroy the finish. She wanted it for Desiree."

"What if it's Dillon?"

"Well, we talked about that. If Dillon left it, what was to stop him from walking right in then and butchering her and the baby, if that was what he wanted? Or taking them away? She said, Arley said . . ."

"What?"

"She said, 'Dillon knows if he wanted me, he could've had me.' "

"Oh God," I said. "Oh my God."

"Anne . . ."

"Well, I'm not going." Jeanine was standing on the porch, watching us argue.

"Anne, listen."

"Are you always this calm?"

"I'm not calm. And I was a lot less calm when she told me about this. But I thought it over—"

"And now you think she's right?"

"I do. I know it feels scary. But I'm still going out there to stay with her until you come back. And—"

"Promise me."

"Don't say that, Anne. It sounds like you think I don't care about her."

"I know you do! But what can you do, anyhow? Are you taking a machine gun with you? What if he comes for her?"

"If he was coming for her, he wouldn't have left that bed. And I am going to tell the police about it, get them there, watching round the clock. That's what I was going to say when you interrupted me."

"You are?"

"Yes. That's what I decided when I thought it over. You don't have to do everything."

You don't have to do everything.

All the way to the airport, I leaned my forehead on the cool glass of the passenger-side window and chewed my fist.

"You're involved with Charley, aren't you?" Jeanine asked. "That's what that was all about."

"I am, but that's not what that was all about," I told her.

"I can't believe you didn't tell me," she said. "I can't believe it. I should be going out with Charley. You were paired off already. . . ."

"You want to go out with everybody, Jeanine?"

"Everybody with a body like Charley's."

"That's not all there is to it—"

"What there is to it doesn't hurt though . . ." I couldn't even chuckle. And I couldn't explain. I was so reluctant to get on the plane that I left my bag sitting with Jeanine's purse, and she had to run to catch up and give it to me. I didn't even put out my hands to take it, just sat there and, the first chance I got, ordered a Bloody Mary, though it was nine-thirty A.M.

Stuart picked me up at the airport, and I didn't know what

happened that same night until many hours later. In fact, no one knew.

There is a little arroyo near Trinidad, Texas, where hundreds of hopeful border runners heading for *el norte* have scratched a tunnel under a section of fence. It's been filled in with a backhoe, and even with paving, dozens of times. But a new passage in the crumbly soil always seems to open up. The country around that dry spot was so remote that it wasn't until the wee hours of the following morning that fellow INS patrols found the two border guards, one of them dead. Med-flighted, the man with the shattered left shoulder survived. He identified Dillon without hesitation. Apparently unarmed, Dillon had come strolling up as if to vault over the fence, down the gully into Mexico. As the two guards wheeled their all-terrain vehicle and shone the lights down on him, calling for him to halt, Dillon's small masked companion—authorities believed it was Spirito—opened up with a thirty-aught-six from a clump of shrubbery, nailing both guards on the first volley. It was a coward's move, a back shot. What the wounded man remembered was Dillon shouting for the gunman to stop.

"That guy's alive," he said. "Let him be." He leaned over the guard, gently removing his pistol from its holster and asking, "Where you hit? In the shoulder? Doesn't seem so bad. You'll make it. Figure your fellas will be along soon. Almost time for the cavalry to come." He'd added then, "You tell them you saw the Highwayman, hear? That I came along here by moonlight and now I'm gone."

Ironically enough, Stuart and I had gone to dinner that night at a restaurant just down the street from the huge whipped-cream mansion where, a few years earlier, a famous artist was gunned down by his spurned lover. Afterward, Stuart had wanted to walk on the beach, but I wanted to call Arley. So we found a pay phone, and Stuart stood there while I called Charley, the cabin, and Jeanine. There was no answer anywhere.

"Do you think something's wrong?" I asked Stuart.

"No," he told me. "I think she's probably outside."

I called again at nine, Florida time. Still no answer.

We went back to Stuart's apartment. The building stood at the end of the strip where South Beach emptied into real Miami, and its stucco front was as pink as raspberry cream cheese. "Now we both have houses our mothers would be ashamed to visit us in," Stuart told me.

"But mine will improve," I insisted.

We went inside and lay down on the bed. I took out pictures of Desiree to show Stuart; but he gently placed them on the night table and kissed me, long and familiarly. The way I wanted him to make love to me was not so much desire as the need for completion you feel when your bed is made with clean sheets and you're so tired only sleep can satisfy you. But when he began to unbutton my shirt, I was suddenly aware of a dozen unfamiliar sounds—the whicker of a ceiling fan, the rattle of the icemaker, a voice fading from a car driving past. I was somewhere else, not home. I sat up.

"So," Stuart said, not moving.

"You know, we have to talk about this."

"Anne, hey, hey. Settle down, babe. I know you have unfinished business in Texas—"

"It's not just that."

"Okay."

"And it's not that I don't love you."

"Oh, Anne. Oh, shit."

"Because I do."

379

"I know you do."

"What I guess we have to face is that if we'd really wanted to get married and have kids, we'd have gotten married and had kids. No one stopped us. . . ."

"It was timing, Anne. The timing was off. . . ."

"But, Stuart, I think the timing will always be off. If you wanted that kind of life with me, you'd have stayed in Texas—"

"I have to work."

"I know you have to. And I respect that. But I want to be wanted more than you want anything else."

"I want you more than any other woman."

"I know. It kills me to say this, Stuart. And it kills me I didn't say it sooner. But you don't want the things I want. And the unfair part is, I didn't know how much I wanted them until now."

"Like I needed to know this sooner. I don't even want to know this now." He sighed. "The thing with Arley—"

"It was only a symptom, Stuart. But it's true, I care about her. More than I could ever have expected."

"Oh, Anne," he said, pulling me down beside him. "I'm sorry for us."

Near tears, drained, we had nothing left to say. We fell asleep.

The shrilling of the phone next to my head sounded like a shriek. I sat up, confused by the angle of the bed, forgetting where I was, as Stuart fumbled, knocked the telephone over, and finally gasped, "Hello? Yeah? . . . Anne, it's Charley Wilder."

"Charley?" I cried, glad Stuart couldn't see my face. "What's wrong?"

"I'm calling to tell you, first of all, that Arley is safe. I'm right here with her and the baby, and everything's all right. Nothing has moved outside this cabin all night long."

"What are you talking about? What happened? Why didn't anybody answer the phone?"

"We were . . . busy. Jack came . . ."

He told me then. And he assured and reassured me. Dillon was gone for sure this time, into Mexico south of Laredo. He'd been spotted twice already. Dragnets set on both sides of the border would snag him at any moment. "Anne, I know you'll want to run right back here," Charley said. "But before you do, listen. The devil himself couldn't give them the slip this time. Jeanine's going to come out here around noon, and I'll be back before five. So there's nothing to worry about."

I didn't even answer him. I simply put the phone down and called the airline. We drove to the airport in silence, still in our slept-in, rumpled clothes. Stuart got us coffee—mine with, his black—and insisted on waiting with me at the gate. When they began boarding first class, I started to cry. "The ring," I said, stupidly, awkwardly. "Maybe you want it. I'll . . . I'll send it, okay?" I was hurting him. Did I *want* to hurt him? Or just hurt myself more?

"Keep it, Anne," Stuart said lightly, rocking up on the tips of his loafers. "Keep it. You're a pearl of a girl, huh? Oh, Anne. Arley will be all right. It will be all right. I . . . Jesus, I have no idea what to say. None of this seems real. And maybe—look, we don't know how you'll feel six months from now. . . ."

But I did know. I couldn't let him hope. "Stuart, there's something else," I said. "You're going to hate me."

He looked away from me, following the incoming arc of a landing plane. "No, I'm not. Maybe there is something else. But this is enough. You remember what your mother used to say? You don't have to tell everything you know."

We went to a bank of phones, and I called Arley to tell her I was on my way. There wasn't much life in her voice, but she said she was glad I was on my way, though I shouldn't feel I had to come.

Then there was nothing left to do but say good-bye.

I kissed Stuart, feeling the jump of his jaw muscle against my cheek. Little nerve. Such a little nerve he was. "Stuart, take good care of . . ."

"You too, babe," he said. "Never change."

On the plane, I sat down and willed tons of aluminum and steel to make its way back faster in the direction it had come from only the previous morning. Whatever maternal gene I possessed for Arley had been activated into rescue mode, and there was no stilling it. The plane was delayed for three hours in Atlanta, and I ate a one-pound bag of peanuts while waiting and pacing. All told, it took twelve hours for me to get back, home from the airport, and into my car. It was while I was speeding toward the cabin, with the pedal jammed to the floor, with my gun in the glove box, that I realized I hadn't called Charley, hadn't grabbed my car phone, hadn't stopped to think whether I would do whatever it took if I had the opportunity.

I'm no warrior.

Even if I could have got to her in time, I don't know what I could have done.

CHAPTER EIGHTEEN

Arley

The cabin didn't have a television. Aside from missing *E.R.*, I didn't really mind. Annie was taping every episode for me anyhow, and when we moved to Azalea Road, we were going to watch the whole thing like some big movie, with no commercial breaks. I made her promise not to even peek at any of the shows, and she kept her promise.

The days passed quickly, even without TV. You'd be surprised how much work a person weighing twelve pounds can give you, when you're going through three or four changes a day (breast-fed babies are really ick when it comes to that!) and washing them by hand, not to mention keeping a baby clean and cleared up of rashes and all that. You wouldn't think a little baby, who can't even walk around outside, and whose head smelled like the makeup counter at Oberly's, would get filthy. I once was washing Desi and found this big old crust of crud behind her ear that looked just like bacon grease, and I was shocked; it was like she was this neglected child or something. So besides taking care of her, and washing my own clothes by hand, I was studying for the SATs, which I planned to take in February, just before my six-teenth birthday. Though I know I'm pretty smart, the fact is that my education is awfully sketchy, GED or not. Even so, after the fire there were these stories about "Robber Bride a Genius," which is not true.

The studying and keeping busy kept me from thinking about Dillon all the time. And I was trying not to think about him. The process of me losing him had started then . . . how could it have been any other way?

When I did think of him, I'd try to guess what he was feeling. His mind had snapped from the confinement, I figured that—he always said, didn't he, that a man like him had to be free? After I heard about what he said to the border guard, I knew he realized that he was going to die. He'd die before he'd let himself be taken back to prison. He would have got the death penalty. And the way Dillon had talked about death, even before "The Highwayman," even from what I've heard of how he was back to the time of that girl he said he loved so much before me, I think he was on the edge of suicidal probably all his life.

I don't think it was our love pushed him over. If anything, our love probably made him better than he was, happier, if you can call it that, at least for a while. When I would think about Dillon, I would try to see him looking at a breathing person and firing a gun, and when I would think that this man was the man who'd been inside me, I would turn sick and my feet and hands would get icy cold despite the heat. One night, I even peed my bed. I couldn't think about it. And yet it was always there.

I was always tired. I ate like a pig, and I still lost weight. I'd been so prissy, but there were times I didn't wash my hair for three days. I thought I'd grow dreadlocks like Cully the cook, back at Taco Haven. Every day after she got home from school, Elena would call me and watch *Days of Our Lives* on the phone, telling me all the parts so I could keep up. Annie wouldn't let her come to the cabin—she said it was police orders—but I still gave Elena the phone number. I missed her a lot. She hadn't seen Desi since the morning after she was born, when Mrs. G. let Elena go in late to school to come see me at the hospital, before I came out here. Ellie said my life was more gruesome than anything on *Days*. Even when I nursed Desi, I would sometimes think of Dillon, but I would try not to. It seemed kind of sick. I didn't want anything bad to come through the circle around Desi and me.

People think little babies are boring, but you can watch them for hours. It's sort of like watching a beautiful plant instead of a person. After I fed her and before her nap, she would make her mouth into a perfect O when she yawned, and a milk bubble would stretch out big and shining and then pop, and her little hands would fly out from the sound. She didn't cry, but I couldn't even stand to see her that upset. As she lay on her quilt, I would kneel down over her and cover her, careful not to put any weight on her, like I was a mountain or a willow tree, so that she would have this impression that there was always something between her and anything in the world that could hurt her.

When Desiree was asleep, generally I was asleep, or I was reading. Often, they were just goofing-off books. I'd still read only half the books Annie gave me. Once, she said that some of those books would probably sound pretty naive to me, given what I'd been through. That wasn't entirely true, though. In spite of being married and having a baby and having the kind of family I had, I was still pretty much a kid at heart. One of the books I read was a play, *Our Town*. And I found that I could identify with all those sweet small-town feelings, about being sheltered and shy and lonesome for being a little girl, even though I'd never been a little girl myself. I could identify with how embarrassed Emily was when her boyfriend first confessed his love to her, I could feel just that way, even though I knew much more of what love was about. So I read, or I listened to my CDs, mostly CDs Charley gave me—folks I'd never heard of, like Tom Paxton and Rick Danko and Joan Baez. It was like country music but not, and even sadder. Folk's my favorite music now, though Annie yells at us every so often to "turn off the damned draggy ballads." I read or I listened to my CD player, and though the CD player had a radio, I never turned the radio on, so everybody on earth knew about the border guards before I did.

It was Charley who came and told me. Jack came later, but Charley was first.

Right away, I went over and snatched Desi up out of that beautiful mesquite rocking bed, even though I'd just laid her down to sleep and, like Annie says, you let sleeping babies lie. I picked her up, and I handed her to Charley and I went into the bathroom and puked up my guts. Before then, I'd been sort of half and half on Dillon. Some nights, after Jack Becker or that cute boy cop Pedro checked on me, I'd lie there and think, C'mon, Dillon. Come for me by moonlight and pull me up off this here floor and onto your black horse . . . like he ever had a horse or anything. I'd try to stop myself from the long, slow, every-word replay of our wedding night, but then I'd give in to it, and I'd make myself so hot I thought you could hear my breathing all up and down that field, not that there was a soul around to listen. And after I came, with the sheet all knotted against my crotch, which was still sore, I'd feel as though I'd done some monstrous, depraved thing. But at least, after I did that to myself, I could sleep, and sometimes, when I'd wake up, well, Desi girl would be laughing in her red-hearted crib. Laughing. That girl woke up laughing at three months old, even if she'd screamed four hours straight from colic after supper the night before.

The last night, I knew Annie was coming home, even though I'd told her not to. She'd called me from the Miami airport and then again from the Atlanta airport, said she was going to drive right out to the cabin whether I wanted her to or not, even if it was midnight. Jeanine came and brought me a sub for lunch, but it was so hot I couldn't eat. Charley called and said he was waiting for a glass delivery at the house and would be by as soon as it came. I slept for a while in the late afternoon and was startled to see that it was getting dark when I woke up.

I got up. And not long after, Desi did, too, and started tuning up for her night of squalling. I figured Charley'd be along any minute. And when Jack Becker came on by with old Pedro, I told him just that. The two of them came up on the porch and turned off their car and asked me for Cokes. I was glad I'd got up enough energy to wash that day and put on clean clothes, though I was embarrassed that I didn't have any food to offer them and that Desi was screaming her fool head off. Sometimes Jack came alone and sometimes he brought Pedro—I guess he was training Pedro or something—but I got a kick out of it the times he'd stop by himself, because he always talked about Jeanine. Jeanine thought Jack didn't know anything about the pediatrician; but he knew everything, and he would tell me—this kid!—about how it hurt him, deep inside, that he wasn't man enough to hold on to Jeanine. "She's wild at heart, Arley," he would say, and I would memorize it to repeat to Elena later on. You never think of people in their thirties moaning on about stuff like that.

That night, a tiny little breeze had just started. It was like the whole field where the cabin was took a deep breath. You could bear heat if the air wasn't totally *still*, but it was so still that winter. I was like to die out there without air-conditioning—lucky thing for me I grew up poor, with no air-conditioning in the house except in Mama's room, and Cam and I only daring to sit in there when she was at work. I don't think I ever put a stitch on Desi except an undershirt and her diaper the first six months of her life, though, it was that hot a time.

"You got enough milk and stuff in the house?" Jack asked me, that night before he left. "You want us to get you some ice cream or something?"

"It'd melt before you got back here," I told him. "Anyhow, Annie'll be here later." We both laughed about that. We knew that Annie would somehow manage, through dark of night, to find a way to bring me enough food to feed an army. Annie never came anywhere without bringing food; she said it was an inherited trait. Jack was just about to leave, and Pedro was rocking on the little porch glider with Desi, when the car radio went crazy.

"Let's go, son," Jack yelled after a minute. "Grass fire up there. Threat to the wealthy. You take care, Arley." He stopped then; I never knew exactly why, because they were in a big hurry to get up there on the ridge, where the six or eight big houses would be in trouble if the fire department didn't get things under control right away (though they always did; grass fires are common as armadillos in Texas). "Arley?" Jack turned back for a second. "You want me to get Jeanine to come out here for you?"

"No. Why?" I shivered then. In all that heat. And I just purely ignored it.

"Just . . . well, that fire will go right up the hill if it goes at all. You'll be fine," We all turned and looked about behind the cabin, and sure enough, you could see a faint red glow, like a line of Christmas lights, a few miles off at the base of the ridge. "Listen, how about I call you on the phone an hour from now. . . ." The radio was squawking again, and he jumped into the driver's seat, and he waved, and Pedro winked at me.

All the while I was giving Desi her bath, I kept looking out the back window of the cabin, the one above my bed, which was low on the floor. I could see flames now, actually sort of bounding along the ground, far off, going up the ridge, and sometimes I could hear a faint pop, like a firecracker, when a tree exploded. The air was full of smell—good scents, like fireplace fires. They say a fire sounds like a bus roaring, but I couldn't hear much sound. What I could hear was the thin yowl of sirens, different kinds—the regular ones and the ones that sound like the German police cars in *Diary of Anne Frank*—and every so often, the loose gutter on the cabin would scrape and bang against the north wall. I plugged in my CD player just to put something in the air to sing to, and I wondered why Jack didn't call. When I tried to call Elena, the phone just clicked and clicked. The fire must have got to some wires. If I'd had a car, I probably would have driven on over to Elena's then, even if I wasn't entirely sure of the way. But since Annie was coming, I wasn't really scared or anything. Charley was usually late for everything. But I knew he'd come.

Then, at about nine o'clock, the power failed.

The lights just winked, and went up, and went down, and Emmylou's voice sank and died away right in the middle of "That Old Loving-You Feeling."

It wasn't dark, because of the fire. That fire was standing straight up like a wave against the hills, and the air outside was filling with little flickers of ash, gathering like smoke. I had no idea how bad it really was, how gasoline had been laid down over days on that wet-and-dried grass. I had no idea that the fire protection service had to pull people off little fires all over the county—there were about forty other grass fires that night—to come and help out on the ridge. I had no idea that one of those big houses was already gone and three would be destroyed by morning. I didn't know there was a roadblock, which had stopped Annie and Charley at the highway, and that Jack had promised them I was okay and said someone was headed over to get me in a few minutes. I didn't know that some of the emergency vehicles had their tires slashed, which sent people running around in circles.

But I wasn't afraid of the fire. I knew that the wind was blowing away from me, and that even though it was only a few miles off, grass fires go uphill because of the way hot air rises. What I was scared of was trying to walk through the pitch dark a mile up a dirt-pack road to the highway with my baby. I figured I'd just lie down and wait, awake, for Annie to come.

And that was what I did. So I lay down, but I guess I slept.

When I heard the crash, I opened my eyes, but I didn't sit up and I didn't cry out. The windows were all lit orange from the fire. It was not closer, but it was bigger. I made that out right away. I could see trees with flaming ribbons waving above them behind Dillon's back and over Dillon's head as he stood there. He had kicked the door in.

I didn't speak.

I lay there with my eyes open, not moving one muscle, thinking, clearly, that I was asleep and dreaming and even understanding why I was dreaming like I was. Hot air came whooshing in the open door, and Dillon came walking across the room, fast, and stood looking down on Desi in her crib. Then he turned, and I could feel his eyes on me, as I lay there not six feet away. Like a little kid, I tried to slit down my eyes and pretend I was invisible. He wore a denim shirt, all shiny with dirt, and his hair was long. When he put his face on mine, I felt a stubble of beard on his chin. He knelt beside me, and he put a hand on either side of my face, and he pressed his cheek against my cheek the way he did the time we made love, so hard it almost hurt, so hard I had a tender spot there for days. And then he kissed me, opening up my mouth bit by bit with his tongue, exploring it like the inside of a cave, so slowly, for so long, as if there was something he was trying to find inside me that would keep him alive if he could drink it. I put up my arms then, to touch him, to put my hands inside his shirt and feel his skin; but he shook my hands off and, in one step and one motion, turned and scooped Desi up from her crib.

In track, they taught us to strengthen our hamstrings by getting to our feet without using our hands. I did it so many times, practicing, it got to be second nature, a single motion, a leap to a stride. And that was the way I was up, across that cabin floor as though my legs were built of coiled springs.

He was standing on the porch, a step outside the door, holding Desiree cradled in his right arm, just looking at her sleeping face, not petting or touching her or anything. I didn't feel real, but felt more as if my soul's transparent shape had lifted out of my body, and my body were still back on that bed, watching.

"Give me my baby," I said to Dillon. He looked up, his head all ringed by orange light, as if it were sunrise—in his eyes there were two little fires. He started to smile. His lips moved. I took Desiree with both my hands under her arms and pulled her away from Dillon so hard I nearly spun around backward.

He was shot already. He must have been.

He was hit before I even heard the second blast. The shot shrieked off the gutter, and the gutter clattered down to the porch. It was seconds. I wouldn't have had time to snap my fingers.

Nobody, not Miss Merrill or even Annie, really believes me

that Dillon was still alive when he was knocked back against the cabin wall. Jack Becker said—he said it over and over, and in the exact same words, like he was trying to get me to understand—that those soft bullets "went in like a peashooter and out like a flying saucer" and that Dillon was dead before his knees hit the porch. At first I didn't notice—though it's hard to believe that you wouldn't notice—all his blood and tissue spattered on the walls like someone had thrown a bucket of black paint. I just saw him look up once at me and then sort of lay himself down, his right arm just hanging. You could smell the burning fabric of his shirt, and the burning skin even through the general smoke of the burning air. He said, "Wait! . . . wait for me . . . ," and his head drooped over and he fell. I got down there, holding Desi against me, and kind of crawled over to him. I don't think I even realized what had happened to him. I wasn't really thinking about some-one out there with a gun.

Dillon's eyes were open, but only halfway, as if he'd tried to drift off to sleep, but forgot in the middle just how. From the front, he looked just like himself, and when I put my face on the part of his chest that wasn't bleeding, he smelled just like himself, like clean wood and salt. I touched the tip of his nose; it was cold as an ice cube.

In my arms, Desi was awake, her little eyes focused straight on my face. But she didn't make a peep. It was only when all the girl's yelling and swearing and screaming got so close behind me that I paid it any mind, there was so much noise from the fire, roaring and squealing and spitting, and the sirens, getting closer.

It was because I knew the voice that I turned to look. I saw two of them in that funny light, going around and around on the lawn like a couple square-dancing. Except the tall one had the little one by the elbows and the little figure was kicking back and throwing his head so hard that his baseball cap finally flew off and all this yellow hair came falling down, and I could tell, even at a distance of thirty yards or more, that it was my sister's voice I'd heard yelling out, "Let me alone, you fucking scum!" The taller one I couldn't see, until they danced up closer to the porch, him trying to wrestle her down.

"You hurt?" the man called out.

I couldn't say a thing.

"Girl? Are you hurt?"

"I'm . . . okay," I gasped out. It wasn't a voice loud enough for anyone to hear an inch away.

A police car came roaring up the dirt road and onto the lawn, and some big guy in a regular policeman's uniform jumped out and bounded over to the porch. And then Jack, right away, with Pedro, pulled in and ran over. Jack put his arm around me. "We're here, honey," he kept saying. "We're here."

I handed Desiree to Jack and went to Dillon. The officer turned him over and Dillon's hand, a hand streaked with his own blood, brushed my thigh. The blood was already drying, but I found some there later on, and had to sponge it off. Langtry was still screaming and fighting. "That's your husband, Arley!" she yelled. "Your perfect husband! He loved you so much, Arley! So much he never let me alone one night! Look at him!"

The officer on the porch looked up and said, "He's dead, ma'am. He never knew what hit him."

I said, "I know."

And then the tall man who'd had hold of my sister came up on the porch, out of the shadows and said, "Arley, hey."

"Hey," I said then. "Hey, Mister Justice."

"The baby's not hurt, is she?"

"No—she's okay."

His face all streaked with sweat and dirt, but his blue eyes seemed to darken with what he said. "I first thought she hit the baby, too. Your sister."

"You know she's my sister?"

"I know who she is."

"How did you see them coming?"

"Well, I'm always around. I found me a little trailer in the woods. Nothing but squirrels living in it before. I just saw the two of them, and it looked wrong to me, people heading up toward a fire. I thought it might be someone looking for you."

"You knew it was me? Out here?"

"Yes," he said.

I didn't even know I was crying until I started feeling drops rolling down, wetting my neck. Then Desi started to cough and fuss, and I just picked up my shirt and put her on my breast. I sat down on the steps, and Mr. Justice sat on the lower step, a couple of feet from me. Jack went down to help the other police get Lang into the car. She was trying to bite. Someone finally put a plastic rod in her mouth, crosswise.

Then, all of a sudden, Charley came loping up out of the shadows. They'd stopped him, then Annie, way up at the top of the road. He kneeled down by me and pulled me against his chest.

"Arley," he was panting, "Arley. Thank God. My God."

Two police officers were shaking out a blanket between them and laying it over Dillon. I looked over Charley's shoulder to try to see Dillon's face, but I could only see his hair, a tuft of his buttermilk hair sticking straight up, like a cowlick a little boy might have to wet down for school. Charley turned my chin away, as if he could stop me from seeing what I saw.

"Who's this, Arley?" he asked, real softly.

"This here's Mister Justice," I told him.

"Pleased," Mr. Justice said, his old face creased in a big broad smile. And that was when I saw the cleft in his chin.

Arley

Desi's very verbal for two. Everyone says so, so it's not as if I'm bragging. For months, she wouldn't hardly say a word but "Mama"—which as far as I can tell is sort of like a reflex—and "light."

She was nearly eighteen months old, and I was getting frantic thinking either there was something wrong with her, or that she remembered the night of the fire and "light" meant something terrible to her. I don't know if babies have memories from the womb; but I do know that they'll feel the way you feel. If Desi's having a hissy fit—Annie calls them "grand mal tantrums"—and I'm impatient when I pick her up to soothe her, it just sets her off worse.

The first time she said "light" was Republic Day. We were all sitting on the balcony outside Annie's bedroom at Azalea Road to watch the fireworks from downtown. At the first big pop, Desi screamed. Now, all babies are scared of loud sounds, but I was sitting very relaxed so she wouldn't be startled, and her whole body went rigid and she hid her face, even when everyone said "Pretty, pretty" and Charley's Claude played "Where's the baby hiding?"

There's no telling.

I guess when she's grown, Desi will have to sort out her feelings about her daddy. Maybe, by then, I'll have sorted out my own.

Two years isn't really so long, when you think of it broken up into seasons, or semesters, or segments of a life. But it's long in other ways. It's long enough for a baby to grow into a little girl with hair you can tie in two tiny pigtails. It's long enough for her to sass you, when you take the Tabasco sauce bottle away from her and tell her, "No way, girl," for her to just look at you and tell you, "Yes way, Mama!"

It's long enough to fear a death, then want it, then recoil from it, and then recover.

But reasoning things out might take forever, especially for me. I've really lived my life backward, being old before I got to be young. Knowing all about birth and all about death but not very much yet about life.

It's still that way.

Didn't go to high school, but now I'm in college. I go two days a week to the University of Texas in Austin. I only take six hours, under a special program for single mothers. And I did get a scholarship, a good thing, since Annie's up to her ears in bills and struggling hard to start her private practice. The classes I take are nineteenth-century British and American poetry and twentieth-century American literature. Slow and easy, I thought, when I signed up. Start with what you know.

I also audit a creative-writing class. That's the one I love best. The professor keeps telling me I ought to be taking it for credit; he says, "You have a natural voice." Sometimes I think he means I sound like a girl who grew up in the river valley. Sometimes I think he just has a sort of crush on me. But I intend to keep at it.

It was reading all those stories and poems for classes aloud to

Desi, while I was studying, that made her start talking for real. She started overnight. There was this little problem with her front teeth. They looked funny to start with, kind of grayish, and then I left her on the bottle too long and the enamel started to come off. Of course, I was going around explaining to Jeanine and Elena and those guys, "Look, the enamel is coming right off her poor little old teeth," never thinking the baby would hear or understand. Then one day, all of a sudden, when she was twenty months, Desi said, "Animal coming out of my mouth." No words for almost two years, and then a six-word sentence! She heard "enamel" as "animal," and by the next day, wasn't she saying, "Mama, a cow coming out of my mouth"? Everybody laughed so hard and made her repeat it so much that it got good on her, of course. But she doesn't just say that. She also says, "Tiger, tiger, burning bright!" and a hundred other things. When she walks out on the balcony in my room, she says, "Now, you be careful, baby," just like she was taking care of herself. Elena says there are seven signs of being gifted and that Desi has all seven. I guess she knows, since she's studying at UT to be a kindergarten teacher.

"Child will be a lawyer, like her grandma here," Charley likes to say, and Annie gives him her lemon-juice-mouth look. "Grandma" doesn't sit too well with her. Myself, I don't think Desi'll be a lawyer. I think she'll be a poet. Dillon's poems were good; no one can argue with that. Some of them were published in this book of writing from prison and in a few magazines. I got that money, and I keep it for Desi in a bank account. When I said to Annie that Desi inherited her gift of words from both sides, Annie just walked away mad.

I know it just means she loves me. If I never mention Dillon's name again, it will be too soon for her. That night at the cabin, when she came running up, the FBI agents were in the yard. We heard one of the FBI agents say, "I'm sorry, ma'am. No access. We're from the Bureau."

And then we heard Annie: "I don't care if you're a fucking chest of drawers. You get out of my way or I'll . . . I'll shoot off your leg!" It almost made me laugh, even then, it was quite a moment. But I don't really like when they joke about it. Someone died that night. You can't erase that. Or that he was my husband. Annie sort of wants to downplay that part, like it didn't happen. But I won't let her do it, I'm done with that kind of thinking forever. The way I figure, there's been enough hidden in my life for seven times my seventeen years, enough connections with people that looked fine and real, but weren't.

I have to know it all, remember it all, and live with it all. There was this one magazine story, about how Mama knew the whole time Lang wasn't dead, that she only cut her leg climbing out the window with Dillon. Mama told the magazine she wouldn't have cared if Lang had walked right out the door. And she didn't care if Dillon found me, either. "Things just happen how they're going to," she said.

Anyhow, in the story, there were some more of my poems. My old friend Eric Dorey read those, and he called me and said, "Arley, your mama's not fit to be around people. I hope she's jealous of you because you're making something of your life." Then he told me, "I won't ever forgive you if you don't go to a four-year school. You should aim at the stars, girl, and then, if you don't make it, you can adjust your sights down." When he said that, something in me just answered, okay, he's right, I can do this. Right then, I guess, was when I gave up for good on that old idea of going to technical school. There was a time when even cosmetology would have been too big a goal for a girl like me, but I'm not that girl anymore. If it ever seemed like some great idea to cover things up so they looked good—even if they're ugly or painful underneath—it seems foolish now. In fact, I think that's why people write, to uncover the lessons of the hard times. Maybe that's why I always felt so drawn to poetry. Those powerful words sort of just grab you by the chin and won't let you look away.

Eric's right. We're sort of going out now, and he says it all the time—that you can regret your whole life stuff you never had the nerve to try. Annie thinks I'm following in her footsteps, being an English major, and I am. But I also think it's because of a part of me, a caring part and a brave part, that didn't come from Mama. I think it came from Mr. Justice.

Eventually, of course, I would have found out that Mr. Justice was my daddy. It wasn't like no one knew. Avalon's small, and even San Antonio and the hilly country have their share of people who knew all about how Mama took to following the Righteous Ramblers—Mr. Justice's cowboy band—all around South Texas and beyond when she was no more than a girl, working for the band. As for her getting pregnant during those years, I don't know why she didn't use birth control. Ignorance and passion sure can go together. But maybe she had a plan, too, because it's hard to believe you could make the same mistake three times.

Eric and I went to the library once and searched the fiche for music reviews. And we saw this newspaper picture of Mr. Justice when he was about thirty, the age he was when Mama met him, when she was no older than I am now. Drink and hard living hadn't claimed any of his looks yet. And he was fine. Handsomer than Cam, who I guess is the one who looks most like him.

I wish that I could ask Mama more about it, but no hope of that. Mama's out of my life for good, and that's the right thing for me, though it can't ever be a cause for happiness. I can speculate, though. Mama probably loved his face, and the way he sang, and loved having his hands on her, beyond good sense or reason. Maybe she wasn't looking to make her a family when she had us all. Maybe she wanted to be a child herself, a child wanted, in the way she never had been by her own mama, and us kids were the ties she used to try to bind Mr. Justice to her. Look at those names she gave us—mine's for the town where they have that old amusement park, Six Flags. Cam's name is for Cameron, Texas; but his middle name is Jeremy, which, though everyone always called him "Remy," is Mr. Justice's real first name. Langtry's middle name is Justine, from Justice. Mama was trying her best to cook up a sort of family tree, doing things that looked the way you would think relationships look if you never had the real experience.

But it didn't work out. Maybe they were both just missing parts, so nothing they made together could be real. By the time she got to me, I guess Mama really knew the score, and she sort of just ran out of enthusiasm. That's why she never bothered with giving me a middle name, only the name of the town where they were the night they slept together and she woke up with me inside her, the way I woke up at Solamente River with Desiree in me.

I'll bet she kept on thinking, until the very end, that if she followed Mr. Justice around enough, he'd turn out to be her colored wagon, the one who made her free. The one who made her a somebody. And probably that was the last time she really tried anything having to do with loving another person.

I guess Lang wanted the same thing, too, though I'll never be able to ask her. She won't be in the women's prison at Taggart forever, but hell would freeze over before I'd have anything to do with my sister. They couldn't rehabilitate her enough so far as I'm concerned. I guess her men friends sort of threw in and got her a pretty hot defense lawyer from Dallas, who tried to convince the jury that she did what she did because Dillon hypnotized a woman too young to know better. But the jury didn't entirely buy that. They gave Lang life for the border guard and twenty-five years for killing Dillon. To be honest, there probably *was* some hypnotism going on. I know what Dillon was capable of—and Lang had nothing to fall back on. He probably talked her up a vision of some tropical paradise they were going off to, just to get her to cooperate with him. And she always just took whatever she could get, even if it wasn't hers. She got that from Mama.

On that night, the night of the fire, it must have hit Lang like a sack of bricks that she'd done everything she'd done for nothing. That everything she thought she had with Dillon was just a lie.

The way Lang's lawyer told Annie, Dillon promised he was just going to go get the baby. And Lang thought Dillon was going to kill me. She actually believed that he was going to kill me, when the real truth was probably that he was just using Lang to find me. Langtry helped him tail me from watching Annie's comings and goings at the places where I was. And she helped set the fire to draw everybody's attention away from me.

But it must have been when she saw me standing in the doorway, and saw me take the baby away from Dillon, that Lang's tumultuous jealous heart just burst. She balanced that deer rifle they'd stolen on a tree limb and aimed the telescopic sight right at Dillon, not giving a damn, either, what happened to the baby or to me.

She'd have killed me. Her greed and Mama's spitefulness almost cost me my life. Lang would have fired again, if Mr. Justice hadn't grabbed her from behind.

He saved my life.

He saved my life, and Desi's, just like he gave me those scarlet ribbons when I worked at Taco Haven, and like he gave me that track stile. Maybe he always cared more than he could ever study out how to show. Maybe he had to wait until I was away from Mama to pay any attention to me at all. I figure that's why I never saw him before I started working at Taco Haven. But I'll bet he was around. Like he said, guys like him are pretty invisible.

Just the little bit of how gentle he treated me makes me see how he must have been, long ago.

I wish I could ask Mr. Justice more about the time before I was born, and about his people. I'd try, but I don't think he'd have the words for it. I see him sometimes, but it's not how you would imagine it being in a novel, a big reunion and him being a good grandpa to Desi and all. Mr. Justice is not well. He still lives in that shell of a trailer out by Uvalde, and he's not all there, in the head, all those years of whiskey and probably a core sadness being the reasons why. Sometimes he comes around, and he always leaves things for Desi, the way he did the coffee and the flowers and her beautiful bed. He leaves little horses carved from wood, but he hardly sticks around long enough for me to thank him. Cam sees him once in a while, too, and I know Cam would like to know him better; Cam also hopes that someday him and me will be friends again. Maybe we will.

If it were mine to choose, I'd have Mr. Justice be a real daddy, and teach Desi and me to play the fiddle, which he still can do, and beautifully. But what Mr. Justice did for me was all he could do, and he did it at the time it mattered, and I have to reckon that it's enough. It seems to me that you have to accept what you're given, and choose what you're able to. That there are relationships in a life that can change the whole course of everything, even if they don't last forever. Even if they don't last the whole length of a life, but instead, just a moment.

It's like what Charley says about a tree being an individual and also a family. Everything that happens to a tree is stored inside it—every disaster, every good season—but it's only the tiny outer part of the tree that is actually alive. Mr. Justice and Mama are part of the wood that formed the living me. Now, my middle name is Mowbray. There's a lot connected with that name that isn't pretty or hopeful, but I keep it, just like I do the name LeGrande, because that is a part of who I am. It's a part, though, that's not living anymore, like the inner circles of a tree. It is what was, not what is. I've had to cut the branches the way Charley prunes our trees in the fall to shape them how they should grow; but that doesn't mean I cut away the parts that are preserved within, even the ones I wouldn't choose again.

Dillon is part of that wood heart too. I have to put him in a place that barricades all that was gruesome and shameful and cruel. I have to accept, and not grieve that in the moment we had, he was all he could ever be to me. I have to believe that those magazine stories about "The Highwayman" are about a boy I never knew, or knew only the shining part of. To the rest of the world, Dillon was the one who crossed over, who terrorized and who robbed. But I was the robber, too, that night in the trailer at the prison. I robbed him of his gold, the best he had in him, without knowing it, and combined it with what was good in me to make the jewel of my life. To make my Desiree. The night he wanted to take her, I robbed him of her again—and if I'd had to, I'd have killed him. Not out of rage or greed, like my sister. But to protect Desiree. I would stop at nothing to protect my baby.

Maybe I was just like Mama and like Lang, wanting Dillon to be the thing that made all the difference in the world. As it turned out, he was—though, like so much in a life, not at all in the way you foresee.

Without Dillon, there'd have been no Desi. Until Desi, I thought I understood what love was, and what family was, but I didn't know a thing. Her deep little voice and the way she comes up to me and says, "My daughter, my daughter," as if I were the little girl and she the mama, is so funny and so glorious I sometimes can't imagine why all the songs musicians write are about love between women and men, instead of love for a child by the grownups in her family.

What I have now really is a family, though it sure doesn't look like an ordinary one. But one of the good things about living in reverse is that most kids start out surrounded by love they have to grow out of. And I grew into mine. Annie and Charley and Desi and I live in the big house, and little Claude, who's six, visits all the time. She loves Desi like crazy, and she spoils her rotten; she walks around calling her "honeybear." Any day now, though, Claude's going to have another honeybear. Annie tells Charley she wants to cover the mirrors so she can't see her reflection until she loses twenty-five pounds. That's why they're not getting married until a couple of months after the baby comes, because Annie is so darned vain she says she doesn't want wedding pictures of her looking like Moby Singer. Charley says they'll be just like the movie stars who never get married till they have a string of kids.

Their baby is a boy. They had to have those genetic tests, because of Annie's being over forty; but he's fine. My suggestion is they call him Thornton Wilder, because they already got a Claude Monet and they could keep up the famous-name tradition. After all, Charley's kind of a hippie, not a big professional like Stuart was and all. He doesn't look like the kind of man for Annie; but you can tell just by looking at them that theirs is a true love, one that will last forever. And you can hear that love—a laugh, a cry—through the walls some nights when our house is quiet. Annie and Charley don't mean it, but those nights torment me.

They are the nights I think of Dillon.

They are the nights I dream.

Those will be the nights I'll dream of the fire, or of Dillon kissing me on that mattress in the cabin, dreams that scare me so I sometimes start sobbing without ever knowing I made a noise.

I know what dreams are supposed to be. They're the inside of your mind talking to the outside, picking at things you can't figure out during the day, or things you try to ignore.

But I'm not sure if that's all there is to these dreams.

Sometimes, I think, maybe they're like ghosts. Maybe they come from what lasts, after a person dies. What would that really be? A soul? And made of what? The evil people did on earth? Or their love?

I wonder most, to be honest, because there's another dream I have. Not as often as the others. I've had it only three or four times. But I think of it even more.

In that dream, I have my legs thrown over Dillon's and my long hair that's been cut off for so many years swoops down over us like a steed's wild black mane, and our motion and our emotion are fused into one moving thing, and I'm not afraid, even though I'm naked and completely unprotected. I look straight into Dillon's green eyes and I feel that I want us to be just this way, face-to-face, until both of us blink out, dissolve, until there is nothing left of either of us but a whisper.

I'm sure that I'll stop having that dream someday. When the time comes.

I want to grow up to be a person like Annie and her sister, Rachael, the two women I admire most in the world. If I'm lucky, I'll be happy and I'll be settled, the way they are, the kind of woman who makes decisions that aren't based on a lust and an appetite that cared no more for the real world than a range fire cares whether it burns a shack or a mansion. I'll teach Desiree to be that way, too.

Then I'll know I'm fully grown.

And that dream won't matter anymore.

But if it does still matter, when I'm old, and my time comes to die, then I'll find out for myself whether there really are ghosts.

Lullaby

Now I lay you down
    my sweet, downy
head beneath my cheek,
    to sleep your deep
and dreamless sleep.
    The angels keep you
safe, I pray; my little one,
    my Desiree,
and I will watch and I will wait
    and rock this bough
that will not break.
    No one will take
your soul this night.
    I'm here.

Arlington Mowbray LeGrande